Bumper Book of

Enid Blyton

Stories

The Ragamuffin Mystery
The Rat-a-Tat Mystery
The Rubadub Mystery

 SCHOOL BOOK FAIRS Ltd.

This edition produced exclusively for School Book Fairs by Armada, an imprint of the Children's Division of the Collins Publishing Group 1989.

The Enid Blyton signature is a trademark of Darrell Waters Ltd

Printed and bound in Great Britain

Contents

The Ragamuffin Mystery

The Ragamuffin Mystery was first published in a single volume in the U.K. in
hardback in 1951 by William Collins Sons & Co. Ltd., and in paperback by
Armada in 1969.

CHAPTER ONE

Off in the Caravan

"THIS IS GOING to be just about the most exciting holiday we've ever had!" said Roger, carrying a suitcase and bag down to the front door. "Diana, bring that pile of books, will you, before we forget them?"

Diana picked them up and ran down the stairs after Roger. At the front door stood a caravan. Diana stood and gloated over it for about the twentieth time.

"Fancy Dad buying a *caravan*!" she said. "And oh, what a pity he can't come with us after all!"

"Yes—after all our plans!" said Roger. "Still, it's a jolly good thing Mummy didn't back out, when she heard Dad had to go off to America—I was awfully afraid she would! My heart went into my boots, I can tell you."

"Same here," said Diana, stacking the books neatly on a shelf in the caravan. "Have we got our bird-book—we'll see plenty of birds on our travels, and that's my holiday task—writing an essay on 'Birds I have seen'."

"Well, don't forget to take the field-glasses then," said Roger. "They're hanging in the hall. I say—what did you think about Mummy asking Miss Pepper to come with us, now that Daddy can't manage?"

Miss Pepper was a very old friend of their mother's. The children were fond of her—but Roger felt rather doubtful about having her on a caravan holiday with them. "You see—she's all right in a *house*," he said to

7

Diana. "But in a small caravan, with hardly any room—won't she get fussed? We shall be so much on top of one another."

"Oh well—Mummy must have someone to take turns at driving the car that pulls the caravan," said Diana. "And she'll be company for Mummy, too. She's quite good fun—if only she won't keep making us be tidy, and wash our hands and knees a dozen times a day, and . . ."

"What are you two gossiping about?" said their mother, hurrying out to the caravan with some more things. "If we're going to start off at eleven, we'd better hurry! We've got to pick Miss Pepper up at two o'clock, you know—and that means going over thirty miles an hour if we don't start punctually. Too fast for a car with a caravan!"

"I wish Daddy was coming," groaned Diana, helping her mother to pack in more luggage. "Miss Pepper's all right—but Daddy's such fun on a holiday!"

"Yes—it's a pity," said her mother. "But at least we haven't got to put up with Snubby this time!"

"Gosh yes—Snubby with us in a small caravan—and Loony too—would be just about the limit!" said Roger. "Who's he staying with these hols?"

Snubby was their cousin, a ginger-haired, freckled, snub-nosed twelve-year-old boy. He had no father or mother, and so spent his holidays with one or other of his aunts and uncles. Snubby by himself was bad enough, but with his quite mad dog, Loony, a beautiful black spaniel, he was enough to drive even the most patient aunt and uncle out of their minds.

"He's staying with Auntie Pat, I think," said Diana. "Isn't he, Mummy? I bet he's driving her crazy. Last time he stayed with her, Loony got a passion for goloshes, and took every single one from the hall cupboard and hid them in the rhododendron bushes . . ."

"And the gardener couldn't believe his eyes when he saw them, and he called Snubby, and Snubby asked him why he had sown golosh seed under the rhododendrons!" said Roger, with a sudden snort of laughter.

"Good old Snubby! He *is* a pest, but honestly you can't help laughing at him half the time," said Diana. "I bet he wishes he was coming on this caravan holiday with us."

"Well, thank goodness he's not," said their mother. "Pack those rugs in the corner there, Diana. I really think that's about all. Now I'll go in and see that we've got absolutely everything—and if we have we'd better start."

She hurried indoors. Diana looked round the neat little caravan, wondering how long it would be before it was anything but neat! She and her mother and Miss Pepper were to sleep in it at night, and Roger was to sleep in the back of the car. What fun to travel round the countryside, going where they liked—not knowing what county they would sleep in at night—waking up when they liked—picnicking in the most beautiful spots they could find. Yes—this was going to be something *like* a holiday!

"There's just one thing I do *wish*," said Diana to Roger, as they went indoors to say good-bye to their cook and daily woman. "I wish and wish that old Barney was coming with us."

"Gosh—so do I!" said Roger. "And Miranda his monkey too. Dear little Miranda. We haven't seen her for ages."

"Well, Barney's been travelling about with his father,"

said Diana. "I wonder if he often thinks how he travelled about before—you know, when he was a child and didn't know who his father was, and went about with the people of circuses and fairs. He did plenty of travelling then!"

"And now he's found his father—and a real family of his own—and he's no longer a poor circus boy, all alone in the world," said Roger. "And Miranda isn't a lonely little monkey, going everywhere with him, often hungry and cold—but a spoilt little pet, loved by every single one of Barney's family! And thank goodness, Barney hasn't changed a bit."

"No—he's still the same kind, strong Barney," said Diana. "I do hope we see him these hols. Mummy! Mummy, where are you? We really ought to start, you know."

"Just coming!" called their mother, hurrying down-stairs. "I remembered I must find the sunburn lotion, in case we all get too burnt for words, in this hot weather. Go and say good-bye, dears—then we'll start."

Diana and Roger said good-bye to their cheery old cook, and she pressed a bag into their hands. "Just a few of my special sugar-biscuits to keep you going till dinner-time," she said. "Have a good time! And see and look after your mother; she's tired after all the packing up."

At last they were in the car, and it moved slowly towards the front gate, pulling the caravan behind it. Fortunately the gates were wide and the posts were not even scraped. Away they went down the lane, the caravan running smoothly behind them, rocking just a little now and again when they went over a rut. Soon they were out on the main road—the holiday had begun!

They stopped for a picnic lunch on the way, and then

drove on towards Miss Pepper's. "We shall be late," said Roger, "but it doesn't matter, Mummy—Miss Pepper would be *most* surprised if we were punctual!"

"I dare say—but she's sure to be quite ready ten minutes beforehand," said his mother. "And I shall feel just as I used to when she looked after me in my teens— very very guilty!"

Miss Pepper was waiting for them on her doorstep, her suitcases beside her. She looked as tall and thin as ever, but her eyes twinkled as usual behind their glasses, and she smiled warmly.

"Well, here you all are, bless you!" she said. "And wonder of wonders not more than fifteen minutes late! Had your dinner?"

"Yes, Miss Pepper," said everyone, and Roger leapt out to take her luggage. He stowed it away in the caravan.

"What a fine caravan!" said Miss Pepper, approvingly. "Well, well—I never thought I'd ever sleep in a caravan —and here I am, quite looking forward to it!"

"I'll drive on for some way," said the children's mother. "Then you can take a short turn at driving if you will. We thought we'd make for that lovely little lake at Yesterley. The children can bathe then. Isn't it a mercy it's such glorious weather?"

"It certainly is," said Miss Pepper, settling herself in the front seat. "Dear me—it seems strange not to have Snubby with us. He's always come with the children when I've been with them before."

"He's staying with Auntie Pat—and I expect he's driving her mad," said Diana. "All the same, I wish his dog Loony was with us—darling Loony—I do love him."

"H'm," said Miss Pepper, doubtfully. "I'm fond of

11

him too—but I don't think I should be fond of him long if he went for a caravan holiday with us. He's not a very *restful* dog."

It was very pleasant driving along that sunny day, with three weeks stretching before them, lazy, lovely weeks, full of picnics, bathes, ice-creams—and perhaps sleeping out in the open air instead of in the caravan? Roger made up his mind to suggest it that very first night—not for his mother or Miss Pepper, just for himself and Diana.

The car purred on and on—where would they stop for the night? Nobody knew and nobody cared. The caravan rolled on behind them, and every now and again Roger looked back to make sure it was still safely there.

"We're going to have fun!" he said to Diana. "For three whole weeks—nothing but fun!"

CHAPTER TWO

Very Unexpected!

FOR FIVE DAYS Roger and Diana had a truly wonderful time. For two nights they stayed by the lovely blue lake at Yesterley, and picnicked and bathed. Miss Pepper surprised them all by producing a bathing suit, and bathing too—and what was more she was a very fine swimmer indeed!

"Goodness!" said Diana, lying panting on the white sand that edged the lake. "Goodness! I had a swimming race with Miss Pepper—and she beat me. And look, she's still swimming, and I've had to come out and rest."

"She's jolly good," said Roger. "So's Mummy, actually. I wish I could float as long as she can—she just goes on and on—and yet it's not salt water! She must waggle her hands about, or something."

"This is the kind of holiday I like," said Diana. "Wasn't it fun last night, sleeping out on the heather? Did you hear that owl hooting just by us? It nearly made me jump out of my skin."

"Didn't hear a thing," said Roger. "I just shut my eyes—and never knew anything till you shook me awake this morning. How long are Mummy and Miss Pepper staying in the water? I'm hungry."

They were all hungry those first five days, even Miss Pepper, who became quite ashamed of the enormous appetite she suddenly discovered.

"I do wish you wouldn't look so surprised, you two, when I take a third helping," she said. "You make me feel greedy—and really, it's only just that I'm very hungry."

"Aha! *Snubby* would like to hear you say that!" said Roger. "You always used to tell him he wasn't *really* hungry when he wanted a third helping—but just Plain Greedy!"

"Dear Snubby!" said Miss Pepper. "I do wonder how he is getting on these holidays. Let me see now— your Auntie Pat hasn't any children, has she—so Snubby won't have anyone to play with. I'm afraid he may make himself a bit of a nuisance."

"More than a *bit*," said Diana. "He can behave like a lunatic when he's bored. He thinks of the most awful things to do. Don't you remember how he thought he'd sweep our chimney one day, when it smoked a little, and then . . ."

13

"Don't *talk* of it," said her mother with a groan. "I can't bear even to remember that day. I know your father nearly went mad, and chased Snubby round and round the garden with the chimney brush . . ."

"And fell over Loony," said Diana.

"Yes. Funny the way Loony *always* gets under the feet of anyone who's angry with Snubby," said Roger. "Remarkably clever dog, Loony!"

Each night the four of them sat in the caravan and listened to the news on their portable radio. They hadn't seen a single newspaper since they had set off on their holiday, but as Miss Pepper said, it didn't do to cut themselves off *completely* from everything.

"Someone might have landed on the moon—or started a war—or had an earthquake," said Miss Pepper. "We had better listen in just once a day."

On the fifth night, they were as usual sitting in the caravan, listening to the evening news on the little radio. The children listened with only half an ear, until the announcer came to the weather. That was *really* important! Was the weather *still* going to be warm and sunny?

The news came to an end. It had been very dull—a new strike—a long speech by somebody important—a new kind of aeroplane tested—and then there came a message that made them all sit up at once.

Miss Pepper was just about to turn off the radio, when the voice spoke urgently.

"Here is a message, please, for Mrs. Lynton, who, with her children, is on a caravan tour. Will she please telephone Hillsley 68251 at once, as her sister is dangerously ill? I will repeat that. Here is a message for . . ."

No one spoke for a few seconds, or even moved, as

the message was repeated. Then Diana whispered. "Mummy—it's us they are trying to reach! You're Mrs. Lynton—and oh Mummy, does it mean . . ."

"It means that something's happened to your mother's sister—your Aunt Pat," said Miss Pepper, getting up at once. "Don't worry too much, my dear—we'll drive straight off to a telephone box, and find out what's wrong."

"Oh dear—what *can* have happened?" said Mrs. Lynton, looking very pale. "I'll have to go back—I'll have to go to Pat. Oh, I feel quite dazed."

The children felt dazed too. What a dreadful thing to happen in the middle of a lovely holiday! Poor Auntie Pat—what *could* have happened? "Dangerously ill"— that sounded very frightening.

"You two children stay here in the caravan," said Miss Pepper briskly, taking charge as usual. "I'll drive your mother to the nearest village and we'll telephone. We'll get back here as soon as possible. Cheer up, Diana —don't look so upset, dear. It may not be as bad as it sounds."

In two minutes Miss Pepper was driving the car down the lane, the children's mother sitting silently beside her. Roger and Diana went outside the caravan, and sat down in the heather. It was a very light night, and, although they could not see to read, they could just see each other's faces. Diana was crying.

Roger gave her a quick hug. "It mayn't be so bad," he said. "I expect Mummy will have to go back, though. We'll have to as well, I suppose."

"But how can we?" wept Diana. "Cook's away now, and the house is shut up. There'd be nobody there."

"I'd forgotten that. And what about old Snubby?"

15

said Roger. "He can't stay at Auntie Pat's if she's ill—
or gone to hospital. What's to happen to *him*?"

"And to us too," said Diana. "Mummy will certainly
stay to look after Auntie Pat. She's so fond of her. Oh
what an *awful* thing to happen in the middle of such a
lovely holiday!"

It seemed a very long time before their mother came
back with Miss Pepper. The children heard the car coming in the darkness and stood up at once. They ran to it
as soon as their mother got out.

But it wasn't their mother! It was Miss Pepper—and it
wasn't their car either, it was a taxi!

"Oh—what's happened? Where's Mummy?" cried
Diana.

"Gone off in the car to see to your auntie," said Miss
Pepper, paying the taxi-driver. "She's had a fall and hurt
her head, and the doctors thought she might die. But
they've just given your mother a better report of her, and
have asked her to get back as soon as she can, as your
aunt keeps calling for her."

"Oh! Poor Mummy!" said Diana, thinking of her
mother driving fast through the night, all alone, worrying
about her sister. "Oh, Miss Pepper—do you think Auntie
Pat will be all right?"

"From the doctors' latest report, I should think she
will," said Miss Pepper, comfortingly. "So don't fret too
much. It's silly to cross bridges before you come to them.
Mummy sent you her love, and says she'll give us the
latest news in the morning, if I go into the village to
telephone. It's not very far."

"Will Mummy come back here, and go on with our
holiday?" asked Roger.

"No. No, I think I can say that quite definitely," said

But it wasn't their mother—it was Miss Pepper!

Miss Pepper. "I'm pretty sure she will want to stay with your Aunt Pat till she's really on the mend. We had no time to decide exactly what to do—but I'm afraid you'll have to put up with *me* for a bit, my dears! I promised your mother I'd be with you till she can have you home again."

"But—but what are our plans now, then?" asked Roger, feeling rather dazed. "We've this caravan—but no car—and our house is shut up. Will we leave the caravan here and go and stay with *you*, Miss Pepper?"

"I really do *not* know, Roger dear," said Miss Pepper. "Shall we leave everything till to-morrow? Things like this do happen, you know—and then we often find out how strong—or weak—we are! Your mother now, was full of courage as soon as she got over the shock; she was ready to face up to anything!"

"What about poor Snubby?" said Diana. "He's staying with Auntie Pat. Oh, Miss Pepper—Auntie Pat didn't fall over Loony, did she?"

"No—she slipped off a ladder," said Miss Pepper. "Now—I'm going to open a bottle of orangeade, and find those chocolate biscuits and macaroons we had over from lunch—and we're going to have a nice little supper."

The two children felt glad to have Miss Pepper with them. She was cheerful and brisk, and even made one or two little jokes. Roger felt more cheerful too, after his supper, but Diana was still scared and upset.

"Roger, would you like to sleep in your mother's bunk to-night, in the caravan with Diana and me?" Miss Pepper asked. "I expect Diana would like you in here with us to-night."

"Yes. Yes, I'd like to sleep here instead of in the car," said Roger, and Diana nodded, pleased. Now if she

18

was awake in the night and felt scared and sad, she could talk to Roger. Brothers were good to have when things went wrong!

Soon the caravan was in darkness, while three people tried to get to sleep. What news would the morning bring? Good—or bad? And what was going to happen to their holiday?

CHAPTER THREE

Good Old Barney!

NEXT MORNING Miss Pepper was up bright and early, and woke the two children. "Wake up!" she said. "We'll have breakfast and then I'll pop down to the village and telephone your mother. Did you sleep well?"

"Yes, I did," said Diana, rather surprised, for she had felt sure that she wouldn't sleep at all. Roger had slept well too, and both of them felt more ready to face up to whatever news they would hear.

Miss Pepper made the tea, and Diana cut the bread. Soon they were eating cold ham, and drinking the hot tea. "Though really, why we don't have orangeade this hot morning, instead of this scalding tea, I can't think!" said Diana.

Immediately after breakfast Miss Pepper set off briskly to the village. She was back in half an hour and the children, who were anxiously looking out for her, ran to meet her, most relieved to see a smile on her face.

"Better news," said Miss Pepper at once. "Your

mother arrived safely, and your aunt was so glad to see her—and she has taken a turn for the better already."

"Good, good, good!" said Diana, thankfully.

"Apparently she fell from the top of a ladder when she was tying up some ramblers on the wall," said Miss Pepper. "And she hit her head on the stone path. Nothing to do with Loony at all! She's in hospital, and your mother is with her. And I'm afraid your mother will have to stay away for quite a while, because there is no one to look after your uncle—so your mother says she'll spend part of her time seeing to your uncle and the other part with your aunt."

"Oh. Then what's to happen to *us*?" said Diana at once.

"Well, I suppose I'll have to try and hire a car and take the caravan back to my own home," said Miss Pepper. "You'll have to come with me, I'm afraid, as your own house is shut up. I'm sorry, dears—very very sorry. This is a horrid end to what was going to be one of your very best holidays. . But I honestly don't see what else we can do."

"I don't either," said Roger, gloomily. "And I think it's jolly good of you to take all this trouble for us, Miss Pepper. I'm sure you don't want us in your little house! Oh dear—isn't this all horrid!"

"Diana can come with me to find out about a car," said Miss Pepper as they cleared up the caravan and made up the bunks. "And Roger can stay here with the caravan. That be all right, Roger?"

"Of course," said Roger, still gloomy, and watched Miss Pepper go off to the village again, Diana by her side. What a mess-up of a glorious holiday! Miss Pepper was good and kind—but the thought of living for two or

20

three weeks in her tidy little house filled Roger with dread.

"We'll be too bored for words!" he thought and then reproached himself for being unkind. Whatever would they have done without Miss Pepper just now! "We *might* have gone to stay with old Barney, if he hadn't been touring about the country with his father," his thoughts ran on. "Oh well—we'll just have to make the best of things, I suppose."

Miss Pepper and Diana came back in an hour's time, looking depressed.

"We can't get a car anywhere in the village," said Miss Pepper. "So we telephoned the nearest town, and somebody is going to try there for us. I do hope we shan't have to take some old crock that will break down halfway home! I'm really not very good at driving cars I don't know."

Their caravan was set on a heathery hill, just off the road, not far from a farm-house. The farmer had given them permission to stay on the hill—and, about three o'clock that afternoon, the three saw him coming up to their caravan.

"Oh dear—I hope he's not going to turn us off!" said Miss Pepper in a fright.

The farmer came slowly up to where they were all sitting outside the caravan, his dog at his heels.

"Good afternoon, Ma'am," he said, in his pleasant country voice. "There be a message come for you, sent to my farm-house by the post office. Telegram it be."

He held out the orange telegram and Miss Pepper took it, suddenly frightened. She tore it open and read it. Then she looked round at the two waiting children, puzzled.

"Listen," she said, "it says, '*Wait till you see us to-night. Barney*'."

"Wait till you see us to-night!" echoed Diana, and her face suddenly lighted up. "Oh, Miss Pepper! Barney and his father must have heard about Auntie Pat's accident, and how Mummy had to go to her, leaving us here! And they're coming here to-night! Oh, how WONDERFUL!"

"They must have heard the message on the radio last night, when we did!" said Roger. "And they rang the Hillsley telephone number and found out what was happening. Miss PEPPER! Everything will be all right now! Barney's father will arrange about a car and everything. Oh, thank goodness!"

Diana gave a long sigh of relief, and her heart suddenly lightened. Barney was coming—and his nice father. Now things would soon be settled for them. Perhaps they could go and stay with Barney?

"Thank you," said Miss Pepper to the farmer, and he nodded, and left, his dog still at his heels.

"*Wait till you see us to-night!*" said Diana, quoting the telegram again. "That must mean that they are driving straight to us, wherever they are—and must be rather far away, or they would arrive before to-night. Good old Barney! Now we can just sit back and not worry."

"You two had better go down to the river and have a bathe," said Miss Pepper. "It's so hot to-day. I won't come with you, because someone had better stay with the caravan. Go along now, and have a good swim. It will do you good."

So off went Roger and Diana, feeling considerably happier because of Barney's telegram. How good it was to have friends—how very very good!

"We shall see dear little Miranda too," said Diana happily. "The best thing about animals is that they don't seem to change, as human beings do! Miranda must have looked the same ever since she was a year old!"

They had a long bathe, and then lay in the warm heather to dry. They were hungry when they got back to the caravan. "Any news of Barney yet? Or another telegram?" asked Roger. Miss Pepper shook her head.

"No—but Barney said 'to-night' in his telegram, you know. We shall have to wait in patience. I'm sure they must be down in Cornwall, or up in the north of Scotland, or in the Welsh mountains—somewhere quite far away from here, anyway."

"I'm not going to bed till they come," said Roger firmly.

"I can't really expect you to!" said Miss Pepper. "But I hope it's before twelve o'clock!"

The evening drew on, and the sun began to sink low down in the west. At every far-off sound of a car going by on the distant road, the three of them stiffened and listened—but car after car purred by in the distance, and not one stopped, or came in their direction.

Then at last, just as it was getting really dark, the sound of a car jolting over the rough road to the old farm-house came to their ears. "That *must* be Barney!" said Diana in excitement. They listened anxiously.

The car stopped—and then, a few minutes later they heard it starting up again in the silence of the evening. It was coming over the rough track that led to them!

"It's Barney! It must be!" cried Roger, leaping up. "The villagers must have sent them to the farm, and the farmer has told them where we are. Barney! BARNEY! BARNEY!"

An answering shout came to their ears. "Hey! We're coming! The track's rough, though!"

Soon a big car came to a stop beside the caravan, and a tall figure leapt out; Roger and Diana ran to meet it —and to greet dear old Barney, with little Miranda the monkey on his shoulder, chattering excitedly.

"Hallo, hallo!" cried Barney, and hugged both Diana and Roger. "Sorry to be so long in coming—we were right away in Scotland! Heard the news on the radio last night, of course, and telephoned to your mother at Hillsley. How are you?"

"Oh, BARNEY, it's so lovely to have you," said Diana. "We simply didn't know WHAT to do when Mummy had to go off and leave us. Is that your father getting out of the car now?"

"Yes. We can leave everything to him," said Barney, very happy to be with his friends again. "Every single thing! He's got a marvellous plan. Hallo, Miss Pepper! Isn't this a surprise?"

"It certainly is," said Miss Pepper. "Ah, here's your father! Good evening—it *is* good of you to come to us like this!"

"We'll soon fix up some plans," said Barney's father, shaking hands. "Sorry about this trouble. Let's go into that fine caravan of yours and talk."

And in they all went, Miranda the monkey too, chattering loudly, leaping from one shoulder to another and making Roger and Diana laugh in glee. Good old Barney —dear little Miranda—it really was wonderful to see them again!

CHAPTER FOUR

A Wonderful Idea

IT SEEMED quite a crowd in the little caravan. Miss Pepper
lighted the safety-lamp, and they all looked at one another,
blinking. Barney's brilliant blue eyes shone as he looked
round at everyone. He was as brown as a berry, as usual,
and his grin just as wide as ever!

His father spoke to Miss Pepper. "We rang up again
to-night to see how Mrs. Lynton's sister was, and she is
just a little better—and will certainly recover well now—
but it will take time."

"Thank goodness it's better news," said Miss Pepper.
"It was such a terrible shock last night. I am so glad to
see you, Mr. Martin—I really was worried about what to
do for the best."

"Well, don't worry any more," said Mr. Martin.
"What I propose is that I should hitch my car on to your
caravan and . . ."

"And take us home?" said Roger. "But our house is
shut up, Mr. Martin!"

"Yes, I know that," said Barney's father. "And I
know too that it must be a great disappointment to you,
to have your three weeks' holiday broken up—so I think
that if you all joined Barney—or let him join you, which-
ever way you like to put it—that would solve your
difficulties."

"You mean—we could have your car to drive the

caravan about?" asked Miss Pepper. "Oh dear—if you mean *me* to drive it, Mr. Martin, I'm afraid I couldn't. It's so *big*, and . . ."

"No, no—I didn't mean that," said Mr. Martin. "I'll explain. Barney and I are on a week's holiday—and it is almost up, because I have to get back. What I propose is that I hitch up to your caravan, and we go off to-morrow and find some really nice place for you all to stay in—somewhere near a little inn, perhaps, so that you and Diana can sleep indoors there, and the two boys can sleep in the caravan, and . . ."

"Oh! What a WONDERFUL idea!" said Diana, her eyes shining. "Some place by the sea, perhaps?"

"We'll see," said Mr. Martin, smiling at her excited face. "If we can find a good spot to-morrow, I'll leave you all there, with the caravan, and drive back home. Miss Pepper will keep an eye on you, I know! When the time comes for you to leave, I'll drive up and fetch the caravan. What do you think of that?"

"Oh—too good to be true!" said Roger. "I honestly thought we'd have to go home and look after ourselves in an empty house! It's awfully good of you, sir—and, of course, solves all our problems—except one!"

"And what problem's that?" asked Mr. Martin.

"Well—about Snubby," said Roger.

"What's going to happen to him?"

"Can't he come with us?" said Diana, eagerly. "There's room in the caravan for three—or he could sleep in whatever inn or hotel Miss Pepper and I go to."

"Dear me—I'd forgotten about Snubby!" said Mr. Martin. "Of course he can come too. He was staying with the aunt who's ill, wasn't he, poor fellow. We'll

26

telephone your mother and tell her to send him up to us, when we've decided where you're going to stay."

Diana heaved a great sigh. "I was so worried about everything," she said. "And now all the troubles are smoothed out. Thank you very very much, Mr. Martin. And to think we'll have Barney and Miranda with us too! Miranda, do you hear that? You're coming on holiday with us now!"

Miranda heard her name, and chattered in delight. She leapt to Diana's shoulder and pulled her hair gently, pretending to whisper into her ear.

"You dear, funny little thing," said Diana, fondling her. "Fancy having you with us too—what a treat!"

"Can I offer you some cocoa—or some orangeade?" asked Miss Pepper. "I'm afraid there's nothing very exciting to give you for supper."

"Oh, I nearly forgot!" said Barney, getting up. "We've got a whole lot of stuff in the car. We didn't stop to have meals at hotels to-day, we just bought bread and ham and fruit and tomatoes, and ate them as we drove along. We so badly wanted to get here as soon as possible. I'll go and bring some of it in."

"How lovely!" said Diana. "I don't know why, but I suddenly feel frightfully hungry."

"It's because your worries are gone, dear!" said Miss Pepper. "I feel a bit hungry myself too! It is truly good of you, Mr. Martin, to come to our aid like this."

"Ah well—you've been kind to Barney many a time," said Mr. Martin. "Hey, what's that monkey doing?"

"Oh—she's got my sponge!" said Diana, with a delighted giggle. "Miranda, give it to me! Oh look, she's washing her face with it, just as she's seen me do at times. Miranda, that's *my* sponge!"

"Now she's put it into her mouth!" said Miss Pepper. "Oh, the naughty little thing! Surely she's not thinking of eating it, Diana!"

Barney deftly removed the sponge, and scolded the little monkey, who at once covered her face with her arms, and sat in a corner giving little moans.

"Don't pretend like that!" said Barney, going out of the caravan. "You're not a bit sorry. I'll be back in half a jiffy, everyone. See Miranda doesn't get your soap, Di!"

Barney was soon back with paper bags and tins. Then they all settled down to a first-rate supper of ham, tomatoes, cheese, ripe plums and orangeade.

"What are you going to do to-night—about sleeping, I mean," said Miss Pepper to Mr. Martin. "It's such a lovely night, I expect the children will sleep out of doors again, on the heather, with a rug around them. But you won't want to do that, Mr. Martin."

"No. I'd rather go to the little inn in the village," said Barney's father. "Barney can stay here with you, of course. I'd like to telephone Mrs. Lynton to-night and tell her we'll have Snubby as soon as we can. To-morrow we'll decide where we'll go—and then I'll let Mrs. Lynton know where to send Snubby. Well—I'll say good-night, I think. I can see Diana yawning her head off!"

"Good night, sir," said Roger, "and thanks most awfully. See you to-morrow!" Everyone went to the car to see Mr. Martin off, and soon he was jolting slowly over the little track that led back to the farmhouse.

"And now it's bed for all of us," said Miss Pepper briskly. "My word, I feel different now—everything straightened out so well! I just wish your mother hadn't had her holiday spoilt, though she won't mind so long as your aunt is on the mend!"

The two boys went out to find a thick patch of heather. "We'll wash in the stream to-morrow morning," yawned Roger, settling down on a rug. "Here—there's enough rug for you and Miranda, Barney."

Miranda cuddled up into Barney's neck, chattering in his ear. He was sleepy and didn't answer, and she tweaked his hair.

"Now look here, Miranda," said Barney, undoing her tiny fingers from his hair, "I will *not* have you pulling my hair when I want to go to sleep. Settle down!"

And Miranda settled down meekly, her small brown face hidden in his neck. Barney patted her and smiled. What a funny little thing she was!

Miss Pepper and Diana slept in the caravan with the door wide open for air. Miss Pepper sighed with relief as she closed her eyes. Things were turning out better than she had hoped!

In the morning quite early, Mr. Martin was back again in the car, complete with new-laid eggs, new-made bread, butter and fresh milk from the farm. "And very nice too!" said Miss Pepper approvingly. "Miranda—leave that egg alone!"

"I've been looking at a map," said Mr. Martin, after breakfast, and spread a large one out on the heathery ground, where they had all sat having breakfast in the warm sun. "The thing we have to decide is where to go! Any ideas, anyone?"

"Somewhere by the sea," said Roger at once. "If this hot weather goes on, we'll want to bathe."

"Not in a big town," said Miss Pepper. "Somewhere small and countrified."

"Somewhere where I can watch birds," said Diana. "I've got a holiday essay to write on 'Birds I have Seen'."

"Oh, don't start talking about that essay again!" said Roger. "I bet you don't watch for a single bird the whole time!"

Diana glared at him, and Miss Pepper hurriedly interrupted. "There are birds everywhere, Diana—we really don't need to look for any *special* bird-haunt. Barney, what kind of place would *you* like?"

"Well—I hate modern holiday spots, where there are crowds of people," said Barney. "I'd rather go to some quiet old place—where we can laze about in old clothes, do exactly what we like, and not have to bother with anyone else at all."

"I think we are all pretty well agreed then," said Miss Pepper. "But where shall we find a place like that in the middle of the summer? Most places by the sea are so crowded now."

"We'll go somewhere on this hilly Welsh coast, I think," said Mr. Martin, tracing a route with his finger. "It's lovely country round there. I vote we start off straightaway, and cruise along by the sea—and we'll stop as soon as we find the place we want. Come along—let's pack up and go at once!"

CHAPTER FIVE

A Halt for Ice-Creams

BEFORE LONG they were all on their way. Mr. Martin's car was a big one, and there was plenty of room for them all. The caravan swayed along behind, and Mr. Martin had to keep remembering that his car was pulling it, and try not to swing round corners too fast!

They drove until lunch-time, and then had a picnic by the roadside, in a little wood. They looked at the map again. "Soon be by the sea," said Mr. Martin, following the map with his fingers. "Then we'll look out for a likely spot for you. We'll drive straight through all the big seaside towns, and dawdle along the coast looking for what we want."

"This is fun!" said Diana. "Oh, Miranda—you'll be sick! Barney, that's the fourth plum she's taken."

Barney took away the plum, and Miranda flew into a rage. She leapt on to his head, pulling one of his ears till he shouted. Then she was sorry and tried to creep down his neck, under his shirt.

"Really, you can't help laughing at the naughty little thing!" said Miss Pepper. "What we shall do when Snubby arrives with that mad spaniel Loony, I don't know! There'll be no peace for anybody!"

"Well, I must say I'm as pleased we haven't that pair in the car with us yet," said Mr. Martin, rolling up the map. "A mad dog, an idiotic boy, and a naughty monkey would certainly be too much for any driver!"

They drove off again. They came to a big seaside town, packed with trippers, noisy and full of litter. "Straight through here," said Mr. Martin firmly. "And the next one too. After that we come to a lonely part of the coast, and we'll keep our eyes open."

Through that town they went, and then right through the next, without stopping. Ah—now they were leaving behind the crowded part of the coast, and coming to deserted bays, lonely sweeps of sand, tiny villages, fishing hamlets. Hills rose up from the coast, and the car had to take a roundabout route, going slowly because of the caravan behind it.

"This looks more like what we want," said Diana, looking out of the car window at the sea on one side and hills on the other. "Mr. Martin—do you think we could stop for an ice-cream sometime? I'm simply too hot for words, even with all the windows open!"

"Good idea!" said Mr. Martin, and he stopped at the next village—a tiny place that ran down to the sea. But there was no shop that sold ice-cream! "You go on to Penrhyndendraith," said the woman they asked. "That's got a fine ice-cream shop there. And if the young ones want a bathe, you tell them to go to Merlin's Cove— there's the finest bathing there in the kingdom."

"That sounds fine," said Roger, and they once more drove on. Round the coast they went, with the sea splashing on one side, and the mountains on the other—for now the hills had grown higher, and some of them towered up into the sky.

"Grand country!" said Mr. Martin. "Now—where is this Penny-denny-draith place. Ah—that looks like it— see, built on a slope of the hill."

They came to Penrhyndendraith. It was a truly picturesque place, a fishing village, with a dozen or so old cottages built along the seafront and others straggling up the slope of the hill behind.

Above the cottages on the hill rose a strange old place with curious turrets and towers. It was set right against a cliff-like hill, so that the back of it had no windows at all. Some of it was falling to pieces, and it looked in places as if only the ivy held it together!

A signboard was set over the great old doorway, but it was too far away for the children to read what was on it. Diana was more interested in finding the ice-cream shop than in looking at the half-ruined building on the hill. She jogged Mr. Martin's arm gently. "Look— would that be where the ice-cream shop is?" she asked, and pointed to the crooked row of cottages.

Mr. Martin stopped the car near them. "Well, as I can see only one that looks like a shop, that must be it!" he said. "Yes—see what it says over the door. 'Myfanwy Jones, General Dealer'."

"And look—it says 'Ice-Cream'!" said Roger. "In the corner of the window, see? Come on—let's get out of the car."

So out they jumped and went to the little shop. What a curious place it was! Inside it was very dark, and there was little space to stand, because of the hundreds of things that the shop sold! The goods were piled on the floor, they hung from the walls, they swung from the ceiling!

"It must sell simply everything in the world!" said Diana in astonishment. "Eatables, drinkables, china, pots and pans, fishing-nets, pails, potatoes, spades, stools —goodness, Miss Pepper, it's like a shop out of an old fairy-tale!"

"And here's the witch!" whispered Roger, and got a frown from Miss Pepper, as an old old woman waddled behind the small counter. Her face was a mass of wrinkles, and her snowy white hair was tucked away under a little cap of black net. But old though she looked, her eyes were startlingly bright and piercing.

She spoke to them in Welsh, which they didn't understand. Diana pointed to a card that said "Ice-Cream" and the old lady nodded, and smiled suddenly.

"Two? Three? Four?" she said in English.

"Oooh—twenty!" said Roger at once, and everyone laughed, the old woman too.

"How big are your ice-creams?" asked Diana. The old woman took a scoop and scooped some from an icebox—a good large helping, which she slapped between wafers.

"Ah—I think two each will be enough for the children," said Miss Pepper, "and one each for the grown-ups. What about Miranda, Barney?"

"Oh, one for her," said Barney. "She'll probably put most of it on the top of her head, because she's so hot!"

"There is big seat outside," said the old lady, nodding her head, as the children took the ice-creams, and they took the hint and went to sit on the hard old wooden bench.

"Not much taste—but VERY creamy and deliciously cold," said Barney. "Miranda, please go and sit on the ground. I do NOT like you to dribble ice-cream all down my neck. Nor do I like it held against my ear. SIT ON THE GROUND!"

The little monkey leapt down to the ground, chattering, holding her ice-cream tightly in her paw. The old lady, who was very interested in Miranda, came out to watch her.

"Very good little monkey," she said, in her lilting Welsh voice. "You come far?"

"Quite a long way," said Barney.

"You go far?" said the old lady.

"We don't know. We are looking for somewhere quiet to stay," said Barney. "Somewhere near here, perhaps. It is such lovely country. We don't want a big place, with big hotels—but perhaps a quiet old inn, and . . ."

"Ah, then you go up there, see?" said the old lady, and pointed up to the strange, half-ruined place they had seen on the hills. "Quiet, very quiet—and the food, it is so good, so good. And here, it is beautiful, with the sea so blue, and the sand so white, and . . ."

"But—is that old place occupied then?" said Mr. Martin, astonished. "I thought it was just an empty ruin."

"No, no—my son, he keeps it," said the old lady proudly. "It is an inn, sir, you understand? And what food! Big men come there, sir, important men—they say how good the food, how good!"

Nobody could believe that important people would stay at the half-ruined place. The old woman saw that they did not believe her, and she grasped Mr. Martin's arm.

"I speak the truth," she said. "To my son's inn come Sir Richard Ballinor, and Professor Hallinan, and . . ."

Mr. Martin knew those names! "One is a famous botanist, and the other is a well-known ornithologist— a man who studies birds," he told the astonished children. He turned to the old lady.

"There are many flowers here, then?" he said. "And rare birds?"

"Yes, many, many—up in the hills—and round the coves and on the cliffs," said the old lady, nodding her head. "Big men come to study them, I tell you, sir. My son, he knows them all. His cooking pleases them, sir, it is good, very good. You go to stay there too, sir? He has not many people now, it is a good time. Very good cooking, sir."

"Well—we might as well go up and see the old place," said Mr. Martin, taking out some money to pay for the ice-creams. "Thanks very much, Mrs. Jones. We enjoyed your ice-creams. Is there a road up to the old inn?"

"It is very rough, sir. You must go slowly," said the old woman, smiling delightedly at the thought that they were really going to see her son's place. "Cooking very good, sir, very very good."

They all went off to their car. "She's got good cooking on the brain," said Roger. "I wonder what the old place is like? It *might* be fun to stay there—there's all we want here, really—fine bathing . . ."

"Wonderful walks, I should think," said Barney, who loved walking. "And a jolly fine view."

"Fishing," said Roger, watching a small fishing-boat on the bay, its sails filling out with the wind.

"No trippers," said Miss Pepper.

"And birds for me!" said Diana happily.

"You and your birds!" said Roger scornfully and Diana immediately gave him a punch.

"Well—up to the inn we go!" said Mr. Martin, as they started off slowly up the steep track, leaving the caravan behind for the time being. "And what shall we find there, I wonder?"

CHAPTER SIX

Penrhyndendraith Inn

THE CAR crawled up the steep hill, on the zig-zagging track. The higher they went, the more magnificent the views became.

Diana gasped when she looked down the hill and saw the wonderful bay, and the great stretch of heaving sea beyond.

"Oh, *look!*" she said. "How lucky the people are who live in that old inn, Miss Pepper, and look out on that view every day. And see—the view across the hills is glorious too—are those mountains beyond?"

"Yes. And beautiful ones too!" said Miss Pepper. "Did you ever see such a blaze of heather—why, the hills look on fire with it! My goodness me—I can't help hoping that it will be possible for us to stay in the inn. I've never seen such views in my life!"

At last they reached the old inn. It really looked rather like a half-ruined castle! The great sign above the open doors gave its name.

PENRHYNDENDRAITH INN

"Goodness knows how it's pronounced," said Diana. "I say—isn't it dark inside! What do we do? Ring the bell?"

"Yes, if there is one—but there isn't," said Roger, looking all round. "No knocker either. What do we do? Yell?"

"IS ANYONE HERE?" shouted Barney obligingly, and they all jumped at his enormous yell. A small boy with an untidy shock of hair came running round a corner, followed by a great grey goose. He shouted out something to them in Welsh, and then disappeared into the open doorway, followed by the waddling goose.

"Well—I *imagine* that he and the goose have gone to find the owner of the inn," said Miss Pepper. "Ah—here comes someone!"

A lively little woman came hurrying up the hallway to the door, followed by the small boy, the goose still tagging along behind.

"Good afternoon," said Mr. Martin politely. "Er—Mrs. Jones down in the village told us of this inn, and . . ."

The plump little woman smiled all over her face, and rattled out an answer at top speed.

"Oh yes, sir, yes, sir, that would be my mother-in-law, sir, she knows this place well, and a good inn it is, no doubt about that, sir, we get important people here, sir, you should just peep into our visiting books, oh, the fine names that are there, and my husband, Llewellyn, he is the best cook in the world, sir, he went to London to learn his cooking, sir, in one of the big hotels, very good cooking, oh very . . ."

"Er—what I wanted to ask," put in Mr. Martin, afraid that the lively woman would never stop, "what I wanted to know was . . ."

"Oh yes, sir, you ask me anything," said the woman, smiling and nodding. "Come in, sir, won't you, and see what a wonderful place this is, and oh, the cooking, sir, well can you smell what's baking now, sir? That's my husband, sir, he's always cooking, he's . . ."

This sounded exactly as if her husband was being baked, and Diana gave a sudden giggle. They followed the woman into the great dark entrance, the boy and the goose behind them. Talking all the time, she showed them an enormous, rather dilapidated dining-room, and then took them up some stone stairs, uncarpeted, to the bedrooms.

"The beds are comfortable, sir, the view is fine, just you look, sir, did you ever see anything like it?"

Certainly the view was wonderful, and everyone gasped to see it. "And we don't charge a great deal, sir," rattled on the little woman. "You come to us, sir, if you want to stay in these parts, I tell you the cooking is fine, sir, very good cooking!"

Miranda, the monkey, stopped the flow of talk quite

39

suddenly, by flinging herself on to the grey goose's back. The goose was simply amazed, and began to cackle so loudly that it made everyone jump. The small boy ran to take the monkey off its back, and Miranda promptly jumped on to his shoulder. He screamed in fright and Miranda leapt back to Barney.

"Sorry about that," said Barney to the surprised woman. "It was just that Miranda wanted to see what sort of creature the goose was. I don't believe she's seen one before. Er—is the goose *safe*?"

The great bird was advancing on him, its enormous wings flapping, cackling at the top of its voice.

"Take Waddle away," said the woman crossly to the small boy. "He must not come indoors. Always I am telling you that." She turned to the others, but before she could begin one of her long speeches again, Mr. Martin spoke firmly to her.

"This is my son, and these other children are his friends. This lady, Miss Pepper, is with them, but I go back home to-day. Another boy, and a dog, will come soon. Can you let them have meals here—and a bed for Miss Pepper and Diana? The others would sleep in a caravan we have."

"Oh, sir, it would be an honour, it would be a pleasure to have them!" cried the talkative little woman. "My name is Mrs. Jones, sir, Mrs. Llewellyn Jones, and certainly we will look after them all, they shall have the best of food, sir, they shall go fishing with our men, they shall have picnics—and very good cooking, sir, and . . ."

"Well, thank you," said Mr. Martin, and turned to Miss Pepper. "Would you like to stay here, Miss Pepper? I can see already that the children approve!"

"Yes, Mr. Martin. I think this is just what we're looking

for," said Miss Pepper. "The views and the walks will be enough for me—and as for the children, if they can fish and bathe and explore, that's all *they'll* want! Yes —I'd like to stay here."

"Good, good, good!" cried Diana, and gave Miss Pepper such a sudden hug that she gasped. "And Snubby will love it too, I know he will. When will he come, Mr. Martin?"

"I'll telephone your mother as soon as I can, and arrange for him to come to-morrow, if possible," said Mr. Martin. "He can come by train to the nearest big town, and then get a taxi to bring him here. And let's hope Loony gets on all right with that goose—what's his name—Waddle!"

"Well—what with Loony the spaniel, Miranda the monkey and Waddle the goose, we may have rather a hectic time," said Miss Pepper, with a laugh. "But I've coped with Snubby and Loony before, so I've no doubt I can manage!"

"You go now? You go back home?" said Mrs. Jones anxiously to Mr. Martin. "You will not stay to have supper here, and taste the very good cooking?"

"No. I think not," said Mr. Martin. "I'll go down and pick up the caravan and bring it up here, now that I know the others will be staying. Perhaps I could just have a cup of tea before I leave?"

"You shall, sir, yes, you shall have tea and good, buttery scones!" said Mrs. Jones, and fled down the stairs as if she could smell the scones burning in the oven!

"Whew—what a non-stop talker!" said Roger. "We're going to have some very one-sided conversation, I can see!"

"I don't mind. I like her," said Diana. "She goes on and on like a babbling stream, but she's quite interesting. Oh, I *am* glad we're going to stay here. Sniff the air, Miss Pepper—isn't it clean and—and—mountainy? I wonder what Snubby will say—I'm sure he'll love it."

"Roger—you and Barney come down and help me with the caravan," said Mr. Martin. "It may be a bit awkward getting it round those zig-zaggy corners—you'd better walk behind and yell to me if I'm not giving it enough room to swing round."

"Right, sir," said the two boys, and went down to the car with Mr. Martin. They hopped in and went off to fetch the caravan, Miranda jigging excitedly on Barney's shoulder. Miss Pepper and Diana took the opportunity of peeping into the other bedrooms. "They really look a bit like cells, with their stone walls and stone floors," said Diana. "Let's choose one with the best view, Miss Pepper."

So they chose one with two windows, one window looking out over the sea, and the other into the mountains that rose one behind the other for miles. There were two small beds there, and the stone walls were partly draped with thick old curtains. A great chest stood against one wall, and Miss Pepper looked at it with interest.

"That must be pretty old," she said. "Our few belongings will be quite lost in there. And look at that ancient fireplace, Diana—you could almost put one of the beds in there!"

Diana went to the fireplace, and put her head up the chimney. "I can see the sky!" she called. "It's a most *enormous* chimney!"

A voice spoke to them from the door. It was Mrs. Jones, nodding and smiling. "I will show you a better

"*It's a most* enormous *chimney.*"

room," she said. "This is not so comfortable as the others."

"But we *love* the view here," said Miss Pepper, smiling. "And it really looks very comfortable!"

"No. It is not the best room," insisted Mrs. Jones. "You must have the best room. Come, I will show it to you."

And she took Miss Pepper's arm, and led her to another room, a little larger and better furnished. The view, however, was not nearly so beautiful.

"No. I'd rather have the other room," said Miss Pepper firmly. "Because of the view, you know."

Mrs. Jones looked suddenly sulky. "I do not like you to have that room," she said. "It is not the best room. I will give you this one."

But Miss Pepper was used to having her own way, and shook her head with a polite smile. "No. I have chosen the other room. Now we will go down and see if Mr. Martin has the luggage!"

And down they went to the great entrance, where Mr. Martin and the boys were already waiting with the car and the caravan, having put the bags and suitcases down on the battered stone steps.

"What about my cup of tea?" said Mr. Martin to Mrs. Jones, smiling. "And then we'll just fix up terms, and I'll go!"

"Your tea—your beautiful scones!" cried Mrs. Jones and rushed off down the dark passage-way, presumably to the kitchen. "Wait just one minute, sir, just one minute. The cooking here is . . ."

"Very good!" finished everyone at once, and Mr. Martin chuckled. "What a woman! I should think she probably talks all night long in her sleep, wouldn't you?"

CHAPTER SEVEN

"*Cocking Good! Very Good Cooking!*"

WHEN MR. MARTIN had gone, all the three children waving to him madly, and Miranda waving too, Roger put his hand over his tummy.

"Whew! What a tea Mrs. Jones gave us! I never tasted such marvellous scones in my life! I had six!"

"Cooking good—very good cooking!" quoted Diana. "Even Miranda had two scones. What's the time—just gone half past five, not too bad. What shall we do?"

"A little unpacking, please," said Miss Pepper promptly. "And a little arranging. I see that your father has put the caravan round the side of the inn, Barney, on that level piece. Is it safe there? There's such a slope down this hill."

"I'd better put heavy stones under the wheels," said Barney. "In case that small boy thinks up anything funny! He looks a bit of a monkey to me. Come and help me, Roger."

While the boys went to drag big stones to the wheels, Miss Pepper and Diana went upstairs to their room. They expected to find their luggage in the room with two windows that they had chosen, but it wasn't!

"Well! Don't tell me that Mrs. Jones has put it in the Best Room that she kept trying to force on us!" said Miss Pepper crossly. "Go and look, Diana."

Diana went off to the Best Room, and came back at

once. "Yes, it's there! What a nerve, really. She *knew* we said this one!"

"Well, we'll just go and get the suitcases and bring them here," said Miss Pepper, deciding that Mrs. Jones must be kept firmly in her place, and do what her guests asked. So in half a minute the suitcases were in the room they had chosen, and were being unpacked. There were great drawers in the chest, and the clothes were hurriedly arranged inside.

In the middle of it there came a knock at their door. "Come in!" called Miss Pepper, in her briskest voice.

In came a tall thin man with thick, untidy hair, wearing glasses and a surly look. "Good evening," he said. "I am Mr. Jones, the innkeeper. You have the wrong room. Please to come this way to our Best Room."

"I've already chosen this one," said Miss Pepper. "It's quite empty and I prefer the view. You have no guest staying in it, I know."

"Madam, you will not like this room," said Mr. Jones, looking even surlier.

"Please don't be so mysterious," said Miss Pepper, deciding that however well Mr. Jones cooked, she was not going to like him. "Why shouldn't I like this room?"

"There are sometimes noises in the night," said Mr. Jones solemnly...

"Oooh, how thrilling! What *kind* of noises?" asked Diana. "Howls—yells—moans—or what?"

"You laugh," said Mr Jones angrily. "But you will not laugh in the dark of night, when the noises come."

"Well, we'll see what they are like," said Miss Pepper, slamming a drawer of the chest shut. "Then we'll know whether to laugh or not. If you're trying to tell me the room's haunted or something, you're wasting your time. I don't believe in things like that."

Without another word Mr. Jones walked out of the room. Miss Pepper looked at Diana. "Well—if I wasn't such an obstinate woman, I'd move out into the other room!" she said. "This is obviously a guest-room, and I see no real reason why we shouldn't have it if we want it. Even the beds are made up and are all ready to sleep in!"

Soon all their clothes were stowed away and they went down to see how the boys were getting on. Miss Pepper peeped into the caravan and was astonished and pleased to see everything put away so tidily.

As she stood there talking to the boys, the great grey goose came round the corner, cackling loudly. Behind it came the small, untidy boy, whistling.

He went right up to the caravan and had a good look inside. The goose looked in too, and made as if to climb in.

"Oh no, you don't," said Roger, and gave it a small push. "Geese not allowed in here!"

The goose hissed and flapped its wings. The boy put his arms round its long neck, and it quietened down. He stared solemnly up at Roger with great dark eyes.

"What's your name?" said Diana, amused.

"Dafydd," said the boy.

"Oh—David," said Diana. "Come and look inside the caravan. Haven't you ever seen one before?"

Dafydd didn't understand what she was saying, but took her hand and went inside the van. He fingered everything with his dirty little hands, and finally took up a small comb from a hair-brush and slipped it into his pocket.

47

"No, no, Dafydd!" said Barney. "That's *my* comb, old son! Put it back!"

But Dafydd shook his head, and picked up a tube of tooth-paste. He examined it with interest. Then he suddenly felt something touching his pocket and looked down. It was Miranda, slipping a paw in, and taking out the comb! She was not going to allow anyone to steal Barney's belongings!

She leapt on to Barney's shoulder, chattering angrily, and began to comb his thick hair. Dafydd stared at her, frowning, rather scared. He said something in Welsh, something rather rude, and shook his little fist at Miranda, who immediately danced about on Barney's shoulder, saying plenty of rude things back to him in monkey-chatter.

"Cackle-cackle," said the goose outside, and flapped its wings impatiently. Miranda felt sure that it, too, was saying something rude, and she leapt straight off Barney's shoulder down to the floor, and then, with another flying leap she was on the goose's back, clinging to its neck, chattering loudly.

The goose was so astonished that it fled at once, hissing like a dozen snakes, with Miranda riding it. Barney roared with laughter, and Dafydd at once battered him with his small fists, angry that anyone should make fun of his goose.

"Now, now," said Barney, holding Dafydd's small fists in one of his hands. "That's enough! The monkey won't hurt your Waddle. You go after him, and I'll call back the monkey. And listen—you're NOT to come inside our caravan if we're not here. Do you understand?"

Dafydd shouted something that nobody could under-stand, kicked Barney on the ankles, wrenched his hands

48

away, and was out of the caravan like a streak of lightning, yelling for Waddle.

"Well—what do you think of *that*?" said Barney to the others. "I vote we keep our caravan locked when we're out anywhere. What a little rascal!"

"His mother ought to keep him in order," said Miss Pepper. "A few good slaps would do him a world of good. Taking that comb right under our noses! We'd better keep our room locked too, Diana, when we're out. Ah, here comes Miranda, looking pleased with herself!"

Miranda did feel pleased with herself. She had put that flappy goose in its place! She had ridden on its back all the way to the cow-shed a little way up the hill, the goose cackling at the top of its voice.

"You'd better behave yourself, Miranda," said Diana, "or Dafydd will be after you! Him and his precious goose! What a pair!"

"Well, the goose will have to mind its p's and q's when Snubby comes with Loony," said Barney. "I can't see either of them putting up with Dafydd and Waddle for long, if they *don't* behave themselves."

"You two boys will be quite comfortable in the caravan at nights," said Miss Pepper. "The bunks are very good. Diana and I have got that room we wanted—the one with the heavenly views—though Mr. Jones tried to scare us out of it with tales of noises in the night!"

"Oh, have you seen him?" said Barney. "He's not what you might call very merry and bright, is he? Roger and I thought he must have some secret sorrow, he looked so glum! But he'd no right to try and scare you with tales of noises at night, Miss Pepper."

"Oh, he and his wife are proud of their Best Room, as they call it," said Miss Pepper. "He just hoped that a silly fib about noises would make us change rooms, that's all. I don't expect he has even *noticed* what wonderful views our room has!"

"Well, I don't mind noises, or pet geese or light-fingered small boys, so long as we get Good Cooking, Very Good Cooking!" said Diana. "We shall see what supper's like."

Well, supper was Wonderful! Miss Pepper stared in amazement at the beautifully cooked meal. It began with chicken soup, went on to a fine joint of beef with mounds of roast potatoes, garden peas and the first runner beans, and finished with an ice-cream pudding set round with dainty biscuits of all kinds!

"I *say*! This is the best meal I've had since Daddy took us out to a big hotel in London!" said Roger. "*Look* at this ice-cream pudding—there's enough for a dozen people. Are we supposed to eat it all, Miss Pepper?"

"Well, supposed to or not, I've no doubt you will!" said Miss Pepper, and they did! Miranda had the last little biscuit off the dish, and sat nibbling it on Barney's shoulder as Mrs. Jones came in, beaming, to clear away.

"You like your supper?" she inquired, and laughed to hear the loud chorus that answered her.

"Cooking good, VERY good cooking!"

CHAPTER EIGHT

"Hallo, Snubby!"

THEY WERE all sleepy after their wonderful supper, and were yawning widely when Mrs. Jones trotted in with a silver tray on which coffee cups were set.

"Dear me!" said Miss Pepper, surprised to see the gleaming silver and the steaming coffee. "Who would have thought that a little country inn like this would do everything so well! No wonder 'Big People, Important People,' sometimes come here, as Mrs. Jones boasted! Coffee, everyone?"

"Anything to keep me awake!" said Barney, with a most tremendous yawn. "Miranda, that sugar is NOT for you. Smack her paw, Diana, please. She's as bad as that monkey of a Dafydd."

Far away, somewhere in the depths of the great dark hall, a bell shrilled. "The telephone!" said Miss Pepper. "I hope that's to say your aunt is getting on well, Diana."

Mrs. Jones appeared. "Someone for you, Miss Pepper, please," she said, and out went Miss Pepper, hoping for good news. She was soon back.

"That was your uncle," she said to Roger and Diana. "Barney's father got held up, and found he couldn't get back to your aunt's home to-night—so he telephoned your uncle, and told him to send Snubby off to us by train early to-morrow. Snubby is absolutely too thrilled for words, he said, and Loony promptly went mad!"

Everyone laughed. Roger rubbed his hands together. "Good old Snubby! Funny we should be so pleased to have such a pest with us, but things always seem to happen when Snubby and Loony are around. What time will he arrive?"

"Probably by the half past twelve train, at Dilcarmock, five miles from here," said Miss Pepper. "It's not a bad train. I'll telephone to order a taxi to meet him and bring him here. Your aunt is going on well, so your uncle sounded quite happy."

"He'll feel even happier to-morrow when he's got rid of Snubby," said Roger. "Last time he stayed there Snubby kept pretending to be a Christy minstrel with a banjo and made banjo noises all day long. Uncle and Aunt nearly went crazy!"

Miss Pepper groaned, remembering the holiday at Rubadub when Snubby had fancied himself at playing all kinds of instruments, not only banjoes. "I only hope he doesn't take it into his head to be a Christy minstrel here," she said. "Anyone want any more coffee?"

Nobody did. One by one they yawned again, and Miss Pepper laughed. "Let's all go to bed," she said. "It's getting on for nine o'clock and we've had a very long day. Off to the caravan, boys—and sleep well! See you at breakfast-time. It's at half-past eight, so if anyone wants an early morning bathe, there'll be plenty of time."

"Right. I'm half asleep already," said Roger, getting up. He gave Miss Pepper a sudden hug that surprised her. "I think you're a brick to stay on with us like this after our caravan holiday broke up!" he said. "I hope to goodness you don't hear any unpleasant noises in the night!"

"Well, we'll lean out of one of our windows and yell

if we do!" said Miss Pepper, pleased at the sudden hug.

"This will be your last peaceful night, boys," said Diana, with a grin. "To-morrow you'll have Snubby in the caravan with you, and mad-dog Loony!"

The boys left, and Miss Pepper and Diana went upstairs, meeting Mrs. Jones on the way. "A truly wonderful supper, Mrs. Jones," said Miss Pepper. "Your husband is surely a trained chef?"

"Oh, yes indeed," said Mrs. Jones proudly. "It was in London Town that he was trained, Miss Pepper, at a big, important hotel. We were so happy there. I was chamber-maid, and he was second chef. I wanted to stay—but no, Mr. Jones he wanted to come back here, where he was born. His cooking is good, very good!"

Miss Pepper nodded, said good night and went on up the stairs, half wondering whether she would find their things removed from their room-with-a-view to the Best Room. But no—their cases were still in the room they had chosen. Good! Miss Pepper was also pleased to see that there was a key in the door.

"Now we can lock our room when we leave it," she said to Diana, "and can be sure that that monkey of a Dafydd won't come in with his cackling goose and pocket whatever takes his fancy!"

She and Diana were soon in bed and fast asleep. Were there any Noises in the Night? There might well have been, even if only the wind in the chimney, but neither of them would have heard a thunderstorm that night! The beds were comfortable, the room was airy, and they slept so soundly that they only awoke when Mrs. Jones came knocking at their door with cans of hot water.

Breakfast was as good as supper had been. Cold ham,

boiled eggs, hot toast, home-made marmalade, creamy butter, and scalding hot coffee . . . Miss Pepper looked at the table with much approval.

"Snubby will like this place," said Roger, taking his second boiled egg. "Have you phoned about a taxi for him yet, Miss Pepper?"

"No. There's time enough after breakfast," said Miss Pepper. "Did you and Barney bathe? I should imagine you did, by your appetites!"

"Well, we didn't!" said Roger, with a grin. "We slept like logs—and I don't think we'd have wakened when we did if that young Dafydd hadn't come peering in at the caravan window and wakened up Miranda. She leapt out of the window and chased Waddle the goose all over the place, and what with Dafydd's yells and the goose's cackles, we woke up with an awful jump! Why doesn't someone smack Dafydd hard?"

"Someone's going to, if he doesn't look out," said Barney grimly, rubbing his hands together.

Miss Pepper went to phone for a taxi for Snubby. "I've ordered one to call here at 11.30," she said. "I thought you three would like to go in it to meet Snubby. It's the only one in the village, apparently, so it's probably a poor old crock."

"Right," said Barney, pleased at the idea of meeting Snubby at the station. "We'll have time to go down for a bathe, then. Are you all coming? Merlin's Cove is supposed to be the best bathing-place, apparently."

Mrs. Jones agreed that it was indeed the best place, when she came in to clear away the breakfast. Dafydd and Waddle also came in with her, and Waddle immediately pecked at a piece of toast left on one of the plates. Mrs. Jones didn't say a word of reproof—but Miranda did!

She snatched the toast out of the goose's beak, and then pulled her tail feathers hard, chattering angrily all the time.

Dafydd aimed a blow at the monkey, and Barney was immediately beside him, holding his hands tightly.

"No! Do you want to be bitten? Miranda has very sharp teeth. I will show you them. Come here, Miranda."

Dafydd stared at the monkey's sharp little teeth, and turned away, gabbling in Welsh.

"He says your monkey must not hurt his goose," said Mrs. Jones, clearing away. "Dafydd, go away. You are not to come in here now that we have visitors. Take Waddle with you."

Dafydd went out sulkily, Waddle following behind. "Waddle was just a little gosling when Dafydd had him," said Mrs. Jones. "He broke his leg, and Dafydd mended it—he put a stick, like so—and tied it well. And Waddle's leg mended, and now he will not leave Dafydd, and what a trouble the two are, I give you my word, and what is the use of my scolding him, he hears only what he wants to hear, he does only what he . . ."

It looked as if Mrs. Jones was launched on one of her never-ending speeches, and Miss Pepper interrupted her firmly.

"We would rather that Dafydd and Waddle did not come into the dining-room or into our bedroom," she said.

"But how can I stop them?" argued Mrs. Jones, deftly folding up the tablecloth. "They go where they please, they . . ."

"Not when *we're* here!" said Miss Pepper. "Er—have you ever tried a good smack, Mrs. Jones?"

"A smack! A smack is no good with that one!" said

Mrs. Jones. "Even if you could get near him with a smack! Like an eel he is, like a slippery eel, and as for Waddle, he is as bad, the way he walks where he wants to walk, and cackles when he wants to cackle, and . . ."

But there was no one to listen to her! The room was empty, the boys had slipped out to bathe, Diana had gone too, and Miss Pepper had hurried quietly out of the room! Mrs. Jones went on talking for a long time before she saw she was alone—and even then she didn't stop, but talked away to herself as she carried out the tray to the kitchen.

The boys couldn't find their bathing things, and there was a great to-do at once. "Miss Pepper! MISS PEPPER! Ask Di if she's got our things with hers, will you?" shouted Barney, as he saw Miss Pepper at her bedroom window. "Ours aren't in the caravan, that's certain."

Diana hunted hurriedly in the drawers where she had put her clothes, and at last found the boys' bathing things. She threw them out of the window, and one pair caught on a rambler growing up the wall.

"Ass!" shouted Roger. "Now I'll have to get a ladder. Why can't girls throw properly!"

"Oh dear—if you don't hurry up, the taxi will be here," said Miss Pepper, looking at her watch. She called down to the boys. "I don't think you'd better bathe, after all—you'll miss Snubby's train if you do!"

And then, what a surprise! A piercing, very well-known voice came to their startled ears—surely, surely, it couldn't be SNUBBY'S?

"HALLO, EVERYBODY! HERE I AM!"

And someone came up the slope to the inn—someone very dirty indeed, with straw sticking out of him at every corner and a black dog careering at his heels.

"Snubby! We were just going to meet you!" yelled
Roger. "How did you get here? Your train isn't even due
in yet! How AWFUL you look! What in the world have
you been doing?"

CHAPTER NINE

Hot Bath for Snubby!

SNUBBY MARCHED up to the astonished Roger and Barney,
grinning all over his freckled, snub-nosed face. His ginger
hair was very wind-blown indeed!

Diana and Miss Pepper ran downstairs most amazed.
How like Snubby to arrive so unexpectedly!

"Have I given you a surprise?" he said. "I thought I
should!"

"Snubby—how did you get here so soon? And why are
you so *filthy*?" said Miss Pepper. "Hallo, Loony—good
gracious, *you're* all covered in straw too!"

"Well, Uncle got me a ticket for an awfully slow train,"
said Snubby, rubbing his dirty face with an even dirtier
handkerchief. "And I heard there was a very early one,
so I decided to catch that. You see, Uncle was getting
pretty fed up with me, really. I arrived at Dilcarmock
ages ago, and I got a lift in a cart that was loaded with
straw and stuff for Penrhyndendraith, or whatever this
place is called. Gosh, it crawled, though, and the straw
was frightfully prickly."

"Snubby, you look too awful for words," said Diana.
"Honestly, I've never *seen* such a tramp!"

"Well, I did think you'd all be more pleased to see me,"

said Snubby, sounding hurt. "I tell you, I couldn't stay with Uncle any longer. He just glowered at me till I almost changed into a worm. Darling Miranda, are *you* pleased to see me?"

The little monkey leapt to his shoulder and put her tiny paws down his neck, chattering softly. Yes—she was very pleased to see Snubby—and Loony too!

Loony was tearing all round the place, sniffing into every corner. He had given everyone a really good lick, and was now interested in all the new smells. And then, quite suddenly, he saw a most fearsome creature coming towards him, hissing like a dozen snakes!

It was Waddle, of course, Waddle, who detested dogs and cats—and monkeys! Waddle considered that the inn belonged to him and to no one else, and woe betide any strange creature who dared to sniff around his domain!

Loony took one look at Waddle and backed away hurriedly. What in the world was this creature? Bird? Animal? Snake? Its head and neck and voice seemed to be those of a snake—but it had wings! Loony let out a terrified yelp and ran to Snubby.

"Don't be an ass, Loony—it's only a *goose*!" said Snubby—and then promptly ran for shelter himself as Waddle, cackling, hissing and flapping, descended upon him and Loony too!

But little Miranda was not going to have her friends scattered like this, and entered into the battle with delight! She flung herself on Waddle's back and clasped her neck as she had done once before, chattering at the top of her voice.

Then it was Waddle's turn to run, and off went the goose into the house, waddling more quickly than ever

a goose waddled before, cackling as if the house was on
fire! Miranda clung to her tightly, and the goose could
not shake her off.

Loony recovered his courage and raced after them,
barking madly. Mr. Jones, coming to see what the noise
was about, met the goose and Miranda with Loony
immediately behind them, and was promptly bowled over.
He sat down very suddenly indeed, knocked over by the
heavy goose, and then trodden on by the surprised Loony.

Miss Pepper put her hands over her face, and groaned.
WHY did things like this always happen when Snubby
was around? He had only to appear, and the whole world
seemed at once to go crazy. And now there was Mr.
Jones, tall and thin and dour, getting up from the stone
hall floor, rubbing himself angrily.

"Oh, Mr. Jones—I hope you're not hurt," said Miss
Pepper, hurrying to him. "The goose frightened the dog,
and then the monkey frightened the goose, and the dog
ran after them both, and, and . . ."

"And the cow jumped over the moon," said Snubby
with a hoot of laughter. Mr. Jones took one look at him
and raised his voice.

"Get out of here, you dirty little tramp! Go where
you belong, into the gutter! Don't dare to come up to
this inn, where decent folks stay!"

There was a surprised silence, while everyone stared
first at Mr. Jones, and then at Snubby. Snubby glanced
down at his dirty clothes apologetically, and then looked
beseechingly at Miss Pepper.

"Er—this is a cousin of Diana and Roger Lynton,"
said Miss Pepper. "The one whom Mr. Martin arranged
to come and stay, you remember. He's had a long—and
—er—a very dirty journey. He needs a—a wash."

59

Mr. Jones was completely bowled over.

Mr. Jones glared at them all, and limped back down the hall without a word. Miss Pepper took hold of Snubby.

"You're going to have a hot bath," she said. "And I'm going to scrub you from head to foot—you—you dirty little tramp! *Really*, Snubby, I *cannot* imagine how anyone can get as filthy as you look."

"Where's that goose gone?" said Snubby, pretending not to hear. "I can't stop old Loony from going for him if he appears again."

"Don't worry about Loony—he'll retire into the darkest corner he can find, if he sees Waddle," said Miss Pepper, keeping a firm hold on Snubby and propelling him towards the hall door. "Thank goodness the creature has disappeared and Miranda's recovered herself. I do wish you'd caught the proper train, Snubby, and not caused all this sensation! We don't want to be turned out of this place. The cooking is so . . ."

"Very very good!" finished Barney, with a grin. He put his arm round Snubby's shoulder. "Cheer up! Where's your luggage? Get out a bathing suit and come and bathe with us—you'll soon be clean then."

"No," said Miss Pepper at once. "I don't see why he should make the sea absolutely black! Is that all the luggage you've got, Snubby—that small case there? My goodness—you can't have much in it."

"Well, I thought Roger could lend me what I've forgotten," said Snubby amiably, going indoors with Miss Pepper. "Gosh, I feel a bit tired now. Come on, Loony. Is there anything to *eat*, Miss Pepper? I do feel awfully empty. I say, what a place this is! I thought it was a ruin, till the van-man told me it was the inn I'd asked him to drop me at. I say, I do hope I'm going to sleep in the caravan with the others, I . . ."

"Snubby! *Stop* talking for a minute," said Miss Pepper quite fiercely. "I want to ask for some hot water for you. Stay here while I go to the kitchen. Don't dare to move from there, because if Mr. Jones sees you again he might quite well pick you up and throw you into the sea—and I wouldn't blame him either!"

"I say—you *are* peppery this morning, Miss Pepper darling!" said Snubby, surprised. "And I'd so looked forward to seeing you again, too. I never . . ."

But Miss Pepper was gone, walking quickly down the dark hallway to the equally dark kitchen, which was huge and rather forbidding. Mrs. Jones was there, doing some washing-up in an enormous sink.

"Oh, Mrs. Jones—do you think I might have a very large can of hot water?" asked Miss Pepper. "The children's cousin has arrived and he's really *very* dirty."

"I will get it at once for you, certainly I will," said Mrs. Jones, reaching for an enormous jug. "I will bring it up to the bathroom, Miss. In two minutes it will be there."

Miss Pepper, thankful that Mrs. Jones did not chatter on and on as she usually did, went to collect Snubby, determined that he should not escape her.

"You dirty little ragamuffin!" she said as she saw him patiently waiting for her on exactly the same spot where she had left him, Loony sitting beside him. "You look as if you've just been sweeping a chimney! I never did know anyone who could . . ."

"Get dirty wherever he goes and whatever he does," finished Snubby with a grin. "I wonder how many times you've said that to each of us, Miss Pepper! Where's the hot water?"

It wasn't long before Snubby was clean and shining all over, even to the backs of his ears. It wasn't any good protesting that he could wash himself, Miss Pepper was determined to get him really clean. Loony sat beside the bath, watching in alarm, half afraid that it might be his turn next!

"Now dry yourself, and I'll go and find something for you to eat," said Miss Pepper. "*Look* at the bath-water— what a disgrace! It will take you quite a bit of time to clean the bath!"

Snubby sighed. He thought it was very hard that no matter what he did, he got into trouble. He rubbed himself dry and talked to the listening Loony.

"She called me a *ragamuffin*! What do you think of that, Loony? Except that it sounds a bit like something to eat, it's a horrid name to give to anyone. *Ragamuffin!* Now what am I supposed to put on? Those clean clothes, I suppose—my own vest, Roger's old shorts—and this looks like Barney's shirt, it's so big! Loony, you don't know how lucky you are to be born a dog, and be able to wear the same old fur coat all your life. Like to try this vest on, old thing?"

Loony retreated to the door at once, and scratched at it, whining, suddenly afraid that it might enter Snubby's head to pop *him* into the bath.

"I'm not ready yet, old chap," said Snubby, looking down into the bath, where the dirty water had already left a black line all round the sides. "I say, Loony— come and look at this! I've got to clean this bath, and it will take me *ages!*"

Loony put his front paws up on the side of the bath and looked down at the water, wagging his tail. He didn't mind looking, so long as he wasn't going to be bathed in it. He couldn't imagine why *anyone* ever had baths. Snubby suddenly sniffed, and bent down over Loony.

"You know, you smell pretty awful," he said. "I've a good mind to pop you in too, and . . ."

But very fortunately for the scared Loony, Miss Pepper's voice suddenly sounded outside the door.

"Snubby! What in the world are you doing? Aren't you dressed *yet*? I hope you've cleaned that bath. There is a piece of meat-pie, and some bread and cheese downstairs, if you hurry!"

Snubby hurried at once. He let out the bath water, and hurriedly tried to remove the black line round the bath with the flannel Miss Pepper had given him, finished dressing, and grinned at Loony as he opened the bathroom door. "Loony—I have a feeling we'll enjoy being here. We're going to have quite an exciting time!"

Well, Snubby, you're right. But perhaps it will be rather *too* exciting!

CHAPTER TEN

Snubby gets into Trouble

SNUBBY THOROUGHLY enjoyed his first day at Penrhynden-draith, and so did the others. They went bathing that morning, and found Merlin's Cove. It was a truly lovely place.

The sands were almost white there, and as smooth as silk to walk on. When the tide was up it swept right into all the caves that made up Merlin's Cove. These ran either a little way or a long way into the high rocky cliff, and two were labelled "DANGEROUS."

"Ha—let's see why they are dangerous," said Snubby,

peering into one, and was at once firmly taken by the arm by Barney.

"Any fatheadedness on your part, and you go straight back to another of your uncles and aunts," he said. "Do you want rocks falling on your head—or to lose your way for ever in a maze of cliff tunnels? Aren't you ever going to grow up, Snubby?"

Loony ran a little way into the dark, low cave, and then turned his head as if to say, "Come on, Snubby!" but Snubby yelled to him at once.

"Come back, ass! Aren't you *ever* going to grow up?"

They explored some of the other caves, and found most of them shallow, going back only a little way. They bathed twice, and lay in the sun. Miranda hated the water and wouldn't go near it, though Barney at last persuaded her to paddle, and held her paw like a child.

Loony splashed past her, and, once out of his depth and swimming, turned his head as if to say "Monkeys are poor creatures! *They* can only paddle!"

"It looks as if we're going to have a pretty good time here," said Roger, lying on the sand, leaning on his elbow. "Look—are those fishing boats coming in? Aren't they lovely?"

They were! They all had brown sails of different shades, and came smoothly in on the wind, the tide taking them to the little jetty not far off. The children scrambled up to go and see the catch. Miranda waited till Loony had come out of the water, and was vigorously shaking himself, and then leapt straight on to his back, clinging there with all her might, jigging up and down as if wanting a ride.

This was an old trick of Miranda's, and one that

Loony didn't approve of at all! He set off at top speed hoping the little monkey would be bumped off, but she clung on for dear life, winding her tail round his tummy.

"Loony, roll over on the sand, you idiot!" shouted Snubby. "Have you forgotten how to get her off!"

Loony promptly rolled over, and Miranda had to leap off, scampering to Barney quickly before Loony could catch her. The children laughed, and ran over to the jetty. They watched the great catch of fish being emptied. There were some large crabs among the catch, and Miranda was most interested in them as they began to walk off sideways.

She tapped one, and almost had her paw caught by one of its big claws! After that she and Loony kept well away from the crawling crabs.

They were all very hungry by dinner-time, and went back through the little straggling village and up the slope of the hill to the old inn. They passed the ice-cream shop, and Snubby at once wanted to go in and buy ice-creams when he heard how the others had sampled them the day before.

"No. You'll spoil your dinner," said Barney. "Do come on. I feel quite hollow inside with hunger."

Miss Pepper had had a peaceful morning, except for twenty minutes when Mrs. Jones saw her wandering round the old garden of the inn, and came out to talk non-stop. Miss Pepper made up her mind that she would rather go down to the beach with the children than risk being found by Mrs. Jones again!

It really was a very pleasant first day, marred only by an accident to Snubby's clothes—or rather to the shirt and the shorts which belonged to Barney and Roger.

Barney suddenly saw that his nice shirt, which had

been almost new, was torn right down the back. He felt very cross.

"What on earth have you done to ruin my shirt like that?" he demanded. "It's my newest one—I hadn't even worn it myself! I didn't mind lending it to you till you had your own clothes sent on—but I do think you might have been careful with it! And gosh—look at Roger's shorts! Have you sat down in a patch of oil or something? You *are* in a filthy mess!"

Snubby tried to screw himself round to see the shorts. "I wondered what that horrible smell was that seemed to follow me around," he said. "Well, I never! When *could* I have sat down in oil? I'm awfully sorry, Roger—and sorry about your shirt too, Barney."

"Well, I don't know what you're going to do to-morrow for clothes," said Roger. "Borrow a skirt of Diana's, I suppose! I'm certainly not going to lend you any more things."

Miss Pepper was also very annoyed, and stared in horror as Snubby presented himself to her and asked her advice about the oil.

"To think I scrubbed you from head to toe this morning—and you look exactly like a ragamuffin again!" she said. "Well, you'll have to stay in bed to-morrow while I wash your own dirty clothes, the ones you took off this morning."

"Oh *no*!" said Snubby, in horror. "Stay in *bed*? I couldn't!"

But Miss Pepper was quite firm about that and the next day Snubby found himself compelled to have his breakfast in the caravan, sitting in his bunk. He was very angry indeed, and Loony simply *couldn't* understand what all the fuss was about.

"I simply daren't borrow anything else of Barney's or Roger's," groaned Snubby to a sympathetic Loony. "And as I've only got this old vest to wear, or my pyjamas, I don't see *how* I can go out of the caravan till Miss Pepper cleans up those torn dirty things of mine."

He lay and thought angry thoughts for a time, and then an idea came into his head. "That ice-cream shop!" he said. "I believe it sells second-hand clothes. I'm sure I saw some hanging up. Loony, what about us slipping out and buying some before the others come back? I'm NOT going to lie here all day! I'll turn my pyjama trousers up to my knees so that they are more like shorts—and keep this vest on."

And, very soon, a rather peculiar figure slipped out of the caravan, and ran down to the little village. Snubby grinned as he looked down at himself, and wondered if the old lady in the shop would notice his peculiar attire.

Old Mrs. Jones, her snow-white hair tucked under the black net cap, didn't seem at all surprised to see a small boy in vest and turned-up pyjama-legs.

"You'll be one of the children up at the inn?" she said in her sing-song voice, with a twinkle in her eye. "Is it an ice-cream you are wanting to buy?"

"Well, yes—among other things," said Snubby, giving her the grin that always made old ladies love him. "Look —I've got into trouble over my clothes, and I want to buy some more. Have you got any that would fit me— second-hand ones, I mean?"

"Well, now, there's that pair of long trousers," said old Mrs. Jones, pointing to a most dilapidated pair, hanging on a hook. "Clean they are, though dirty they look, for I washed them myself. And there's this jersey, red and yellow, gay it is, and not badly worn."

"Long trousers would be fine," said Snubby, pleased, and put them on over his pyjama legs. "Hey, Loony, how do I look?"

Loony barked sharply and wagged his tail. "He says I look about sixteen, instead of twelve," said Snubby with a grin. "Now for the jersey—my word, I've gone gay, haven't I! Is it clean, because if it isn't, Miss Pepper will rip it off me at once."

"It is clean," said Mrs. Jones. "And you shall have a cap too—a good one. See the big peak!"

Snubby put it on and fancied himself very much in it. "Thanks awfully," he said. "How much do I owe you?"

"That will be two shillings for the cap, four shillings for the trousers, and three for the jersey—nine shillings— and an ice-cream thrown in for nothing," said Mrs. Jones, laughing at Snubby's peculiar appearance.

"Oh, I say—that's jolly kind of you," said Snubby, and paid up at once. He took the ice-cream wafer, and grinned gratefully.

"It is my son who has the inn where you are staying," said Mrs. Jones. "So good he is at cooking! He went to London to learn. Ah, to think that a poor boy like my Llewellyn, with never two pairs of trousers to his name, should have gone to London and learnt to cook! And now that inn is his! Always, all his life, he has said to me, 'Ah, if only that inn was mine!' How I laughed! 'I have five pounds in my old stocking,' I said, 'and that has taken me eighteen years to save—and you want to own that inn'!"

"Gosh—how did he get it, then?" asked Snubby, licking the last of the ice-cream.

"He made friends in London," said the old lady proudly. "Important friends. And they lent him the money to buy the inn he so much wanted. How happy my Llewellyn is now!"

Snubby thought of the cross-looking, dour man he had seen the night before. "Goodness—he doesn't *look* very happy!" he said. "I say! I must go! Miss Pepper will be sending out a search party for me or something. Good-bye and many thanks!"

And away he rushed, really a very peculiar figure indeed. What in the world would the others say!

CHAPTER ELEVEN

A very Queer Happening

SNUBBY HAD a few moments of doubt as he walked up the steep slope to the inn. "If they jeer at me I shall run away!" he said to Loony, who wagged his tail sympathetically.

The first person he met was the boy Dafydd, with his faithful goose. Dafydd gave a loud shriek when he saw him and tore off with Waddle behind him—though whether the shriek was because Snubby looked so peculiar, or because he was scared of Loony was not clear! Snubby stared after him, frowning. If that was the effect he was going to have, things were not going to be easy!

Roger, Diana and Barney came out of the inn at that moment. They had been looking everywhere for Snubby, having missed him from the caravan. They looked at him, not recognising him in the least, and wondered why Loony was following this peculiar-looking lad.

Snubby had pulled the big peaked cap down over his

face, and he grinned when he saw that the others did not recognise him. He swaggered up to them, hands in pocket, and pretended to speak in Welsh, in a peculiar-sounding hoarse voice.

"Colly-inna-dooly-hector-sonkin-poppyll?" he said, his cap still pulled down over his face.

"What on earth is this fellow saying?" said Roger, astonished. "And why is Loony with him?"

Diana gave a sudden shriek, and pulled at Snubby's cap. "It's Snubby! SNUBBY! Where have you been? Where did you get those *awful* clothes?"

"They're not awful. They're fine—*and* clean," said Snubby, turning himself round and round so that they could admire him. "I bought them at the ice-cream shop —second-hand."

"Snubby! How *could* you buy clothes like that—you don't know *who's* worn them before!" said Roger.

"What does that matter? I tell you, they're *clean*!" roared Snubby. "Oh gracious goodness—here comes Miss Pepper!"

What the others had said was nothing to what Miss Pepper said! She insisted that he should go straight back to the caravan and take off "those TERRIBLE clothes, ESPECIALLY that cap," and wait till she came with clean ones.

"I'm not going to," said Snubby obstinately. "Fancy expecting me to waste a lovely morning like this in that caravan, when I've gone and got myself clothes to wear. It's no *good*, Miss Pepper, I'm going to wear these clothes till my others are clean—and if you all think I'm not fit company for you, all right, Loony and I will keep away from you! Come on, Loony—they're looking at us as if we were a couple of bad smells!"

And with that Snubby marched quickly off down the hill, his peaked cap at a very cheeky angle indeed. Diana called crossly after him. "Well—you *do* smell in those clothes! You smell dreadful!"

Snubby took no notice at all, and soon disappeared round a bend. Miss Pepper suddenly began to laugh.

"Oh dear!" she said. "What a *sight* he looks—and yet I really do believe he's quite proud of those awful clothes. I only hope to goodness he won't want to go on wearing them when his own are ready. Well—what are you three going to do to-day?"

"Bathe—have a walk, perhaps fish if we can get a boat," said Barney. "It's a pity Snubby's behaving like this. Why didn't he think of putting on his bathing things—it's warm enough for him to wear them all day on the beach. I'll take them down with me, shall I—in case he does join us, and then I can tell him to wear them, and stay with us."

So, when the others went down to the beach, they took Snubby's bathing things with them. But there was no sign of him, or of Loony either!

Snubby was angry and hurt. Fancy calling him a bad smell! He caught sight of himself in the glass window of the ice-cream shop as he went by, and stopped. H'm! He did look a bit queer, perhaps. Pity the trousers were so big and sloppy—and the jersey certainly *was* a bit loud. But the cap was fine!

"I suppose we look a bit ragamuffinish again, Loony," he said sorrowfully. "Now—what shall we do? I know —we'll find a quiet place, and read that code-letter from old Bruce. I'll tell you what he says."

Loony wagged his tail. He knew who Bruce was— a very close school-friend of Snubby's, a rascal almost as bad as Snubby, the bane of their form-master. The two of them had invented a most involved secret code, using both figures and letters. It took Snubby about two hours to write a letter in their secret code—and even longer to decipher any he got from Bruce! Still, it made them both feel very important indeed, and they enjoyed that.

"We'll go somewhere out of sight of the others," said Snubby to Loony. "Look—what about going down to that broken bit of cliff over there—see? We could hide among the fallen rocks nicely, and see what old Bruce has got to say in his letter."

So down they went together and were soon ensconced among the warm rocks, the sea not very far away. Snubby took out Bruce's letter. It was on a squared piece of paper, neatly torn out of his maths book.

Snubby looked at it and gave a small groan. "It's rather a long one," he said to Loony, gazing at the mass of neat little figures, interspersed with letters. "It'll take us ages to decode. Still, it's all good practice, Loony. You never know when you might have to use a code. Now—let's see—12—6—J—567—P—gosh, what does P stand for now? I wish I had my code-book with me. Hallo—who's this?"

A man was coming over the rocks towards them. He was short and wore a black beard, and dark sun-glasses. Snubby glanced up at him, expecting him to pass by. But he didn't.

He came towards Snubby, and stood beside him. "Give that to me!" he said in an angry voice.

Snubby was extremely startled. He hastily stuffed his precious code-letter into his pocket. "What's up?" he said. "What do you want?"

"That letter!" said the man savagely. "How dare you open and read it?"

73

"Well, why shouldn't I? It was sent to me, not to you," said Snubby, beginning to feel that the man must be crazy. "Don't be daft!"

"You know you had to meet me here and give me that letter," said the man, his voice shaking with rage. "And I find you have opened it and are trying to decipher it! How dare you! I shall see that your uncle beats you well!"

"What on EARTH are you talking about?" said Snubby, absolutely at sea. "This is NOT your letter. It's mine, and I'm certainly not going to give it to you. It's in a very secret code that my friend and I know."

"Your friend? Your *friend* knows the code—and you too? You lie!" said the man. "You are a foolish boy who hopes to make me give you money for handing over my letter."

"Oh, don't be an ass," said Snubby, getting up. "If this is a joke, it's pretty silly. I'm going!"

But to his enormous surprise the man threw him roughly back on the rocks, dug his hand into Snubby's pocket and tore out the letter. He slapped Snubby hard across the face, and turned to go. But this was too much for Loony! He began to growl angrily.

What! This man dared to knock Snubby over and slap him! With a very fierce snarl indeed Loony flung himself on the surprised man, who shook him off with great force. He picked up a piece of rock and flung it at Loony, who only just dodged it in time.

"Loony! Come here! He'll kill you!" shouted Snubby. "He's absolutely mad. Let him go."

Reluctantly Loony sat down and watched the bearded man clamber up the cliff and on to the roadway. The little spaniel growled angrily till he was out of sight, sad that he could not chase him. He turned to Snubby and whimpered, pawing him as if to say, "Are you hurt, master? Is everything all right?"

"I'm not hurt, only angry," said Snubby, "and jolly puzzled too. Why did he come here to me? Did he think I was someone else? And what on earth was he gassing about—a letter in code, he said—and took my letter from old Bruce! I suppose he saw it was in code. Look

here, Loony, there's something peculiar about this. Let's go and find the others."

And off they went along the beach. They soon saw the others sitting on the sands, sunning themselves after a bathe. Snubby went up to them and sat down.

"Got something to tell you all," he said in a low, mysterious voice. "Listen!"

At once they sat up, grinning at Snubby's peculiar appearance, but eager to hear him. He began to relate what had happened.

They all listened, most astonished. Barney whistled.

"You're not making this up by any chance, are you?" he said, for Snubby had at times invented some very curious stories.

"No! No, of course I'm not," said Snubby indignantly. "It's true, every word of it—and here's the bruise I got on my elbow when that fellow flung me down on the rocks."

He showed them quite a massive bruise. Barney looked at it and frowned.

"Either that fellow was quite mad—or there's something queer going on," he said. "Why did he mistake you for someone else, though? You must have looked like the person he was to meet—a real tramp, if you don't mind my saying so, Snubby. A proper ragamuffin! The kind of person who *might* be a go-between, if something dirty was going on."

"I'll take these things off at once then," said Snubby hastily. "Got my bathing things? I'll just pop behind that rock. A go-between! Phew—just wait till I see the real one, if ever I do!" He went behind a rock and hastily flung off his awful clothes, putting on a pair of bathing trunks. And then, *just* as he joined the others, someone passed them, dressed in clothes very like Snubby's—long, dirty-looking trousers, a bright woollen jersey, a peaked cap—and behind him ran a small black dog!

"There you are!" whispered Barney, nudging Snubby very hard indeed. "See? I bet that's the fellow *you* were mistaken for—a regular ragamuffin! He's even got a little black dog—a mongrel poodle—and he's making for the rocks over there where *you* were sitting. Now what do we do?"

CHAPTER TWELVE

Snubby and the Ragamuffin

THEY ALL WATCHED the little ragamuffin go to the patch
of fallen rocks where Snubby had sat. The small dog
leapt about at his heels, and then sat down by him, as
he settled himself on one of the rocks.

"See? He's waiting for someone," said Roger. "I bet
he's got the *real* secret code-letter all right—the one that
mad fellow thought *you* had!"

"I expect that man was told to look out for a ragamuffin
of a boy, sitting on those rocks, with a black dog," said
Barney. "And the boy would hand him a letter—secret
instructions about something or other, I should think—
and . . ."

"And old Snubby happened to go to that very spot,
looking like a ragamuffin himself—with Loony who's as
black as any dog can be expected to be!" said Roger.
"And what was more, Snubby happened to be reading a
letter in code—his code and Bruce's—but how was the
man to know that? He must have been certain it was his
own code-letter!"

"Gosh—no wonder he was furious with me then!"
said Snubby. "He must have thought I was actually
trying to decipher his secret instructions or whatever they
were! You know, he might have killed old Loony, if
that rock he threw had hit him!"

"I think this is pretty serious," said Barney. "Do we
tell Miss Pepper, or not?"

"We *don't*!" said Diana at once. "She might want to leave immediately! And it *is* so nice here! I don't expect anything horrid will happen now, especially as Snubby has taken off those frightful clothes. You're *not* to wear them again, Snubby."

"Not even the cap?" said Snubby, disappointed. "I rather fancied myself in that."

"*Certainly* not the cap," said Barney. He stared round at the boy still sitting patiently on the fallen rocks some way along the beach. "That kid will have to sit there a long time! The bearded fellow won't be back, that's certain. He's probably going slowly mad trying to decipher Snubby's code, and making it fit in with his!"

"I'm going to talk to that boy," said Snubby, getting up. "I might find out something."

"Better not," said Roger.

"Why?" said Snubby, walking off in his bathing things. "We're sure that horrible fellow with the beard won't come back again—he thinks he's got the letter he wanted. The boy will just think I'm some tripper or other."

And off he went with Loony, whistling a dance tune, jigging along in time to it. When he came near to the waiting boy, he suddenly remembered his Christy minstrel pretence, and began to make a noise like a banjo, pretending to strum with his fingers.

It was a very very peculiar noise and the boy looked up at once, thinking he was hearing a real banjo. He was astonished to see Snubby's pretence, and laughed.

"Twang-a-twang-a-twang-twang-twang-a-twang-a-twang-twang!" The sounds that Snubby made between his teeth were exactly like a cheap banjo!

"Hallo!" he said, sitting down grinning, "I like your little dog. What's his name?"

"Woolly," said the boy, running his hand over the poodle's woolly back. "What's your dog's name?"

"Loony," said Snubby. "Short for lunatic. You waiting for someone?"

"Yes. A man with a beard," said the boy. "Got to give him a letter from my uncle."

"Who's your uncle?" said Snubby, strumming his pretend banjo again.

"Morgan the Cripple," said the boy, beginning to imitate Snubby. "Twang-a-twang-a-twang! He was a fisherman, but he broke his leg—and he lets out fishing boats now instead of fishing."

"Why didn't he *post* the letter?" said Snubby. "Lazy fellow!"

"How do I know?" said the boy. "I say, look at your dog and mine making friends! I do wish that man would come for his letter. I thought I was late—but he's later still. And I did want to go out in a boat with my Pa this morning."

"All right. You give me the letter and I'll wait here for him," said Snubby. "And if he comes I'll give it to him, see? He won't know I'm not you, will he—we've both got a black dog!"

"Well—I'd get a fine thrashing if anyone found out," said the boy. "But I'm not waiting here all morning. Here—take the letter—and wait till he comes. Don't say a word about me, though!"

"Right. You go off," said Snubby, feeling suddenly very excited. "I'll wait about on these rocks with Loony, my own black dog!"

The boy thrust a letter into Snubby's hands and went off quickly, his poodle at his heels. Snubby sat there on the rocks, and waited, his heart beating. The man wouldn't come back, of course—but he must stay here on the rocks till the boy was out of sight!

It seemed ages till the boy disappeared. Snubby looked along the beach, to where he had left the others. They were all there, watching intently.

Snubby stood up as soon as the boy was out of sight, and then he and Loony raced over the sands to the other three. He flung himself down beside them, panting.

"The boy *was* waiting for the man with a beard," he said. "His uncle—a man called Morgan, who hires out boats —gave the letter to him to deliver. The boy didn't say why—I don't think he knew. He's a bit simple, I think. He said he was late, and he hoped the man would soon come, because he wanted to go out in a boat with his father."

"And so you offered to wait in his place and deliver the letter?" said Barney. "We wondered what was happening when the boy suddenly went off."

"Yes. And he gave me the letter!" said Snubby, triumphantly slapping his bathing trunks where he had hidden it. "What do you think of that?"

Everyone stared at Snubby, and nobody really knew *what* to think. Snubby always did such surprising things!

"Let's go back home and examine the letter," said Barney. "I don't know whether we ought to or not— but it does seem as if something peculiar must be going on. Why should Morgan, whoever he is, send a letter in code to a man like the one who knocked you about so roughly? Why *in code*? If Morgan is only a fisherman, presumably *he* didn't write it—so someone must have given it to him to hand to someone else—it was too secret and precious to be trusted to the post!"

"*Do* let's go and examine it," said Diana. "We might

have to take it to the police, you know. But what could be going on in a dear little place like this—full of country folk and fishermen?"

"Smuggling perhaps?" said Roger hopefully.

"What kind of smuggling could go on here!" said Barney. "No, I don't think it's that. In fact, I can't *imagine* what it is. Come on—let's get back. Anyway, it's getting on for lunch time."

Snubby smacked his lips at once. "Ha—good cooking— very good cooking!" he said. "Oh, by the way, I learnt something from old Mrs. Jones at the ice-cream shop this morning, when I went to buy these smashing clothes. She told me that Mr. Jones, who keeps our inn, is her son— and she said it's always been his dearest wish to own it, and now he does, because some rich friends he met when he was learning to be a chef in London, lent him the money to buy it."

"And I suppose those rich friends are Sir Somebody This and Sir Somebody That, whom she told us so often came down to stay," said Roger. "I bet they don't have to pay a penny when they come."

They were nearly at the inn now, and Barney gave Snubby a nudge. "We'll go to the caravan and see your letter there," he said. "We've plenty of time."

Soon all four, with Loony and Miranda, were shut in the caravan. Snubby was just about to show them the letter, when Loony barked sharply.

"I bet that's Dafydd again, with that Waddle of a goose," said Diana, crossly, and opened the door. Yes, it was! He was up on the wheel, peering in at the window.

"Go away, you little snooper," said Diana, half amused, half cross.

"Soon be dinner," said Dafydd solemnly, his arm round the goose's neck.

"Well, we'll be in good time," said Diana, "Run away, now!"

She shut the door and they peered at the envelope Snubby took from his bathing trunks. "It's a bit squashed, because I've sat on it," he said, and slit the envelope. He drew out a one-page sheet of paper, folded in four, and opened it out flat.

"There! It's in code, as we thought!" said Barney, excited. "We'll never decipher it, of course. Look at all the little figures and letters!"

"No wonder he thought that Bruce's letter which I was trying to read, was *this* one," said Snubby, staring at it. "All this mess-up of figures and letters! Gosh—I wish we could decipher them."

"Well, we can't," said Barney, folding up the sheet. "What are we to do with it? Shall we just wait and see if anything happens? The man who took *your* letter, Snubby, will soon find out that it's not the right one, because he won't be able to decode it—and if he could, he'd only read a lot of rubbish!"

"Well, I like *that*!" said Snubby indignantly. "Bruce and I don't write rubbish, let me tell you."

Nobody took any notice of his indignant remark. Diana spoke to Barney.

"And when the bearded man finds out that he's got the wrong letter—from a boy who wasn't the messenger after all—and that therefore someone else took the *right* letter from the fisher-boy and went off with it, what will he do?"

"Aн—what *will* he do?" said Barney, tickling Miranda under her chin. "I think we'd better wait and see—and in the meantime, we'll keep this letter very very carefully!"

CHAPTER THIRTEEN

Two More Visitors at the Inn

MISS PEPPER came to the caravan, just as the four children were getting up to go. She looked sharply at Snubby, fearing that he might be wearing his dreadful clothes—but he was still in his bathing trunks. The old clothes were on one of the bunks.

"You can throw those away, Snubby," she said. "See, here are your own things, washed and cleaned up. Please put them on."

"Can't I come in to lunch like this?" said Snubby, looking down at himself.

"No," said Miss Pepper definitely. "Diana, how brown you are getting! Did you have a nice morning?"

They went off together talking. Barney had been thinking deeply, and now he turned to Snubby and Roger. "I think it wouldn't be a bad idea to take a walk over to the fishing jetty this afternoon, and see if we can spot Morgan the Cripple, and perhaps talk to him," he said. "I'd like to see what kind of a fellow he is—and wouldn't I like to know what he's mixed up in!"

"Good idea!" said Snubby at once. "Do you hear that, Loony? Walkie-walk this afternoon!"

Loony promptly went mad, and raced round the little caravan at top speed, jumping from bunk to bunk, barking.

"Er—Loony," said Barney, "sorry to disappoint you,

old fellow—but you're *not* coming with us this afternoon!"

"Why ever not?" demanded Snubby, astonished.

"Use your brains!" said Barney. "If that boy who gave you the letter is there, he'd recognise Loony at once, and, even though you wouldn't be in bathing things this time, he'd perhaps recognise you if you had Loony with you. But without Loony, and wearing ordinary clothes, I don't see how he *could* recognise you."

"Loony won't like not coming," said Snubby gloomily. "And he'll bark the place down if we leave him in the caravan."

"Well—we'll get Di to stay with Miss Pepper this afternoon, and keep Loony with her," said Barney. "It's either that, or we leave *you* behind with Loony, Snubby."

"Oh, Diana will have Loony all right," said Snubby. "Stop showing off, Loony please—we know all about your wonderful jumping—look what you've done to my bed-clothes, you ass!"

They went off to the dining-room of the inn, and found Diana at the table, and Miss Pepper at the sideboard, putting slices of cold ham on to plates. Snubby went to help her, and Loony at once sat himself exactly below Miss Pepper's right arm, hoping she might perhaps drop a slice of ham!

Barney told Diana in a low voice what he proposed to do that afternoon, and she was quite willing to stay behind with Miss Pepper and Loony. "We could all three go for a little walk," she said. "Miss Pepper would like that. By the way—there are two more visitors at the inn!"

"Who?" asked Barney, looking round the table, pleased to see an enormous salad, and mounds of new potatoes. "My word—what a fine spread!"

"I don't know their names," said Diana, "but look—
here they come now!"

Two men walked into the room, one tall and command-
ing, with a monocle in his eye, and a smart, upturned
moustache. The other was a short man, with a black
beard and dark sunglasses.

Snubby turned at that moment to take two plates of
ham to the table, and at once saw the two men. He
jumped violently and a piece of ham leapt off one plate,
and was at once snapped up by a delighted Loony.
Snubby went quickly to the table and hissed at the surprised Barney and Roger, nudging them, and nodding
over towards the table by the window where the two
men sat with their backs to them.

The boys knew immediately what he meant! The man
with the beard and the sunglasses was the one who had
snatched Snubby's letter from him! Good gracious—and
he was staying in the hotel!

"Has he seen Loony, do you think?" whispered Snubby.
"He might recognise him. He can't recognise me, I'm
sure, now I'm properly dressed."

"Take Loony out at once," ordered Barney. "Quick—
before they see him. Here, stick a bit of my ham into his
mouth, then he won't mind what you do with him! Lock
him into the caravan."

Snubby snatched a piece of ham off Barney's plate,
picked up Loony, and put it into his mouth. Loony was
so amazed at this extraordinary generosity that he didn't
even bark. Snubby was able to streak out of the room
with him at top speed, certain that the men hadn't seen
him.

Miss Pepper was astonished to see him carrying Loony
out of the room. "Was he sick or something?" she asked,

sitting down at the table. "Poor Loony! Perhaps he swallowed too much sea-water this morning."

"You never know," said Barney, and changed the subject at once. "This must be home-cured ham, mustn't it, Miss Pepper. It's got a wonderful flavour!"

"It probably is," said Miss Pepper. "Diana, pass me the salad cream, please."

Snubby came back, grinning. "I'm sorry that Loony felt sick," said Miss Pepper.

"He'd better stay behind this afternoon," said Barney solemnly, "and perhaps go for a walk with you, Miss Pepper—and Diana, too?"

"Yes. That's a good idea," said Diana. "Would you like me to go for a walk with you, Miss Pepper?"

Miss Pepper was really delighted. "We'll go up into the hills," she said. "And you could take your field-glasses with you, Diana, and your bird-book, and we could try to spot some interesting birds for your school essay."

Roger winked at Barney. Everything was going along very nicely!

Snubby kept on staring at the two men, and Barney kicked him to make him stop. Who were these men? It should be easy to find out from Mrs. Jones. He grinned secretly to himself to think that one of them probably had Snubby's code-letter from his friend Bruce in his pocket—and had probably tried a dozen times to decode it, and failed!

Barney had a chance of finding out who the men were immediately after the meal. The two of them walked out of the room and went upstairs, and Mrs. Jones came in to clear away, with Dafydd and Waddle hovering about outside in the hall as usual.

"Two more visitors, I see, Mrs. Jones," said Barney,

as she stopped to stroke Miranda, and give her a titbit.

"Oh, yes—they come often," said Mrs. Jones proudly. "They are Sir Richard Ballinor, and Professor Hallinan —he's the great bird expert, you know. They are friends of my husband, he met them in London, and they know his cooking is good, very good, so they come here often, and they love the place, they love the mountains and the hills and the sea, and . . ."

The boys waited patiently till she had run on for some time, and then Barney interrupted.

"I expect they were pleased when your husband bought this place," he said, "it makes a nice holiday spot for them, doesn't it?"

"Ah, the good kind men, they lent my husband the money to buy the inn he so much wanted," said Mrs. Jones, in her lilting Welsh voice. "So always I welcome them and give them my very best."

"I expect they've got that Best Room of yours then!" said Diana at once. Mrs. Jones nodded.

"But that is not the room they *like* best," she said. "The room they always have is the room you have— with the two windows. But there—that Miss Pepper of yours is not one to change her mind, is she?"

"No, she's not," said Roger and Diana together, remembering how many many times in the past they had tried to make Miss Pepper change her mind about something! And then they heard Miss Pepper's voice at the door.

"Aren't you coming, children? Loony is barking his head off in the caravan!"

"Right," said Barney, and they left Mrs. Jones, who would certainly have chattered for an hour if they had stayed!

Miss Pepper and Diana and Loony set off for their walk in the hills, Diana with the field-glasses slung over her back. Loony was rather puzzled that Snubby didn't come with them, and was inclined to stay with him—but when Snubby artfully rolled into his bunk and pretended to go to sleep, Loony at once decided that a walk with Diana was better than an afternoon in a boring caravan, with everyone shushing him.

"Now let's take our bathing things, and go all the way along the beach to the fishing jetty," said Roger. "We can bathe whenever we like—either before we look for Morgan the Cripple, or afterwards."

"Better be afterwards," said Barney. "It's idiotic to bathe too soon after lunch."

They set off with Miranda scampering in front of them, only leaping on to Barney's shoulder when they met a dog or a shouting child. The sun shone out of a cloudless sky, and became very hot indeed as they walked over the white sand, past the caves.

They came near the little stone fishing-boat jetty. Not many people were there. A few old boatmen sat on the low sun-warmed wall, and a woman sat knitting on a wooden seat. Barney and the others lay down on the sand nearby.

A dirty, unkempt boy in a bright woollen jersey came running on to the jetty with a mongrel poodle, and Barney sat up at once, nudging the others. "That's the boy who gave Snubby the letter," he said. "There can only be *one* mongrel poodle in this little place, surely!"

They all sat up and watched the boy. He went to where a boat was being untied, and helped to push it off. It was a pretty sight to see its sails unfurling and filling with wind.

A man came on to the jetty at that moment, dressed in fisherman's clothes—a man who limped badly and walked with a stick.

"Morgan the Cripple, do you think?" said Roger, as the fisherman went to talk to some old cronies on the wall. "Come on—let's go up on the jetty. We might be able to get into talk with him."

But before they had got up from the sands someone else strode on to the jetty—a man with a dark beard, wearing sunglasses. He called sharply to Morgan, who got up at once. "Here, Morgan—I want a word with you!"

"I bet there's going to be a quarrel!" said Barney excitedly. "Let's hope we hear it. Come on—we'll get nearer to the wall!"

CHAPTER FOURTEEN

An Exciting Afternoon

"COME OVER HERE," said Morgan to the bearded man, and took him to one side of the jetty, out of hearing of the other fishermen there. Barney and the others crawled over the sand as near as they dared, and lay down hidden by the stone jetty wall.

"Morgan—that letter you gave your nephew to deliver to me," began the man. "That wasn't the one you were given for me, you know it wasn't."

"What you talking about, Sir Richard," said Morgan in a deep, puzzled voice. "That letter never left my pocket, and that I swear, from the time it came to me till the time I gave it to Dai this very morning. Didn't he go to the pile of rocks we arranged?"

"Yes. He was there—dressed as you said, and the little black dog too, so I knew it was the right boy," said the bearded man. "But I tell you *he gave me the wrong letter*. I can't make head or tail of any of it!"

"That were the letter given to me for you," said Morgan obstinately. "Jim give it to me as usual, straight from his pocket to mine it went, and all he said was, 'We'll be back Friday. Be ready,' and off he sailed again. That letter was what he give me, I tell you."

"I don't understand it," said the bearded man, staring at Morgan. "Where's that nephew of yours? I'll have to question him—though how *he* could have changed the letter beats me. Morgan, if you're double-crossing me I'll pay you out in a way you won't like!"

"I'm not double-crossing anyone!" said Morgan, raising his voice angrily. "Do I want to double-cross myself? I'm in this as much as you are, aren't I?"

"Don't shout like that," said the other man, looking round anxiously, afraid of the other fishermen hearing.

"I'll call Dai," said Morgan surlily. "He's there, watching that boat. He'll soon tell you it was the letter all right. Dai! DAI! Here a minute!"

The small boy and the poodle came running up. "Yes, Uncle Morgan?" said Dai, glancing at the bearded man, and looking scared.

"Did you give this gentleman the letter I gave you for him this morning?" said his uncle sternly.

"Yes," lied the boy. "Yes, of course I did."

The bearded man suddenly caught hold of the small

90

boy, and held him in such a fierce grip that he began to howl. "You didn't give me any letter! You're not the boy I saw! He was bigger—and his dog was a black spaniel —not a poodle."

"Let go the boy," said Morgan sternly, seeing that Dai was scared almost to death. "You said you had a letter given to you by a boy—who *was* the boy then, if it wasn't Dai?"

"I don't know—I tell you, it was a boy with a spaniel— a real ragamuffin, like your nephew," said the man, glaring at the terrified boy. "And when I came up to him, I saw he was actually *reading* the letter! It was in

R.M.   D

code. I immediately thought it was the letter he should have delivered to me and took it, though he tried to stop me."

Morgan laughed harshly, and turned away. "Then you are a fool, Sir Richard. The boy wasn't the right ragamuffin, and the letter was his, not yours."

Sir Richard grasped Morgan's arm and swung him round. "Man, this is urgent, you know that. I've not got the right letter, I tell you—the letter you gave to Dai. Where's *that* letter? You, boy, answer me at once!"

"I—I gave it to a boy who came to talk to me," wept poor Dai, terrified out of his life. "I waited and waited for you, and this boy said he'd give it to you for me. I didn't know you'd already been—and gone off with the wrong letter."

Sir Richard pushed the boy away from him with such force that he almost toppled over the jetty into the water. Morgan scowled. "Leave the boy alone. What harm's been done? You got a letter you couldn't read—and someone else has got a letter *he* can't read. I'll get in touch with Jim and he'll send another."

Sir Richard took out a handkerchief and mopped his forehead. He came close to Morgan and spoke in his ear, so that the three boys listening down on the sand below the jetty could only just hear his words.

"You deliver the next letter to me yourself, Morgan. If anything goes wrong, it'll be laid on *your* shoulders for thinking that idiot nephew of yours was trustable. If Jim's letter hadn't been in code, there'd be someone else now who would know enough to spoil all our plans for Friday—yes, and for always!"

"Aw—shut up," said Morgan rudely, and turned away.

"And if I find that boy whose letter I took—and who

got *my* letter from Dai—I'll wring his neck!" said Sir Richard in such a bloodthirsty tone that Snubby, who could hear every word, felt suddenly scared. What had seemed rather a peculiar joke, was turning into something that wasn't a joke at all! Why on earth had he gone and talked to Dai and persuaded him to hand over the letter?

"I'd know the boy anywhere," went on Sir Richard, still in the same angry voice. "Awful ragamuffin—a tramp of a fellow in long, dirty-looking trousers, a horrible jersey, and a peaked cap too big for him—and a black spaniel. Dai is dressed much the same, but he isn't as big as this other fellow—and the black dog misled me, of course."

Snubby was feeling distinctly uncomfortable now, and so were Barney and Roger. How maddening that this bearded fellow was staying at the inn! Would he recognise Loony? And then Snubby?

Morgan strode off, leaving the other man by himself. The fishermen on the wall looked at Morgan curiously as he passed. They had been too far away to hear anything that was said—but they knew there had been a quarrel.

"Your grand friend upset, Morgan?" called one old fellow. "Wasn't your last catch of fish good enough for his lordship?"

Morgan didn't answer. The fishermen nudged one another and grinned as the bearded man walked after Morgan, but nobody dared to call out to him. Dai had disappeared entirely, hidden somewhere out of sight.

The three boys on the sand lay there silently for some time, and then, hearing no more voices, rolled over and looked at one another. "Let's go and bathe," said Barney, in case anyone was listening. He added in a low voice, "We'll talk later. Come on."

"Yes—a bathe would be fine, it's so jolly hot," said Roger loudly. Snubby said nothing. He was still very shaken by what he had overheard. He hoped the letter was safe in the caravan. Had he better destroy it?

They said no more till they were well away from the jetty. Then Barney mopped his head and said "Whew! what on earth do we do next? You've landed us into something now, Snubby—all through that idiotic code-letter from Bruce."

"It wasn't idiotic," said Snubby in a rather meeker voice than usual. "Anyway, that fellow—fancy him being the Sir·Richard Mrs. Jones told us about—that fellow couldn't puzzle out our code. It's a jolly good one, and not idiotic as you seem to think."

"Let's bathe," said Barney, "and perhaps when we feel a bit cooler, we can think this business out. Good thing we didn't bring Loony, Snubby—that fellow might have spotted him—and us."

"I say—what on earth are we going to do with Loony now?" said Snubby in sudden dismay. "We mustn't let that fellow, Sir Richard, see him at all—but you know what Loony is—rushing about all over the place!"

They all splashed into the cool sea, and when they came out they felt decidedly better. They sat on the sand and talked.

"To-day's Wednesday—and whatever is to happen is planned for Friday. *I* think it's smuggling," said Roger. "There are only two more days to go. Do we go to the police, do you think?"

"No. No, I don't think so. If we do, they will question that bearded fellow, and whatever's planned won't happen," said Barney, frowning. "I'm just thinking of something we heard one of the fishermen yell out to Morgan. He said 'Wasn't your last catch of fish good enough for his lordship?' Well now, what did that mean? It means that Morgan hires out a boat to Sir Richard, presumably for catching fish—but perhaps brings in *something else*—either instead of fish, or hidden in the catch."

"Something that he wants brought here to be hidden, do you think?" asked Roger.

"Yes. Perhaps something he wants to hide for some considerable time," said Barney thoughtfully. "I wonder who this Sir Richard really is—and his friend Professor Hallinan, the bird-expert. I think they are just *posing* as Sir Richard and the Professor—using their names instead of their own. I think I'll walk into Dilcarmock and telephone my father after tea, and ask him if he can find out."

"They must be rich, to lend Mr. Jones the money to buy the inn," said Snubby, screwing his toes into the sand.

"I can't think *why* anyone should lend a few thousand pounds to a fellow like Mr. Jones, just because they liked his cooking so much," said Barney. "I mean—when you lend money, you expect to get some good return from it—the profits made on the visitors that come to the inn, for instance. But very little profit can be made on *that* inn, I'm sure. Besides ourselves there are only these two men there!"

"Well—what *does* he give them in return then?" said Snubby. "Do you imagine he lets them use his inn as a kind of headquarters for whatever they are really up to?"

Barney sat up straight and smacked his knee. "Of *course*! You've hit it! What other reason could there be? There's a little gang here—Morgan—and Jim, whoever he is—and Mr. Jones—all in some game together, and this inn is somehow the heart of it. Gosh—we *have* tumbled on to something!"

"But what have we tumbled on?" asked Snubby, excited. "How can we find out what it is? I SAY—this is pretty exciting, isn't it? I simply can't wait till Friday!"

CHAPTER FIFTEEN

Oh, Loony!

LOONY WAS extremely glad to see the boys when they came back, and rather astonished to be shut up immediately in the caravan, when everyone went to have tea. He barked dismally, and Miss Pepper was surprised at Snubby's seeming hard-heartedness.

"I really can't see why he can't come in to tea," she said. "He was as good as gold with us this afternoon. We had a wonderful walk—and Diana spotted some most unusual birds with the field-glasses."

"There was one I couldn't make out," said Diana. "A green bird with a red top-knot."

"Mrs. Jones tells me that there is a Professor Hallinan staying here," said Miss Pepper. "A famous ornithologist, and . . ."

"A *what*?" said Snubby, astonished.

"Bird expert," said Miss Pepper. "So I suggested that

Diana should ask him about the bird. He'd be sure to be able to identify it."

The three boys felt extremely doubtful about this, as none of them now believed that the Professor was a real bird-man, any more than Sir Richard was really a Sir Anybody! But Barney winked at the boys, and said cheerfully, "Yes, Di—good idea. I'll come with you and listen to what he says. Might learn something—you never know!"

Snubby gave a sudden chuckle. "No—you never know!" he said. "Miss Pepper, we're going to walk in to Dilcarmock after tea—coming?"

"Good gracious no! I've had enough walking to-day," said Miss Pepper. "You'd better catch a bus part of the way, it's quite a distance."

The two men came in to tea at that moment and nodded to Miss Pepper. Diana determined to catch Professor Hallinan when he went out of the room. So she hovered about with Barney, while Snubby and Roger went to comfort poor Loony in the van.

At last the men came walking out, and made for the stairs. Diana darted to the tall moustached one, with a monocle in his eye.

"Oh please do excuse me, Professor Hallinan," she said breathlessly. "But I know you are a famous ornith-ornith—whatever it is, and know all about birds—so *do* you think you could help me to name a bird I saw to-day?"

"Er—surely! I'd be pleased to try," said the Professor. "Where did you see it?"

"Flying over the hills," said Diana. "Green, with a red top-knot."

"Ah well, I fear I couldn't identify a bird on so little description," said the Professor, courteously. "It *sounds* as if it might be a rare immigrant, which is sometimes seen here—Latin name *Lateus Hillimus*. Yes, it might be that."

"Oh—thank you," said Diana. "I hope I remember such a queer name!"

Barney now entered into the conversation, very politely. "I saw a Short-Necked Curlikew," he said, "just outside the inn, it was. Surely that was unusual sir?"

"Very unusual," said the Professor.

"And would you say that the Dotty Shade Warblers could be found in these hills?" asked Barney. "I have heard they nest here at times."

"Er—well, yes, I believe they *have* been known to nest here," said the Professor. "Excuse me—I must join my friend." And away he went up the stairs.

Diana stared at Barney in the utmost amazement. "Short-Necked Curlikews! I've never heard of them in my *life*," she said, "and I know the names of *most* of our birds now. And who ever heard of the Dotty Shade Warblers?"

"Nobody," said Barney, taking her arm. "Your Professor is a fraud, dear Diana. What did he say that green bird of yours was—a *Lateus Hillimus*? Poppycock! You won't find *that* bird in any of your bird-books! He's no more a bird expert than I am. I only wish I'd asked him if he had ever seen the curious nest of a Poppy Cockbird."

Diana giggled. "Gracious—I've a good mind to put the Poppy Cockbird into my school essay, just for a joke —and draw one too. But I say, Barney—do you *really* think the Professor is a fraud? He was so polite and knowledgeable too."

"All tricksters are," said Barney. "And I bet that his

friend, Sir Richard as he calls himself, is no more a botanist than the Professor is a bird expert! They're frauds, both of them—using other people's names—pretending to be what they're not. My father knew their names—but I bet if he'd met them here, he would have spotted that they were bogus. Anyway, I'm going to phone him and ask him to make some inquiries, so that we can be certain."

"Well let's go and break the news to the others," said Diana. "Come on. Goodness—to think that the bogus Professor said he thought your equally bogus Dotty Shade Warblers could be found in these hills! How do you *think* of names like that, Barney?"

"It's easy!" said Barney. "Come on, Di. I want to be off to Dilcarmock to telephone my father. And we *must* keep Loony out of Sir Richard's sight, there's no doubt about that. He'd recognise him at once!"

They went half-way to Dilcarmock by bus, and then walked the rest of the way. Loony was delighted. Two long walks in a day—he was truly in luck!

Barney telephoned his father. "Dad? It's Barney here. Can you hear me?"

"Yes—speak up a little though," said his father. "Are you all right?"

"Fine," said Barney. "But there's a bit of a mystery on about two men here—the famous experts that old Mrs. Jones at the ice-cream shop told us about. . . . Sir Richard Ballinor, and Professor Hallinan—they've arrived at the inn, and I've a feeling they're *frauds*—no more experts than I am! The Professor doesn't know one bird from another. What are they like, Dad? The real men, I mean?"

"One is tall, with an upturned moustache, and wears

a monocle," said his father. "And the other, Sir Richard, is rather short, and has a beard."

"Gosh," said Barney, surprised to hear his father give such a close description of the two men at the inn. "That pretty well describes the two fellows here, Dad—the ones I think are frauds. I say—could you possibly find out if the real Sir Richard and the real Professor are at their homes? If they are, I'll know for certain these two fellows are frauds, and we'll watch them to see what they are up to. But if you hear they're away in Wales—well—I suppose they won't be frauds after all. I think they are, though, in fact, I'm sure of it!"

His father chuckled. "Quite a mystery!" he said. "I'll certainly find out where the real Sir Richard and Professor are—they're both members of my Club and I can easily inquire there. I'll let you know at once whether your two men are false—or genuine."

"Thanks," said Barney. "Don't telephone though, Dad—in case one of the men answers. Send me a telegram—and put just one word—'False' if the real experts are not the ones here—and 'Genuine' if they are. Then I'll know what to do."

"Right. But don't get mixed up in anything unpleasant, Barney," said his father. "Let me know if there's any more I can do to help. I'll find out what you want at once, and you'll get a telegram to-night. I'll put the inn's telephone number, so that the post office will phone it through to you personally. Now don't get into any trouble—if these men aren't what they seem, they may be most unpleasant if they think any snooping is going on."

"Right, Dad. Thanks and good-bye," said Barney and put down the receiver. He went out of the box and told the others what his father had said. "We'll know for certain to-night if what we think is correct," he said. "I *bet* we're on the right track!"

The four walked half-way back, and caught the bus the rest of the way, feeling quite tired. Even Loony decided that it was possible to overdo this walking habit! Miranda, of course, loved it all, for she sat on Barney's shoulder most of the time—and was thoroughly spoilt by all the passengers in the bus!

"You'll be sick down my neck if you accept any more sweets from people," said Barney at last. "Stop nibbling my ear, Miranda, you tickle!"

At a few minutes before eight, the telephone bell rang, and Mrs. Jones came hurrying into the room where everyone was sitting. "For you, Master Barney, please."

Barney shot out, and a voice over the phone said, "I have a telegram for you, sir. It has only one word though, and that is—'*False*'."

"Thanks," said Barney, and put down the receiver. "False! Well, we guessed right. Mr. Jones's rich and important friends are no more than rogues who are making money in some dishonest way with his help! Rogues who are working in disguise and using other men's names! Now we can go right ahead, and try and find out what's happening. Friday night is apparently *the* night. If only we knew what to look out for!" He went to tell the others. Diana wanted to tell Miss Pepper, but nobody agreed.

"But all this sounds as if it might be dangerous," said Diana. "And surely the *police* ought to be told those men are frauds."

"We'll wait till Friday comes, and see if we can find out what is happening," said Barney. "And for goodness' sake, let's keep Loony out of sight. If one of those men spots him, and guesses that he belongs to one of us, there will be danger—because they'll know Loony's owner has got the real letter, and they'll go for Snubby at once to get the precious letter!"

"All right. Let's destroy it then!" said Snubby promptly.

"No," said Barney. "We might have to produce it, to show we really did get hold of it—when the police come in on the job—as they'll have to, sooner or later. I'll take it and hide it somewhere safe. I'll get it now."

He went out of the room, and down to the caravan. The letter had been put into Snubby's pillow-case, on his bunk. Barney slipped in his hand and took it out. Then he found some drawing-pins and took them and the code-letter outside the van. He crawled underneath it and pinned the letter on the under-part of the caravan, very firmly indeed.

He crept out, grinning. If anyone found it there he would be very very clever!

Loony was sitting sadly by himself in the van, wondering why he wasn't allowed in the inn. Barney felt sorry for him and left Miranda there for company. The little monkey sat close to Loony, chattering in his ear, but he took no notice at all. He was waiting for his beloved Snubby to come for him!

Everyone went to bed early that night, for they were very tired.

"What with bathing and walking, and all the rest of the excitement we've had, I can't keep awake another minute!" said Snubby with a tremendous yawn that set all the others off too, Miss Pepper as well.

"Come along, Diana," she said, getting up. "You go off to your caravan, boys. Sleep well!"

They all slept very well indeed, and Diana didn't want to get up when the hot water arrived next morning, brought as usual by Mrs. Jones, followed by Dafydd and the goose!

"Oh, Mrs. Jones—I don't think we need have the goose in here," protested Miss Pepper, and Mrs. Jones shooed both the little boy and Waddle away.

"I didn't even know they were behind me," she said. "That Dafydd—he puts his nose everywhere, and that goose, he is just as bad—in my larder he was yesterday, Miss, as sure as I stand here, pecking at the scones I had made for tea. Sir Richard and the Professor, they make such a fuss of my Dafydd, Miss, he follows them all day long, they spoil him, I say, and . . ."

"Well, thank you, Mrs. Jones, we'll be down in half an hour," said Miss Pepper firmly, knowing quite well that if she didn't interrupt Mrs. Jones, she would be standing there talking till breakfast time!

Everyone was punctual for breakfast for once, and Sir Richard and the Professor were at their table too. Nobody knew that Dafydd and his goose were once more peeping in at the window of the caravan—and that Dafydd was feeling very very sorry for poor lonely Loony, left there to wait for Snubby to return.

"Poor dog Loony," said Dafydd softly, and tapped on the window. "Poor dog!"

Loony saw Dafydd's small face peering in at the window and barked hopefully, pawing at the window-pane as he stood on his hind paws on one of the bunks.

"Dafydd will undo the door for poor dog Loony," said the small boy pityingly. "Wait, dog Loony."

He scrambled down from the wheel he was standing on, and with his goose behind him, went to the door. It was shut, not locked, and he opened it easily.

Loony shot out at top speed, barking, and the goose fled for its life, cackling as if it had laid a hundred eggs. Dafydd was cross. He had at least expected a word of thanks from Loony!

Loony tore across the slope of the hill and into the hall of the inn, the door of which was always left open. Where was Snubby? He flung himself against the door of the dining-room and scampered in, barking delightedly.

"LOONY!" said Snubby in horror. "You bad dog! How did you get out?"

Loony threw himself on Snubby and licked him, whining as if he hadn't seen Snubby for a month. Barney glanced quickly round at the two men at the window table, with their bacon and eggs in front of them. Sir Richard was staring at Loony in amazement, and he nudged the Professor. "That's the dog!" he said. "I'd know him anywhere. He belongs to that boy, see?"

Barney couldn't hear what was said, but he could guess. Blow! Now the men would know that Snubby was the boy who had their letter. "Quick, Snubby!" he said, "let's get out of here with Loony. Buck up! Those men have spotted him—and you too!"

CHAPTER SIXTEEN

A Day Out for Snubby!

SNUBBY WAS really scared. He got up at once, and followed by Barney, left the table and went quickly out of the door. Loony went too, barking in delight. Miss Pepper was most astonished, and stared after them indignantly.

"Where have they gone—and why did they leave the breakfast table without a word to me?" she said. "Is one of them feeling ill, Diana?"

Roger gave Diana a little kick under the table, afraid she might say something that would make trouble. "Er —didn't you think Snubby looked a little pale?" he said. "Perhaps it's a touch of the sun. He may have said a word to Barney about it."

"I'd better go and find out," said Miss Pepper.

"Oh, wait till Barney comes back," said Roger. "Don't leave your hot bacon and eggs! I expect old Barney will be back in a minute."

He shot a glance at the two men sitting at the window-table. They were talking earnestly, and the bearded man looked angry and troubled. Roger wished he could hear what they were saying.

Snubby was now safely in the caravan with Barney, Loony at his feet, and Miranda cuddled in Barney's arms. They were talking earnestly.

"How did Loony get out? He can't open the door

105

himself!" said Snubby. "I bet it was that little nuisance of a Dafydd—always snooping round! Well, *now* the fat's in the fire! Those men spotted Loony all right— and know I'm the boy who took the code-letter from that fraud Sir Richard."

"Yes—and they're certain to try and get it now," said Barney. "How, I don't know—but it might be jolly unpleasant for you, Snubby, if they catch you! I think the best thing for you to do is to hide."

"All right. But where?" asked Snubby dismally. "In the caravan? They'd soon find me here."

"No, certainly not in the caravan," said Barney. "I almost think the best thing to do would be to catch the next bus to Dilcarmock and spend the day there. Unless the men happened to see you getting on the bus they'd never guess you'd gone there. I'd better come with you."

"Yes, do," said Snubby, still looking dismal. "But what on EARTH are we going to tell Miss Pepper?"

"The truth!" said Barney, getting up. "I'll see if I can catch Roger's ear and tell him what we're going to do— and he can tell Miss Pepper we decided to go to Dilcarmock, and rushed out to catch the bus—and apologise for us."

"I never finished my bacon and eggs," groaned Snubby. "Oh, why did I ever get mixed up with that idiotic letter?"

"I'll see if I can catch Roger," said Barney, and ran up to the inn. He was careful not to be seen from the dining-room window, for he knew the men sat there. He went to the dining-room door and peeped in. Miss Pepper had her back to him, and he was able to signal to Roger unseen.

"Excuse me a moment, Miss Pepper," said Roger, and slipped out of the room before she could ask him any questions. She was puzzled and annoyed.

"What *is* everyone doing this morning?" she said. "I hope *you* feel all right, Diana. I think I'd better go and see what is happening."

"Well, have some hot toast first," said Diana, trying to give the boys as much time as she could. "Take this nice brown piece."

Barney told Roger their plans in a few words. "We think Snubby had better clear off for the day—so we're going to Dilcarmock by bus and won't be back till supper time. Then I'll lock Snubby into the caravan, and we'll say he's tired—and I'll take him something to eat there—and perhaps have it with him, in case those men try to get him. Got it?"

"Yes," said Roger. "But Miss Pepper is getting very suspicious. For goodness' sake go now—she'll be out in half a minute, I know she will."

"Right. We'll go at once," said Barney, and went to fetch Snubby from the van. Roger watched them go racing down the slope to the village below. Would they catch the bus? It was about due now, and if they missed it they would have to wait a whole hour. He went back to the inn and met Miss Pepper hurrying out, having eaten her bacon and eggs and toast very quickly indeed.

"Oh, Roger! What *is* happening?" she asked. "Really! Leaving the table like that, one after the other, without a word of explanation! Where are Snubby and Barney?"

Roger looked round carefully before he answered, in case the men might be within hearing. "Well, it's all quite simple," he said, smiling brightly. "Apparently they made up their minds to go to Dilcarmock for the day, and had to rush off very suddenly to catch the bus. They asked me to apologise to you."

"Well—why in the world couldn't they have said just one word to me about their plans," said Miss Pepper, still puzzled. "Aren't you and Diana going?"

"Er—no—we thought we'd stay and keep you company," said Roger. "What about going out in a boat, Miss Pepper, just us three?"

"Well, that would be very nice," said Miss Pepper. "Very nice indeed. But I shall have a few words to say to Barney and Snubby when they come back this evening —tearing out of the room like that in the middle of breakfast!"

The two men came out of the inn at that moment, talking in low tones, looking all round. Roger was sure they were looking for Snubby. They looked at him, and Sir Richard took a step forward as if he were going to say something. Then the other man pulled him by the arm, to stop him. Obviously nothing was going to be said in front of Miss Pepper!

"I bet they know she'd call the police if they began to make a rumpus about Snubby and secret letters!" thought Roger. He was glad to see Diana coming out behind the men.

"Di! We're going boating!" he shouted. "Just the right morning for it—hot sun and a wind off the shore."

"Oh *good*!" said Diana, longing to know what had happened to Snubby and Barney, but not daring to ask in front of Miss Pepper. Roger took Diana's arm and hurried her off to the caravan. "Just going to tidy up the bunks!" he called. "We'll be ready in ten minutes' time."

Diana thought it was a very good idea of Barney's to go to Dilcarmock for the day. "If only we can get Friday over, with whatever's supposed to happen then, I'll feel safer!" she said. "Oh dear—why does Snubby *always* get into trouble? And us with him! And he never seems to mind, does he? I bet he's sitting happily in the bus now, pretending to play a banjo or something, and keeping everyone in fits of laughter.

Diana was almost right in her guess! Snubby *was* in the bus—but he wasn't playing a pretend banjo, he was playing a mouth-organ—or rather, pretending to, his hand up to his mouth, making a most realistic zz-zz-zz noise, exactly as if he were playing a jiggy tune! And as Diana had surmised, everyone was delighted, laughing and egging him on. No—Snubby wasn't feeling nearly as worried as the others!

When Miranda slid down to the floor and began to dance in time to Snubby's horrible noises, even the bus driver had to look round—and the bus almost went into a ditch!

"Shut up now, Snubby," said Barney, alarmed. "You'll cause an accident."

Back at the inn the others were preparing for a morning's boating. Miss Pepper insisted on large sunhats being taken, for the sun would beat down on the boat and there would be no shelter at all. They had to go and buy some at old Mrs. Jones's shop, which meant an ice-cream each, of course.

While they were eating them, the two men from the inn passed slowly by, and peered in. They said nothing, much to Roger's relief, and walked on.

"I don't somehow like those men," said Miss Pepper. "I can't imagine why they're down here—they don't seem to fish or bathe—and look, they're in their city suits even on a day like this! If they weren't who they are I'd think they were up to no good!"

"I wouldn't be surprised if you're right, Miss Pepper," said Roger solemnly, and Diana gave a sudden giggle.

They had a glorious morning quite far out in a boat. They took turns at rowing and steering and lying flat with a hand over the side dragging through the water. The two children bathed from the boat as well, and slowly their faces, arms and legs turned a bright red-brown. Miss Pepper was extremely glad of her enormous sunhat!

Barney and Snubby also had quite an amusing time in Dilcarmock. It was a big seaside town, full of trippers, and had a tremendous lot of side-shows. Barney, who had once been a circus-boy, used to going round with fairs, enjoyed joining in the amusements he had known so well—hoopla stalls—dodgem cars—swings—round-abouts and so on. He even met someone he had once known at Rilloby Fair, and they had a wonderful talk which poor Snubby couldn't even share.

Miranda loved it all, of course, and Loony met so many stray dogs tearing about that he had the time of his life. He thought that Dilcarmock was much more interesting than Penrhyndendraith!

"Time to get the bus back," said Barney at last. "We shall miss supper at the inn if we don't—even though you must have had at least a dozen ice-creams, Snubby, and goodness knows how many shrimps, and some of that awful gingerbread, and three meat-pies, and—let me see—how many cheese sandwiches was it?"

"Well, I'm beginning to feel hungry for my supper, all the same," said Snubby. "So don't let's miss the bus,

Barney. Loony, keep to heel. I don't want to lose you just as the bus is due."

They went to the bus stop, and the bus came rumbling along in about two minutes. They settled into the front seats, Miranda on Barney's shoulder, eager to see everything as usual. Loony lay at Snubby's feet.

"I do hope those two men won't try to get me this evening," said Snubby suddenly. "I'd forgotten all about them, I was enjoying myself so. Do you think I dare go in to supper?"

"Yes—you'll be all right if we're all with you," said Barney. "But we *must* go about together, all four of us *and* Loony, till bedtime. We can say we're jolly tired and go off early, see?"

They were glad to walk up the slope to the caravan, for they really *were* tired. Roger was there, waiting for them with an anxious face.

"I say!" he said, as soon as he saw them. "Something's happened—the code-letter's gone from under the caravan where Barney pinned it. I think that silly, snooping little Dafydd found it. I can't find the little wretch anywhere, or I'd take it from him—and I only hope the men don't see him with it! Isn't he a *pest*?"

CHAPTER SEVENTEEN

Where is the Code-Letter?

BARNEY AND SNUBBY looked at Roger in horror. The code-letter gone! Who would have thought anyone could possibly find it, pinned so neatly to the underside of the caravan?

"Not only that—but our caravan lock was broken when I went to it after tea—and the whole place was upside down!"

"*That* must have been the two men searching it for the letter," said Barney at once. "Dafydd wouldn't dare to do that. He wouldn't be able to break the lock for one thing."

"Why do you think Dafydd has the letter?" asked Snubby.

"Well, I'll tell you," said Roger. "You see, Miss Pepper, Di and I came back for lunch, and I went to get something out of the caravan—and I saw Waddle the goose standing by it. The lock wasn't broken then. I was surprised to see Waddle all by himself, because he's like a dog, always at Dafydd's heels . . ."

"Where was Dafydd then—under the caravan?" asked Barney.

"Yes! I looked all round for him, and couldn't see him —and then the goose stuck its head under the caravan and cackled as if to say 'Buck up, Dafydd!' And *I* looked under and there was the little pest, as quiet as a mouse!"

"Did you see if he had the letter?" asked Snubby.

"No. I didn't think about the letter then!" said Roger. "I just shouted at Dafydd and told him to come out, and said he wasn't to go near the caravan. He's too light-fingered—takes anything he fancies, like a monkey. Oh—sorry, Miranda, I forgot you were present!"

Miranda chattered as if she understood, and Roger went on with his tale. "Well, Dafydd shot off with Waddle—and then I suddenly remembered the letter and crawled under the van to have a look. And the letter wasn't there—but the drawing-pins were scattered on the ground below so *somebody* must have taken them out to get the letter. And I'm dead certain it *was* Dafydd, because if it had been the two men they wouldn't have come in the afternoon and searched the caravan for it, would they?"

"Not if they'd taken the letter in the morning," said Barney. "Well now, the thing is—has that little pest got the letter still? We'd better find out as soon as we can."

But Dafydd had gone to bed! "He is fast asleep," said Mrs. Jones. "Such a boy he has been to-day, and that goose of his! Into my larder they were, and up the stairs, and into mischief everywhere, and . . ."

"Er—would he like this little clock we won at hoopla in Dilcarmock?" said Barney, bringing a gay little clock out of his pocket.

"Indeed and he would, oh indeed to goodness!" said Mrs. Jones. "But not to-night, sir, he is asleep! To-morrow I will give it to him myself."

"No, *I'd* like to give it to him," said Barney, putting the clock firmly back into his pocket, and went off before Mrs. Jones could say any more.

"We'll make him give up the letter in return for the clock," said Barney. "The little wretch! He's everywhere! Fancy crawling under the caravan!"

"Well, kids do silly things like that when they're as small as he is," said Snubby. "I remember thinking it was grand fun to crawl under my uncle's car when I was his age, and let oil drip on me."

"You *would*!" said Diana. "Ugh! Thank goodness I didn't want to do things like that."

They had a pleasant supper, and, much to their surprise, the two men were not there.

"Have they gone, Mrs. Jones?" asked Barney, nodding his head towards the window-table. She shook her head.

"Oh no, young sir. They had an early meal and have gone to see some friends. Busy men they are, sir, even when they are down in quiet Penrhyndendraith—rich men, important men, sir, and proud I am to think they like our inn—but it's the cooking, the very good cooking! You too like my husband's cooking, I know! You . . ."

"Yes, yes, Mrs. Jones," said Miss Pepper, and the cheery little woman took the hint and scuttled out of the room.

"She's absolutely non-stop!" said Snubby. "Honestly, I never know why you stop her, Miss Pepper. I could listen to her for ages."

"I dare say," said Miss Pepper. "But you and I have slightly different ideas, Snubby."

"Don't squash me like that," said Snubby crossly. "Anyone would think I was an orange."

Miss Pepper simply couldn't help laughing, and the others chuckled. "You *can't* squash old Snubby," said Roger. "We've all tried—but he's made of rubber. He bounces up again immediately."

They all went off to bed early again, really tired with their long day. The three boys held a conference in their caravan.

"I'll nab Dafydd first thing to-morrow morning if I can, and get that letter from him," said Barney. "And Snubby must be very very careful not to go near the two men, in case they think he's got it on him—they know it's not hidden in the caravan, because they've searched for it—what a mess they made, the wretches!"

"How am I to stay away from the fellows to-morrow?" demanded Snubby. "I can't *keep* going off to Dilcarmock."

"We'll think of something," said Barney. He yawned. "I'm going to sleep—and woe betide Dafydd to-morrow if he doesn't give me that letter!"

The next morning they looked for Dafydd and Waddle as soon as they got up, but they were nowhere to be seen. Barney went along to the kitchen, where Mr. Jones was cooking a breakfast that smelt too delicious for words.

"Er—good morning. Do you know where Dafydd is?" asked Barney politely.

Mr. Jones turned, scowling, holding a frying-pan in his hand. "No, I do not. I will not have him here when I cook."

The boys went out of the kitchen hurriedly, feeling that Mr. Jones did not want them there either when he "cooked."

"What a dour, surly fellow," said Roger. "You'd think he'd be jolly cheerful, having this inn for his own."

They kept a sharp eye out for the two men, but did not see them. Barney went cautiously into the dining-room to see if they were there—and found Mrs. Jones clearing dirty plates away from the men's table.

"Oh—have they had their breakfast already?" asked Barney.

"Yes—early they were to-day!" said Mrs. Jones. "Sir Richard, he said they had much business to do to-day, and . . ."

"Oh, he did, did he?" said Barney. "I wonder what kind of business he does in a little place like this."

"Sir Richard owns two fishing vessels," said Mrs. Jones, "and many other things. He . . ."

But just then Miss Pepper came in with Diana, and Mrs. Jones hurried out to the kitchen to tell Mr. Jones they were down.

The boys went hunting for Dafydd again after breakfast, keeping a sharp look-out for the two men, who, however, were not to be seen. It wasn't until nearly lunch-time that they found Dafydd, wandering along with Waddle as usual. He came up to them at once.

"Mum says there is a clock you have," he said. "A clock for me."

"Oh, she told you, did she?" said Barney, taking the gay little clock out of his pocket.

Dafydd gazed at the clock in delight, and rattled something off in Welsh. He reached out for it—but Barney held it away.

"Dafydd," he said, "if I give you this—*you* must give *me* something."

"My knife!" said Dafydd, and dug his hand into his pocket.

"No, Dafydd—I want that paper you found under our caravan," said Barney. "You were bad to take it. But if you give it to me now, you shall have the clock."

"Paper gone," said Dafydd solemnly.

"Gone? Where's it gone?" demanded Roger.

"Men took it," said Dafydd, pointing in the direction of the inn.

"When?" said Barney sharply.

Dafydd did not seem to know. He suddenly began to cry. "They shout at Dafydd," he said. "Dafydd sit there, to make a boat with the paper," and he pointed to a little wooden seat in the inn garden. "And man come and say 'You give me that!' and he take it—like this!" And Dafydd made a grab at the clock Barney was holding.

"Good gracious!" said Roger. "That's a blow, isn't it! Dafydd, when was this?"

"Man hit Waddle," said Dafydd, aiming a blow in the air. "Bad man. Steal from Dafydd. You give me clock now?"

"No. You haven't got the letter to give me," said Barney sternly. "You were a bad boy to take the paper away to make a boat."

"He probably didn't think it was ours," said Roger, as the little boy began to cry bitterly. "After all, you don't usually find a paper sheet stuck under a caravan! He couldn't have guessed it was so important."

"I suppose he couldn't," said Barney, looking at the sobbing child. He suddenly put his arm round him. "Stop crying. We forgive you. See, here is the clock—you wind it up like this—it says tick-a-tock, tick-a-tock!"

Dafydd was overjoyed. He stopped crying at once and took the clock. He held it to Waddle's ear. "Listen!" he said. "Tick-a-tock, tick-a-tock."

The goose backed away, not at all sure about the clock.

"And this is how you set the alarm bell going," said Barney, hoping the child would understand. "See—you wind *this* little handle—and now listen!"

The alarm bell shrilled out and the goose raced off in fright, cackling loudly. Dafydd was entranced. He suddenly put his arms round Barney and gave him a great hug.

"You nice boy," he said. "Dafydd get back paper for you. Yes, Dafydd give it to you."

"I wish you could, old chap," said Barney. "But it's too late now! Run along."

Dafydd went to find his goose, and the others looked at one another hopelessly.

"No good," said Barney. "Those two men have the letter—and know all they want to, whatever it is—they know what 'Jim' has told them to do to-night, and everything. Well, it's about lunch-time. Where's Miss Pepper?"

"I'll go and get her. She's upstairs," said Snubby. "Come on, Loony, let's go and tell Miss Pepper she's VERY late!"

And away he went at top speed with Loony, racing up the stairs. But Miss Pepper was not in her room, and Snubby turned to go down again, Loony running in front of him.

He stopped dead as he saw Sir Richard coming along the landing, out of the Best Room. The man saw him and rushed at him, catching him by the collar.

"You! You pest! How dare you take that letter from that boy Dai! How much do you know? You tell me, or I'll throw you down the stairs."

He swung Snubby over the stairway as if he really meant to keep his word. Snubby, half choked, was terrified out of his life.

He gasped out something, but the man could not understand, and shook him as if he were a rat. "Answer me! I'll get the truth out of you if I have to choke you!"

Loony heard the angry voice and came tearing up at

"Tell me, or I'll throw you down the stairs."

119

top speed. The little spaniel gave an angry snarl and flung himself on the man, nipping him sharply in the calf of the leg. Sir Richard let Snubby go, and yelled with pain, and the boy at once fled into Miss Pepper's room, and locked the door behind him.

He listened, gasping and choking, and heard the man rush down the stairs, pursued by a very angry Loony. Gosh—now what was he to do? He simply DARE not slip out of Miss Pepper's room—that fellow might get him again!

CHAPTER EIGHTEEN

Dafydd's Discovery

ROGER, BARNEY and Diana waited patiently for Snubby and Loony to come down with Miss Pepper. In a short while Miss Pepper appeared from the garden of the inn, where she had been sitting, reading a paper.

"Oh—are you ready for lunch?" she said. "Where's Snubby?"

The others looked at one another. Where *was* Snubby —and why hadn't he come down when he found that Miss Pepper wasn't in her room? Barney felt suddenly alarmed.

"I'll fetch him," he said, and went into the inn. He tore up the stairs, and came to Miss Pepper's room. It was shut and locked. Loony was there scratching at the door and whining. Barney knocked.

"Snubby! Are you there?"

Snubby's voice answered him, sounding rather weak. "Yes. Oh, Barney, is it you? I'll unlock the door."

He unlocked it and Barney went in at once. "What have you done to your head?" he said. "My word, you look awfully pale, Snubby. Has something happened?"

"Yes," said Snubby, lying on Miss Pepper's bed again. "That bearded man attacked me—half choked me, and almost flung me down the stairs. I must have hit my head somehow—against the wall, I suppose, when he shook me till my teeth rattled! Loony went for him and bit him—good old Loony!"

"Grrrrr," said Loony, fiercely, remembering.

"Gosh!" said Barney in horror. "What a brute the fellow must be! You'd better stay out of his way, Snubby. He's furious with you for getting his letter from the little fisher-boy, Dai, of course. Pity we couldn't read it!"

"I'm staying up here," said Snubby. "I don't know what you can tell Miss Pepper, but to-day I'm quite definitely keeping out of Sir Richard's way."

"I'll tell her you hit your head and hurt yourself," said Barney, troubled. "I'll suggest to her that you stay up here as it's much quieter than downstairs. Perhaps after to-night those men will go. Do you want any lunch? I could bring a tray up for you."

"No thanks," said Snubby. "I couldn't eat a thing. My tummy feels all of a wobble."

"Bad luck, old son," said Barney, thinking that Snubby must indeed feel queer not to want his lunch. "Try to get a bit of sleep."

"My head's begun to ache," complained Snubby. "Oooh, Loony, I *am* glad you went for that spiteful wretch!"

Loony leapt on the bed, and Snubby pushed him down.

"Sorry—this is Miss Pepper's bed, not mine," he said. "Though I dare say if I went to lie on Diana's bed, *she* wouldn't mind you coming beside me."

Barney went downstairs and told Miss Pepper that Snubby had somehow hurt his head, and wanted to lie down quietly, and that he didn't want any lunch. Miss Pepper was quite alarmed to hear this and ran up the stairs at once. Barney quickly told the others what had happened, and they listened in dismay. Poor old Snubby.

Miss Pepper came down at last and they began their dinner. Miss Pepper was quite worried. "I cannot *imagine* what Snubby was doing to bang his head like that," she said. "How very sensible of him to want to lie quiet this afternoon—of course my bedroom is just the place! Nobody will disturb him there. I'll pop up after lunch to see if he's all right, and then leave him in peace till tea-time. He says he has a most terrible headache, poor boy."

"I bet he'll be all right by tea-time," said Roger, eating an enormous chunk of home-cooked meat-pie. "I say, wasn't that little monkey of a Dafydd pleased with his clock! He must have set that alarm off about twenty times since we gave it to him. I keep hearing it trilling away somewhere or other."

Miss Pepper went up to see Snubby after lunch, and was glad to find him fast asleep, with Loony on guard. She tiptoed out of the room, hoping that he would sleep till tea-time and then feel quite recovered.

"Wouldn't you like to bathe this afternoon?" Miss Pepper asked the three children. "And then lie out in the sun?"

"Sounds fine," said Roger. "Let's go a good way along the beach this afternoon, where there are those rock-pools. I bet some of them would be as warm as toast to wallow in."

So they all went over the white sands, and settled down by the rock-pools. The rocks were quite high there, and the tide was going out, leaving warm, shallow pools in which swam small grey shrimps.

They bathed, and then lay either in the deliciously warm pools, or on the hot sand. Miss Pepper put up a huge sun umbrella, lay down under it and fell asleep.

Barney lay in one of the pools, amused to feel a shoal of little shrimps trying to nibble his leg. He sat up to tell the others—and caught sight of two people coming along the sands, deep in talk together.

"Hist!" he said in a low voice. "I spy Sir Richard and the other fellow coming along. Keep your heads down. I wonder where they're going?"

The two men walked quickly past on the sand, talking in low voices. "Gone to chat to Morgan and Jim, I suppose," said Barney. "About the Doings to-night, whatever they are! What do you bet that one of Morgan's boats is coming in at dead of night with some mysterious 'catch' that they don't want anyone else to see unloaded?"

"Look—isn't that Dafydd and his goose?" said Roger, in surprise. "Following some way behind the men? I wonder what he's up to? See how close he's keeping to the cliff—as if he doesn't want them to see him?"

"Doing a bit of snooping again, I suppose," said Diana. "You just never know where that child will pop up next!"

They all lay down again in the pool, their heads propped against convenient rocks. Diana yawned. "I think I'd better get out and lie in the sun. I'm almost asleep, and I don't want to wake up choking in the water!"

It was a truly lazy afternoon, and the four, with

Miranda too, thoroughly enjoyed it, though they missed Snubby and Loony very much. Miranda sat near Barney on a rock just above his head, sad because she could not sit on his shoulder as usual. But nothing would persuade her to lie in the pool too!

After about an hour Miranda began to chatter quietly, and Barney sat up in the pool. "What's up?" he said. "Someone coming?"

A small brown face, with a shock of untidy hair above it, peered round the rock at him. It was Dafydd! A long curving neck peered round as well, and Barney saw that Waddle was there too.

"Shhhhhh!" said Dafydd mysteriously, and then began to point with his finger some way up the beach, jabbing the air with it.

"What is it? What do you want to tell me?" said Barney in a low voice.

"Men," said Dafydd. "Two men. Dafydd see where they go. Dafydd want paper back, and follow men. Up long hole."

"What on earth does he mean?" said Barney to Roger, who was listening. "Do you suppose he went after the men with some wild idea of getting back that letter for us?"

"Up long hole," said Dafydd, nodding. "Dafydd take you."

"This sounds interesting," said Barney. "Let's go with him and see what he means. Wait a bit, though—is that voices? Maybe it's the men coming back. Dafydd, come down here."

Dafydd and the goose scrambled over the rocks and sat beside Barney, Dafydd's bare feet in the water, and the goose paddling solemnly round the pool.

"Men come back," said Dafydd, peering over the rock. Barney pulled him down.

"Keep still," he said, and Dafydd understood and sat quite still, swinging his feet to and fro in the warm pool.

The men passed by once more, on their way back, and were soon out of sight. Dafydd stood up. "Up long hole?" he said, pointing over the sands. Barney and Roger scrambled out of the pool, shook themselves like dogs, and followed the small boy and goose back along the way the men had come.

They came at last to the caves that led into the cliffs, and Dafydd disappeared into one of the two marked "DANGEROUS". Barney pulled him back.

"No! This cave is dangerous," he said.

Dafydd obviously didn't understand. He ran right into the cave, and the two boys followed him, feeling rather scared in case part of the roof fell.

"I suppose if the men *did* go into this cave, it can't be very dangerous!" said Roger.

"Or maybe they labelled it 'Dangerous' themselves," said Barney grimly. "Perhaps they've got a convenient hiding-place up here!"

"Well—it's not much of a cave!" said Roger, as they came to the end of it. "Nowhere to hide anything here!"

"Look at Dafydd," said Barney. "He's climbing up that rock—now he's running along a ridge—he's gone!"

So he had! He disappeared half-way along the ridge of rock, and Waddle the goose, left behind on the sandy floor of the cave, sent a sorrowful cackle after him.

Dafydd appeared again, beckoning. They could only just see him, outlined against the dark cave-wall, standing on the ridge.

"Up long hole!" said the small boy. "You come too. Up long hole."

Barney and Roger began to feel excited. They climbed part of the rock at the back of the cave, came to the ridge, and walked along it. Half-way along there was a hole in the wall of the rock, and it was through this that Dafydd had disappeared. He had now slipped through it again, and the two boys peered after him in the dim light, for the cave was almost dark.

"You come too?" asked Dafydd, and added something in Welsh that they didn't understand.

"Rather!" said Roger, and scrambled through with Miranda at his feet. "Where in the world does this lead to? What a pity we haven't a torch. I say—it really *is* a long hole, isn't it—as far as we can see, anyway! Come back, Dafydd—we can't go scrambling about in pitch darkness!"

CHAPTER NINETEEN

Very Exciting!

THE TWO BOYS and Miranda climbed back into the cave where Waddle greeted them with loud cackles. Dafydd leapt down and joined them.

"Long, long hole," he said. "Men go up long hole. Dafydd too. Long, long, long."

"All very mysterious indeed," said Barney. "Thanks, Dafydd. Did the men see you?"

"Not see Dafydd. Dafydd not get letter," said the

small boy, looking doleful. "Dafydd make clock go Tr-r-r-r-r-ring, and men call out quick!"

Barney laughed. "You little monkey! You crept behind the men, and set off the alarm! My word, they must have been scared. Good for you, Dafydd. Now you must go home."

Dafydd set off across the sands, and the boys went to tell Diana where they had been. She was intensely interested.

"The men *must* be smuggling something," she said, "and hiding it up Dafydd's 'long, long hole.' I bet to-night there will be fresh goods to take up there."

"Yes, quite probably," said Barney. "I wonder why they went there to-day, though. Perhaps to make room for the new goods? I wish we'd had a torch—we'd have gone right up to the very end of the hole. It's a steep passage really, of course, but Dafydd kept calling it a long, hole hole! Funny little chap—he went up the rocky cave-wall like a monkey—well, like Miranda did, actually—with a spring and a leap and a jump! He must have eyes like a cat—I believe he would even be able to see in the darkness of that passage! It seemed to go up pretty steeply, as far as we could tell."

"Barney—let's watch to see if those men go out to-night," said Roger eagerly. "They'd have to pass fairly near our caravan if they did, and old Loony would be sure to bark. We could creep after them, and see what they take into the cave, if they do go there."

"Yes. I don't see why we shouldn't," said Barney, suddenly excited. "Snubby can come too if he's feeling better—but not you, Di. Miss Pepper would hear you slipping out of your room."

"I do hope old Snubby *is* better," said Diana. "Fancy

127

that man attacking him like that! The sooner I hear those two men are in prison, the better I'll be pleased. Passing themselves off as a Sir Somebody and a Professor!"

Miss Pepper suddenly woke up with a jump and looked at her watch. "Good gracious! It's tea-time!" she said. "You run on ahead, children, and tell Mrs. Jones to get tea. I'll follow at my own pace."

"Good," said Barney, as they ran off over the sand, "now we can slip upstairs and tell Snubby what we've discovered, without Miss Pepper overhearing."

They found Snubby feeling much better, and began to tell him of their afternoon's excitement—but Snubby interrupted.

"Listen!" he said, "something awfully peculiar happened this afternoon, when I was lying here, half asleep. Loony heard the noise first, and barked. I sat up, thinking those men might be coming into the room—but I hardly thought they would, with Loony barking like mad! But the noise didn't come from *outside* the room—it seemed to come from *inside*."

"What noise?" asked Barney, puzzled.

"I don't exactly know how to describe it," said Snubby. "It was a—a sort of bumping and banging—and it came from that side of the room near the fireplace, but—well, as if it was *under* the room, sort of muffled."

"Oh, Snubby!" said Diana, looking suddenly scared, "it must have been the Noises that Mr. Jones warned us about, when he said we'd better not have this room, we'd far better have the Best Room. He said that Noises sometimes came in the night—but I've not heard any so far. Miss Pepper and I thought it was just nonsense, of course. And now *you've* heard them!"

"Yes. I certainly heard them," said Snubby. "I didn't

dare to get off the bed—and Loony began to bark his head off, and ran all round the floor, trying to find out what was making the noises."

"What on earth *were* they, do you suppose?" said Barney, puzzled. "Is there a door behind the chest— a cupboard, or something?"

"Look and see," said Snubby, and the three children peered round the back of the great chest. But no door was there, only the stone wall.

"It's a mystery," said Barney. "But I say, we'd better not stay up here discussing it. Miss Pepper will wonder what's up again. Are you coming down to tea, Snubby?"

"Rather! I feel jolly hungry—and I don't particularly want to stay alone in this room of noises any longer," said Snubby. So down they all went, to find Miss Pepper patiently awaiting them, and a very fine tea on the table.

The four children, with Miranda and Loony, went to have another talk after tea, in the caravan. They shut the door and spoke in low voices. Barney told Snubby of their idea to follow the men, if they went out that night, and see if they went up the "long, long hole."

"I'd like to come—but I don't think I will," said Snubby. "I feel a bit shaky now I'm up. I'll tell you what I will do, though—when you two have left the caravan to follow the men, I'll nip upstairs and lie on the couch in the room next to Diana's, and wait till I hear them come back—and report to you as soon as you reach the caravan."

"Righto, if you want to," said Barney, understanding quite well that Snubby wasn't particularly anxious to stay all by himself in the caravan that evening!

"Better find our torches," said Roger. "We shall certainly need them. Do you mind if we take Loony with us, Snubby?"

"Er—no," said Snubby, wishing he could say yes, he did mind! He knew he would feel much safer with Loony somewhere near him!

They found their torches, and then put on warm jerseys, for the wind had changed and now blew cold. They went to join Miss Pepper, and set off for a short walk in the hills behind the inn. A bird flew up as they walked over the heather, and Barney pointed to it solemnly.

"Is that a Crazy Corn-Crake, or a Yellow Black Bird?" he said. "We'd better ask the Professor when we get back!"

They all began to feel excited when they were back from their walk, and had had supper.

"It's not dark till about ten," said Barney, "so we'll have a game of cards, shall we? Anyway, the men are still here, so we needn't worry about them slipping off without us seeing them!"

The two men were walking up and down outside the window, well in sight. At about ten they came indoors and went upstairs.

"Getting ready to go, I expect," said Barney. "Come on, we'll be off to the caravan and keep watch. We'll say good night to Miss Pepper now."

Miss Pepper and Diana went upstairs to bed. "Good luck!" Diana whispered to the boys, as she left. Snubby went off to the caravan with Roger and Barney, who slipped on their warm jerseys again and put their torches into their pockets. Snubby began to wish he was going too, but they wouldn't let him.

"You still look groggy," said Barney. "We don't want you fainting, just as we go up the long, long hole, and watch for the men. They won't guess we're watching, so they'll probably come straight out of the front door."

The caravan was in darkness, and the three boys peered out of the window, Miranda too. At about half past ten they heard footsteps, and by the light of a half moon saw the two men coming down the slope.

But wait—there were *three* men, not two! Barney nudged Roger sharply.

"See who the third man is—Mr. Jones! I *thought* he was in this, didn't you?"

"Wait till they've gone round the bend, then we'll follow," said Roger, excited. "Gosh! Fancy Mr. Jones going too!"

They slipped out of the caravan with Loony as soon as the men were round the bend, leaving poor Snubby alone. He didn't like being on his own and shot up to the house, creeping up the stairs and going to the room next to Diana's as he had planned. He lay down on the couch there wishing heartily that he had Loony with him.

Meanwhile Roger, Barney, Miranda and Loony were stalking the three men. They were now down on the beach, making their way to Merlin Cove, where the caves ran back into the cliffs. The moon gave enough light for the men to be clearly seen in front of them, and the boys were careful to keep out of sight by walking close to the cliffs.

"Tide's coming in," said Roger, "and it's going to be pretty high to-night, with that strong wind blowing off the sea. Hallo—look! Is that a boat coming ashore?"

They stopped, keeping close to the cliffs, and watched a boat being rowed ashore. Two men were in it, and the boys felt sure that the man rowing was Morgan. Who was the other?

"Jim, probably, whoever he is," said Barney. "I can't see that they have much in the boat—if they are bringing in goods they have smuggled in a fishing catch."

The three men did not go down to the boat when it grounded on the sands but waited while it was pulled up on the beach by Morgan and the second man. Then Morgan and his friend began to lift what seemed to be

big packets out of the boat, and went up to the caves with them.

The men took them and disappeared into the cave marked "Dangerous."

"The one we were in this afternoon, of course!" said Barney.

Then Morgan and his friend went back to the boat and staggered up the beach with more packets, evidently the last ones for they, too, disappeared into the cave. One of them then came back and pulled the boat right up to the cave entrance, making it fast.

Then he too went into the cave, and it seemed as if

all of them had gone to some hiding-place where the packets were to be placed.

The two boys and Loony went right up to the cave and stood outside, listening. Not a sound was to be heard except the little waves breaking on the sand as the sea came in.

"Come on," said Barney. "Into the cave we go, and up the wall at the back and on to that ridge. Maybe we can hear the men if we listen at that hole that goes up and up."

They went in quietly, not switching on their torches at first, for the moon shone into the cave and lighted it.

"Up we go!" said Barney, leaping up the wall on to the ridge, and pulling up a most surprised Loony. "And don't let's make any noise, for goodness' sake. Loony, not a growl or a bark from you, or you may put us in danger. Here's the hole, Roger. I'll lead the way!"

CHAPTER TWENTY

The "Long, long Hole"

THE TWO BOYS shone their torches up the hole.

"It goes up and up and up!" said Barney. "It's rather like a shaft, only not so steep, of course. I can't hear a thing, can you?"

"No," said Roger. "The men must be a good way up—come on!"

They began to clamber up the long, steep passage, switching on their torches every now and again to show them their footing. Not a sound could they hear until at last Loony gave a little growl of warning. They snapped off their torches at once.

"Voices!" whispered Barney. "Voices some way in front. We'd better be careful now. Shade your torch with your hand, Roger, when you switch it on. Come on—they're a long way ahead yet. Quiet now, Loony!"

They went on again, listening for any sound from above, but could hear nothing. Either the men had now gone beyond hearing, or were being very quiet. The boys came to a very steep part indeed, and discovered that rough steps had been cut there. They climbed up them, and came to what seemed to be a small cave in the very heart of the cliff. They sat down to rest for a moment, panting with the long, steep climb. Loony ran round, sniffing here and there.

"Loony! Miranda? Where have you gone?" whispered Barney, switching on his torch and shining it round the little cave. "*Now* where are they, Roger? I can hear them, but can't see them!"

He got up cautiously, and went farther into the cave. He found the two scraping about behind a big rock, unearthing the bones of some small animal. "Leave that alone!" whispered Barney. "Come with us. We're going on up the hole."

Miranda leapt on to his shoulder and Loony reluctantly left his find. Once more they all scrambled up the steep passage, which was, in truth, more like a "long, long hole," as Dafydd had said.

"Have you any idea of the direction we're going in?" asked Roger.

"No—except that we seem to slant to the left all the time," said Barney. "We must have got beyond the cliffs by now and be burrowing up the hills at the back of them."

They heard noises again a little later, and stopped to listen. The noises went on and on, and sounded as if goods were being moved or stacked.

"I bet they're opening those packets and stacking the contents somewhere," said Roger. "Shall we go any nearer?"

"Yes—but I think perhaps only one of us," said Barney. "You stay here with Loony and Miranda, and I'll go as near as I dare. Keep your hand on Loony's collar."

Barney went on up the steep passage, and soon the sound of voices was quite loud. Counting was going on—"100 —200—300" Barney heard. He looked up the passage, which was not so steep here, and saw a bright circle of light not far ahead.

"That's where the passage stops and the hiding-place is," thought Barney. "They're all up there together. I can hear Morgan's deep voice now—I wish I could hear what he's saying—but I hardly dare creep any closer."

He stayed for about ten minutes, listening to the sound of goods being shifted about and stacked, and voices arguing. Then suddenly he got a shock.

The men were coming back, and the lamp or whatever it was that he could see shining some way up the passage, in the hiding-place, was suddenly switched off. The beams from torches appeared instead! Barney scrambled back to Roger quickly, finding it much easier to go down than it had been to climb up!

"Roger—they're coming down!" he whispered. "Pretty quickly, too. Come on. Where's Miranda?"

"She slipped off," said Roger. "I didn't see her go. She's probably gone down again."

They went down farther, hoping to see Miranda waiting for them, but she was nowhere to be seen. Loony didn't like slithering down any better than he liked scrambling up! They came to the little round cave where Loony and Miranda had unearthed bones. "There she is!" said Barney, exasperated, shining his torch on the little monkey, who was busily scraping in the sand again.

She leapt up to a jutting piece of rock and chattered at him. "Come here at once," ordered Barney in a low voice, but Miranda chose to be annoying, and sat up on the rock, swaying about and chattering all kinds of nonsense.

"We'll have to go on, Barney," said Roger. "I can hear the men getting quite near."

"Well, I'm not leaving Miranda," said Barney. "Come on—let's hide behind that rock where Loony unearthed those bones. The men will never guess anyone is here— they don't know they were followed."

"All right," said Roger, feeling uneasy as the men's voices became louder and louder. He and Loony went quickly to the big rock and stood silently behind it, Loony pressing against his legs. Miranda at once dropped on to Barney's shoulder and put her tiny paws down his neck.

The voices came very near, and the sound of the men's feet was almost deafening as they slipped and slithered down the steep rocky passage. Loony couldn't help giving little growls as they passed the entrance of the small cave in which the boys were hiding.

Roger tapped him sharply, afraid that the men would hear, and stop to investigate. But mercifully they didn't, and soon the sound of their voices and feet grew less and less, until finally the boys could hear no sound at all.

"It's all right now—we can go," said Barney, relieved, and switched on his torch. "Miranda, take your hands out of my neck, you tickle terribly. And stay on my shoulder, or I'll never bring you out on an adventure again!"

The boys went down the hole, slithering over very steep parts, making far more noise than when they went up! They came at last to the end of the hole, and stood on the ridge of rock on the wall of the big cave. The moon shone into the cave—and what a shock the boys had!

The moon now shone, not on white sand, but on heaving water! Water that was already as high as the ridge they stood on! It caught the moonlight at the entrance, and then shimmered in the light of the boys' torches, at the dark rear end of the cave.

"The tide's come in to the cave—*right* in—and it's still coming!" said Barney in horror. "I never thought of that. It's swept into this cave—and all the caves, of course—and the wind is piling up the waves high enough to swamp the lot. What shall we do?"

"I reckon the men only just got away in time," said Roger. "But, of course, they had a boat. Look out— that wave will sweep us off the ridge!"

They leapt back a little way up the hole just in time to avoid being swept away as an enormous wave splashed right over the ridge. They retreated back up the hole, scared.

"Well," said Barney, "it certainly looks as if we're going to be penned up here for some time, because the tide isn't full for an hour or two. It's that strong wind that's making it so high. Blow! Snubby will be waiting and waiting for us to get back—and he'll be worried stiff."

"I say—let's go back up the hole and see what the men have hidden in that hidey-hole, or whatever it is, right at the top of the passage," said Roger, excited. "Come on—it's a fine chance for us, Barney! We know the men can't come back, because they wouldn't be able to get through the water in the cave."

"You know—that's an idea!" said Barney, delighted. "A really good idea! If we find out what's hidden there, we can go to the police to-morrow, and tell them, not only about the men, but about what they've hidden, and where it is! If only we hadn't to make that wearisome climb all over again!"

"Oh, come on—it won't seem so bad this time, because we don't need to be afraid of the men hearing us," said Roger, and Loony barked at the excitement in his voice.

So back they all went again, up the long, shaft-like passage—and certainly this time it did not seem so long, for they could go as carelessly as they liked, and not be afraid of making even the slightest noise! They let Loony bark, and allowed Miranda to scamper ahead as much as she liked.

They came to the last part of the passage, which was steeper than ever.

"There's a rope-ladder here, at the very end," panted Barney, shining his torch in front of him.

Roger saw a strong rope-ladder stretching up from the end of the rocky passage to the entrance of the hiding-place. He held Loony while Barney went up the rope with Miranda. Then he went up too, leaving Loony below.

The boys stared round at the hiding-place. It was about eight feet square, a natural hole in the rock that someone had made into a kind of cell by chipping the walls smooth, and the floor level. It was stacked with oblong packets, marked with numbers. Except for a few empty bottles which had held drink of some kind, and a couple of old rugs, there was nothing else to be seen.

"Gosh—what a wonderful hidey-hole!" said Roger, looking round. "I wonder who first discovered it. Barney, what do you suppose is in those packets?"

"I think I know all right!" said Barney. "They're packets of stolen bank-notes! Bank-notes that can't be passed for some considerable time, because the numbers are known—but which could be shipped across to Ireland easily enough, perhaps from this Welsh coast—or stored till the hoo-ha and excitement has died down, and then used some time in the future!"

"I *say*! But there must be millions here!" said Roger, amazed. He patted a big packet. "This will be about the only time in my life that I shall ever be able to say I have laid my hands on hundreds of thousands of pounds! Barney—*now* I can see why those men got Mr. Jones into their power—they badly wanted some good head-quarters down here on this coast—where they could bring their goods by boat and hide them, and take them away again by boat—over to Ireland, perhaps, as you say!"

"Yes. Or help themselves to a packet or two when they knew they could get rid of the notes undetected in London, or some other big town!" said Barney. "Do you remember the last Bank raid, Roger—where the thieves ambushed the driver of a Bank van—and drove off in the van with hundreds of thousands of pounds? Not one note has been traced so far—and I wouldn't mind betting it's all here!"

Roger's heart began to beat fast as he glanced round at the stacked packets again.

"Could we open one just to see?" he said.

"Better not," said Barney. "We'll tell Miss Pepper to-morrow—and I'll telephone my father. He'll get on to the London police. The village policeman here couldn't possibly deal with it."

Roger sat down on a pile of the packets. "To think I may be sitting on half a million pounds!" he said. "Oh, Barney—I *wish* we could get out of here and tell everyone! To think we're penned up here for hours because of that high tide."

Barney glanced all round the little room, and then happened to look upwards. What he saw so astounded him that he stood as if turned into a statue, staring, staring. Roger was quite alarmed.

"What's the matter?" he said, and looked upwards too. He was as amazed as Barney at what he saw.

"A *trap-door*! A wooden trap-door! Set in the roof of this funny round hole. BARNEY! Let's open it and get out and see where we are. Quick, Barney!"

Barney was as excited as he was, but more cautious. "Wait a bit, wait a bit! We don't know where the trap-door leads to, ass. We might walk straight into trouble! Shut up, Loony, shut up barking! Gosh, we've excited him now, too, and he'll bark the place down. I'd better go down the ladder and drag him up here. Perhaps he'll be quiet then."

They stacked up the packets high enough to reach the trap-door, and then mounted them. Both boys raised their arms, and pushed at the wooden trap-door, which fitted closely into a square of the roof. But it would not budge.

"Must be fastened the other side!" panted Barney. "Oh, *blow*! Try again, Roger!"

They tried again, banging at the trap-door in their impatience, making a tremendous noise.

"I expect it opens into some deserted cellar or pit," said Roger. "Probably nobody will hear us, Barney. Try again! Oh, Loony, DO be quiet!"

"I suppose the men prefer to use the cave way when they bring the money in," said Barney, taking a rest, "because it's so easy to bring it by boat. Nobody would suspect a boat going out by night, and Merlin's Cove would be quite deserted then. But the men don't need to help themselves to the money by way of the cave and the hole. When they want it, they've only to open the trap-door and drop neatly down, collect what they want, and go back through the trap-door again. Very clever!"

"Let's try the trap-door again," said Roger. "We might use one of the packages as a battering-ram—they're solid enough! Do stop barking, Loony—it's quite deafening in here!"

The two boys stood on the packages—and then they suddenly leapt down in fright. Loony growled fiercely, making Miranda jump in fear on to Barney's shoulder.

"Someone's opening the trap-door!" said Roger. "I can hear noises up above. Oh, gosh, Barney, it's not those men, is it? We're trapped if it is. We've no getaway at all!"

141

CHAPTER TWENTY-ONE

The Trap-Door Opens!

AND NOW how was Snubby getting on, lying alone in the little room next to Miss Pepper's, missing Loony very much—listening anxiously for the two men to return to their room nearby?

He was quite determined to creep behind the big couch he was on, if he heard so much as a footstep! But he heard nothing at all for what seemed like hours, and at last fell asleep very suddenly indeed.

Diana too, in the next room was fast asleep, but Miss Pepper was still reading a book. At last she yawned, shut her book and blew out her candle. She was just going to sleep when she thought she heard a little noise. She opened her eyes and listened—no—it must have been an owl outside.

She fell asleep, and then awoke again some time later. She sat up. What had awakened her? She listened intently. There—a noise—it came again and again. It almost sounded as if it was in the room!

Miss Pepper was not easily scared, but her hand was trembling a little as she lighted her candle again. Diana woke up, as the light flickered in the room.

"Are you all right, Miss Pepper?" she asked, sleepily, thinking it was the middle of the night, although she hadn't really been asleep very long. "Ooooh—what's that?"

"I don't know," said Miss Pepper, puzzled. "I heard

noises—but there doesn't seem anything to cause them."

"Oh, Miss Pepper—they must be the noises Mr. Jones told us about!" said Diana. "He didn't want us to have this room because of them—nor did Mrs. Jones."

"Oh yes," said Miss Pepper. "But I really thought that was only a bit of nonsense. There—did you hear that? A deep-down sort of noise—bump!"

"Yes," said Diana, scared. "I don't much like it. Where's it coming from, Miss Pepper?"

"I don't know," said Miss Pepper, getting out of bed, and holding the candle into every corner. Diana thought she was very, very brave! Bump! Boomp! Bump!

"It's coming from the old chest!" said Diana, with a little scream.

"No, dear, no," said Miss Pepper. "Don't be silly. There's nothing in the chest but our clothes. You know that."

Miss Pepper went to the door of their room and opened it, looking out, holding her candle up to make sure that the three boys were not playing some sort of a silly joke in the middle of the night to scare her and Diana. They could be very annoying at times!

But no—no one was there. She noticed that the door of the next room was a little open, and went to it. Was anyone hiding in there?

She had the surprise of her life when she saw Snubby fast asleep there, sprawled on the big sofa, still in his day clothes! What on *earth* was he doing there? She went over and shook him. He awoke in a hurry, scared stiff, thinking the men had got hold of him!

"Why are you here, Snubby? Did you hear any noises?" asked Miss Pepper, wondering if by any chance she could be dreaming it all.

"Oooh—you *did* frighten me," said Snubby. "What noises? No, I've heard none—but I did hear some when I was resting in your room to-day—bump—boomp—bump!"

"Yes—that's what *we've* been hearing, Diana and I," said Miss Pepper. "Come and listen, Snubby."

So Snubby joined Diana in the next room, and they all listened. But they could hear absolutely nothing at all now.

"Funny!" said Snubby. "Not a sound to be heard. Can I sleep on your couch at the foot of the bed, Miss Pepper—to—to see that you're safe, you know."

Miss Pepper smiled a little smile. "Of course, Snubby—but now tell me why you were sleeping in the next room, instead of in the caravan with the others? What's happened? Have you quarrelled?"

"I can't tell you just yet, Miss Pepper," said Snubby awkwardly. "Tell you to-morrow, perhaps."

He snuggled down on the sofa, with a blanket thrown over him, and Diana and Miss Pepper got into bed again. The candle was blown out, and they all lay in darkness, hoping to goodness that there would be no more disturbing noises. None came, and one by one the three fell asleep once more.

Some time later Snubby woke again, and sat up, astonished. He heard a MOST surprising noise—so surprising that he thought he must have been dreaming. But no—there it was again—wuff-wuff-wuff-wuff! It was Loony barking!

"Miss Pepper! I can hear Loony barking!" he cried, shaking her awake. "But it can't be! Di, wake up! Can you hear Loony?"

Now they were all awake and listening. Wuff-wuff-wuff!

Yes, that was Loony all right. But where was he? The barking sounded near, and yet muffled.

"This is really mysterious," said Miss Pepper, worried. "Where in the world can Loony be?"

Then loud noises came—bang! Bang-bang-bang. They sounded almost as if someone was knocking at a door somewhere, very fiercely indeed.

"The noises *are* coming from the chest," said Diana, almost in tears.

"Let's move it out," said Snubby. "I thought the same myself this afternoon, when I heard them. Come on—help me, both of you—it's most FRIGHTFULLY heavy!"

It certainly was—but they managed to shift it at last—and there, where it had stood, was a wooden trap-door, shut tightly down!

"Gosh—look at that! No wonder they didn't want you to have this room!" said Snubby. "This trap-door must be used for something secret—for whatever dirty work those two men are doing! There—I can hear Loony again! AND Barney's voice—listen!"

"But—but who put them down there and shut the trap-door on them?" said Miss Pepper, overcome with amazement. "I never heard of such a thing in my life! Can we lift up the trap-door, Snubby? Oh dear—I feel as if this *must* be a dream!"

"Can't be," said Snubby. "It's much too noisy. Gosh, they're banging at the trap-door again. They couldn't open it while the chest was standing on it, of course. Hey, wait a bit—I'll pull this handle—ah—UP she comes!"

And the trap-door gradually lifted as Snubby and Diana pulled at the iron handle!

145

Down below, there was great consternation of course. Barney and Roger were absolutely horrified to see the trap-door being raised from the other side! They at once thought that somehow the two men were there, and that now they would be discovered—and properly trapped. They ran to the rope-ladder and began to climb down it. But Loony wouldn't come. He began to bark excitedly as the trap-door opened, and he heard Snubby's beloved voice.

"Hey!" called Snubby, taking the candle from Miss Pepper, and sticking it down the hole. "Loony! What on earth are you doing there! LOONY!"

Loony nearly went mad, trying to jump as high as the trap-door and failing miserably. Barney and Roger and Miranda paused when they heard Loony's happy barking, and heard Snubby's voice.

"That *can't* be Snubby opening the trap-door!" said Barney, amazed. "But it's his voice! Quick, let's get back into that little room and see." So back up the rope-ladder they went—and saw Snubby peering through the open trap-door, waving a candle, and Loony almost mad with joy.

"SNUBBY! How did you get there?" yelled Roger. "Where are you?"

"In Miss Pepper's room. Under the old chest," said Snubby, getting muddled in his excitement. "But I say—how did YOU get down there? Gosh, this really MUST be a dream. Hand Loony up, will you, before he goes stark raving mad!"

Loony was handed up, and promptly did go completely mad, tearing round and round the room, leaping on the beds, and barking at the top of his voice. Miranda leapt through the trap-door too, and poor Miss Pepper's bedroom became a complete mad-house, as the two animals chased round and round.

Barney and Roger climbed through the trap-door, helped by Snubby, and were soon sitting on the beds, laughing and most relieved at their extraordinary escape.

"*Well!* To think that passage from the cave led right up to Miss Pepper's bedroom!" said Barney. "I never even dreamed it would go to the inn—but of course, now I think of it, it went so very steeply up a slope and veered this way all the time right to the hill that rises up against the back walls. So easy to make a secret entrance! Everything fits in beautifully now—the men staying here —and wanting this bedroom—because it's the entrance to their hidey-hole—and . . ."

"I simply cannot *imagine* what you are talking about," said poor Miss Pepper. "Will you kindly enlighten me?"

"Oh, don't go all starchy, Miss Pepper darling," said Snubby, hugging her. "We've had a secret from you— listen."

And he and the others poured out their strange story to the amazed Miss Pepper. She could hardly believe it.

"Why didn't you tell me anything of this?" she demanded. "I would have taken you all away from here AT ONCE."

"That's just why we didn't tell you!" said Roger. "We couldn't bear to leave in the middle of something mysterious like this. Isn't it *exciting*, Miss Pepper?"

"It's certainly *exciting*," said poor Miss Pepper, quite overcome. "I wonder why it is that I can never go away with you children without getting mixed up in something really undesirable!"

"But Miss Pepper—don't you think it's *desirable* to catch thieves?" said Barney. "Those two men must be two of the cleverest rogues in the country—and we've found out! Oughtn't we to do something about it at once?"

"Oh dear—in the middle of the night?" said Miss Pepper. "Well, perhaps we ought."

"Roger, you and Snubby see if you can get some of those packages up into the bedroom," said Barney. "And I'll go down quietly to the telephone, and wake up my poor father—and tell him to inform Scotland Yard— or his local police if he thinks it best—of our discoveries."

So, while Snubby fetched a rope from the caravan to fix to the strong handle of the trap-door, and then slid down it to pass up packages to Roger, Barney went quietly down to the telephone, woke up his astounded father and told him the news. He kept an ear open for the two men to come back, but not until he had put down the receiver and gone upstairs again did he hear quiet footsteps.

He slipped into Miss Pepper's room, shushing the others, and listened until he heard the men's door quietly shut. Then he slipped out again, and came back looking so triumphant that Miss Pepper was astonished.

"What have you been up to now, Barney?" she said. "Nothing much," said Barney. "The men left the key of their room outside in the lock, so I just slipped out, and locked them in. They will have to wait there till the police come and let them out—because I've got the key in my pocket!"

It was very late when at last the three boys, with Loony and Miranda, went down to the caravan to get a little sleep. Diana and Miss Pepper crawled into bed, but could not go to sleep for a long time, because they had to talk and talk and talk!

"It will be an exciting day to-morrow!" said Diana—and it certainly was! Two cars arrived about nine o'clock, full of plain-clothes police, and poor Mr. Jones had the shock of his life when they appeared in his kitchen!

The two men also had a terrible shock when they found their door well and truly locked on the outside—and were faced by four sturdy policemen when at last it *was* opened!

"What's the meaning of this!" blustered Sir Richard angrily—but he calmed down at once when an inspector reached out and tugged off his beard!

"Ah—George Higgins," said the inspector. "I thought so. You look more like yourself now, George. You and your friend took some fine-sounding names, didn't you! Would you please come with us—and your friend too. Don't worry about the bank-notes—we'll take care of those!"

And within twenty minutes the police cars had gone, taking with them the false Sir Richard and the equally bogus Professor, both of whom they had been looking for for some considerable time. Alas—Mr. Jones went with them!

Poor Mr. Jones! As Mrs. Jones said, "He's not bad is my Llewellyn, not wicked at all. It was those men, with their lies and their promises. They tempted my poor Llewellyn, they lent him money to buy the inn. How was he to know they were bad men—a Sir and a Professor! And his cooking, it was so good, so very good cooking!"

Morgan and Jim were also paid visits by the police, and disappeared from the little village of Penrhydendraith for a long long time.

Mrs. Jones, in tears, begged Miss Pepper not to leave. "I have no money!" she wept. "Stay here with the children, and let me have your payment. What else shall

I do? My cooking is fair, not very good cooking like Mr. Jones's, but it is not bad. Have pity on me, Miss Pepper."

"Well, we don't *really* want to leave," said Miss Pepper. "We can none of us go home at the moment—and I'm very very sorry about all this, Mrs. Jones. We'll stay for another two weeks at least. And let's hope it will be a *holiday*, not a peculiar mystery to be solved, with noises in the night and all the rest of it!"

And a holiday it is, with sunny days, blue seas, white sands—boating, fishing, bathing, walking! All the four are as brown as berries—and they have been joined by another boy, small and just as brown. Dafydd has tagged on to them, with his faithful goose Waddle—and his precious alarm clock!

Everyone knows when the five are coming down to the beach. Wuff-wuff-wuff! Chatter-chatter! Cackle-cackle-hiss! R-r-r-r-r-ring! R-r-r-r-r-ring! R-r-r-r-r-ring!

"Somebody ought to write a book about those children and their doings!" says old Mrs. Jones, as they go by.

Well, Mrs. Jones—somebody has!

The Rat-a-Tat Mystery

The Rat-a-Tat Mystery was first published in a single volume in the U.K. in hardback in 1951 by William Collins Sons & Co. Ltd., and in paperback by Armada in 1970.

CHAPTER ONE

Christmas Holidays

"How LONG do these Christmas holidays last?" said Mr. Lynton, putting his newspaper down as a loud crash came from upstairs. "I sometimes think I'm living in a madhouse—what *are* those children doing upstairs? Are they practising high jumps or something?"

"I expect it's Snubby as usual," said Mrs. Lynton. "He's supposed to be making his bed. Oh, dear—there he goes again!"

She went to the door and called up the stairs. "Snubby —what in the world are you doing? You are making your uncle very angry."

"Oh—sorry!" shouted back Snubby. "I was only moving things round a bit—and the dressing-table fell over. I forgot you were underneath. Hey, look out— Loony's coming down the stairs, and he's a bit mad this morning."

A black spaniel came hurtling down the stairs at top speed and Mrs. Lynton hurriedly got out of the way. Loony slid all the way along the hall and in at the sitting-room door almost to Mr. Lynton's feet. He was most surprised to receive a smart slap on the head from Mr. Lynton's folded newspaper. He shot out of the door almost as fast as he had come in.

"What a house!" groaned Mr. Lynton, as his wife came back. "As soon as Snubby arrives peace and quiet vanish. He makes Diana and Roger three times as bad, too—as for that dog Loony, he's even more of a lunatic than usual."

"Never mind, dear—after all, Christmas only comes once a year," said Mrs. Lynton. "And poor old Snubby must have *some*where to go in the holidays—you forget he has no father or mother."

"Well, I wish he wasn't my nephew," said Mr. Lynton. "And WHY must we have his dog Loony every time we have Snubby?"

"Oh, Richard—you *know* Snubby wouldn't come here if we didn't have Loony—he *adores* Loony," said his wife.

"Ha!" said Mr. Lynton, opening his newspaper again. "So Snubby won't go anywhere without Loony—well, tell him next holidays we won't have that dog here—then perhaps Snubby won't inflict himself on us!"

"Oh, you don't really mean that, dear," said Mrs. Lynton. "Snubby just gets on your nerves when you're home for a few days. You'll be back at the office soon."

Upstairs Snubby was sitting on his unmade bed, talking to his cousins, Diana and Roger, and fondling Loony's long silky ears. They had come to see what the terrific crashes were.

"You'll get into a row with Dad," said Roger. "You never *will* remember that your room is over the sitting-room. Whatever do you want to go and lug the furniture about for?"

"Well, I didn't really *mean* to move it," said Snubby. "But a sixpence went under the chest-of-drawers, and when I moved it out I thought it would look better where the dressing-table is, but the beastly thing went over with a crash."

"You're going to get a whacking from Dad pretty soon,"

said Diana. "I heard him say you were working up for one. You really are an ass, Snubby. Dad goes back to the office soon. Why can't you behave till then?"

"I *do* behave!" said Snubby indignantly. "Anyway, who spilt the coffee all over the breakfast-table this morning? Not me!"

Roger and Diana stared at their red-haired freckle-faced cousin, and he stared back at them out of his green eyes. They were both fond of the irrepressible Snubby, but, really, he could be very irritating at times. Diana gave an impatient exclamation.

"Well, I don't wonder Dad gets tired of you, Snubby! You and Loony rush about the house like a hurricane— and WHY can't you teach Loony to stop taking shoes and brushes from people's bedrooms? Did you know he's taken Dad's clothes-brush this morning? Goodness knows how he got it off the dressing-table."

"Oh, golly! Has he really?" said Snubby, getting off the bed in a hurry. "There'll be another explosion from Uncle Richard when he discovers that. I'll go and find it."

Christmas had been a mad and merry time in the Lynton's house. All the children had come home from school in high spirits, looking forward to plenty of good food, presents and jollifications. Snubby had been a little subdued at first, because he was afraid that his school report might be even worse than usual, and his uncle and aunt had been pleasantly surprised to find him most polite and helpful.

But this wore off after a few days, and Snubby had now become his usual riotous, ridiculous self, aided in every way by his black spaniel, Loony. His uncle had quickly become very tired of him, especially since Snubby had forgotten to turn off the tap in the bathroom and flooded the floor. If it hadn't been Christmas time Snubby would certainly have got a first-class whacking!

All the same, everyone had enjoyed Christmas, though the children wished there had been snow.

"It doesn't *seem* like Christmas without snow," complained Snubby.

"Oh, we'll get plenty as soon as Christmas is gone," said Mrs. Lynton. "We always do. Then you can go out the whole day long, and snowball and toboggan and skate—and I shall be rid of you for a little while!"

But there had been no snow yet, only a drizzling rain that kept the children indoors for most of the time, much to Mr. Lynton's annoyance. "Why must they *always* talk at the tops of their voices?" he said, in exasperation. "And is there any need to have the radio on so loudly? And will *someone* tell that dog Loony that if I fall over him again he can go and live out of doors in the shed?"

But it wasn't really any good telling Loony things like that. If he wanted to sit down and scratch himself, he *sat* down, no matter whether someone was coming along to trip over him or not. Even Snubby couldn't make him stop. Loony just looked up with his melting spaniel eyes, thumped his little tail, and then went on scratching.

"I don't know *why* you scratch!" said Snubby, in exasperation. "Pretending you've got fleas! You know you haven't, Loony. Oh, get up, do!"

One rainy morning Diana was mooning about, getting in her busy mother's way. "Oh, Diana, dear—*do* get something to do!" said Mrs. Lynton. "Have you done all your morning jobs—made your bed, dusted your room, done the——"

156

"Yes, Mother—*everything*," said Diana. "I really have. Do you want me to help you?"

"Well, will you take down all the Christmas cards?" said her mother. "It's time they were down. Stack them neatly in a big cardboard box, so that we can send them to Aunt Lucy—she makes scrap-books of them for children in hospital."

"Right!" said Diana. "Oh, there's Snubby with his mouth-organ. Mother, doesn't he play it well?"

"No, he doesn't," said her mother. "He makes a simply horrible noise with it. Let him do the cards with you, then perhaps he'll put it down and forget it. I really do believe your father will go mad if Snubby wanders round the house playing his mouth-organ."

"Snubby, come and help with the Christmas cards," called Diana. "Look out, Mother—Loony's coming down the stairs."

"Christmas cards? What do you mean?" said Snubby, coming into the room. "Oh—take them down? Right oh! It's always fun to look at them again. Let's put all the funny ones into a pile."

He and Diana were soon happily taking down the gay cards. They read each one and laughed at the funny ones, stacking them all neatly into a box.

"Oh, here's the one Barney sent us!" said Diana. "Look—isn't it marvellous! Just like old Barney too."

She held up a big card, on the front of which was a picture of a fair ground. Drawn neatly in one corner was a boy with a monkey on his shoulder.

"Barney's drawn himself and Miranda on the card," said Diana. "Snubby, I wonder how he enjoyed Christmas-time with his family for the very first time in his life!"

Roger came into the room just then, and took up Barney's card too. "Good old Barney!" he said. "I wish we could see him these hols. I say—wasn't it MAR-VELLOUS how he found his father—and discovered that he had a whole family of his own?"

"Yes," said Diana, remembering. "He spent all his life in a circus with his mother, and thought his father was dead. And when his mother died, she told him his father was still alive, and he must find him. . . ."

"And he went out to seek for his father, and hunted everywhere," said Roger. "And do you remember how at last he met him—last hols, it was, at Rubadub, that dear little seaside place where we were holidaying—and what an awfully nice man he was, *exactly* like Barney . . ."

"Oh, *yes*," said Diana, remembering it all clearly. "And then dear old Barney discovered that he hadn't only a father, but a grandfather and grandmother and an uncle and aunts. . . ."

"And cousins!" finished Snubby. "Gosh, what a wonderful Christmas Barney must have had. I bet he's forgotten all about us now!"

"I bet he *hasn't*!" said Diana at once. "I say—I've got a smashing idea! Let's ask Mother if we can have Barney to stay for a few days! Then we'll hear all his news."

"And we'll see Miranda, his pet monkey, again," said Snubby, thrilled. "Do you hear that, Loony? We'll see Miranda!"

"Come on—let's go and ask Mother this very minute!" said Diana, and flew out of the room. "Mother! Mother! Where are you?"

CHAPTER TWO

Barney

THE THREE CHILDREN raced upstairs to find Mrs. Lynton. Loony went with them, almost tripping them up, he was so anxious to get to the top of the stairs first. He barked as he went, sensing the children's excitement and wanting to join in.

Mr. Lynton, trying to write letters in his room, groaned loudly. "That dog! I really *will* have him kept out of doors if he goes on like this!"

"Mother! We've got such a good idea!" said Diana, finding her mother putting clean towels into the bathroom.

"Have you, dear?" said her mother. "Snubby, could you tell me HOW you get your towel as black as this? You haven't been climbing chimneys by any chance, have you?"

"Ha-ha! Funny joke!" said Snubby, politely.

"Oh, Mother, do listen. We've got a *splendid* idea!" said Diana again.

"Yes! Can we have Barney to stay for a few days, Mother?" said Roger, going straight to the point. "Do say yes! You like Barney, don't you?"

"And we haven't seen him since the summer holidays," said Diana. "Not since he found his father and all his new family, and went to live with them."

"And we simply MUST see him," said Snubby, snatching the bathmat away from Loony, who was shaking it as if it were a rat.

"Well, dears," began Mrs. Lynton, looking most uncertain. "Well . . . I really don't know *what* to say."

"Oh, why? *Why* can't we ask Barney—and Miranda too, of course?" said Diana, astonished. "You always liked him, Mother, you know you did."

"Yes, dear, and I do still," said her mother. "But I don't feel that Daddy will welcome anyone else here while you are all three turning the house upside-down, and——"

"Oh, we *don't* turn it upside-down!" cried Diana. "Haven't I been tidying things all the morning? Oh, Mother, we'll be as quiet and tidy as anything if you'll let Barney come. We simply *must* hear his news before we go back to school again."

"Well, you must ask Daddy, Diana," said her mother. "If he says yes, Barney shall certainly come. I'll leave it entirely to him."

"Oh," said Diana, looking gloomy. "Can't *you* ask him, Mother?"

"No," said her mother. "Stop turning on the taps, Snubby. I said *stop*. And take Loony out of the bathroom please. He'll have that sponge next, out of the bath-rack."

"Come on, Loony," said Snubby, in a sorrowful voice. "We're not wanted here. We'll go and have a game together in the garage."

"No, you won't," said Roger firmly. "You'll come and back us up when we ask Daddy if we can have Barney."

"I can't," said Snubby. "Uncle said he didn't want to set eyes on me again this morning. Or Loony either."

"Oh, well—you come, Di, and we'll tackle Dad together," said Roger. "And for goodness' sake, Snubby, don't start playing your mouth-organ outside the study door just when we're inside."

Loony shot down the stairs at top speed as usual, followed by Snubby three steps at a time. Mrs. Lynton shook her head and smiled to herself—nobody, NOBODY would ever teach Snubby and Loony not to hurl themselves downstairs.

Mr. Lynton heard a discreet knock on his study door and raised his head from his letters. "Come in!" he said, and in came Diana and Roger.

"What is it?" asked their father. "Surely you don't want any pocket-money yet, after all the money you had given to you at Christmas?"

"No, Dad, no," said Roger hurriedly. "We shouldn't *dream* of asking you for any yet. Er—we just wondered if —er—well, we thought it would be nice if——"

"Nice, and *kind* too," said Diana. "If we—er—if Barney could——"

"What *is* all this?" said her father impatiently. "Can't you ask a straight question?"

"Well, we wondered if Barney could come to stay for a few days," said Diana, bringing it all out in a rush. "You remember Barney, don't you, Dad? The circus-boy we got to know so well."

"Yes, I remember him," said Mr. Lynton. "Nice boy— very blue eyes—and didn't he have a monkey?"

"Yes, Dad!" said Roger eagerly. "Miranda—a perfect darling. Could we have them to stay?"

"Ask your mother," said her father.

"We have," said Roger, "and she says we're to ask *you*."

"Then I say No," said Mr. Lynton firmly. "And I'm pretty certain your mother really wants to say No as well —you're all wearing her out these holidays! Also, I've got your Great-Uncle Robert coming for three days, and I've really been wondering if I can't send Snubby and Loony off to Aunt Agatha while Great-Uncle is here— I don't feel that the old gentleman will be able to cope with the three of you—and that mad dog Loony too."

"Oh, Dad! You didn't ask Great-Uncle in the Christmas holidays, surely!" cried Diana. "He talks and talks and talks, and we daren't say a word, and——"

"Perhaps that's why I asked him!" said her father, a sudden twinkle in his eye. "No—actually the old fellow asked himself. He hasn't been well—which is why I'm sure he can't cope with Snubby and Loony—and the mouth-organ."

"Oh," said Diana sadly. "Well, it's no good asking Barney then—there wouldn't be room, for one thing. Oh, and I *did* so want to see him these hols—and now we shan't see him for ages. Couldn't you *possibly* put Great-Uncle off, Dad?"

"No, I couldn't," said her father. "And even if I did, I wouldn't have Barney here—one more to add to the madhouse! And you might warn Snubby he may have to go to his Aunt Agatha's soon."

Snubby was horrified at this news. "But I don't *like* being there!" he said. "Loony has to live in a kennel— and I have to wash at least twenty times a day! I say, I won't play my mouth-organ any more. And I'll stop whistling. And I'll tiptoe down the stairs, and——"

"Ass!" said Roger. "That would only make Mother think you were ill, or sickening for something! Blow! All our plans made for nothing!"

"And we shan't see Barney now," said Diana. "*Or* that darling little Miranda."

"I say," said Snubby suddenly, "look—it's snowing!"

They ran to the window and looked out. Yes, big snowflakes were falling steadily down. Diana looked up at the sky, but the snowflakes were already so thick that they hid it completely.

"If it goes on like this, we'll have some fun," said

Roger, feeling more cheerful. "And when Great-Uncle comes to stay we can keep out of his way all day long—we'll be out in the snow, tobogganing!"

"And skating, if there's any ice," said Diana, thrilled.

"But *I* shan't be here!" said Snubby, in such a desperate voice that the others laughed. "I shall be with my Aunt Agatha and Uncle Horace, with poor old Loony howling by himself out in his kennel."

"Poor Snubby. Never mind. Perhaps Great-Uncle won't come," said Diana.

But the next day there was a letter from Great-Uncle announcing that he was arriving in two days' time. Snubby looked at his aunt in despair. Would he be sent away? He was ready to promise anything rather than that. Especially as the snow was now beautifully thick and deep, and the ponds had begun to freeze. There would be no tobogganing or skating at his Aunt Agatha's, he knew that.

But Mrs. Lynton was quite firm. If Great-Uncle Robert was not very well, then the worst thing in the world for him would be a dose of Snubby and Loony. He might even have a heart-attack at some of the things Loony did.

"I must telephone to your Aunt Agatha at once," she said. "Don't look like that, Snubby—the world isn't coming to an end."

She went into the hall to telephone—and almost as she touched the receiver, the shrill bell rang out. Ring-ring! Ring-ring! Ring-ring!

"I hope it's to say Great-Uncle can't come!" cried Snubby. But it wasn't. Mrs. Lynton turned round, smiling. "Who do you think wants to speak to you?" she said. "It's Barney!"

"Barney!" cried everyone, and they all rushed to the

telephone. Roger grabbed the receiver first. "Barney! Is it really you! Did you have a good Christmas?"

Then he listened to Barney's reply—and suddenly a look of utter delight came over his face. "Oh, BARNEY! What a wonderful idea! Yes, I'll ask Mother—hold on. I'll ask her straight away!"

Snubby and Diana could hardly wait for him to ask his mother whatever it was that Barney wanted to know.

"Mother!" said Roger, "Barney and one of his cousins are going to stay at a house his grandmother owns, by a little lake surrounded by hills—the lake is frozen and the hills are covered with snow—so there will be tobogganing and skating. And he says, can *we* go too?"

There were shrieks of delight from Diana and Snubby. "Of course we'll go, of course!"

"Barney says, if you say yes, his grandmother will telephone all the arrangements to you," said Roger, his eyes shining. "Oh, Mother—it's all right, isn't it? We can go to stay with Barney, instead of him coming here—and Snubby won't have to go to his Aunt Agatha's—and Great-Uncle Robert can come here in peace, without any of us to worry him. Oh, Mother—we *can* go, can't we?"

CHAPTER THREE

An Exciting Invitation

MRS. LYNTON LOOKED at the three eager children, and nodded her head, smiling round at them.

"Yes. I don't see why you shouldn't. In fact, I think it's an excellent way of solving all our difficulties. Oh, Snubby, dear, DON'T!"

Snubby had caught hold of his aunt and was waltzing her round and round in delight, shouting, "Hip-hip-hip, hurray, it's a hap-hap-happy day!"

Mr. Lynton came out into the hall in surprise, and was told what the excitement was about. He listened with approval.

"Ha! That will give your Great-Uncle a little peace and quiet—and us too," he said. "I hope you're not going to leave Loony behind. I really should like to see the back of that dog for a little while."

"You will, you will!" shouted Snubby, approaching his uncle to give him a waltz-round too, he was so very relieved. But fortunately he thought better of this—his uncle did not take kindly to such idiotic manners.

Roger was already telling Barney of his parents' consent, and getting a few more details. Diana snatched the receiver from him after a minute or two, longing to have a word with dear old Barney. A little chattering noise greeted her.

"Oh, is that you, Miranda!" she cried, enchanted to hear the familiar monkey-chatter once more. "We'll be seeing you soon, Miranda, soon, soon, soon."

"Woof, woof!" said Loony, not understanding what was going on at all, and quite amazed at all the excitement. He tried to tug the mat from Mr. Lynton's feet and run off with it, but Snubby stopped him just in time.

Everyone was thrilled to hear from Barney. After Snubby had had a few words on the telephone with him too, the receiver was put down and they all trooped into the sitting-room to talk over the exciting news.

"Fancy—a house in the middle of the snowy hills— and by a frozen lake too—it couldn't be better!" said Roger exultantly. "I must look out my skates. You're lucky, Snubby, you had new ones for Christmas."

"What about our toboggan?" said Diana. "I don't believe it's any good for us now—too small. We haven't used it for about three years. Blow!"

"I'll buy a new one with my Christmas money," boasted Snubby. "Oh, I say—I wish I could buy skates for Loony!"

Roger laughed. "I wish you could. Loony would look priceless on skates—he wouldn't know which skate to use first!"

"Oh, it's too good to be true!" said Diana, sinking into a chair. "Mother, you don't mind us going, do you? You won't be lonely, will you?"

"Dear me, no," said her mother. "I shall be glad to have time to devote to your Great-Uncle. Thank goodness Loony won't be here. When is Barney's grandmother going to telephone about the day and time and other arrangements, Roger. Did Barney say?"

"Yes. She'll phone to-night," said Roger. He turned to the others. "Barney sounded *exactly* the same, didn't he?" he said.

"Exactly," agreed the others.

"But why shouldn't he?" said Mrs. Lynton, surprised.

"Oh, I don't know," said Roger. "After being a circus-boy so long—with ragged clothes and often hardly enough to eat—and no schooling to speak of—and then finding a whole new family, and having to have lessons—and decent clothes and table-meals instead of camping out —well, somehow I thought he might have changed."

"Barney will *never* change," said Snubby. "Never. I say —think of toboganning down steep hills—whoooooosh!" He slid at top speed over the polished floor, and stopped when he saw his aunt's face. "And skating round and round—and in and out. . . ."

He skated into a little table and Diana just caught it as it fell. "Don't be more of an idiot than you can help!" she said. "I bet you'll fall down a thousand times before you can skate even half a dozen steps. Ha—I'm looking forward to seeing you sitting down bump on the ice!"

Barney's grandmother telephoned to Mrs. Lynton that evening. She had a kind, very soft voice, and Mrs. Lynton thought how lucky Barney was to have a grand-mother who sounded so nice. She told the waiting children what the old lady had arranged.

"She says that this house in the hills has been shut up for some time," said Mrs. Lynton. "Her sons and daughters used to use it for winter sports when they were young. She is sending someone to clean it up and air it, and it should be ready for you to go to in two days' time."

"Is any grown-up going with them?" asked Mr. Lynton. "They must have someone *sensible* there."

"Barney's *very* sensible," said Snubby, at once.

"Mrs. Martin—that's Barney's grandmother—says she is sending her cook's sister to look after them," said Mrs. Lynton. "She will cook for them, and dry their clothes, and see that they don't do anything *too* idiotic. But I hope Roger will see to that, as well. He's quite old enough to take charge, with Barney."

"We'll be all right," said Roger. "You needn't worry, Mother. My word—only two days and we'll be down at this little house!"

"It doesn't sound very little," said his mother. "There are five or six bedrooms, and a big old kitchen, and two or three other rooms. You'll have to help to keep it tidy, or the cook's sister will walk off and leave you!"

"I'll help her," promised Diana. "And we can all make our beds—though all Snubby does is simply to get out of his in the morning and pull the sheets and blankets up again."

"Tell-tale," said Snubby at once. "It's *my* bed, isn't it?"

"I think to-morrow we'd better look into the question of skates and boots and clothes," said Mrs. Lynton. "And you will all need good wellingtons, of course. I hope you've brought yours back from school, Snubby. You forgot them last term."

"Yes, I brought them back. Anyhow, I quite well remember bringing *one* back," said Snubby, helpfully.

"What's the house called?" asked Diana.

"Well—I think I must have heard it wrongly over the

telephone," said her mother; "but it *sounded* like Rat-a-Tat House."

Everyone laughed. "How lovely!" said Diana. "I hope that *is* its name. Rat-a-Tat House—why ever was it called that, I wonder?"

Next day was a busy one. Boots, socks, gloves, sweaters, skates—all were pulled out and carefully examined. The weather remained very cold and frosty, and snow fell again in the night. The forecast was cold weather, much snow, and hard frost—just right for winter sports, as Snubby kept announcing. He produced his mouth-organ once more, and nearly drove everyone mad by trying to learn a new tune. In the end Mrs. Lynton took it away and packed it at the very bottom of one of the suit-cases that were going with them.

But, not to be outdone, Snubby then went about pretending to strum on a banjo, and made a peculiar twanging noise with his mouth half-closed as he strummed an imaginary banjo with his fingers and thumb. This was really worse than the mouth-organ, and unfortunately, as the banjo was purely imaginary, it could not be taken away from him.

"Can't that boy be sent to Rat-a-Tat House to-day?" demanded Mr. Lynton, hearing the banjo passing his door for the twentieth time that morning. "My word, it's a good thing he won't be here when Great-Uncle Robert comes."

At last the suit-cases were all packed, the skates strung together, and clothes set out fresh for the next morning, when they were to join Barney. Loony rushed about eagerly all the time, trying to help, and making off with shoes and bundles of socks whenever they were put ready to pack. Even Snubby got a bit tired of him when he met Loony rushing *up* the stairs, just as he, Snubby, was rushing down, and both arrived in a bruised and tangled heap at the bottom.

"Ass of a dog!" said Snubby fiercely to the surprised Loony. "I'll leave you behind if you do that again. I nearly broke my leg. Grrrrrr! Bad dog!"

Loony put his tail down and crept under the hall chest. There was a smell of mouse there, and he had a wonderful time scrabbling round and round to find it, snuffling loudly all the time, much to Mr. Lynton's amazement.

"We're to go to Barney's home first, and then go on with him and his cousin to Rat-a-Tat House," said Roger to the others. "I wish to-morrow would come. I say —I wonder what the cousin's like. Mother, how long can we stay away?"

"Till the snow's gone, I should think," said his mother. "That's what Barney's grandmother said. But, of course, if it lasts more than a week or so, you'll have to come back because of getting ready for school again."

Roger groaned. "Don't mention the word! Snubby, STOP that noise. Or play another instrument for a change. That imaginary banjo of yours is getting boring."

Snubby obligingly changed over to a zither, which was certainly much pleasanter. He really was a marvel at imitating sounds. Mrs. Lynton hoped he wouldn't start on a drum next!

The morning came at last—a brilliant morning, with a clear blue sky and pale yellow sun—and the snow underfoot as crisp as sugar. "Heavenly!" said Diana. "Just exactly right for us!"

Off they went in a taxi to catch the train to Barney's town, Loony too, so excited that he had to be put on the lead. Now for a good time—now for some sport— hurrah for the winter holidays!

CHAPTER FOUR

At Barney's Home

BARNEY'S HOME was at Little Wendleman, and a car was at Wendleman station to meet them—a nice big utility van with plenty of room for luggage. Best of all, Barney was there to meet them too, with Miranda sitting excitedly on his shoulder.

"Barney! Old Barney! And Miranda; hey, Miranda!" shouted Snubby, hanging out of the compartment window as the train drew in. He opened the door and he and Loony fell out together. Barney ran up in delight, his brilliant blue eyes shining as brightly as ever. Miranda, the little monkey, leapt up and down on his shoulder and chattered at the top of her voice. She knew everyone immediately.

"Barney! Dear old Barney!" said Diana, and gave him a hug. Roger clapped him on the back, and Snubby grinned all over his freckled, snub-nosed face. As for Loony, he went completely mad, lay on his back, and did one of his bicycling acts at top speed, barking loudly.

"Hallo!" said Barney, his brown face glowing with pleasure at seeing the children who had befriended him when he was a down-at-heel circus-boy. "Gosh—it's grand to see you all again. Isn't it, Miranda?"

The little monkey leapt on to Diana's shoulder and whispered in her ear, holding the lobe in her paw the way she often did. Diana laughed. "Darling Miranda—you

171

haven't changed a bit, not a bit. And you do look smart in your little red coat and bonnet and skirt!"

Barney looked different. He was no taller and no fatter, and his face was as brown as ever. But now he was dressed well, his hair was cut properly, and he wore a tie, which he had rarely done when he had been a circus-boy. In fact, he looked extremely nice, and Diana gazed at him in admiration.

Barney laughed, as he saw the eyes of all three on him. "Do I look different?" he said, in the voice they knew so well, with the slight American twang he had picked up in his circus travels. "I'm not a circus-boy any more— I'm a gentleman—whew—think of that! Me, Barney the hoop-la boy, the boy who took any job he could, who never wore anything but canvas shoes, dirty old trousers, and a ragged shirt. . . ."

He paused and twinkled round at the three listening children. "Yes, I'm a gentleman now—but I'm still the same, see? I'm just Barney—aren't I, Miranda?"

Miranda leapt on to his shoulder again and jigged up and down, chattering in monkey-language. What did she care how Barney was dressed, or where he lived, or whether he was a circus-boy or a gentleman? It was all the same to her. He was just Barney.

"Yes, you're still just Barney," said Diana, and gave a little sigh of relief. She had wondered just a little if having a family, and a fine house and money to spend would have changed Barney—but no, it hadn't.

"Come on," said Barney. "The car's here, see, and there's my father driving it." He said the words "my father" in a very proud voice. Diana felt touched. How very, very glad Barney must be to have a father of his own, and to have found him after so many years of thinking he was dead!

172

Barney's father, Mr. Martin, was sitting at the wheel
of the car. The children marvelled at the likeness between
the two—bright blue, wide-set eyes, corn-coloured hair,
a wide mouth, ready to smile. Yes, they were certainly
father and son. The only real difference between their
faces was that Barney's was so much browner than his
father's.

"Hallo, kids!" said Mr. Martin, and smiled, looking
more like Barney than ever. "Nice of you to come all
this way to see Barnabas—or Barney, as you call him.
Hop in! We're to have lunch at his grandmother's, and
then I'll take you to Rat-a-Tat House."

"Thank you very much, sir," said Roger politely. "It's
good of you to meet us like this—and jolly good of
Barney's grandmother to invite us to stay with him at
Rat-a-Tat House. We're thrilled."

The boys piled the suit-cases into the utility van. Loony
clambered in, and sat up in a corner so that he could look
out of the window. He loved hanging his head out of a
car, his long ears flapping in the breeze. He was delighted
to see Barney again, though he wasn't so sure about
Miranda the monkey. He had suddenly remembered how
she used to ride on his back, jigging up and down in a
most aggravating manner. He looked at her out of the
corner of his eye. Would she try that old trick again?

The car drew up in the drive of a pleasant-looking
house, timbered, with white walls, tall chimneys and wide
casement windows. As they drew up, the front door
flew open, and a little old lady stood there, as brown-eyed
as the monkey that sat on her shoulder.

"Ah, here you are!" she cried. "Welcome, welcome!
I've longed to meet dear Barney's friends. Come along in,
come along in!"

The children liked Barney's grandmother at once. She

173

had curly white hair, a very pink, soft-cheeked face, brown eyes, and a lively smile. They smiled to see the monkey on her shoulder as they shook hands.

"Ah—you see I have a monkey just like Barnabas!" she said in a merry, bird-like voice. "Monkeys run in our family—my mother kept two. Jinny, here are good friends!"

Jinny, the little monkey, was not dressed like Miranda. She wore a little yellow cape round her thin shoulders. She held out a tiny, wizened paw in a very solemn manner and shook hands with each of them. Loony stared in astonishment at her. What—*another* monkey—or was he seeing double?

Soon they were all sitting in a cosy room, with a blazing fire, gay curtains and a lovely meal laid ready on a round table. Snubby looked at it approvingly. Hot tomato soup to begin with—now that was just what he felt like! He took his place at once and beamed round. This was the kind of thing Snubby enjoyed.

"What comes next?" he asked Barney, in a loud whisper.

"Ah—Barnabas has told me what you like," said the old lady, who had very sharp ears. "Sausages—plenty of them—and fried onions *and* tomatoes—and potatoes and peas. Barnabas has had many a meal with you, I know—and now I am proud you should have a meal with him."

Snubby thought this sounded fine. What a nice old lady. Barney was certainly lucky to have such a splendid family belonging to him. For a second Snubby was just a little jealous when he looked at Barney's handsome, smiling father. *He* would have liked a father like that— but he had no parents at all, worse luck. Snubby simply couldn't understand children who grumbled at their

174

parents—they didn't know how lucky they were to have them!

It was a very pleasant meal. Barney told them all about the lessons he had had during the last term. He had never been to school, and his father had thought he must have plenty of private coaching before he sent him anywhere. The boy was very intelligent, and enjoyed his lessons immensely.

"He's as good at them as he is at walking the tight-rope or turning cart wheels!" said his father, with a laugh.

"How marvellous!" said Snubby, enviously. "I'm no good at either! Barney—do you ever miss the circuses and fairs and shows you used to belong to?"

"Sometimes," said Barney. "Not often. But just at times I think of what fun it was sleeping out under the stars—or having a tasty meal out of some cook-pot in a fair when I was very hungry—and I miss the show people a bit."

"You can always go off for a taste of that life again, whenever you want to, Barney," said his father, smiling at him.

"I know," said Barney. "But I shall always come back home—come back here to you and Granny. I like the freedom of the show-life—but I like putting out roots too, as I can here. That feeling of *belonging* somewhere—to a place or a family—that's what I've missed all my life, and now I've got it, I'm going to keep it."

The talk went on during the meal, happy, jolly talk, friendly and intimate. Loony lay beneath the table, amazed at the variety of titbits that came down to him from Snubby, Roger and Barney. Miranda, curious to see why Loony was so peaceful, slid down a table leg to investigate, and joined in Loony's little feast, much to his annoyance. Jinny, the other monkey, seldom left her mistress's shoulder, and gravely took little titbits in her tiny paw. Sometimes she patted the soft old cheek near to her, and often did what Miranda did to Barney—slid a small paw down her mistress's neck to warm her tiny fingers.

"Now, after lunch, the car will take you all to Rat-a-Tat House," said Barney's grandmother. "Mrs. Tickle, the cook's sister, is already there."

"Mrs. Tickle—is that *really* her name?" asked Snubby. "Is she ticklish?"

"I have no idea," said Mrs. Martin. "And if I were you I wouldn't try to find out."

"I thought a cousin of Barney's was coming too," said Roger. "Where is he? Are we going to pick him up somewhere?"

"No. He has started a cold," said Mrs. Martin. "He may be along in a day or two, but not to-day. You'll have to settle in without him."

This pleased everyone very much. They badly wanted to have a long, friendly talk with old Barney, and a strange cousin would have embarrassed them.

They piled into the utility van, and waved good-bye to Barney's grandmother and little Jinny, the monkey. Then away they drove over the snowy roads towards the white-clad hills.

"Wake me up at Rat-a-Tat House," said Snubby, suddenly feeling sleepy after his enormous lunch. "What fun we're going to have there!"

You're right, Snubby—you just wait and see!

CHAPTER FIVE

Rat-a-Tat House

THE CAR HAD to go slowly along some of the roads because they were already slippery. It took about an hour to reach the little village of Boffame, which was two or three miles from Rat-a-Tat House.

"Now we shall soon be there," said Barney's father, who was at the wheel. "My word, we had some fun at Rat-a-Tat House when I was a boy, and played there with my brother and sisters and cousins. You'll have fun too, Barnabas, with your friends."

They went through the little village, and then up a small, very steep hill. The car stopped half-way up, and would not go on. Its wheels slid round and round in the same slippery place.

"Get the sacks out and the spade, children," said Mr. Martin. "I thought this might happen, so we've come prepared!"

They got the spade and dug away the snow under the wheels, slipping the sacks beneath them instead. Then Mr. Martin started up the car again, the wheels gripped the sacks instead of the slippery snow, and the car slowly reached the top of the hill. It stopped and Mr. Martin waited for the children to come along to the car with the sacks and spade.

"It's a good thing I took all the goods yesterday that you'll need at Rat-a-Tat House," he said. "I doubt if a car will be able to get through if we have any more snow."

"Perhaps we shall be cut off from everywhere!" said

Snubby in delight. "Lost in the snowy hills. Marooned in Rat-a-Tat House. We shan't be able to go back to school. Hurrah!"

Loony barked joyfully. If anyone said "hurrah" it meant they were happy, so *he* had to join in too. Miranda leaned across the car and tweaked one of his long ears, and there was a scrimmage immediately. Mr. Martin looked round for a moment. "I don't know what's happening at the back, but it's most disturbing to the driver," he remarked, and Loony at once got a smack from Snubby, and yelped in surprise.

The car went slowly on. They came to another hill— would the car stick half-way up this time? No, it went up steadily and everyone gave a sigh of relief.

The countryside looked enchanting in its thick blanket of dazzling white snow. Every little twig was outlined in white, and every sharp outline of fence or roof was softened by the snow. Diana looked out of the window and thought how beautiful it was.

"We'll have marvellous tobogganing," said Roger. "Best we've ever had. And plenty of skating if the frost holds."

"It's sure to," said Barney's father, driving the car down into a little valley surrounded by snow-clad hills on every side. "Now we're nearly there—you'll see Rat-a-Tat House in a minute—it's round this corner. Ah, there's the frozen lake, look."

"Oh, it's quite a *big* lake!" said Diana, surprised. "What a pity we can't go boating and swimming, as well as skating."

Everyone laughed. "Rather impossible," said Barney's father. "Perhaps you can come again in the summer and have some fun here with Barney and his cousins then."

"So this is the house," said Snubby, in approval, as

they swung in at a small drive. "Ha—I like it! It's—it's rather *odd* looking, isn't it? All those turrets and towers and tucked-in windows and things."

"It's old," said Mr. Martin; "but was so very sturdily built that it has lasted well for a great many years. It's seen a bit of history too. Oliver Cromwell once stayed here, and it is said that a celebrated Spaniard, who was taken prisoner, was brought here and hidden—and what is more, was never heard of again."

"Gosh!" said Snubby, thrilled. "I hope he isn't still there. I can't speak a *word* of Spanish. I like the look of Rat-a-Tat House. I feel as if plenty of exciting things have happened here."

As they swung slowly up the drive, the front door opened, and someone stood there smiling at them—a very small woman with plaits of dark hair wound round her head, and merry dark eyes. She wore a flowered overall, and over it a spotless white apron. The children liked her at once.

"Is that Mrs. Tickle?" asked Snubby, leaping out of the car before anyone else.

"Yes," said Barney. "But *don't* ask her if she's ticklish, because hundreds of people have asked that already and she's tired of it. Hallo, Mrs. Tickle! I hope you haven't been lonely."

"Not a bit, I've been too busy!" said the little woman, coming to help with the suit-cases. "Are you cold? Come away in, then, I've a fine fire for you. Good afternoon, Mr. Martin, sir—I'm right down glad to see you all, I was afeard you'd not get through the snow."

"We were only stuck once," said Mr. Martin. "I'll just see the children in safely, Mrs. Tickle, and then I must go, because I want to get away before more snow falls. It looks as if the sky is full of it again."

"That's right, sir, you get home before it's dark," said little Mrs. Tickle. "Oh, my word, who's this?"

It was Loony, prancing round in the snow, getting into everyone's way as usual.

"I didn't know you were bringing a dog," said Mrs. Tickle. "I've got no dog biscuits for him."

"Oh, he doesn't mind having what we have," Snubby assured her. "He loves a slice off the joint or a chop."

Mrs. Tickle looked quite horrified. "He won't get anything like that while *I'm* in charge!" she said, leading them all indoors. "I like dogs to be kept in their place. And monkeys too," she said, with a look at Miranda sitting on Barney's shoulder. "Well, here you are—sit down and warm yourselves!"

She led them into a big, panelled room, at one end of which was an enormous fireplace with a fire of logs, crackling and blazing.

"Oh, it's lovely!" said Diana, glancing all round. "It's like a house in a story book. And how light the room is!"

"That's the reflection of the snow outside," said Mrs. Tickle. "Bless us all, what's the matter with that dog?"

Loony was growling in a most peculiar manner, and backing away from the fireplace, towards which he had run for warmth. Barney gave a bellow of laughter.

"He's just seen the bearskin rug in front of the fire! It's got a bear's head at one end and he thinks it's real!"

Certainly poor Loony had had a terrible shock! He had run towards the fire, and had suddenly seen the bear's head at the end of the rug, its two glass eyes shining balefully at him. Loony imagined that the bear was crouching down ready to spring, and had backed away at once, producing his fiercest growls.

"Idiot," said Snubby. "Look at Miranda—she's braver than you are, Loony!"

Miranda had also seen the bear—but she had seen bearskin rugs before and was not at all worried. She leapt down and sat on the bear's head, chattering away at Loony, and jigging up and down.

"She's telling you not to be such a coward, Loony," said Snubby, severely. "Really, I'm ashamed of you!"

"Well, children, Mrs. Tickle will take you all round the house and show you your rooms," said Barney's father, looking at his watch. "And no doubt she has a fine tea waiting. Help her all you can, please. Barney, you are in charge here, remember, and if anything goes wrong, let me know at once."

"Yes, sir," said Barney. "I suppose Rat-a-Tat House is on the telephone?"

"Yes," said his father. "So you'll be quite all right. Mrs. Tickle knows where the toboggans are, and your skates—we brought them here when we drove her over with all the food and bedclothes and so on. Well, have a good time. Mrs. Tickle, keep them in order—and don't stand any nonsense."

"I'll keep them in order all right, sir," said little Mrs. Tickle, looking quite fierce. Then she smiled. "I'll enjoy having them round me," she said. "Mine are all grown up now, and it will be like old times to have them rampaging round. I hope you get back all right, sir."

They all went to see Mr. Martin off in the car. It was getting dark already, though the gleaming snow threw its white light everywhere. "Good-bye!" shouted everyone, and waved till the car had crawled out of the gate.

They all went back into the fire-lit sitting-room, with

its wide window-seats, its enormous fireplace, and gleaming old furniture. Snubby stood by the fire, rubbing his hands in glee.

"Isn't this smashing?" he said. "I wish we could go out into the snow now, and toboggan. Fancy sliding down those hills at top speed. Loony, do you think you'll like tobogganing?"

Loony had no idea what tobogganing was, but he was sure he would like anything that Snubby liked. He felt the general excitement and decided to show off. He rushed round the room at top speed, barking, then suddenly lost his footing on the highly polished floor, rolled over and finished by sliding along swiftly on his back. Everyone roared.

"Is *that* how you're going to slide over the snow?" said Snubby. "You'll get along fine like that, Loony."

"Would you like to come and unpack?" said Mrs. Tickle's voice at the door. "And by that time, you'll be ready for tea, I've no doubt!"

She was right—they certainly would!

CHAPTER SIX

Settling In

A WIDE STAIRCASE led up to the first floor of Rat-a-Tat House, and many rooms opened off the upstairs landing. Everywhere there was panelling, and Snubby went along knocking at the walls, rat-a-tat-tat!

"Snubby, *must* you do that?" said Diana. "What's the idea?"

"Ha—secret passages of course!" said Snubby at once.

"You never know! This place might be riddled with them!"

"Well, I hope you're not going to knock on the walls every time you pass them," said Diana.

"It's *Rat-a-Tat* House, isn't it?" said Snubby, with a grin, and knocked again on some wooden panelling—rat-a-tat-tat! "I say, I wonder why it's got such a peculiar name? Do you know, Barney?"

"No," said Barney. "But maybe Mrs. Tickle does. We'll ask her sometime."

Mrs. Tickle was away along the landing opening doors as she went. "You can choose your own rooms!" she called. "Barney has one to himself, and so has Diana, but you other two boys are to share. The dog can sleep down in the kitchen."

"Well, he can't," muttered Snubby under his breath. "And what's more, he won't! He'll be sleeping on my bed as usual."

The rooms were rather exciting. They all had panelled walls, which Snubby proceeded to knock on smartly with his knuckles, cushioned window-seats, old-fashioned wash-stands, and cupboards that opened out of the panelling.

"You can hardly tell they're cupboards!" said Diana, opening hers. "They look just like part of the oak walls. I never had a room like this before. I feel as if I've slipped a few hundred years back in history!"

"Our room's smashing too," announced Snubby. "Where's Mrs. Tickle? Oh, she's gone. Good. I just wanted to say something she's not to hear. I am *not* going to let her shut Loony up in the kitchen to-night, so I shall think of some way to prevent it—and then he can come on my bed as usual. He'd be miserable if he had to sleep in the kitchen."

Diana opened her suit-case and unpacked and put her things away neatly, while the boys explored the other part of the house. Mrs. Tickle called up the stairs. "Tea will be ready in five minutes—and the scones are hot, so don't be too long."

Diana shouted for the others. "Roger—Barney—Snubby! Tea's almost ready, so buck up and un-pack!"

Roger and Barney came along and put their things away in the great old chests and dark cupboards. Snubby rushed up with Loony at the very last minute, covered with dust and cobwebs.

"Where in the world have you been?" said Diana, looking at him in disgust. "Don't come near me, *please*! You're so cobwebby that you've probably got spiders crawling all over you!"

"Am I?" said Snubby, surprised, and brushed himself down so vigorously that dust flew everywhere. "I found a little attic place—rather exciting, with old boxes and trunks in it. Hey, what's that!"

It was the booming sound of the old gong in the hall. Mrs. Tickle was tired of waiting for them to come down and had suddenly remembered the gong. How it made them jump! Miranda leapt to the top of the curtains at once, and Loony ran under the bed.

"That's calling us for tea, I expect," said Diana. "Snubby, you've *got* to undo your suit-case and put your things away before you come down. Go on, now—buck up!"

"All right, all right, teacher," said Snubby. "Don't start trying to boss *me*! It won't take me long to un-pack."

It didn't. He simply undid his suit-case, opened his cupboard door, and emptied everything into it, pell-mell.

He shoved the suit-case in at the back and then shot downstairs at top speed, Loony just in front of him. The staircase ended in a wide, polished hall, and Loony was able to slide all the way to the front door with the greatest ease.

"Jolly good, Loony," said Snubby admiringly, and walked sedately into the sitting-room, where the others were just about to sit down. Diana stared at him accusingly.

"You haven't had time to unpack. You go back and do it!"

"Everything is safely in my cupboard," said Snubby. "*And* the suit-case is empty, teacher!"

"Don't keep calling me that," said Diana, exasperated, but Snubby didn't even hear. His attention had been caught by the meal on the tea-table. On a spotless white cloth were six different plates of food. Where Diana was sitting was a very large brown teapot, a large blue milk jug, and a large basin of sugar lumps. Two dishes of jam were on the table and one pot of fish-paste.

Snubby looked in awe at the six plates of food. "Stacks of new bread-and-butter—hot buttered scones, at least three each—gingerbread squares, all brown and sticky— a giant of a chocolate cake—a jam sponge twice as large as usual—and home-made macaroons! *Macaroons*—my very favourite goody. Hey, Mrs. Tickle, Mrs. Tickle!"

And the delighted Snubby with Loony at his heels went rushing out into the kitchen to the surprised Mrs. Tickle to tell her what he thought of the tea. He debated whether to give her a hug but decided that he didn't know her well enough yet.

Mrs. Tickle was very pleased with his admiration of the first meal she had provided. "Go along with you," she said, beaming. "You're a caution, you are! You'd better be careful that the others haven't eaten everything by the time you get back to the table!"

That made Snubby rush off in a panic, but to his relief there was still plenty left. He had to gobble to catch up with them, but Snubby never minded that.

"Your table manners haven't improved at all," said Diana primly. She felt quite like her mother, sitting in state behind the big brown teapot.

"Sorry, teacher," said Snubby, in such a humble voice that everyone laughed. "I'll stay in and write out 'I must please dear Diana, I must please dear Diana' one hundred times!"

"I shall throw something at you in a minute," said Diana. "Probably the teapot."

"Right," said Snubby. "But wait till it's empty. I may want another cup of tea. I say, look at Miranda, Barney —she's dipping her fingers into the strawberry jam and then licking them."

"Miranda—how *can* you?" said Barney, reprovingly, and the little monkey hid her face in his neck as if she was ashamed—but the next minute, down went her little paw into the jam dish again!

It was a happy, merry tea, and Barney enjoyed it more than any of them. He had been a lonely boy for so many years, longing for the companionship, the teasing, the family talk that he had never had. Now he was quite at home in the fun, and entered into all the teasing with delight. But nobody ever had a readier answer than the cheeky, irrepressible Snubby—he was never at a loss as to what to say or do!

They all helped to clear away tea. By this time, of course, Mrs. Tickle had had to light the lamps. These were old-fashioned oil-lamps, because there was no electricity in Rat-a-Tat House.

"You be careful of these lamps," she warned them. "And if you want to rush about with that mad dog of yours, Snubby, don't knock them over or you'll have the place afire."

"I'll be careful," promised Snubby.

"There are candles upstairs on the landing," went on Mrs. Tickle, "and candles waiting in the hall for when you all go up to bed. And if you want wood for the fire, it's in that cupboard there, by the fireplace. I'll bring you more from outside if you want it."

"No, you won't," said Roger at once. "*I'll* do that—and just tell us whatever jobs you want done, Mrs. Tickle, and we'll do them straight away."

"That's what I like to hear!" said the little woman, pleased, and went out smiling.

Soon they were all sitting round the fire. "Let's have a game," said Snubby. "I brought some cards. I'll go and fetch them." He went off upstairs, knocking on the panelling all the way—knock-knock-knock—rat-a-tat-tat, rat-a-tat-tat!

"I wish he wouldn't," said Diana. "Why does Snubby always have to make *some* kind of noise?"

Snubby came back with the cards, and the children heard his knock-knock-knock on the panelling again. Loony listened with his head on one side and so did Miranda. It was rather an eerie sound, hollow and irritating.

"Let's put some more wood on the fire before we begin," said Roger, and opened the door of the little cupboard beside the fireplace, where logs were kept. He hauled one out, threw it on the fire and shut the cupboard door. Then he went with the others to the table and they all sat down to play cards.

But they hadn't dealt more than one hand when some-

thing made them jump. It was a hollow, knocking sound
—knock-knock-knock—rat-a-tat-tat! Knock-knock-knock
—rat-a-tat-tat!

Loony growled, and that made them all jump, too. It
wasn't Snubby knocking this time—he was there at the
table with them, listening, half-scared.

"Pooh—it must be Mrs. Tickle knocking or hammering
something in the kitchen!" said Roger, seeing that Diana
looked frightened.

"It isn't," said his sister in a low voice. "It's in this
room. But there's nobody here but us!"

Knock-knock-knock—rat-a-tat-tat! It was exactly the
same knocking as Snubby had drummed on the panelling
when he went up and down the stairs.

"It *is* in this room," said Barney, starting up. "Whatever
can it be? Who is it? I don't like it."

"Let's get Mrs. Tickle," said Roger, and shouted for
her. "Mrs. Tickle! We want you. Quickly!"

In came Mrs. Tickle, most surprised. "Whatever is the
matter?" she said, seeing their startled faces.

"Listen," said Roger, as the soft knock-knock-knock
came again. "That knocking, Mrs. Tickle . . . what can
it be?"

CHAPTER SEVEN

Knock-Knock-Knock!

MRS. TICKLE STOOD in the middle of the room, listening.
She looked alarmed. "The knocking!" she said. "The
knocking! It's come again after all these years!"

"Whatever do you mean, Mrs. Tickle?" said Barney.

"My father didn't tell me about any knocking—and he knows all about this house."

"Maybe he doesn't know about the knocking, though," said Mrs. Tickle, looking relieved as the noise stopped. "I heard the tale in the village of Boffame yesterday. It's because of the knocking that this house got its name."

"Sit down, Mrs. Tickle, and tell us," said Barney, and the little woman sat down at once, on the very edge of a chair. She began to speak again in a low voice.

"I'm only telling you what's said," she said. "A tale that's handed down through the years, you understand. I heard it from old John Hurdie, in the post office, and he got it from his great-granny, so he said."

"Go on, go on," said Roger, as she stopped for breath. A piece of wood broke in the flames of the fire and the burning log fell to the bottom of the hearth, making them all jump.

"Well," said Mrs. Tickle, "it's said that the house was called Boffame House after the lake and the village—but soon after people came to live here, there were strange knockings on the front door. . . ."

"On the front door?" said Roger. "Do you mean someone hammered there with their fists?"

"No. They used the great knocker there," said Mrs. Tickle. "Didn't you see it when you came in this afternoon?"

"The door was wide open, so we didn't notice," said Diana, trying to remember. "Is it a very *big* knocker?"

"Enormous," said Mrs. Tickle. "And you wouldn't *believe* the sound it makes—thunderous, Mr. Hurdie at the post office told me. But when the footman went to answer the door all those years ago and see who was there —there was nobody."

"The one who knocked might have run away," said

Snubby, hopefully. "Lots of people *do* knock at doors or ring bells, and then run away. They think it's funny."

"Well, it isn't, it's stupid," said Mrs. Tickle. "We've got a boy in our village who does that—but he did it once too often to me. Aha—I put glue all round the knocker—and what a mess he was in!"

Everyone laughed. "But why didn't the person who knocked all those years ago stay till the door was opened?" asked Snubby. "And who was he?"

"Nobody ever saw him, though often he came knocking day or night," said Mrs. Tickle, enjoying the telling of such a dramatic story. "And what was more, that knocking went on for a hundred and fifty years, so the old story goes!"

"Ha—then it couldn't have been the *same* person knocking all that time," said Snubby. "But what did the knocking mean—anything at all?"

"Yes, it was said to give warning that there was a traitor in the house!" said Mrs. Tickle. "So there must have been a good many traitors then, it seems to me! And old Mr. Hurdie, he says that when the knocking came, there was always a searching of the old place to see if anyone was hiding there—and the servants were always questioned to find out if one of them was untrustworthy. Oh, there were some goings-on in those old days, you mark my words."

"How long ago did the knocking stop?" asked Barney. "You said it only lasted a hundred and fifty years—but this house is much older than that."

"It's more than a hundred years ago now since Mr. No-One hammered at the door with that knocker!" said Mrs. Tickle. "It's so old now that I reckon it would fall off the door if anyone touched it!"

Mrs. Tickle's story was so very interesting that the

children had quite forgotten about the mysterious knocking they themselves had heard a little while back—but they soon remembered it when it suddenly came again!

Knock-knock-knock . . . rat-a-tat-tat! There it was again, soft and hollow and mysterious—*and somewhere* in the room! There wasn't a doubt of it.

Barney sprang up at once. "We've got to find what it is!" he said.

"Oh, dear!" said Mrs. Tickle, beginning to tremble at the knees. "Oh, dear—I've gone and scared myself with that old story. I'm all of a shake. It's the knocker back again—Mr. No-One after all these years. But what's he knocking for? There's no traitor here!"

"Cheer up!" said Roger. "He's not knocking at the *front* door, Mrs. Tickle. Come on, Barney—let's trace where the knocking is!"

They waited for it to come again—and it did, as soon as they were quite silent. Knock-knock-knock . . . rat-a-tat-tat!

"It's over there—in that corner of the room!" said Barney, and ran towards the corner. The knocking stopped and then began again. Knock-knock-knock.

"It's coming from the wood cupboard!" cried Mrs. Tickle. "Bless us all, that's where it's coming from. But there's only logs there, that I do know."

"We'll soon see," said Barney grimly, and flung open the little door of the wood cupboard.

And out sprang a very indignant and rather frightened Miranda! The little monkey ran chattering to Barney and leapt straight up to his shoulder, burying her little furry head in his neck.

"Miranda! MIRANDA! Why—it was only *you* in the cupboard after all," said Barney. "You little pest—

you gave us such a fright! But why did you knock like that?"

"She was imitating Snubby!" cried Diana. "She heard him keep on knocking on the panelling as he went up and downstairs—and you know how she loves to copy what we do—so when she got shut in the cupboard, she did what Snubby did—and knocked on the wooden door in exactly the same way—knock-knock-knock . . . rat-a tat-tat!"

"That's it," said Roger, most relieved. "Phew—I didn't like it much. When did Miranda get shut in?"

"When you opened the wood cupboard door to put more logs on the fire," said Barney. "She must have slipped in without your noticing it, and you shut the door on her. Funny little thing—knocking like that!"

"Well, I hope she doesn't do anything else to give us such a scare," said Mrs. Tickle, getting up, and looking herself again. "Right down feared I was! And don't you start thinking about that big old knocker on the front door—Mr. No-One hasn't been at it for a hundred years, and it's not likely he'll start now."

"Anyway—there are no traitors in this house now," said Barney. "Only four kids, you, Mrs. Tickle, and a monkey and a dog. Miranda, don't do such an idiotic thing again. I'm surprised we didn't miss you, but I ч. е thought you were asleep in that rug on the sofa."

"Why didn't Loony go to the cupboard and scratch at it as he usually does when he hears a noise coming from somewhere?" wondered Diana.

"Easy," said Snubby, with a grin. "He's not awfully keen on getting Miranda out of trouble! I bet he thought she could jolly well stay there as long as possible!"

"Yes. I believe you're right," said Barney, looking at Loony, who was busy scratching himself. "Bad dog,

Loony—to let poor little Miranda stay in the dark cupboard without lifting a paw to help her."

"Wuff," said Loony politely, and went on scratching. Snubby poked him with his foot.

"Stop it!" he said. "Sit up and listen when you're spoken to."

Loony wagged his tail, and it thumped on the floor—knock-knock-knock!

"Oh, my goodness—don't *you* start rat-a-tatting now!" said Snubby, and Diana giggled. She was very relieved to find that their scare had been groundless—and she half-wished that Mrs. Tickle hadn't told them that queer old story.

"Let's get on with our game," said Snubby. "Let me see—we'd better deal again. Come on!"

They dealt again and Snubby looked at his cards. "Ha!" he said. "Couldn't be better! I can tell you this —even if Mr. No-One comes and hammers at that knocker now, I shall go on with this game—I've got a smashing hand!"

Fortunately for him, there was no hammering at the front door, and he won the game easily, looking very pleased with himself.

It was cosy and warm in the sitting-room, with the log fire blazing away. The children felt very happy, thinking of the next day and all the fun they would have. Diana drew the curtains after a while, shutting out the starry night and the white snow.

Later on Mrs. Tickle came in with a tray. "Supper!" she said, beaming. "Will you lay it for me, Diana, while I go and see to the poached eggs?"

"Poached eggs! Mrs. Tickle, how did you know I was simply longing for one?" said Snubby at once.

"Well, I had a feeling you were longing for *two*, not one," said Mrs. Tickle, who had taken quite a liking to the snub-nosed, freckle-faced "imp" as she called him to herself. Snubby grinned in delight.

"Two! How well you know me already!" he said. "Loony—salute Mrs. Tickle, please—your very *best* salute!"

And Loony, proud to show off his very newest trick, sat up and saluted quite smartly, much to Miranda's interest.

"There now—he's as sharp as his master!" said Mrs. Tickle, putting down her tray and laughing. "You're cautions, both of you. I'll be back with the poached eggs in a minute." And off she went, chuckling over Snubby and Loony. Really—what a pair!

194

CHAPTER EIGHT

What Fun!

SUPPER WAS a very pleasant meal, a simple one of poached eggs, hot cocoa, and biscuits and butter. Diana began to yawn before she was half-way through it. Miranda immediately copied her, yawning delicately, showing her tiny white teeth, and patting her mouth as she did so, just like Diana.

Both Miranda and Loony were enjoying a buttered biscuit. Each of them licked off the butter first, Loony with his large pink tongue and Miranda very daintily with her tiny, curling one.

"*Not* very good manners," said Roger, lazily. "My word, I'm sleepy. It's this big fire, I suppose. Snubby, how are you going to prevent Loony having to sleep down in the kitchen? I bet Mrs. Tickle will insist on it."

She did, of course. She appeared at nine o'clock, carrying her candle to go up to bed.

"Time for you all to go up," she announced firmly. "And I'll take that dog to the kitchen now, Snubby."

"You won't mind if he chews up the rug there, and the cushion on the chair, and any slippers or towels you've left out, will you, Mrs. Tickle?" said Snubby solemnly. "I'll pay for them all, of course, if he does much damage— but it's very, very hard on my pocket."

Mrs. Tickle was taken aback. She looked at Loony who stared back her her unwinkingly.

"He can't *help* being a nibbly, chewy dog," said Snubby

195

earnestly. "It's his *nature*, you see. The funny thing is, he NEVER chews anything when he sleeps with me. Never."

Mrs. Tickle made up her mind at once. "Well, you let him sleep with you then," she said, "if you can abide a smelly dog in your bedroom. I won't have him chewing up my kitchen, and that's flat."

"I'll do *anything* to please you," said Snubby, rather overdoing it now. "Anything. I'll even have a smelly dog in my bedroom. Won't I, Loony?"

Loony thumped his tail on the floor and Miranda at once pounced on it. Loony swung round at her and she leapt on to his back, hanging on to his silky fur for all she was worth.

Loony raced round the room with her on his back, trying hard to remember how to unseat her. "Roll on the floor, ass!" cried Snubby. "Roll on the floor!"

But, as soon as Loony rolled over, Miranda was off like a bird, springing here and there till she came back to Barney's shoulder.

"Good as a play they are!" said Mrs. Tickle, laughing. "Now—are you all coming up or not? I'm not leaving you down here—not with an oil-lamp to upset and cause a fire! Mr. Martin did leave strict instructions about that."

"Right," said Barney, getting up. "Come on, everyone. Light your candles!"

He waited till they were all in the hall, lighting their candles, then put out the oil-lamp in the sitting-room. Miranda was annoying everyone by blowing out their candles as soon as they lighted them.

"Hey, Barney!" called Snubby indignantly. "Come and stop this fat-headed monkey from blowing out our candles! She must be dotty!"

Barney gave one of his uproarious laughs. "Oh, Miranda!" he said. "Do you *still* remember Grandmother's birthday cake?" He turned to the others and explained.

"You see, my grandmother had her seventieth birthday a little while ago, and our cook actually put seventy little candles on it—and Miranda helped Granny to blow them all out. She loved it!"

"So I suppose she'll blow out any candle she sees now," groaned Roger. "Stop it, Miranda. Gosh, she's blown mine out *again*! Barney, get hold of her. We'll never get to bed."

Miranda was safely captured, and then the little procession made its way up the wide staircase, Loony tearing on ahead as usual, and Miranda firmly tucked in Barney's right arm, well away from his candle.

"Good night!" he said. "Sleep well. We're all near one another, so if anyone's scared in the night, give a yell!"

But they were all far too sleepy to be scared by anything. The beds were very comfortable, and there were plenty of blankets to keep out the cold, for the rooms were none too warm. Snubby decided that the water in his jug was really far too cold to wash in—he would tackle that in the morning. He decided too, that he would tidy his belongings in the morning; it would take him so long now to sort them out from the heap he had thrown on the floor of his cupboard!

Loony was already asleep on the middle of the bed. Snubby pushed him firmly down to the end and then got into bed himself, quite pleased at the warm patch Loony had made in the middle. He lay for half a minute, wondering at the utter quiet and stillness of the old house —not a sound to be heard, not one!

How awful if the great old knocker began to knock as in the olden days! Snubby was giving himself quite a pleasant thrill about this when he suddenly fell sound asleep—so sound that he didn't even feel Loony creeping up the bed and lying heavily on his middle.

The morning was bright and clear and the sun shone so brilliantly that the snow on the pond began to melt fast. "That's good," said Roger, looking out of his window as he dressed. "If the snow melts on the pond and we get no more, it will freeze again to-night and we can skate to-morrow, because the ice will be free of snow. To-day we'll go tobogganing."

After what Snubby called a "super-smashing" breakfast of porridge, bacon, eggs and toast, they went to see what jobs they could do for Mrs. Tickle. Her kitchen was enormous, and had a pump at one end to pump water for her sink. At the other was a large old kitchen range, but beside it was a new oil-cooker on which she managed to cook everything.

She had the fire going in the range to heat the kitchen, and it all looked very cheerful. She looked up as the children came in carrying the breakfast things, and smiled all over her pleasant face.

"What else can we do for you?" asked Diana. "I'll help you with the washing-up."

"Well, you don't need to do that," said Mrs. Tickle. "But if you could see that you each make your bed— and get some wood in for me—and clean the lamps— that would be fine. I'll be able to get on well then."

"Upstairs everyone," ordered Diana, taking charge. "Roger, you get Snubby to help you with your bed, then you help him with his—or he'll just leave it as it is. Do you hear, Snubby?"

"No, teacher," said Snubby, and skipped out of the way of a slap from Diana.

Everything was soon done, and well done too. Snubby's bed was as well made as the others—the lamps were cleaned and ready for the night—and so much wood was got in that Mrs. Tickle said she had almost enough for a week! She was very pleased. Snubby decided that he now knew her well enough to give her a hug.

"Now then, get away with you," she said, surprised. "Squeezing all the breath out of me like that. You're a caution, that's what you are. Oh, bless us all, there's that dog got my brush again. I'll give him such a larruping if I catch him."

But she never could catch the artful Loony. He enjoyed himself running off with her brush, her duster, and her mop—till she took to keeping a big broom at hand and chasing him every time he appeared.

"Let's go and get our things on now," said Roger, when all the jobs were done. "I'm longing to get out into the snow. Let's toboggan first of all, before we have a snow-ball fight or anything."

It wasn't long before they were all in their outdoor things—wellington boots, scarves, gloves, thick jerseys. It was bitterly cold out of the sun, but they soon got warm.

They had two toboggans—each big enough to take two or three of them at once. They set off up the nearest hill, dragging the toboggans behind them. Loony tried to gallop off at a furious speed as usual, but to his dismay found that his legs sank right into this soft white stuff that so mysteriously covered the ground—and for once in a way he had to get along very slowly indeed.

Miranda wouldn't leave Barney's shoulder. She didn't like the snow, though it did occur to her that it would be fun to put some down Barney's neck. She kept her little paws under his collar to warm them. Barney liked feeling them there.

The hill was steep enough to give the children a very thrilling run down to the bottom. There they all tumbled off into the soft snow, roaring with laughter. Loony soon learnt to sit on the toboggan with Roger and Snubby, his long ears flying backwards in the wind. He loved it, and barked all the way down.

Miranda went with Barney and Diana. She was a bit scared of the sudden rush down the hill and cuddled under Barney's coat, her tiny head just peeping out. "You're scared, Miranda!" said Barney. But when he tried to make her stay behind on the top of the hill, she wouldn't. No, she wanted to be with Barney every minute of the time.

They had races on their toboggans—two on each toboggan, and then one on each. Barney won easily. His brilliant blue eyes were bluer than ever on this dazzling snowy day, and he looked very happy. In fact, they were all very happy. It was Snubby, as usual, who was the first to feel the pangs of hunger.

"You *can't* be hungry already," said Roger. "Not after that colossal breakfast, Snubby. Why, you had six pieces of toast on top of everything else. It can't possibly be lunch-time yet." He undid his glove to look at his watch.

But at that moment a bell sounded clearly through the frosty air—Mrs. Tickle ringing to tell them lunch was ready.

"What did I tell you?" said Snubby, triumphantly. "*I* don't need to look at the time to know when a meal's due. Come on, Loony—race you to Rat-a-Tat House!"

CHAPTER NINE

A Happy Day

"WHAT A LOVELY SMELL," said Snubby as soon as he reached Rat-a-Tat House. "What is it?"

"Stew!" said Roger, sniffing. And stew it was, full of carrots and onions and turnips and parsnips. Loony almost pulled everything off the table in his anxiety to see what it was that smelt so good.

"Now you stop that!" ordered Mrs. Tickle, pushing him away just in time. "If you come out to the kitchen with me you'll see I've got some delicious stew-bones for you. Paws off the tablecloth, please."

"I'm quite tired," said Diana, sitting down with a flop. "Aren't you, Barney?"

"No, not really," said Barney. "But I'm used to a strenuous sort of life and you're not. I remember the days when I was a hoop-la boy and got up at half-past five to help to get the fair ready—worked all the morning —took charge of the hoop-la stall in the afternoon, and after that worked as gate-boy, taking the money—and then helped the fellow on the swing-boats."

"Oh, Barney—your life must seem so different now," said Diana, beginning to eat her stew. "Barney, didn't you feel queer when your father first found you and took you home to a family you didn't know?"

"Yes, I did," said Barney. "I was shy for the first time in my life, I reckon. I couldn't seem to shake hands properly, or say how-do-you-do, or even look them in the face—except my grandmother. I wasn't shy of her. But

I guess that was partly because she had a monkey on her shoulder like me—and the two monkeys took to one another from the first. They even shook paws."

"Are your cousins nice?" asked Snubby, holding out his plate for a second helping of stew.

"Yes. Very," said Barney. "You know—it was queer—I've never been ashamed of being a circus-boy, or of any of the jobs I've ever done in my life, but when I met my clean and tidy cousins—they even had clean nails—and saw their fine manners—well, I sort of felt ashamed, and wished I could sink into the ground."

"You didn't!" said Snubby, surprised. "I bet you're worth six of any of your cousins. Why, you're even worth six of me and Roger. *I* think you're a marvel."

"You may be a bit of an ass, Snubby, but you're a real sport," said Barney, touched. "But I'll tell you a queer thing—instead of my cousins looking down on me because I'd lived in caravans and tents, and done all kinds of queer circus jobs, they thought it was all marvellous—and they were *proud* of having me for their cousin. Think of that!"

"You deserve it," said Diana. "You had a jolly hard time, and you were all alone—but you never gave up. I *am* glad we met you that day—it seems so long ago now. We've had some exciting times together, haven't we, Barney?"

"Yes," said Barney, getting up to take some things to the kitchen. "But I'm afraid they're ended now. When things run smoothly and happily there don't seem to be so many adventures—or mysteries."

Snubby forgot his manners and pointed his fork at him. "How do *you* know? Saying things like that is enough to *make* things begin to happen at once. I smell something in the air."

"Yes, you smell the remains of the stew," said Barney, laughing. "Get up, you lazy fellow, and help me to take these things out and get the pudding."

"Right," said Snubby and stood up. "Gosh!" he said in surprise. "Something's happened to my legs—I can hardly stand on them."

Roger and Diana found exactly the same thing. Their legs were stiff, and hurt when they walked. Barney laughed at them.

"It's all that trudging up the snowy hills," he said. "We must have walked up and tobogganed down fifty or sixty times. You'll be as stiff as anything for a day or two."

"I can't possibly walk up even the smallest hill this afternoon," groaned Snubby, in dismay. "Honestly, I think I'll have to have crutches."

"*I* can't go tobogganing any more to-day, that's certain," said Diana, sinking into a chair. "But, oh—I *don't* want to miss being out of doors on such a heavenly day."

"Cheer up," said Barney. "We'll go out and build an enormous snowman—and we'll have a snowball fight— you'll find you can do that all right!"

Barney was right. Although they found that they could hardly walk when they left the table to stagger out with the dirty plates to Mrs. Tickle, their legs gradually became less stiff—and by the time they went out into the snow again they could walk quite well—though none of them except Barney felt that they could possibly climb up a hill dragging a toboggan behind them.

"The snow's just right for snowballing!" called Diana, gathering some into her gloved hand. They all wore leather gloves, knowing from experience how woollen ones became soaked at once, and then the cold bit their fingers and chilled them through and through.

"I'll take Diana for my side, and you two can be together," said Barney. "Diana, you can make me snowball ammunition, and I'll do the throwing. Look— this is our little fort—if we are driven out of it the other side have won—but we'll stand firm!"

He made a big circle for himself and Diana, and Roger and Snubby made one for themselves too. Miranda was on Barney's side, of course, and Loony was on the other side.

Ammunition was soon made and the battle began. Snubby was a very wild thrower, but Roger was excellent, and most of his snowballs found their mark. Diana gasped and ducked and yelled, while Barney tried to protect her by sending a fast volley at Roger. Miranda was puzzled by the fight, and, finding herself in a dangerous place on Barney's shoulder, leapt off to a nearby tree.

She landed on a snowy branch, and watched the fight with great interest, sometimes jigging up and down on the branch and scattering snow from the tree.

Loony, of course, went completely mad as he always did when there was any kind of contest between the children. He floundered about, getting in everyone's way, and finally, for some reason of his own, dug an enormous hole in the snow, sending it flying out behind him as if he were a rabbit digging a burrow.

The fight went on until Barney became too strong for Roger, and, leaving his own circle, advanced on the two panting boys, sending a stream of well-directed snowballs at them.

"Pax, pax!" yelled Snubby, as Diana also advanced, and snowballed him mercilessly as he slipped and rolled in the snow.

"All right—you win!" panted Roger, collapsing into the snow. "Gosh, that was the best snowball fight I've ever had! Pax, Diana, pax—don't you dare to put that down my neck. Help, Loony, help!"

The funniest thing that happened that afternoon was when Miranda suddenly discovered the meaning of all this snowballing. She had sat on her tree, watching the others in astonishment as they rolled the snow into balls, and hurled them through the air—and all at once she understood the game.

Quickly she leapt off the bough and gathered up some snow in her tiny paws, making a tight little snowball—and then, with a very good aim, she flung it straight at Loony, and hit him—biff, on the nose. He gasped and spluttered in surprise.

"Good shot, Miranda!" yelled Barney, and laughed his infectious laugh. "Did you see that, you others? Miranda threw a snowball at Loony and hit him. Look out, Loony—she's made another."

Miranda thought this was a wonderful way of teasing Loony—but soon her fingers began to feel very cold indeed, and, whimpering with the pain in them, she leapt up to Barney's shoulders, and stuffed her cold paws down his warm neck.

"Hey!" he said, startled. "Are you putting snow down my neck, Miranda? You'd better not. Oh, they're your cold, cold paws—all right, warm them, then!"

The snow was exactly right for building a snowman too. Snubby had the ambitious idea of building a snow house as well, alongside the snowman.

"You build the snowman, Barney; you and Miranda and Diana," said Snubby. "Roger and I will build his house—a proper little snow house with a chimney and everything."

Barney and Diana set to work on the snowman, and made a fat fellow, with a large round head and big feet sticking out at the bottom. "His name is Mr. Icy-Cold," said Diana, with a giggle. "Let's get him a hat."

Roger and Snubby were hard at work on their snow house. They had borrowed two shovels from Mrs. Tickle, which made the building a good deal quicker.

Soon they had built the rounded walls, as high as themselves, and somehow managed to make a roof that stayed on—a rounded one, like an Eskimo's igloo. They also added a little chimney.

"Now a window," said Snubby, excited. "Get *away*, Loony. Go and mess about with the snowman, not with us. You'll find yourself being built into the roof soon!"

They made a little round window, and left a round opening for an entrance. They were really quite proud of their work when they had finished.

"It's a proper snow house," said Snubby, pleased. "Big enough to sit in. Come on, Roger—let's squeeze into it for a few minutes and see what it's like to live in a snow house."

They got inside, and sat down. Snubby peered out of the little window. "I can see our sitting-room window," he said. "And Mrs. Tickle is inside, cleaning. Ooooh, I feel jolly cold! What about lighting a fire in our little house?"

That made Roger laugh. Loony came up to see what the joke was, and tried to squeeze himself in through the door and join them. He almost knocked down part of one wall, and Snubby protested.

"You're so *rough*, Loony," he complained, pushing him out. "You *ruined* the snowman's feet by scrabbling for rabbits or something underneath them. I'll snowball you hard if you don't behave yourself."

"Come on," said Roger, "I'm getting cold sitting here·

I can't imagine how Eskimos can live and sleep in a snow house—I should freeze to death."

He squeezed out carefully, followed by Snubby. Miranda came and watched them with interest. *Now* what were they doing? She hopped in through the window and then stared out cheekily. Loony made a rush at her, but Snubby caught his collar.

"No! If you and Miranda have a scrimmage in the snow house that will be the end of it. Roger—Barney— what about going in now? It must be nearly tea-time—or so the clock in my tummy tells me—and I could do with some scalding hot tea to drink."

It was a very tired set of children who sat down to a late tea—tired but happy. Diana said she could really hardly lift the big brown teapot.

"We've forgotten to draw the curtains across the window," groaned Roger. "I meant to—and now I really feel I can't get out of my chair!"

The light from the big oil-lamp on the table streamed out of the window across the snow outside, and just caught the outline of the snow house, and fell on the big snowman too.

"He looks as if he's watching us longingly," said Snubby. "I bet he'd like to come in and join us. Poor old Mr. Icy-Cold!"

Snubby was just lifting his cup to his mouth, gazing out of the window as he did so, when he suddenly put down his cup again, and stared fixedly.

"Hey!" he said, startled. "Who's that out there—look, beyond my snow house? Somebody standing quite still. Look!"

Everyone looked, but no one could see anything or anyone. "It's only the snowman, ass," said Barney. "Don't scare Diana. Who on earth would come and stare at our window at this time of night in this lonely district?"

"I don't know," said Snubby, still gazing out. "I can't see anyone now. I suppose I *must* have been mistaken. But *honestly*, I thought there was someone standing quite still, watching us."

Barney got up and drew the curtains so that they met. "I tell you, it's only our snowman," he said. "Anyway, it can't be very nice for the poor thing to stand out in the cold and watch us eating a fine supper like this in the warm room. Good night, Mr. Icy-Cold. See you in the morning."

CHAPTER TEN

Whose Glove?

"IT CAN'T have been anyone," said Diana. "Loony would have barked."

"Yes. So he would," said Snubby, relieved. "It was just my imagination."

Both Barney and Roger forebore to say that Loony would probably not hear any footsteps on the snow, and certainly could not *see* anyone out of the window. They didn't want to scare Diana, and they both honestly thought that Snubby had made a mistake.

All the same, Barney resolved to go and have a look round for footprints in the morning—if it was possible to make out any strange ones amid the marks made by their own feet. The talk soon went on to something else, and they all forgot about Snubby's fright. They enjoyed their supper immensely and, as usual, carried out the dirty things to Mrs. Tickle. Miranda collected the forks and handed them over proudly in her little paw.

"There now!" said Mrs. Tickle, delighted. "What a clever creature she is—but how you can wear her on your shoulder like that, Barney, I don't know—and her putting her hands down your neck too, to warm them!"

At half-past eight everyone was asleep—but not in bed. No, they were all asleep in their chairs by the fire, books on their knees or fallen to the rug below. Loony too, was asleep, making little excited grunts as he chased a rat in his dreams. Miranda had cuddled under Barney's jacket and could not be seen, but she, too, was asleep.

There Mrs. Tickle found them when she came in to ask if anyone wanted hot milk before they went to bed, for the night was really very cold.

"Do any of you want . . ." she began, and then chuckled to herself. Well, well, well—all fast asleep! They ought to be in their beds, poor things, tired out like that!

She woke them all, and to their great astonishment they found that they were not comfortably in bed as they imagined, but slumped in their chairs by the fire. So that was what a morning of tobogganing could do! Groaning and yawning, they lighted their candles and crawled up to bed, with Mrs. Tickle laughing at them and lighting the way. What a set of yawners!

They all slept late the next morning, and Mrs. Tickle rang the gong in vain. In the end she had to go up and wake them all, and even pull Snubby out of bed and take all the clothes away!

However, they were bright and cheery after breakfast, though all but Barney were very stiff. They gazed out of the window at the lake as they ate fried sausages and fried bread. The surface was quite free from snow and the ice looked blue and inviting.

"What about skating this morning?" said Barney. "Or are you all too stiff?"

"Well, I don't feel like using my aching muscles to climb up those hills in order to toboggan down them," said Diana. "But I'd like to try skating. I'll probably use a different set of muscles, and they won't hurt."

They did their usual jobs, and helped Mrs. Tickle willingly. When she heard they were going skating she gave them each a packet of biscuits.

"Skating's hungry work," she said. "You'll need a snack—and maybe if you have that you won't want to eat me out of house and home when you get in for your lunch."

"I've got to stay behind to mend my sweater," said Diana. "I tore it yesterday and if I don't mend it before I go out it will all unravel. I'll catch you boys up later, down at the pond."

The others left her to ask Mrs. Tickle for a needle, and went off with their skates. On the way they passed the big snowman they had built the day before, and stopped to look at him.

"He's a real beauty," said Barney. "Quite the biggest I've seen. We ought to have given him a coat to wear to make him look real."

"I say, just let's have a look and see if there are any strange footmarks about," said Roger, remembering Snubby's scare the night before.

"Oh, no!" said Snubby, quite ashamed now of the alarm he had raised. "It was just that my eyes were tired with the glare of the snow, I expect. I saw things that weren't there!"

"We'll have a squint round, all the same," said Barney.

He walked round the snowman, but saw nothing unusual at all—merely a large number of jumbled footmarks made by their wellington boots the day before.

Then he looked at the snow house and all round about. There was again a mass of footsteps and it was impossible to tell whether any of them belonged to a stranger—though Barney's sharp eyes showed him one or two that he thought were *not* made by rubber boots. But, no; it really *was* impossible to tell.

"Come on," he said. "Nothing here. Snubby *must* have been mistaken after all."

Snubby went into his little snow house just for the fun of it. He sat down for a few moments, imagining that he was an Eskimo in an igloo. Then, hearing the others' voices getting faint in the distance, he stooped to go out again.

And then it was that he saw the glove. There it lay, half-hidden by the snow, just at the side of the little entrance to the snow house. Snubby stared at it and picked it up, thinking for the moment that it must belong to Barney or Roger.

But it was a big glove—made of thick navy-blue wool. Not one of the children had hands large enough to fit this glove. Snubby turned it over, his heart beginning to beat fast. So there *might* have been someone out here last night after all—someone staring in through the lighted window, watching them. It wasn't at all a nice thought. He ran after the other two boys, shouting.

"Barney! Roger! Wait, I've got something to tell you!"

They turned round, recognising something urgent in his voice. Loony, who had run on with them, turned back at once and floundered over the snow to Snubby.

"What is it?" said Roger.

"Look what I found in my snow house," said Snubby, panting. "This glove! I was just crawling out when I found it. Surely it isn't one of ours—it's so big."

"No. It's not ours," said Roger. "We've all got leather gloves, Barney too. This is someone else's. I suppose Loony couldn't possibly have taken it from somewhere and dropped it there, could he?"

"No. Not possibly," said Snubby. "He didn't even *go* to the snow house with me. He ran on with you. I say, you know—I think there *was* someone out here last night after all. But why? Out in all this cold and snow!"

"Don't say a word to Diana or Mrs. Tickle," said Roger. "You'll scare them stiff if you do. This may be just nothing. Anyway, we can't do anything about it now— we'll just have to keep watch this evening and see if we can spot anything. I must say it's rather queer."

212

"*Could* somebody have crouched in the snow house last night, and watched us?" said Snubby, "I must have seen someone either getting in or getting out—I don't know which."

They sat down at the edge of the shining pond to put on their skates. Barney had some fine new ones given to him for Christmas by his grandmother. He had never skated in his life, and he was much looking forward to it. He puzzled over the glove that Snubby had found, but soon forgot about it as he stood up, wobbling, on his skates.

Snubby and Roger had skated before. Snubby, oddly enough, was better than Roger, and he was soon off and away, calling to the others.

Loony was most excited to see his master apparently flying over the ice, he went so fast and so lightly. With an excited bark he rushed over the snow to the ice and tried to bound after him.

But to his intense surprise he found that all his four legs slid away beneath him, and there he was, sliding on his back, just as he sometimes did in a slippery hall.

But it was much more difficult to find his feet again on the slippery pond than in a polished hall—each time he tried to stand he slipped over again, and at last he managed to sit down on his tail, looking very miserable.

"Bad luck, Loony!" shouted Snubby, circling round him. "You can't manage your legs this morning, can you? You'll have to learn to walk slowly for once."

But Loony leapt to his feet to follow Snubby, and again he found himself off his balance, his paws slithering away beneath him, and his nose bumping the ground. He somehow managed to sit down again and howled dismally.

"All right—I'll take you back to the bank," said Snubby.
"And just be sensible and stay there."

Roger was now on the ice, skating carefully, afraid of
falling, but soon getting into the way of it. Barney stood
and watched Snubby, and the ease with which he flew over
the ice. It looked to be just a question of balance—
and Barney knew all about that. Hadn't he walked the
tight-rope a thousand times? Hadn't he stood on horses'
backs when they galloped gracefully round a circus
ring?

Without another thought Barney stepped on to the ice
and set off smoothly and rhythmically. Immediately he
felt at home, and his feet felt as if they had wings. He gave
a shout.

"Ho! This is wonderful! Why didn't I ever skate
before?"

Roger and Snubby watched him in amazement. They
themselves a winter or two ago had had to go through the
painfully slow process of learning skating the hard way—
falling, slipping, bumping down on the ice, scrambling
up only to fall again—before they could balance themselves
and skate for more than a few yards.

And here was old Barney skating at thirty miles an hour
as if he had done nothing but skate all his life long. Look
at him now, going round in circles, then shooting off
again, then spreading his legs wide and circling once more.
What a boy!

"You *knew* how to skate, you fibber!" shouted
Snubby.

"I did not! It's the first time!" called back Barney, his
blue eyes gleaming brightly. "It's heavenly—superb—best
sport I've ever tried!"

Diana came on the ice just then, also full of astonishment to see Barney skating so easily, Miranda on his

shoulder, enjoying this new game to the utmost. Diana was a graceful little skater, and went over to Barney, holding out her hand.

"Skate with me," she said. "That's right, hold my hands like that. Oh, Barney—you skate beautifully!"

It was grand fun to be on the ice that clear winter's morning. Roger fell over quite a lot and groaned, and rubbed himself, quite envious of the others, especially of Snubby. Snubby did not skate as gracefully as either Barney or Diana but he was as usual, full of idiotic tricks, leaping in the air on his skates, twisting himself round in never-ending circles till he fell over in giddiness—and altogether behaving in what Diana called a "very Snubby-ish way."

They had a wonderful morning on the ice, and were glad of the packets of biscuits that Mrs. Tickle had given them, which they shared generously with Loony and Miranda.

"Let's skate this afternoon too," said Barney, who felt as if he could never have enough of flying through the frosty air so easily. So the whole day was spent on the pond. It was quite clear of snow now, except at the far end, where trees overhung it, and the surface was still snow-bound.

They were very tired that evening—so tired that they dragged themselves upstairs very early indeed, immediately after supper. Mrs. Tickle was amused—and pleased too, because now she also could get to bed early.

They all lighted their candles in the hall, and Barney held Miranda tightly so that she couldn't blow them out. Then up the stairs they went, yawning.

"I don't mind telling you that *nothing* will make me wake up to-night!" said Snubby, smothering a really enormous yawn.

"A thunderstorm would," said Diana. "It always wakes *me*."

"No. A thunderstorm wouldn't wake me—nor an earthquake—nor even a bomb!" said Snubby.

But he was quite wrong—as wrong as ever he could be!

CHAPTER ELEVEN

Noise in the Night

SNUBBY WAS asleep almost before he had climbed into bed. He felt his eyes closing as he groped for the bedclothes, and then he knew nothing more. He didn't even dream.

The others were almost as sleepy. Even little Miranda was tired out with her day in the frosty air, and snuggled down at the foot of Barney's bed before he was in it. Mrs. Tickle was the last of the household to go to sleep.

But she had not been skating for miles all day long. She undressed slowly, folded all her things as she always did, washed herself in the icy-cold water, and undid her plaited hair to brush it out.

She thought about the four children. Nice children, she said to herself, always willing to give a hand, and always jolly together. But that caution of a Snubby! He was the best of the lot, thought Mrs. Tickle, deftly plaiting her long hair again.

"Him and his freckles and jokes! He reminds me of what my Tom used to be—always up to mischief and as artful as a monkey—yes, as artful as that little Miranda! I didn't take to her at first, but she's got such funny little ways. And that Loony! If ever a dog had the right name, it's him. Taking my cloths and brushes all day long and hiding them."

She was in bed at last, having done all the things she did so meticulously every evening—said her prayers and read her Bible and rubbed cream on her rough hands. She blew out her candle and settled down with her hot-water bottle, hugging it to her with pleasure—and then, like the others, she fell fast asleep.

The night was still and the frost was hard. There was not a sound to be heard, for even the owl was too cold to hoot, and flew sadly on his silent wings, looking for mice that he could not see. They were far under the snow, safe in their cosy holes.

And then a thunderous sound split the deep silence—a tremendous noise that echoed through the old house and awoke everyone immediately.

Nobody knew what it was. It had sounded in their dreams, and by the time they had awakened, only the echo of the noise was left in their minds.

Snubby leapt up in fright. Diana cowered under the bedclothes. Roger sat up and Barney sprang out of bed. Mrs. Tickle covered her head with the bedclothes. "A storm!" she said. "Oh, my, what a crash!"

Loony barked madly without stopping, partly with fright but mostly from anger. He had been so sound asleep —not even one ear open—and now this strange noise had awakened him without warning.

Roger, who shared a room with Snubby, called across to him: "Snubby, did you hear that crashing noise? What do you suppose it was?"

"The end of the world I should think!" said Snubby, his heart still beating fast. "It can't be a storm—look, you can see the stars in a clear sky."

"I'm going to Diana, to see if she's scared," said Roger,

and he got out of bed and ran to Diana's room. He met Barney on the landing, holding a lighted candle.

"Hallo. Did you hear that row?" said Roger. "Whatever was it? An explosion of some sort?"

"No. I don't know *what* it was," said Barney. "I was fast asleep. It sounded pretty near, anyway."

They went into Diana's room. "Diana! Are you all right?" called Roger to his sister. She was still under the bedclothes. She put her head out and looked at him in the light of the wavering candle-flame.

"Oh, Roger—Barney. Whatever *was* that?" she said, in a shaky voice.

"Can't imagine—perhaps a crash of thunder," said Roger, speaking cheerfully. He hated Diana to be frightened.

"You needn't worry," said Barney. "The sky isn't stormy—the crash won't come again."

But even as he finished speaking, it did come again. And this time they heard it clearly, not muddled as in a dream.

RAT-A-TAT-TAT! RAT-A-TAT-TAT!

The noise echoed all through the house, and then slowly died away. Diana disappeared under the bedclothes with a cry of fright. Roger clutched at Barney.

"The knocker!" he said. "It's someone hammering at the front door with that enormous knocker. Good gracious—who is it coming here in the middle of the night?"

"Perhaps—perhaps it's my father," said Barney. "No, he would have telephoned. Gosh! I really don't feel as if I want to go down and open the door."

The light of another candle flickered outside Diana's door. It was Mrs. Tickle, who, although really too scared to get out of bed, had felt obliged to come and see if the children were all right. She shook so much that she could hardly hold her candlestick level.

"What was that?" she said. "Someone knocking at the door? But—it's midnight! I'll not open the door. I daren't go down the stairs!"

"I tell you what," said Barney, speaking as cheerfully as he could, "we'll lean out of the window over the front door and ask who it is. It may be someone who is lost and needing help."

Snubby had now joined them with a very frightened Loony, who produced a string of growls but no barks.

"WHY did you say that nothing in the world would wake you to-night, Snubby?" said Diana. "Something *always* happens when you say silly things like that."

"Come on," said Barney. "Let's go and shout out of the window. Or would you rather stay here with Diana, Mrs. Tickle?"

"I'll stay here," said Mrs. Tickle. "I'll look after Diana—and she can look after me. And mind, if it's someone lost, don't let them in till you've told me. Waking us all up like this at midnight! It's disgraceful!"

The three boys, with Loony and Miranda, went along the landing to the big window that overlooked the front door. They opened it with difficulty, for it was very stiff.

Outside lay the thick snow, and the snowman and snow house loomed up dimly in the bright starlight. Barney leaned out of the window, trying to see down to the front door.

"Who's there?" he shouted. "Who's there?"

They all held their breath to listen for the answer. But none came. There was not a sound from below. Barney shouted again.

"Who knocked on the door? Answer, please!"

But still there was no answer. The night was silent and

still. Barney shut the window, for the air was bitterly cold. He shivered.

"Nobody there," he said. "Not a sound to be heard."

"Do you think we'd better go down and open the door—just in case?" said Roger.

"In case of *what*?" said Barney, fastening the window.

"Well, in case there's somebody ill there—or exhausted with being lost," said Roger.

"Anyone who can hammer at that knocker with such fury can't be ill or faint," said Barney grimly. "And we *don't* go down! That's quite certain."

They went back to Mrs. Tickle and Diana. "Nobody there," said Barney briefly.

Mrs. Tickle began to shiver again, partly with fright and partly with cold. "It's that Mr. No-One," she said. "The one that used to come all those years ago—and hammer on the door to warn the family that there was a traitor inside."

"Stuff!" said Roger. "Rubbish! Fiddlesticks! That's a silly old legend. Anyway, there *isn't* a traitor of any sort or kind in this house, Mrs. Tickle. *I* think it's someone playing a fat-headed joke on us."

"Well, if that's so, we're not going to fall for it," said Barney firmly, though he felt very doubtful indeed that it was a joke. "We're going to go back to bed and get warm and go to sleep—and in the morning we'll do a little exploring for footprints up to the front door. Our Mr. No-One had to go up those steps, and we'll at least see what his feet are like—big—small—middle-size."

"Yes. That's a good idea," said Snubby. "Come on then—let's go to bed."

"I'm going to sleep on the couch in your room, Diana," said Mrs. Tickle. "We'll be company for each other. You'd like that, wouldn't you?"

"Oh, *yes*," said Diana, and kind Mrs. Tickle went off to collect her bedclothes and hot-water bottle, and then made her bed up on the little couch at the other side of Diana's room. Diana felt very comforted to know that she was there—and Mrs. Tickle was also glad to have Diana's company. That Mr. No-One—what a fright he had given them all!

Snubby and Roger talked things over for a few minutes and then Snubby fell fast asleep again. Barney, in the next room, puzzled over the knocking for some time, and over the curious fact that nobody was at the door. He didn't for one moment believe in the old legend.

"We'll find out a few things to-morrow morning," he thought, turning over comfortably. "Oh, sorry, Miranda —did I squash you?"

The little monkey had been so frightened by the noise that she had crept right to the bottom of Barney's bed, and had cuddled by his feet.

The clock down the hall chimed the half hour—half-past midnight, thought Barney. Well, look out, Mr. Knocker, whoever you are—we'll all be on your trail to-morrow morning!

CHAPTER TWELVE

The Footprints

EVERYONE but Mrs. Tickle slept soundly for the rest of the night. Mrs. Tickle, who had not tired herself out with vigorous skating, as the children had, was not as sleepy as they were, and she lay and worried about the strange knocking for a long time.

At a quarter to seven she slid off the couch in Diana's room, put on her dressing-gown, and opened the door quietly to go to her own room. It was time to get dressed and go down and see to the lighting of the fires.

Later on, Barney went into Roger's room to dress with him and Snubby and to talk about the night's alarm. They none of them felt scared now; they felt brave and rather scornful of last night's fears. Outside was the brilliant sunshine and the dazzling snow, and the thought of skating and tobogganing drove away the alarms of the night.

Diana came knocking at the door. "Are you ready to go down to breakfast? I'm dressed."

"Yes, we're ready," said Roger, opening the door. "I vote we go and have a squint at the knocker that was used so vigorously last night."

So, with Loony streaking ahead of them, the first thing they did was to race down the wide stairs, and go straight to the front door.

"We've not used this door since we first came," said Barney. "We came in this way when we arrived, but ever since then we've used the side door to go in and out."

"We haven't had any fall of snow since we came," said Roger, considering. "So let's think now—about foot-prints. We drove up in the car to the stone steps that run up to the door. . . ."

"So there should only be the marks of the car tyres in the drive—and *our* footmarks going up the steps to the door," said Barney. "And that means, there should now be *another* set of footprints—Mr. No-One's—coming up the drive right to these steps, where they will unfortunately be muddled with ours. My word, isn't the door difficult to open!"

It certainly was. It had two great bolts, one at the top and one at the bottom—two locks—and a heavy chain. The locks were stiff to turn, but at last they clicked and the children were able to open the great door.

"We've never even *seen* the knocker yet!" said Diana, and she looked to see what it was like.

It was magnificent. It was in the shape of a great lion's head, and to use it one iron lock of its mane had to be grasped in order to lift the knocker. Diana and the others marvelled at it. They had never seen such a knocker in their lives—no wonder it made so much noise!

"I'll just feel it to see how heavy it is," said Snubby, and took hold of the handle made by the lock of the lion's mane. He raised the knocker, but it was so heavy that it fell back again immediately.

CRASH!

Loony fell down the steps in fright, and Miranda shot under Barney's coat. Diana jumped violently and turned on Snubby at once. "DON'T! I can't bear being made to jump like that. WHY must you be so silly?"

"Sorry," said Snubby, very much startled himself. "I'd no idea it was so heavy."

Mrs. Tickle came running into the hall, looking as scared as could be. "What . . ." she began, and then saw the children standing there. "Oh, bless us all, I thought it was that Mr. No-One again. I was just coming to give him a piece of my mind."

"It was only me," said Snubby. "Sorry! My word, isn't it an ENORMOUS knocker, Mrs. Tickle. No wonder it gave us all a fright last night. Whoever knocked must have been a strong fellow, to crash it on the door like that."

"Well, don't *you* do that again, or the breakfast will be spoilt," said Mrs. Tickle, still rather cross. "I dropped

the egg I was holding and it splashed all over my shoe—
look!"

"Loony, lick it!" ordered Snubby, but before the dog
could get to the shoe, Miranda was there, licking the egg
yolk with much enjoyment.

"How *can* you, Miranda!" said Diana, in disgust.

"Let's look for footprints," said Roger, and he went
to the top of the steps and looked down.

There was not much help to be got from the mass of
footprints there, nor from those just in front of the
door, under the porch. A jumble of footmarks flattened
the thick snow, and it was difficult to tell one from
another.

"We all stood here together when we arrived," said
Diana. "Your father, Barney—and we four—and Loony
of course leaping about everywhere—but we shan't find
Miranda's tiny paw-marks because she was on your
shoulder."

"There'll be the marks of the suit-cases too," said
Barney. "Yes, you can see them here—and here."

They all went down the steps, trying to keep to the
sides, so that they did not make any further prints to
confuse those already there. It was when they came to
the bottom of the steps and into the drive that they really
discovered something.

The marks of the car tyres were there, of course, coming
up the drive, and stopping by the door—then swinging
round and back when Mr. Martin drove off again. But
there was a strange line of footprints, all by itself, coming
right across the drive, from the snow-clad lawn nearby.
The children followed them to where they themselves
had made hundreds of prints when they snowballed one
another.

"Look at these!" said Barney, in excitement. "These

prints aren't made by us—they're enormous! They are made by someone wearing really big boots—they look like wellington boot prints, many sizes larger than ours."

The children looked down at them earnestly. Yes, these prints were not theirs. What a pity they were lost in the jumble of footmarks they themselves had made, and could not be followed any farther. They thought they could make them out here and there, but it was very uncertain.

"Let's follow them back to the front door," said Roger. "Everyone's got to be jolly careful NOT to tread on them or spoil them."

They followed them across the lawn and over the drive to the bottom of the steps, where, of course, they were then lost in a jumble of others.

Mrs. Tickle came to the front door, looking rather impatient. "Aren't you *ever* coming to breakfast?" she said. "And do you want to catch your deaths of cold, messing about outside without even a coat on?"

"Mrs. Tickle, come and look; we've found Mr. No-One's footprints!" called Snubby. "Do come!"

Mrs. Tickle pricked up her ears at once. She went cautiously down the front-entrance steps, afraid of slipping, and was proudly shown the set of prints leading up to the bottom step.

"Follow us and we'll show you where they come from," said Roger, and took her to where they had had their snowball fight. "See, they are lost here—but Mr. No-One went over the lawn from here, right across the drive, and then he must have gone up the steps to knock on the door."

"Yes," said Mrs. Tickle, looking extremely puzzled. "Yes, but why is there only *one* set of prints?"

"Because he was by himself!" said Snubby, thinking
that Mrs. Tickle was not very clever.

"Yes, I know that. But why isn't there a set of prints
leading *back* from the front-door steps?" said Mrs.
Tickle. "I mean—he'd got to walk *back*, hadn't he?
And there are no footmarks showing that he walked away
again."

Nobody had thought of that at all. How very stupid!
Barney frowned, very puzzled. "Yes, we didn't think of
that—we were so excited at finding strange footmarks
that we never thought that there should be *two* sets; one
coming and one going."

"This is *horrid*!" said Diana. "How can anyone come
to our front door and knock, and then not go away?
He's not standing there now! Then *how* did he go
away?"

"For goodness' sake come and have your breakfast,"
said Mrs. Tickle, shivering with the cold. "I'll have you
all in bed with bad chills if you stay out here any longer.
Leave Mr. No-One and his antics to himself and come
away in."

They obeyed her, very silent. It certainly was very,
very strange that there were no footmarks going away
from the house—only one set, walking towards it! How
did Mr. No-One, as they all called the night visitor, go
away if he didn't use his feet? It was a puzzle—a real
mystery!

They sat down to breakfast, and helped themselves
to hot porridge. Snubby remembered the fright he had
had two nights before when he thought he had seen
someone standing near the snow house while they were
having their supper. He reminded the others.

"I bet that was Mr. No-One too," he said. "And I bet
that's his glove we found!"

"Oh, yes," said Roger. "I expect it was. Well, we now know he was a man with large hands and large feet, and he has probably got one odd navy glove. But what we *don't* know is why on earth he's messing about Rat-a-Tat House."

"I wish he'd go somewhere else," said Diana, pouring out large cups of milky coffee for everyone. "And I hope to goodness he doesn't come knocking at our front door again."

"Do you think we'd better telephone to my father and tell him about it?" said Barney. "After all, this is my granny's house, and if anyone intends to burgle it, we ought to do something about it."

"Yes, of course. We'll telephone and tell the whole tale!" said Roger. "Good idea. Perhaps your father will come over and have a fight with Mr. No-One, Barney."

But when they went to telephone, there was no reply. The snow had brought down the wires, and until they were mended Rat-a-Tat House was completely cut off from everywhere!

CHAPTER THIRTEEN

A Few Interesting Things

"WELL!" SAID BARNEY, hanging up the telephone receiver. "That's that. We're cut off from everyone at the moment. Couldn't even get a doctor if we wanted one."

"We could get to the village of Boffame somehow, if we had to," said Roger.

"It would take us *ages*," said Barney. "All through that thick snow! I bet we'd get lost, too. All the countryside looks alike when it's covered with snow. We'd need skis to make any headway."

"So we'll have to solve the Mystery of Rat-a-Tat House by ourselves!" said Snubby cheerfully. "Oh, well, we're jolly good at mysteries, I think. We've had four already —the Rockingdown Mystery, the Rilloby Fair Mystery . . ."

"The Rubadub Mystery," said Diana, "and what was the other? Oh, yes, the Ring o' Bells Mystery."

"We'll call this the Rat-a-Tat Mystery then, as Snubby said," put in Barney. "How queer—they all begin with R."

"Is there any more bacon and eggs?" asked Snubby, hopefully.

"Certainly not," said Diana indignantly. "You've had twice as much as anyone else."

"Oooh, I haven't. Have I, Loony?" said Snubby, looking hurt. Loony thumped his tail on the ground and licked Snubby's hand.

"Stop thumping," ordered Diana. "I don't want to hear any knocking or thumping or hammering for ages. Loony, stop it!"

"Does anyone feel like tobogganing to-day?" asked Roger. "My legs feel quite all right now."

Barney would have liked to skate all day long, but when the others voted for tobogganing he nodded too.

"Right," said Roger. "That's settled then. But don't let's choose such a steep hill for our tobogganing this time —it really is such a drag up."

So they chose another hill, and dragged their toboggans up joyfully, after they had done all they could to help a rather silent Mrs. Tickle. She wasn't at all happy about Mr. No-One!

When they came to the top they had a fine view over

the white countryside, and suddenly saw something they had not been able to see from the other hill they had tobogganed down.

"What's that?" said Snubby, pointing to what looked like a small house, whose roof was white with snow. It stood very close to one bank of the lake, and, in fact, looked almost as if it were *on* the lake.

Everyone looked down at it. "It's a boat-house, of course!" said Roger. "Built partly on land and partly over water. There'll be boats in there, won't there, Barney?"

"Yes," said Barney, remembering that his father had told him that boats were stored for use on the lake in the summer. "I'd forgotten there was a boat-house. We might go and explore it when we're tired of tobogganing."

The snow was beautifully crisp for tobogganing again and the children really enjoyed themselves—especially when Snubby went down the hill alone with Loony, and the toboggan struck something, leapt in the air and flung both Snubby and Loony into the snow. Poor Loony fell in so deep that he was lost to sight!

"Loony, Loony, where are you?" yelled Snubby in a panic. "Come and help, you asses, don't stand laughing your heads off there. Loony will suffocate in the snow."

"Not Loony!" shouted Roger. "He's having a nice little rest!"

Loony was, in fact, tunnelling under the snow, too out of breath even to bark. He popped up just by Snubby and made him jump. He leapt on him in delight and over went poor Snubby, deeper in the snow than ever, with Loony leaping about on top of him. The others laughed till they ached, but Snubby was most annoyed.

"Let's eat our morning biscuits in the boat-house—if we can get in," said Barney when they began to feel tired and hungry. So they went over the snow to the boat-house, which with its white-painted walls and snow-clad roof, was really quite difficult to see from a distance.

It was shut and locked. "Blow!" said Barney. "We can't get in."

They went to look in at a window, and saw three boats there, in the dimness of the shed. Snubby wandered right round the shed and then suddenly shouted.

"Hey, here's a broken window. We can get in after all."

The others went round to him, but before he came to the broken window, Roger suddenly saw something else. Footmarks! Large ones, very much the same size as those they had seen in the drive.

"I say, we're on to something now," said Barney, excited. "Perhaps our Mr. No-One lives here—trespassing in my father's boat-house. Anyone got a torch?"

No one had, which was a pity. Barney looked at the broken window and saw that he could easily get in without tearing his clothes. "I'll just have a snoop round," he said, and was up on the wooden sill easily and in at the jagged window.

The others waited eagerly. He soon came back with a bit of news. "Yes, I think our Mr. No-One is staying here. One of the boats is lined with boat cushions, as if someone sleeps there. And I found an empty cigarette packet. Look!"

He gave the packet to Roger and then climbed deftly out of the window, his eyes shining. He looked at the large footprints again, just under the window. Yes, Mr. No-One used the window to get in by, that was certain. Now, where did the footmarks go? They might lead to Mr. No-One himself!

But the prints merely went to the front of the boat-house, which, instead of standing on piles in the water, as it usually did, was now standing in thick ice, for the lake was frozen. As soon as the footmarks reached the ice, they disappeared, of course, for no footprints showed on the ice.

"At least the footprints go *both* ways this time," said Roger thankfully. "Look, there are sets leading up to the window and sets leading away again—all jumbled up, but clear enough to see that the fellow came and went."

"Who is he—a tramp?" wondered Diana. "But why would a tramp come and knock at Rat-a-Tat House? And, anyway, how did he make footprints that only led there—and not away? That's been puzzling me all day!"

"Oh, let's not worry about that," said Snubby, who had

231

finished his biscuits and wanted to toboggan again. "Come on—it's cold just standing here."

They were all bright-eyed and red-cheeked when they went in for lunch, feeling quite ravenous.

"Has Mr. No-One been knocking at the door again?" asked Snubby cheerfully, as Mrs. Tickle brought in a dishful of chops surrounded by fried potatoes and tinned peas. "Oh, I say—look at that! It makes me feel hungrier than ever."

"That Mr. No-One wouldn't dare to come in the daytime," said Mrs. Tickle. "I've got my rolling-pin ready, and a kettle boiling on the stove. I'm ready for him if he comes banging at any door, front or back."

They all laughed at the determined little woman. She laughed too. "There you are—you get on with your lunch—and there's a big treacle pudding to follow so leave a bit of room for that."

It was a lovely meal as usual, and the children felt lazy after it. But the day was again so beautiful that no one wanted a long rest. Soon they were on their way to toboggan again and spent the whole afternoon racing down and climbing up the snowy hills. They were very tired when they dragged themselves back to Rat-a-Tat House just as it was getting dusk.

"I can't find enough strength to throw a snowball at anyone," said Snubby sorrowfully. "As for Loony, he's so tired I'm having to drag him back on my toboggan, the lazy fellow."

"Our snowman is still standing on guard over our snow house," said Roger. "Hallo, Mr. Icy-Cold? Your hat's gone crooked. Pray let me put it straight for you."

He tipped the old hat straight, and they all went on to the garden door to take off their wet boots and gloves. Mrs. Tickle heard them and came to welcome them.

"You're late," she said. "I've had hot buttered toast ready for you for twenty minutes. Hurry up and wash, or the toast will be cold."

"I can't even hurry for buttered toast," said Snubby. "I'm an old, old man, Mrs. Tickle, bent and stooping, and my legs will hardly bear me. Oh, what tobogganing does to you!"

"Go on with you," said Mrs. Tickle. "Bent old man you may be, but you'll eat more than your share of the toast, I'll be bound!"

They all sat at the laden white-clothed table, enjoying their meal, with Diana pouring out huge cups of tea for everyone. They were happy but so tired that they could hardly tease one another. Loony flopped down under the table with an enormous sigh. He was very much afraid he would go to sleep before the titbits began to arrive for him below the table.

"Let's draw the curtains," said Barney. "I don't want to feel that Mr. No-One is hiding in our snow house again and watching us while we eat."

"All right. Draw them," said Roger. "I don't feel able to stand on my legs at the moment."

Barney got up to draw them. Before he pulled them across the lighted window, he looked out into the darkness, pierced only by the rays of the bright oil-lamp. He swung round suddenly.

"I SAY! Our snowman's gone! He's not there!"

"Gone! But he can't be! Why, he was there when we came in, half an hour ago!" cried Diana. "Roger put his hat straight."

"Well, he's not there now," said Barney. "Come and see. You can just make out the snow house—but no snowman! Gosh! What queer things are happening? Where *has* Mr. Icy-Cold gone?"

233

CHAPTER FOURTEEN

Another Mystery

THE FOUR CHILDREN really were astounded at the disappearance of their snowman, especially as they had passed him such a short time ago on their way back to tea.

"Someone must have knocked him down," said Barney at last. "It's the only explanation. Snowmen don't walk away on their own—not even our nice Mr. Icy-Cold."

"Well, shall we get a torch and go out and see if he's been knocked down and made into just a heap of snow?" said Roger.

"Yes. And we may perhaps spy the person who spoilt him," said Barney, getting his torch off the mantelpiece. "We'll take Loony too; he'll soon smell out anyone hiding nearby, watching to see if we've noticed the disappearance of the snowman."

"I don't see any *point* in knocking him down," began Diana, really puzzled, and then she stopped. A cry had come from the kitchen, and then the children heard hurried footsteps running down the passage to the sitting-room. The door was flung open, and there was Mrs. Tickle "all of a shake" again.

"What's the matter?" cried Barney.

"The snowman! Your snowman! He came and peeped in at the kitchen window when I was having my tea," panted Mrs. Tickle. The children stared at her unbelievingly.

"But—Mrs. Tickle—you must know that a snowman

234

doesn't walk!" said Roger. "It must have been a——"

"I tell you, it was your snowman, all white, and with that hat on," said Mrs. Tickle, sinking down into a chair. "Such goings-on! We'll get back to Little Wendleman as soon as possible. You telephone your father, Barney."

"The telephone is out of order," said Barney, and Mrs. Tickle groaned. Then she looked out of the window and gave a little scream.

"He's gone—your snowman's gone!" she said. "I *thought* it was him, peering in at my window and frightening the life out of me. Hat and all."

This was really very puzzling. None of the children believed for a moment that it actually was their snowman that Mrs. Tickle had seen. But *who* was it? And why was he all in white? And how was it that their own snowman had disappeared so very suddenly?

"I believe that wasn't a snowman at all, out there," said Mrs. Tickle, nodding her head towards the window. "He may have been once, but after that it was someone covered in snow, watching us."

"Oh, no, Mrs. Tickle!" said Barney. "Honestly, we walked close by him this morning *and* this afternoon, and there is no doubt at all but that he was a snowman made of snow. Why, Roger even put his hat on straight for him. Didn't you, Roger?"

"Well, then—you explain to me how he walked away and came and looked in my kitchen window," said Mrs. Tickle fiercely. "You tell me that!"

They couldn't. It was just as much a puzzle to them as to poor Mrs. Tickle. Barney and Roger went out to the kitchen with her to see if the snowman was still doing some peeping. But he wasn't. Barney took his torch into the backyard and shone it everywhere, but there was nothing to be seen, except a jumble of footmarks all mixed up together—obviously Mrs. Tickle's and some of theirs. It was impossible to tell if there were any others as well.

They came back, and Mrs. Tickle firmly locked and bolted the door behind her. "I won't have that snowman walking into my kitchen," she said.

"It's a pity he doesn't," said Snubby. "He would go and warm himself at your big fire, Mrs. Tickle; and in a few minutes all you'd have to do would be to mop up a big pool of water, and empty the snowman down the sink."

Mrs. Tickle had to laugh. "You're a real caution, you are," she said. "Have you finished your tea yet?"

"Gosh, no!" said Snubby, quite shocked to think that he could have left his tea and forgotten about it. "I was in the middle of my third piece of toast and butter."

"You'd better go and finish it, then," said Mrs. Tickle, giving him a little push.

The children went back to the sitting-room to finish their tea. They all felt rather excited, but they found it difficult to believe that Mrs. Tickle had seen anyone *really* like a snowman. It must have been a trick of the dusk.

"But that doesn't solve *our* problem—of why our snowman suddenly disappeared," said Snubby.

"He might have melted," suggested Diana. "The weather might have got warmer. It feels like it."

"You can't possibly tell what the weather's like sitting in this hot room," said Roger. "I'm sure it's as cold as ever. I hope it is, anyway. I want to go skating to-morrow."

"Yes!" said Barney, beaming. "Yes, let's all go skating."

They had a very pleasant evening with no more disturbances. They thought that Mrs. Tickle seemed a bit

scared of being in the kitchen by herself, so they decided
to ask her to come and have a game of Snap-Grab with
them—that would cheer her up, and make her forget the
snowman who had peeped in at her window.

They set the cork in the middle of the table and Roger
dealt the cards. Whenever anyone saw that two cards
were the same, he not only had to call "Snap!" but had to
grab the cork as well. This saved a great many arguments
as to who it was who had called Snap first! Snubby
grabbed at the cork so fiercely every time he called Snap
that they made him go and fetch his gloves and put one
on.

"You've scratched my hand twice," complained Diana.
"You really are rough at this game, Snubby. I shan't
play unless you wear a glove."

So Snubby fetched his gloves and put one on his right
hand. Now, when he grabbed the cork, he couldn't
scratch anyone!

Miranda loved a game of snap, and kept trying to grab
the cork herself when anyone yelled "Snap!" Once she
really did get hold of it and leapt away to the mantelpiece
with it, holding it so tightly that Barney couldn't get it
away from her.

"You really are naughty," he said, but Miranda refused
to give up the cork. She put it into her mouth and held it
there, looking wickedly at Barney.

Snubby laughed. He got up and put a few old cards
on the mantelpiece beside Miranda.

"Here you are," he said. "You can have a game of
Snap all to yourself, cork and all, you little wretch!
We've got another cork in the card-box."

Miranda picked up the cards in delight, and began to
chatter to herself. She took the cork out of her mouth as
soon as Barney was safely settled again at the table, and

set it down beside her. Then she began to deal out the cards.

"Look! Do look at Miranda!" said Diana, amused. "She'll be yelling out 'Snap!' in a minute."

But she didn't get as far as that, of course! She did, however, think that it would be more fun to play cards *with* someone, rather than by herself, and in a few minutes she leapt off the mantelpiece, cork in mouth, and cards in one paw. She scuttled along the floor to where Loony was lying in a deep sleep under the table, and woke him by biting his tail.

She dealt out the cards and put the cork on the floor. Diana, peeping under the table, went off into fits of laughter and Barney produced his uproarious laugh, that always set everyone else laughing too.

Loony wasn't at all pleased. He sniffed at the cork, looked scornfully at the cards and once more went to sleep. Miranda had to play on her own again.

Snubby soon had all the cards, as usual, though Mrs. Tickle ran him very close. She was surprisingly good at grabbing the cork, much to Snubby's annoyance. It was, in fact, a very jolly evening, despite the upsets of two or three hours before.

"Bedtime," said Mrs. Tickle at last. "And let's hope Mr. No-One doesn't come hammering at the door again. If he does, I don't stir out of my bed. Let him knock all he likes."

"And so say I," said Roger, yawning. "Yes, let's go to bed. Diana's nearly asleep already."

They turned out the oil-lamp, collected Loony and Miranda (who still clutched her cards and cork), lighted their candles and set off upstairs. In half an hour's time the house was in darkness, and everyone was sound asleep, except Loony.

It is true that Loony was *asleep*, but to-night he had one ear open, which meant that that one ear was awake, and so Loony was not really *sound* asleep. The upsets of the night before, and the excitement over the snowman had put him on his guard. He meant to keep one ear awake all night—just in case!

It was just about midnight when that one ear heard something unusual—not the crashing of the knocker on the front door this time—but a small sound, somewhere downstairs. Loony's ear took in the noise, and he awoke at once and sat up. Snubby was lost in a deep sleep, and took no notice. Loony ran to the door and listened.

Yes, something was going on downstairs. He ran to Snubby, and gave a little warning growl. Then he pawed at him. Finally he jumped up on to Snubby's middle— that always awoke him, as Loony very well knew.

It awoke him now and he sat up indignantly. "Ass! What did you want to do that for? Haven't I told you . . . I say—what are you growling for?"

Loony's growl put Snubby on his guard at once. Aha! Perhaps someone was about to crash that knocker again, and Loony had heard footsteps. Right—Snubby would go down and watch for Mr. No-One, and catch him hammering at that knocker. Grrrrrr! Snubby growled softly into Loony's silky ear—they would both go on the warpath immediately!

"Come on," said Snubby. "Something's up!"

239

CHAPTER FIFTEEN

Look Out, Snubby!

SNUBBY SLIPPED on his dressing-gown, and looked across at Roger, shining his torch on him. He was fast asleep. Should he wake him? No, he would go down and pry around a little first, and then if there *was* anything exciting, he could come back and get Roger.

Loony was still growling in a low tone, his hackles up and his body stiff. There was no doubt that he could hear *something* going on.

Snubby began to feel excited. "Adventure in the night!" he whispered to Loony. "Come on, old fellow."

They went out of the room quietly, and Snubby shut the door behind him. They crept along the wide landing, and came to the top of the stairs. Snubby shut off his torch and listened. He could hear sounds now—muffled sounds —he thought they came from the kitchen.

"Who's there?" he wondered. "Mr. No-One perhaps! Loony, we'd better go carefully. Gosh! It might be the snowman, of course. I never thought of that."

Snubby would never have dreamed of thinking he might *really* meet a snowman, if it had been broad daylight— but somehow, in the dark, silent house, with queer sounds going on, it seemed quite possible that he might meet the snowman round the next corner. He tightened his dressing-gown belt, and went softly down the stairs, torch in hand.

Yes, the sounds quite definitely came from the kitchen.

They were curious sounds, and Snubby couldn't quite make them out. There were bumps—and scraping noises —and grunts as if someone was carrying something heavy. What could be happening?

Snubby came to the bottom of the stairs and went down the hall towards the big kitchen door. Mrs. Tickle always left it open at night, but now it was shut. Snubby crept towards it, Loony close at his heels, still growling very softly.

Snubby put his eye to the keyhole, but the kitchen was in darkness, except for what seemed to him to be a ray from a stationary torch. He heard a low voice, and then a bump from the far side of the kitchen. Snubby tried to think what was just there—was it the larder? No. Was it the cupboard where Mrs. Tickle kept the crockery and pans? No. Of course—it was the *cellar*! He and Barney had noticed the door there, and had tried to open it, to see where it led to, but it had been locked.

"The cellar's locked, and I don't know where the key is," Mrs. Tickle had told them. "I expect your granny has something stored down there, Barney. It was open when I was here last summer—your cousins were here boating and swimming. I expect your granny locked it when we all went home."

But whoever was in the kitchen now had evidently got hold of the key to the cellar, because Snubby, straining his ears, could quite well hear someone going down the steps. What in the world was happening? Were thieves robbing the cellar of any goods stored there? What a time to choose—in the middle of a snowy spell, when there was no chance of a lorry or van to take them away.

Loony continued to growl, and Snubby got tired of looking through the keyhole. He suddenly decided that he would slip out of the garden door and go round to the kitchen window. He would have a much better view there.

"Come on," he whispered to Loony, and they went back up the hall together. They passed the open sitting-room door and, in the light of the dying fire, Loony suddenly caught sight of the gleaming eyes of the bearskin rug. He backed heavily into Snubby and growled loudly.

"Look out!" whispered Snubby, almost falling over. "What's the matter? Oh, it's the old bear. My word, doesn't he look life-like to-night!"

He was about to go on when a sudden idea struck him. Why shouldn't he drape the bearskin over him, and pull the head over his—if the men happened to see him looking in at the kitchen window, they would have the fright of their lives to see what appeared to be a live bear!

"Also," thought Snubby, shivering, "it would be nice and warm to wear. I expect it will be terribly cold outside."

All thoughts of waking Roger went from his mind and he felt a tingling feeling run down his back as a tremendous excitement suddenly took hold of him. Yes, he would wear the bearskin. He would give those thieves a fright, and he would find out what they were doing. What a tale to tell the others! Snubby's chest swelled in pride, and he patted Loony on the head.

"I'm going to wear that bearskin," he whispered. "So don't get excited about it. The bear won't eat me!"

And then, to Loony's everlasting amazement, Snubby went to the bearskin, lifted it up, and draped it round his shoulders, with the big head on top of his! When he bent his own head the bear's head flopped down lower and it looked exactly as if it were alive.

It was very heavy—heavier than Snubby had imagined. But he was quite determined to wear it! Loony gaped at him, his tail well down. He couldn't understand this at all, and he was all ready to leap on the bearskin if it showed any sign of biting Snubby or clawing him.

Snubby went slowly to the garden door, weighed down by the skin over his shoulders. He unlocked the door and he and Loony went out into the cold, frosty night. The snow was thick and deep as he went round the house to the kitchen entrance, Loony obediently at his heels.

The spaniel growled as they came near the kitchen door, and Snubby tapped him on the head. It was essential that the men should not hear anything. As they rounded the corner, they saw that the kitchen door was open—and, to Snubby's amazement, some hefty boxes, about the size of small trunks, were piled in the little kitchen yard.

He stared at them. They were only very dimly outlined in the starlight, for there was no moon, and Snubby could not make out anything at all except their size. What were the men doing with them—hiding them in the cellar?

"Or perhaps taking them *out*!" thought Snubby. "Yes, of course—they are taking them out. That's why the cellar door was locked and the key was gone. These men must have come to the house while it stood empty, and hidden something down in the cellar, knowing it would be safe in an empty house, with nobody to pry and peep."

He stole past the boxes to the kitchen window, and peered inside, just as the snowman was supposed to have looked in at Mrs. Tickle that evening. A torch lay on a table, its beam pointing towards the cellar door—which, of course, was open.

Loony did his best to peer through the window too, putting his paws on the sill. He almost choked himself trying not to bark—especially when a man appeared at the top of the cellar steps, going backwards as if he were helping another man to carry something very heavy.

Snubby watched in excitement. Yes, it was another box—very heavy too. Good gracious, no wonder the men had locked the cellar door and taken the key! Mrs. Tickle would have been amazed to find the cellar full of heavy boxes! Snubby supposed that the men hadn't had time to remove them before Mrs. Tickle and the rest of them came down to Rat-a-Tat House—they must have thought that the house would certainly stand empty all the winter.

The first man came right out of the cellar followed by a second man; they carried a big box between them.

"Put it down for a moment, Jim," said the second man, panting. He was fat, as Snubby could see in the light of the torch that lay on the nearby table, but he could not see the faces of the men at all.

Loony could bear this no longer. He suddenly gave a terrific growl, and the startled men turned to the window at once, one of them flashing a torch there. He almost dropped it when he saw a great bear's head, apparently looking in at them with gleaming, staring eyes—and, much lower down, just above the sill, another furry head, black this time, with another pair of gleaming eyes!

"Look! What's that? No, it *can't* be a bear!" said the man called Jim, in a startled voice. "What is it, Stan?"

Snubby dropped down as soon as he saw that the men had seen him, and so did Loony. "Quick!" said Snubby. "We must get back to the others, Loony, and wake them up."

He slipped as he shambled along in the deep snow and went down on all fours, looking now for all the world like a real bear. Loony, glancing at him in amazement, half-wondered if the bear had eaten Snubby, for there was little to be seen of the boy now.

The two men rushed out of the kitchen door together, shining their torches. They saw the bear shambling along with Loony. One of them took out a revolver, but the other motioned to him to put it away. "We don't want to rouse the whole household with the sound of a shot," he said. "Besides, somehow I don't think that bear is real."

Poor Snubby didn't know what to do now. If he stood up to get along more quickly, the men would see that it was only someone wearing a bearskin, and not a real bear. On the other hand, he couldn't get along at all fast on all fours in the snow.

The bearskin solved his difficulties by slipping right off his shoulders, and the men at once saw that there was only a small boy on all fours in the snow. They were most relieved. Loony stood by Snubby growling in a most alarming way, ready to fly at the men at a word from the boy.

"Get up," said the man called Jim, to Snubby. "What's the meaning of this foolery?"

"Well," said Snubby indignantly, standing up straight, "I like *that*! What's the meaning of *you* delving about in our cellars in the middle of the night?"

"No cheek from you," said the other man roughly. "Get back into the kitchen at once—go on—and the dog too. And I warn you, if that dog begins to bark or try any funny business with his teeth, I'll kick him over the wall."

"No, don't," said Snubby in alarm, looking at the man's great wellington boots. He hitched his dressing-gown round him and went back to the kitchen, glad to be in the warm, for it was freezing hard outside.

His heart was beating fast. What was going to happen now? Something very unpleasant, that was certain.

CHAPTER SIXTEEN

Down in the Cellar

SNUBBY WENT OVER to the fire that was still gleaming in the grate, and faced the men. His red hair stood on end, and he felt very scared. But he put on a bold face, and even tried to whistle.

The men stood together, talking in a low voice. Snubby's heart sank. They must be discussing what to do with him, and there were so many unpleasant possibilities! Could he make a dash for it? He eyed the door that led into the hall. He knew that it was locked, but the key was on this side. He *might* be able to dash over, unlock the door, open it and rush upstairs.

He suddenly made up his mind, and raced for the door, putting out his hand to turn the key. But the men were on to him like a flash. Loony, now thoroughly aroused, and eager to defend Snubby, bared his teeth and went for the men, snapping at their legs. But the thick rubber boots they wore went up to their knees and Loony only got mouthfuls of hard rubber.

Snubby yelled and slipped between the men, now making for the open door that led into the yard—but Jim was there, to prevent him. Then Snubby saw the opened cellar door and ran to that. Down the stone steps he went, falling down the last four, with Loony on top of him. Snubby was up at once, and ran to the farthest corner, fumbling and stumbling in the dark, afraid that the men would be after him down there.

But no—they didn't come down the steps. There was

only the thud of the cellar door shutting, and then Snubby
heard the turning of the key in the lock.

"Gosh! I've made myself a prisoner," he groaned.
"I bet those fellows planned to lock me up here anyhow,
while they go off with those boxes—they must be going
to take them away somewhere. I wonder if they've got a
van. No, how could they in this snow?"

He sat down on an old broken chair, and Loony
pressed close to him. He didn't understand this at all.
Why had Snubby come down here into this cold dark
place? Why didn't he go back to his warm bed and let
Loony cuddle against his legs? The spaniel gave a little
whine, and Snubby patted his silky head.

"*Why* did you give that frightfully fierce growl, when

247

we were looking in at the window, Loony?" he groaned. "It was all because of that that we got caught. Honestly, you really *are* a loony dog!"

Snubby listened to see if there were any more noises upstairs. He rubbed his bruises and decided to go up to the locked cellar door and see if he could hear anything useful. So up he went, Loony pressing behind.

He could hear low voices, but could not make out a word. "They're moving that box they put down in the kitchen," he thought. "Putting it outside with the others, I expect. What's in them, I wonder? And where are they going to put them? I might have found out all that if I'd been more sensible—or if Loony had."

It was so cold and draughty at the top of the stone steps that Snubby went down to the cellar again.

"Looks as if we've got to spend the night here, Loony," he said miserably. "Blow! WHY didn't I wake Roger and let him come too? He'll go on sleeping all night long, and it won't be till Mrs. Tickle comes down to the kitchen in the morning that anyone will hear me yelling. Brrrrrr! It's cold here!"

He flashed his torch round the cellar. It was very big and rambling. Shelves ran up to the ceiling here and there, and were laden with all kind of stores, especially tinned food. Snubby stared at the labels—pineapple, peaches, pears, grapefruit—his mouth watered. What a pity he hadn't a tin-opener with him.

There was an old wringer there, and various broken chairs stood in corners. A space had evidently been cleared for the boxes, and Snubby could see where they had stood for they had left their outlines in the dust.

He shivered. What a horrid cold place this was. "Loony, let's see if we can find something a bit warmer than the stone floor to lie on," he said, and he and the spaniel went round the big cellar poking into everything.

They made a good find at last—an old mattress, rolled up and tied with rope. "Good!" said Snubby. "Got a knife to cut the rope, Loony?"

Loony wagged his tail, knowing this was a joke. Snubby had no knife, of course, in his dressing-gown, so he had to struggle with the knots. He got them undone at last and the mattress unrolled itself. Snubby lay down on it, gathered his dressing-gown round him and cuddled Loony, who was better than any hot-water bottle!

"Now we'll try and go to sleep, and hope that Mrs. Tickle will hear me yelling in the morning," he said. But it took him a long time to fall asleep. For one thing, he was very excited, and for another he was very cold. But he did sleep at last, Loony curled up against him as close as possible.

Nobody knew that Snubby was not in his bed. Upstairs the rest of the party slept soundly, the three children tired out with their day's sport. Mrs. Tickle heard no sound either, and hardly stirred in her bed—till the alarm clock went off and awoke her.

She got up, dressed and went downstairs. The kitchen fire was still in, thank goodness, so she only had to rake the embers together and put on some coal. Then she took her brooms and dusters and set off to get the sitting-room clean and tidy, and to light the fire there too.

She was most astonished to find the bearskin rug gone. She stood and stared at the empty place where it usually lay and wondered what had happened to it.

"It's that dog Loony," she decided. "He must have come down in the night and fought it, and taken it off somewhere. Where has he put it? What a dog! I can't leave a duster or brush about anywhere but what he's off and away with them. I'll have to tie them all round my waist soon. Where *can* he have taken that bearskin rug?"

She didn't hear poor Snubby yelling in the cellar, because the sitting-room was a good way from the kitchen. She finished cleaning it and then went to mop and dust the hall.

Upstairs Roger was awake, and rather surprised to see Snubby's bed empty and Loony gone too. "He must have dressed and gone out early," he thought. "No, he hasn't; his clothes are still there. Perhaps he's in Barney's room."

He went to see, but Snubby wasn't there either, of course. Barney was already half-dressed, looking forward to another day of skating. Roger looked round the room in surprise.

"Isn't Snubby here?" he said. "He's not in our room. His clothes are there, though."

"I bet he's gone down to ask Mrs. Tickle for a snack before breakfast," said Barney, and Roger thought that was very likely.

Diana came out of her room fully dressed, as he went back. "Buck up, Roger!" she said. "I'm going down to help Mrs. Tickle." And down she went. Barney followed almost at once. They met Mrs. Tickle in the hall, just finishing the polishing.

"Hallo, Mrs. Tickle!" said Barney. "I hope the old snowman didn't visit you in the night!"

"Go on with you!" said Mrs. Tickle. "Are you going to lay the breakfast table for me, Diana, seeing that you're up nice and early?"

"Barney and I will do it together," said Diana, going to the sideboard where the cloths were kept. "Oh, where's the bearskin gone?"

"That dog Loony's taken it, I think," said Mrs. Tickle. "Mad as a hatter, he is."

She went off into the kitchen, and then, a minute later, she came hurrying back, looking puzzled and indignant.

"I went to shake my dusters in the yard," she said, "and bless us all, if the bearskin isn't lying out there in the snow! But how COULD Loony have taken it through a locked door?"

"Isn't Snubby downstairs?" asked Barney in surprise. "He's not in his room—we thought he'd probably gone down to the kitchen to ask you for a snack. You're sure he's not in the larder, Mrs. Tickle?"

Mrs. Tickle began to look astonished. "No. I've not seen Snubby—or Loony—this morning and yet there's the bearskin out there in the snow. Perhaps Snubby's playing some joke?"

"He's an ass," said Barney impatiently. "What can he be up to? He *must* be somewhere in the kitchen, Mrs. Tickle—hiding for some reason of his own."

Diana, Barney and Mrs. Tickle went back to the kitchen, and Roger, coming downstairs, joined them. As soon as they were inside the room, they stopped in surprise. From somewhere came a voice—Snubby's voice—yelling loudly. And with it came a hammering on the other side of the cellar door.

"Help! Help! Open the cellar door. Help! MRS. TICKLE, ARE YOU THERE? HELP!"

"Good gracious! It's Snubby—down in the cellar, of all places," said Barney, and ran to the door.

"But it's locked," said Mrs. Tickle. "And there's no key to it, you remember. How could Snubby get in? And look—there's no key *now*."

Barney was at the cellar door, tugging at the handle. "Snubby! Why are you in here? Where's the key? There's none this side."

251

"Oh! They've taken it with them, the beasts!" said Snubby, with a groan. "I might have guessed. Can you break the door down, Barney?"

Everyone was astounded to know that Snubby was locked in the cellar! And who were "the beasts" who had apparently taken the key—a key that hadn't been there before, as Mrs. Tickle very well knew.

"Try the key of the kitchen door, or of the door into the hall," said Diana, suddenly remembering that the keys at home were often interchangeable. "Quick, Roger, get them. Snubby must be freezing cold in there."

Roger got the two keys, and oh, what a bit of luck— the kitchen door key fitted the cellar lock! He turned it and out came poor Snubby, with Loony barking madly at his heels.

CHAPTER SEVENTEEN

Barney Thinks Things Out

"SNUBBY! How did you get in there?"

"What happened? Gosh, you look cold!"

"Come over to the fire, Snubby; your hands are like ice."

Everyone spoke at once, and Diana dragged the shivering Snubby to the fire, which was now blazing well. Mrs. Tickle was simply amazed that he should have been in the cellar all night. Whatever next!

Snubby got as close to the fire as he could and held his hands out to the flames thankfully. "My word, it was cold down in the cellar," he said. "If I hadn't had Loony for a hot-water bottle I'd have been frozen stiff."

"But Snubby, how did you get locked in there? What were you *doing*, wandering about at night!" cried Mrs. Tickle.

"I had an adventure," said Snubby, beginning to feel pleasantly warm, and very much the centre of attention. "I heard a noise in the middle of the night and came down to see what it was. . . ."

"Snubby, how brave of you," said Diana, admiringly. "I couldn't possibly have done that."

Snubby went on with his tale of the night's doings; how he had looked through the locked kitchen door, and had had the idea of going to look in at the kitchen window clad in the bearskin, and had gone out of the garden door and round to the window.

"There were boxes out there, piled up," said Snubby, "and the kitchen door was open wide."

"But I locked it!" said Mrs. Tickle, amazed. "And what's more, I bolted it too!"

"Well, it was open," said Snubby. "Is it locked now?"

Barney went to look. "Yes, locked *and* bolted! They must have got in somewhere else, and opened the kitchen door from inside. And then, when they went, they must have locked and bolted it again on the inside, and gone out the way they came in."

"Probably a window somewhere. We'll look in a minute," said Roger. "Go on, Snubby."

Snubby told the rest of the tale. How he had been caught and how he had bolted down the cellar steps to escape the men, who had promptly locked him in.

"The box I saw them carrying up the cellar steps must have been the last one," he said. "There aren't any more boxes like it down there. I had a look. My word, it was cold in the night; I was lucky to find an old mattress to sleep on."

It really was an extraordinary tale. Nobody knew quite what to make of it. So many queer things had happened since they had been at Rat-a-Tat House, but this last one, of boxes hidden in the cellar, and taken away in the middle of the night was the most puzzling of all.

"I suppose all the queer things fit together somehow," said Barney, when at last they were in the sitting-room having breakfast, with Snubby now dressed and comfortably warm again. "But the question is—how?"

"Yes, how does Mr. No-One, banging at our door in the middle of the night fit in with the Somebody who watched us by the snow house one night?" said Roger.

"And how does the walking snowman fit in too?" wondered Diana. "Why should he wander about and look into the kitchen window, frightening Mrs. Tickle out of her wits?"

"I rather think I know!" said Barney suddenly. "Yes, I'm beginning to see how all the happenings can fit together like pieces in a jigsaw."

"What do you mean?" said Roger, surprised.

"Don't talk to me for a bit while I think it out," said Barney, buttering a piece of toast. "It's just beginning to dawn on me."

Snubby was eating his fifth piece of toast, and was now feeling extremely pleased with himself and his adventure. He was even inclined to boast, but this the others would not allow.

"It wasn't *really* very clever to hear a noise in the night and go down by yourself instead of waking me and asking me to come with you," said Roger. "If I'd been with you we might even have caught the men, locked them into the cellar in the same way that they locked *you* in! You never know."

254

"I think I've got it," announced Barney suddenly. "Yes, I think I begin to see things now."

"What? Tell us," said Diana eagerly.

"Well, listen. Coming down here was quite a sudden idea of my father's and grandmother's," said Barney. "To all intents and purposes the house was closed till next spring—shut up and empty. Well, along comes someone who wants a very, very good place to hide something in—perhaps stolen goods—perhaps smuggled goods. I don't know——"

"And what could be better than an empty house which won't be visited for months," cried Roger. "Yes, go on, Barney."

"Right. They decide to bring their goods here, and probably plan to hide them in our cellar till it's safe to take them to wherever they want to," said Barney. "So they break in somewhere, or get a key that will unlock one of the doors, and one night they arrive here with a car, or van, or lorry——"

"And carry those boxes I saw down into the cellar," said Snubby. "Gosh, yes! That's it. Meaning to collect them in their own good time! And they locked the cellar door and took away the key just in case anyone should come here to do a bit of cleaning and perhaps even pop down into the cellar, and discover what was hidden there."

"Exactly," said Barney. "It certainly was a splendid hiding-place. No one would see the van or lorry arriving in this lonely spot, far from any other house—no one would see the boxes being unloaded and taken into the house—and no one would see them being taken away again when the right time came."

"And then suddenly we come and spoil all their plans," said Diana. "What a shock it must have been for them to hear that we had arrived to stay for a while. How do you suppose they heard?"

"Oh, probably someone in Boffame village told them," said Barney. "Or they may have come along to have a look to see if their hidden goods were all right, and discovered us here."

"And one of them spied on us in the snow house," cried Snubby. "And dropped his glove there."

"But I don't see how Mr. No-One, banging at the knocker, fits in," said Diana, puzzled. "Or the walking snowman that went and peeped in at Mrs. Tickle's window last night. Somehow I don't *think* she made that up."

"She didn't," said Barney. "I'll tell you how I think Mr. No-One, the knocker, and the snowman all fit into the picture. I think they were meant to *frighten us away* —so that we would go off, and leave the coast clear for them. They would be able to load up their lorry again, or whatever it was they used—and hide the goods somewhere else."

"Gosh!" said Snubby, lost in admiration at Barney's explanations. "You're right. Mr. No-One was simply one of those men—Jim or Stan—hammering away at the knocker to make us think it was the old legend coming true. I nearly did think it too—we were all scared to death."

"It's a wonder we didn't leave at once," said Diana. "Mrs. Tickle would have loved to go, I know."

"Yes, but to the man's great annoyance, we still stuck here—and they had to watch us tobogganing all day yesterday, instead of rejoicing to see us pack up and go."

"We couldn't go, anyway," said Roger. "Unless a car came to fetch us, and we couldn't get Barney's father over because the telephone is out of order."

"They wouldn't know that," said Barney. "So they they tried to scare us once more, by dressing up in a white sheet, or something like that and stealing the snowman's hat, and then peering through the window at poor Mrs. Tickle."

"No wonder she was scared," said Diana. "We all thought she made it up, or was quite mistaken, but she wasn't. Poor Mrs. Tickle! How awful to see the snowman peering through the window, hat and all."

"And when we still didn't get in a panic last night, I suppose they gave up trying to scare us and decided to get the boxes out in the middle of the night, hoping we wouldn't hear, and hide them in a safer place," said Barney. "But old Snubby heard them, and rather messed up their plans."

"But not enough to *ruin* them," said Roger. "They've got the stuff away all right, that's clear. I wonder what it was."

"I think we ought to try and find out," said Barney. "This may be something pretty serious, you know. If only we could telephone my father! I wonder how long it will be before the telephone wires are mended."

"Ages, I expect," said Diana. "What do you plan to do now, Barney?"

"I plan to follow the tracks the men made carrying those boxes away," said Barney. "They'll show easily over the snow."

"Well, we'll have to buck up then," said Roger. "Look, the sky's full of snow, and it's beginning to fall already. Any tracks will soon be covered."

"What *I* want to know is how Mr. No-One made tracks to the front door, and got away without leaving another set," said Snubby. "Who'll tell me that?"

Nobody bothered to answer him. They were all rush-

ing to get their hats and coats to go and find the tracks
the men made when they took away those big heavy
boxes.

CHAPTER EIGHTEEN

On the Trail

DIANA STAYED behind to tell Mrs. Tickle a little of what
Barney had said, and to carry out some of the dirty
dishes. Mrs. Tickle, looking astonished, tried to follow
all that Diana was saying, but she soon gave it up.

"All I know is, there's very funny goings-on here,"
she said. "And I don't like it. If the telephone was all
right, I'd phone Mr. Martin and tell him it's dangerous
to stay here and get him to fetch us. Knockings in the
night, and wandering snowmen, and Snubby locked in the
cellar! It just isn't right."

"Never mind, Mrs. Tickle," said Diana, comfortingly.
"I don't think we'll have any more 'funny goings-on' now
—if Barney's right in what he says. So you needn't be
scared, or carry your rolling-pin about with you."

"Indeed I shall—it goes with me wherever I go,"
declared Mrs. Tickle, brandishing it. "Upstairs and
downstairs."

"And in my lady's chamber," said Diana, with a laugh.
"All right, you do what you want to do, Mrs. Tickle. *I*
think you've been marvellous." And with that she went
out to join the others. They were examining the snow
house, and the place where the snowman had once
stood.

"Look, Di," said Barney, as she came up. "The

snowman has simply been knocked down and then trodden on. The only things left are his two feet."

"And someone's broken down the back wall of the snow house," said Roger. "Walked into it, probably, or leaned on it when he was watching us through the window."

"AND we've found out how Mr. No-One walked through the snow to the front door, and apparently didn't go back again," said Snubby. "*I* worked that out, actually."

"Oh, the clever boy!" said Diana, amused at Snubby's boasting. "How did Mr. No-One do it?"

"Well, watch. I'll go to that tree through the snow, and come back, and yet you'll see only one set of prints," said Snubby; "and *all* going one way!"

"Go on, then, show me," said Diana disbelievingly. Snubby grinned. He walked slowly to the tree, making well-defined footmarks in the snow—and then, when he reached the tree, he stopped. He looked carefully over his shoulder to see the last footmark he had made, and put his foot in it; then the other foot into the neat print, and the next.

"He's walking backwards, and putting his feet into the same footmarks he's already made," said Diana, astonished. "What an idea!"

"Yes. So there is only *one* set of footprints all going to the tree, though Snubby has gone there *and* back," said Roger, as Snubby arrived beside Diana again, grinning all over his freckled face.

"And that's how our Mr. No-One managed to puzzle us, when he walked up to our front door in the middle of the night, and hammered on it, and apparently didn't go back again," said Barney. "He just walked backwards in the prints he had already made."

"It was clever of you to find that out, Snubby," said Diana. "I never thought of that. I say, it's snowing quite hard. Have you looked yet to see if you can follow the tracks the men made when they carried off the boxes?"

"No. We'll go and do that now," said Barney. "If we don't, the tracks will be covered. Let's take our toboggans with us, then we can do a bit of sliding down the hills again. Skating's no use at the present moment."

But when they got to the outdoor shed where the toboggans were kept, they had a great shock. The toboggans were not there!

"Blow!" said Barney. "Who's taken those?"

"Stan and Jim, I bet," said Snubby, feeling quite brilliant. "AND I know what for."

The others stared at him. "You don't mean—you don't mean they've taken them to drag away those boxes," said Roger. "Oh, goodness! I hope you're not right."

But Snubby *was* right. When they made their way to the back door, outside which he had seen the big boxes set ready to take away, they found the toboggan tracks deeply indented in the snow there.

"Look—here's one set—and another," said Barney. "The runners of the toboggans have cut right down into the snow, almost to the ground."

"Yes. That's because those boxes were so heavy," said Snubby. "I bet those men saw our toboggans out in the shed there when they were snooping round, and one of them suddenly had the bright idea of using them to carry away the boxes. They'd be far too heavy to carry between them for any distance."

"Snubby's quite a detective," said Roger, half in earnest and half joking. "Get away, Loony; you're spoiling the tracks we're following. Go and play with Miranda."

But Miranda didn't want to play with Loony. She was

sitting on Barney's shoulder, trying to catch the snow-flakes as they floated down round her. She couldn't make out why they disappeared as soon as she caught them.

"Let's see if we can follow the tracks now," said Barney. "They may go to that boat-house—you never know. They'll be easy to follow, because the men can't have taken all the boxes at once on the toboggans—not more than two at a time, I should think—so they'd have to come to and fro a good many times, and make quite a track over the snow."

"Well, the tracks are beginning to go already," said Diana. "The snow is falling so thickly. Look, they go right round the house. Come on, let's follow them."

They began to follow the deeply-rutted tracks made by their toboggans. Snubby was feeling quite worried in case they would not find the toboggans; he had been so much looking forward to some more fun on them. Blow those men! What silly tricks would they be up to next?

The tracks led around the house and down the drive and then out of the gate. They led across the road and over the bank beside the pond. Then they led round the pond to where the boat-house was.

"There you are! We *thought* the men might have made the boat-house the next hiding-place for the boxes," said Barney, pleased.

"I'm surprised they didn't realise we could easily follow their tracks," said Roger.

"Well, they probably knew a thick fall of snow was coming, and they hoped the tracks would be hidden," said Barney. "Look—there's the boat-house. Let's go carefully in case the men are there."

So they went very carefully indeed, not talking or laughing, and not allowing Loony to bark even a small

bark. The boat-house loomed up, all white, with a new layer of snow on the roof.

The toboggan tracks, still deeply indented in the snow, led right round the boat-house to the front of it, where the lake itself began. There the tracks stopped.

"It looks as if the men brought the boxes here, and unloaded them into the boat-house," said Barney, in a low voice. "I wonder where our toboggans are?"

"Look! Is that them over there?" cried Snubby suddenly. "Loony, go and look."

Loony leapt over the snow to where the newly-fallen snow was half covering something brightly coloured. He scraped at it and barked loudly as the children walked towards the snow-covered heap.

"Yes, it *is* our toboggans," said Diana. "They emptied

them, and then threw them into the snow, hoping they would soon be hidden. I hope they haven't damaged them."

The children pulled them out. No, they were quite all right, although the paint had worn off where the heavy boxes had scraped them.

"Well, that's *something*, at any rate!" said Diana thankfully. "I was afraid we might not find them again, and they're such beauties."

"What are we going to do next? Look in the boat-house?" said Snubby eagerly. "The men can't be there, or surely they would have yelled at us."

"Well, we can at least go and peep through that broken window," said Barney. "I wonder how the men got the boxes into the boat-house. I suppose they have a key to the big doors that open above water-level to let the boats out in the summer."

They went round the boat-house to the broken window. Barney looked boldly inside, but it was so dark in there that snowy morning that he could not make out even the outline of the boats. He felt for his torch, but he had left it behind.

"Blow!" he said. "Oh, you've got yours, Snubby— good." He flashed it quickly through the window, and all round the shed. There was no one there at all; at least, no one that he could see. "Empty!" he said. "Not a soul here. The men must have gone off, now that they have disposed of the boxes. I expect they think they've hidden them so well that no one will discover them. They don't know that we've spotted this old boat-house for a hiding-place."

"Can you see the big boxes anywhere, Barney?" said Snubby, trying to peer in through the window too. "Let *me* look!"

"There's nothing to see in the way of boxes," said Barney. "But there wouldn't be. I expect they are under one of the boats, or covered with tarpaulins—sure to be, in fact. I bet they're here somewhere."

"Well, let's get in and look," said Roger. "We ought to be able to find them—it's not a very big place. Gosh, what a thrill to come across them! Do let's explore the boat-house, Barney. After all, it belongs to your family, so we won't be trespassing. Do let's."

CHAPTER NINETEEN

Rather Disappointing

BARNEY DID NOT NEED much persuading. As for Miranda, she didn't even wait for him to say yes. She leapt in through the broken window, and bounded here and there, looking at this and that with the greatest interest.

Barney began to break away the few remaining bits of broken glass in the window. "Very sharp edges!" he explained. "I don't want any of you to get bad cuts. Diana, you be very careful. Roger will help you up and I'll help you down inside the boat-house."

"I don't see *how* we can cut ourselves," said Snubby, impatient at having to wait. "We're all wearing thick gloves and boots. Buck up, Barney!"

Barney leapt inside the boat-house, and then Roger helped Diana up, and Barney helped her down. Roger followed and then Loony was handed up, and, last of all, Snubby came.

The boat-house was very dark indeed, for the daylight hardly penetrated through the dirty windows. And, in any case, it was a dark day with the sky full of snow; quite a different day from any they had had.

The children had two torches, and with them they began to look all over the boat-house. It was a typical place for keeping boats, full of all kinds of gear, ropes, tarpaulins and half-empty tins of paint. It smelt musty, and the boats were fast-locked in the ice. They had once floated in water there in the boat-house, but now their keels were no longer afloat, they were ice-bound. Barney quickly realised that there was no possible chance of finding any boxes under the boats. He set to work to look under the tarpaulins and sails that lay about here and there.

"I don't believe the boxes *are* here," said Diana, at last, tired of floundering about the dirty boat-shed without finding a single box.

"I'm beginning to think the same," said Barney, puzzled. "After all, Snubby said they were big ones, and there were a lot of them, and they just *can't* be here. We've hunted everywhere."

It was very disappointing indeed. "We followed the toboggan tracks here, where they ended, and yet we can't see any sign of the boxes," said Diana. "Could the men have hidden them anywhere under the snow, do you think?"

"Well, they *could*, I suppose," said Barney. "But even one box would need a big pile of snow to hide it, and a lot of boxes would certainly make quite a mountain under the snow. Still, we can look."

So the next thing they did was to flounder about in the thick snow round the boat-house. They felt sure that the men would not have carried such heavy boxes very far. Loony leapt about like a mad thing, not knowing what they were looking for, but hoping it might be something eatable. Miranda watched him from Barney's shoulder, wishing they could go home to the nice warm fire. She didn't like the snow that kept falling, falling, falling.

There were *no* boxes hidden anywhere round or about the boat-house. Snubby was most disappointed. What a waste of a morning! He was amazed when Barney said it was time to go back to lunch.

"Do you mean to say we've spent the whole morning looking for those beastly boxes?" he said, in disgust. "No tobogganing—no skating—not even a spot of snow-balling. What a waste. Well, anyway, I'm at least going to have a slide on the pond.

"It's got a covering of snow now. You won't be able to slide properly," said Diana.

But Snubby was on the pond, making a little slide of his own. Whooooosh! He slid along quite well and then fell over and slid the rest of the way on his trouser-seat.

As he was turning over to get up, he felt something under his hand and grasped it. What was it? He looked to see and gave a little exclamation.

"A cigarette packet—like the one Barney found in the boat-house. One of the men must have thrown it away last night, when he arrived at the boat-house with the toboggans."

He went back to the others and showed them the packet. "Same as before," he said. "The man must have chucked it away over the lake."

Barney took it to compare with the packet he had found in the boat-house. "Just the same," he said. "Hallo, it's not empty. It's half-full! Look!"

He was right. "Wasteful fellow, throwing away

cigarettes," said Snubby. "I shall really have to speak to Stan or Jim about it when I next see them!"

"Ass," said Roger. "I say, isn't it snowing fast! By the time we've had our dinner all tracks will have been covered with another fall of snow. It's a good thing we followed the toboggan tracks when we did."

"Not that it did us much good," said Diana. "We didn't find a sign of the boxes. I wonder where they can be. Well, I suppose they simply *must* be somewhere in the boat-house."

They were quite ravenous when they got back to Rat-a-Tat House. Mrs. Tickle was looking out anxiously for them. "You're late," she said. "I began to think you'd got lost in the snow."

"Has Mr. Icy-Cold been wandering about again, or Mr. No-One?" asked Snubby. "What—nobody been peeping in at your window? Life is getting dull for you, Mrs. Tickle."

"Go on with you," said Mrs. Tickle, giving Snubby a push. "You've got far too much to say. My word, how wet you are! You'll have to change your things before you sit down to your lunch."

"Oh, blow!" said Snubby. "There's such a nice smell coming from the kitchen. What is it, Mrs. Tickle?"

"You go and get those wet things off," said Mrs. Tickle. "And dry Loony too. What a mess he's in. Stop pouncing at my feet, Loony. Stop it, I say! And just you take one more of my dusters away and I'll put you in the dustbin."

Soon all the children were sitting down to hot vegetable soup. Miranda was given an apple, and nibbled it daintily, sitting on Barney's shoulder. But when she came to the black pips in the middle she was not so dainty. She picked them out with her tiny fingers and dropped them into Barney's soup.

"I don't know *why* we keep you and Loony," said Barney, fishing out the pips. "I really don't. Pests, both of you."

The monkey took hold of the lobe of Barney's ear, put her mouth close and chattered in a whispery voice. Barney listened gravely.

"All right. As you apologised so very nicely, I won't say anything more, Miranda."

Diana chuckled. It always amused her when Miranda whispered into Barney's ear, and Barney pretended to know exactly what the little monkey had said.

After rather a big meal, the children sat round the fire, talking about the peculiar happenings of the last few days. There was no point in going out, for the snow was still falling, and they even had to light the oil-lamp because the day was so dark.

Mrs. Tickle came in to see what they planned to do. "Don't you go out again," she said. "You might easily get lost in this. I can hardly find the way from my back door to the dustbin."

They all laughed. "Mrs. Tickle," said Snubby, "there's something worrying me. How are you going on for food? No tradesmen can come here, and we certainly can't get to Boffame village now."

"That *would* worry Snubby, of course," said Diana. "Food is his biggest interest."

Mrs. Tickle laughed. "You don't need to worry," she said. "I brought in a car-load of things from Boffame village when I came. Old man Hurdie at the post office, he said we were in for more snow, and told me to take all the food I could. Our larder is as cold as a refrigerator, and things keep fresh for a week. The bread's too stale to use now, though, so I'll bake some myself."

"Good idea," said Snubby, approvingly. "Shall I come and help you?"

"No, thank you," said Mrs. Tickle. "I don't want you messing about with my bread. All *you* want to do is to go and poke your nose into my larder. Just like my Tom, you are."

"What's going to happen if this snow goes on and on, and we get even more snowed up?" wondered Roger.

"I don't quite know," said Barney. "I wish we could telephone. I can't see that we can do anything except stay here till my father thinks it's time we came home, and somehow finds a means of transport."

"A large sleigh and a few husky dogs is what we really want," said Diana. "You know, the dogs the Eskimos have."

"Yes, a sleigh with bells on," said Snubby. "Jingle-jingle-jing——"

R-r-r-r-r-ring! Rr-r-r-r-ring!

A sudden, shrill ringing noise made them all jump. Then Barney gave a shout and leapt to his feet.

"The telephone bell! The wires must have been mended. *Now* we can get on to somebody and tell them about the queer happenings here. Hallo, hallo?"

Everyone sat up eagerly. Yes, it was Barney's father, anxiously asking how they were all getting on.

"Fine, Dad, fine!" said Barney. "But, I say, Dad, listen. Some very peculiar things have been going on here. . . . Yes, *peculiar* things, I said. . . . What? . . . Yes, I'll tell you if you'll hang on. Actually, I don't quite know what we ought to do about them. Well, here goes. . . ."

And Barney launched into the story of the last few days and all their strange happenings. What a tale it was!

CHAPTER TWENTY

The Telephone at Last!

MRS. TICKLE CAME RUNNING eagerly when she heard the welcome sound of the telephone bell once more. She and the others stood round Barney while he told the curious tale of the happenings at Rat-a-Tat House.

Barney's father was astonished.

"But what *is* all this?" he said, his voice ringing clearly through the telephone, so that even the others could hear it. "Disturbances in the night—breaking into the house and taking things from the cellar. Why was it locked when you came—it never is! And whatever had these fellows got hidden down there? Barney, is there anything more to tell me?"

"Yes, but I've told you all the *important* things," said Barney. "Can you possibly come down here, Dad? We are pretty well snowed up, and I'm not sure if a car can get through now. Thank goodness the telephone wires are mended."

"Yes, thank goodness," said his father. "Your grandmother was so worried about you all that I really think she was planning to put on my old skis and ski over hill and dale to you."

"Good old Granny!" said Barney, proud of the old lady. "I wouldn't be surprised to see her arriving here on skis—or even on a sledge drawn by reindeer. But, Dad, *is* it possible for a car to get through now, do you think?"

"No, we couldn't risk it," said his father. "Not to-day,

at any rate, with more snow falling. We'd probably get stuck in a snowdrift, and be marooned there for days. Why, some of the villages that are completely snowbound are having to be helped by helicopters. They drop food down, as you know. By the way, you've got plenty, haven't you?"

"Oh, yes," said Barney. "Dad, are you going to tell the police? I don't know what is in those boxes they hid in the cellar here, but it's quite certain they couldn't have got them away far, because no van or lorry could stir from here; so they must be hidden somewhere near, though goodness knows where."

"Yes, I thought that too," said his father. "I shall telephone the police at once, and let you know what they say."

Everyone was very thankful that the telephone wires were mended again. It was a real relief to be in touch with the outer world now that such strange things were happening. Barney put down the telephone and smiled round at the others.

"My father's on the job now," he said. "We needn't worry at all."

"Well, I'm glad to hear *that*," said Mrs. Tickle, as they all turned to go back to the warm sitting-room. As they went, they heard the little "ting" sound from the telephone that meant that someone had lifted the receiver. Barney swung round at once. It was Miranda, pretending to chatter into the telephone just as Barney had done!

"You little mimic," said Barney, snatching it from her paws and putting it back into place again. "Why we put up with you and Loony I really don't know."

Miranda scampered into the sitting-room and sat on top of the bear's head, looking very comical. Then she pretended to whisper something into the bear's ear.

"That monkey—she's a real comic!" said Mrs. Tickle. "Well, Barney, I'm relieved to think your father knows everything. What's he going to do?"

"Tell the police," said Barney promptly. "But what they can do at the moment I don't know—nobody can get through the thick snowdrifts, Dad says."

"Anyway, the men are not likely to worry us any more," said Diana. "They've got their goods, whatever they are, so we needn't expect any more rat-a-tatting, or snowmen wandering about."

"That's true," said Roger. "Anyway, I expect the men have gone off somewhere now they've hidden their boxes. It must have been very cold and uncomfortable sleeping in the boat-house."

"Well, they can't have gone far in this thick snow," said Barney, looking out of the window. "They're probably hiding in some outhouse or other, but I wonder what they do for food?"

"Don't forget that the cellar had plenty of tins on its shelves," said Snubby. "They could help themselves to those when they took the boxes."

"So they could," said Roger. "I never thought of that. And you know, we've never discovered yet how they got into the kitchen. We know they didn't come through the kitchen door, because Mrs. Tickle locked *and* bolted it, so even if they had a key, they couldn't have opened it."

"I'm going to have a look," announced Snubby. "A little detective work! Come on, let's see who can find out how the men got in."

Mrs. Tickle remembered that she had bread to make, and hurried back to her kitchen. The others began to go round the different rooms and try the windows to see if they were all closed and fastened.

"They're all well and truly shut, and fastened tight,"

said Barney. "All the downstairs windows, anyhow. I simply can't imag . . ."

He stopped as Mrs. Tickle came running into the room, looking excited.

"I've found out how they came in," she said. "Through my larder window! It's never had a very good catch, and they've forced it, so that they could climb in. Then they shut it after they went, and I never noticed that the catch was broken."

They all went to examine the broken catch. "Yes, you're right," said Snubby. "They got in this way. My word, what a big larder this is, Mrs. Tickle. And, I say, look at that pie. When is that for?"

"You keep your fingers off my shelves," said Mrs. Tickle, pushing Snubby out. "And who said you could take that jam tart? You're a caution, you are!"

Barney was glancing up at the top shelves. "I suppose nothing has been taken from here by the men, has it?" he asked. "They'd be glad of food now."

Mrs. Tickle fetched a chair and stood on it to look at the shelves above her head. "I don't know exactly what was here," she said. "There were tins and bottles and packets which I didn't touch. Ah, yes, they've taken a few things. I can see marks in the dust where tins or something stood. Yes, I think they took a few tins. Well, I never did!"

"Taking food off the shelves and boxes from the cellar. They'll be sleeping in our beds next," said Snubby. "You'd better look out, Mrs. Tickle."

"I'm certainly going to look *under* my bed to-night— with a rolling-pin in my hand," said Mrs. Tickle fiercely.

"We'll let Loony do that," said Snubby. "He'll simply *love* to go hunting under everyone's bed. Won't you, Loony?"

273

"Wuff!" said Loony, joyously, and tore up the stairs as if he meant to begin that very minute.

They all went back into the sitting-room, and gazed out of the window. What a change in the weather! No clear sky, no pale, clear sun, no view over the gleaming lake; only endless snowflakes falling from a leaden sky.

"I don't envy those men, Stan and Jim, wherever they are," said Snubby. "They must wish to goodness we'd never come down here. I bet they planned to shelter in Rat-a-Tat House if it got too cold in the boat-house."

"They probably hoped to remove those boxes by lorry sometime this week," said Barney. "Their plans have certainly been upset. I do wonder where they hid those heavy boxes. They *can't* be very far away. They could never carry them any distance."

"It's odd," said Roger. "They put them on our toboggans and dragged them down to the boat-house, then took them off the toboggans and hid them. But where?"

"I'm tired of thinking about it," said Diana. "Let's play a game. Let's have a jigsaw battle. We've brought plenty, haven't we?"

"Yes," said Snubby. "I'll get four. They're in the cupboard."

Soon they were all sitting at the big round table, each with a box of jigsaw pieces. "Go!" said Roger, and they all emptied out their pieces quickly, and began to sort them at top speed.

"I always pick out the blue sky bits first," said Diana. "Snubby, you've dropped a piece on the floor already."

Miranda was a little nuisance when jigsaws were being done. She was fascinated by the tiny coloured pieces, and longed to help.

"*Don't*, Miranda," said Snubby, exasperated. "That

piece doesn't go there. Now you've knocked out another piece. Barney, put her on your shoulder."

But she wouldn't stop there, and Diana thought that the only sensible thing to do was to give the little monkey a jigsaw of her own to play with, so she fetched another from the cupboard.

Miranda was delighted and proud. She settled down on the table, her jigsaw pieces spread in front of her, and fiddled about with them, chattering in her little monkey voice. Mrs. Tickle could hardly believe her eyes when she came in with the tea-tray later on, and saw her.

"Well, I never!" she said. "That monkey beats everything. Are you ready for tea—or shall I leave the tray here till you've finished?"

"I've won!" said Snubby, fitting in his last piece. "I'm first! What do I get? The biggest slice of chocolate cake, and more scones than anyone? I've won!"

And just then the telephone bell rang again urgently—r-r-r-r-ing—r-r-r-ring-ring—r-r-r-ring-ring! Ah, what was the news now from Barney's father?

CHAPTER TWENTY-ONE

Diana has an Idea

BARNEY RAN to the telephone at once. Had his father told the police? What had they planned?

"Hallo!" he said. "Hallo! . . . Yes, it's me, Barney, Dad. . . . Yes, I'll listen carefully."

He stood with his ear glued to the telephone, nodding his head and saying "yes—oh, yes" now and again in an excited manner, his eyes sparkling. The others crowded round trying to hear what was being said, but Barney had clamped the receiver so close to his ear in order not to miss a single word, that they could make out very little.

Snubby could hardly stand still, he wanted so badly to know what Barney's father was saying, and at last he heard Barney say good-bye.

"Right, Dad. I'll do all you say, you can depend on me. I'll tell Mrs. Tickle too. I say, how *very* exciting! See you to-morrow. Good-bye!"

He put the receiver back and turned to the others, his eyes still shining.

"What did he say, what did he say?" almost shouted Snubby.

"I'll tell you. Come into the sitting-room," said Barney. "Mrs. Tickle! Oh, there you are! You come too. I've got exciting news."

They all went into the sitting-room, Loony as excited as the rest, though he didn't know what about. Miranda jigged up and down on Barney's shoulder, a piece of jigsaw puzzle still in one tiny paw.

They all sat down, and Barney began:

"My father got in touch with the police and told them everything. The police were *very* interested indeed. My father says he thinks they know what is in the boxes, but they didn't tell him. They're coming down here to-morrow morning to investigate."

"To-morrow—in this snow!" said Roger, looking out of the window where the snow was still falling gently. "No car would get through."

"They're coming by *helicopter*!" said Barney. "And we've got to prepare a landing-place for them."

"Whew!" said Snubby. "This *is* exciting! How do we do that?"

"Well, there's a big lawn at the back of the house,"

said Barney. "Very big, and quite flat, of course. And we're to clear as large a space as we can in the middle of it, so that the helicopter won't land in deep snow."

"Let's go and begin now," said Snubby, leaping up, quite forgetting that it was almost dark.

"Ass," said Roger. "Shut up, and let Barney go on."

"We're to mark the landing place somehow," said Barney. "With dark cloths, or something."

"We can take down all the navy-blue curtains upstairs," said Mrs. Tickle at once, as excited as the rest. "We can clear a big square and lay the curtains all round it. If they're likely to blow away we can weight them down with something heavy—tins of food, or something like that."

"But how many people are coming?" said Diana. "I thought helicopters couldn't take many."

"Three people are coming," said Barney. "My father, an inspector of police, and a sergeant, I think, Dad said. It's the only way they can come, and the inspector says it's absolutely *essential* that they should get those boxes."

"What can be in them?" wondered Snubby, jigging up and down in his chair just like Miranda. "I say, isn't this a thrill? I hope those men won't hear the helicopter coming."

"Dad says it doesn't matter if they do," said Barney. "He says they'll merely think it's been sent to drop food or to see if we're all right. Anyway, he says it's more important at the moment to find the boxes than the men."

"Whew!" said Snubby. "Let's have another hunt for them then. We *know* they can't be far away; they're too heavy to carry any distance."

"Well, we did look all round and about, and in the snow and in the boat-house," said Diana. "Honestly, I

don't think the men could have carried them any distance
at all, once they took them off the toboggan."

"No. That's quite true," said Barney thoughtfully.
"I've puzzled about that too. We know quite well where
the toboggan tracks ended—by the lake-side."

"I suppose," said Diana suddenly, "I suppose . . .
No, it couldn't be that."

"Couldn't be what? What have you thought of?" said
Barney at once.

"Well, we found that the toboggan tracks ended by
the lake-side, and we found the toboggans themselves
nearby in the snow," said Diana. "But it's quite possible,
I suppose, for the men to have slid the toboggans *across*
the lake, to the bank on the other side, and have hidden
the boxes there. And then slid the toboggans all the way
back to where we found them in the snow?"

The others stared at her, taking in this new idea. Barney
slapped his knee and made Miranda jump in surprise.

"Yes! Yes, it's not only possible, it's very, very likely.
If you remember, the lake was free of snow that night.
We'd been skating on it all day, and the toboggans would
slide over it easily enough. And then the snow fell and
hid any tracks made over the lake! Even a thin layer
would hide any cuts made by the runners of the toboggans
as they slid over the ice, weighted down by the heavy
boxes."

"And I've thought of something else," almost shouted
Snubby, making Loony jump this time. "That cigarette
packet I found some way out on the lake—with cigarettes
still in it. It wasn't thrown there by the men, it was
dropped by one of them as he pulled a toboggan along."

"Yes. That's right," said Roger, clapping Snubby on
the back. "That puzzled me too. Now you've solved
that little mystery, Snubby. Of course, it was *dropped*, not

thrown. I say, I wish it wasn't dark. We could go across the lake and hunt for hiding-places somewhere on the opposite bank."

"Let's take our torches and go," said Snubby, jumping up and making Loony bark.

"No, certainly not," said Mrs. Tickle at once. She had been listening to all this in astonishment, not uttering a word. But now she had *her* little say. "Going out into the thick snow at this time of night, when it's pitch dark and freezing cold—you'd all be lost, and frozen to death by the morning."

"Stuff!" cried Snubby, too excited to listen to reason. "I'm going. Come on, Barney."

"No, Snubby, Mrs. Tickle's right," said Barney. "It would be a mad thing to do. We can easily wait till morning. We'll have to be up early. It will take us ages to clear the thick snow off the lawn, and make a square big enough for the helicopter to land in safety."

"We'll have to find spades," said Diana.

"There are some in the gardener's shed," said Mrs. Tickle. "We'll get them out to-morrow. Now, look, don't you *want* any tea? The buttered toast and the scones will all be cold."

"Gosh! I'd forgotten all about tea. However *could* I do that?" said Snubby, sounding most surprised. "Di, lay the cloth, quick. I'll help to set out the things. Buttered toast all going cold. What a thing to happen!"

Mrs. Tickle laughed and went back to the kitchen to get the tea made in the big brown teapot. That Snubby! Just like her Tom, he was, always hungry, always one for a joke. She heard the patter of feet and looked round quickly. It was Loony, and even as she turned she saw him make off with her hearth brush. By the time she had put down the kettle and teapot she was holding he had

279

disappeared upstairs. Goodness knew where he would put that brush!

Tea was a most excited meal, with everyone discussing helicopters, police, possible hiding-places for the boxes on the other side of the lake, and where Stan and Jim, the two men, could be.

"They might be with the boxes," said Snubby, putting potted meat on to his fourth piece of toast. "They might have built themselves a snow-house like ours, and have made a fine hide-out, with plenty of our tins for food, and snow for water."

"In that case we'd better go carefully," said Diana, alarmed. "*I* don't want to find those two men. Let the police do that. But I'd love to find the boxes."

"We'll take the toboggans with us when we go across the lake to-morrow," said Roger. "Then if we *do* find the boxes we can bring two back, one on each toboggan. Wouldn't the police be pleased to see them!"

They were not at all tired that night, for they had had too little exercise, and Mrs. Tickle found it very difficult to get them to bed. She badly wanted to go herself, for she had baked and cooked a good deal that day, and was tired. She peeped in at the sitting-room door at half-past nine.

"Aren't you ready?" she said. "I've lighted all your candles for you out here. Please come quickly."

"Right," said Barney, hearing the tired note in Mrs. Tickle's voice. "You go on up, Mrs. Tickle. We're just coming. We'll knock at your door to tell you we're safely upstairs."

They talked for ten minutes more and then went into the hall to get their candles, but not one was alight! The hall was in complete darkness.

"Don't turn out the oil-lamp!" shouted Barney to

Diana. "Someone's blown out our candles. NOW what's up? Surely our Mr. No-One isn't up to his tricks again. It's pitch-dark here in the hall. I'll just feel about for the candles and see what's happening."

"Oh, *dear*!" said Diana. "Surely we're not going to have any upsets to-night! Buck up, Barney. Wait, I've got a torch. I'll shine it round the hall and see if anyone's about."

She shone it nervously round the dark hall. And yes—someone *was* hiding there. The beam fell on a small furry head, peeping out from behind the back of a chair, with two bright eyes gleaming mischievously.

"It's *Miranda*!" cried Snubby. "Oh, you little wretch! *You* blew out all the candles, didn't you? Loony, get her!"

But before Loony could get near her the little monkey was bounding up the stairs in glee, chattering away in delight. Aha! *She* had played a trick that Loony would never even think of.

CHAPTER TWENTY-TWO

Here Comes the Helicopter

NEXT MORNING dawned clear and bright. The snow had ceased falling, and once again the sun shone from a clear, pale-blue sky. All the children were pleased, because this would make things much easier for the helicopter.

They were up nice and early, and gobbled their breakfast. Diana went to help Mrs. Tickle with the washing-up, and the boys brought in wood for the fires. Then they went to look for spades in the big gardener's shed not far from the kitchen. It was locked, but Mrs. Tickle gave them the key. They unlocked it and looked round for spades.

"Good!" said Barney, as his eyes fell on quite a selection. "Big ones and little ones. Here, have this nice little one, Snubby."

"Don't be a fat-head," said Snubby, annoyed. "I'm as strong as you are—stronger, if anything."

Diana and Mrs. Tickle came out to join them as they were arguing about the spades. Mrs. Tickle rolled up her sleeves and chose a hefty spade. Barney looked at her admiringly. Whatever she did, she did *very* thoroughly.

They went to the lawn, their spades over their shoulders. The snow was quite thick and deep here—about two feet, Barney thought. "Let's mark out a good-sized square," he said. "And begin to clear it at once."

They marked out the square, and then began to shovel away the snow vigorously. It was very hard work. Snubby began it much too vigorously and was forced to take a rest before the others did. "You should have taken the small spade as I told you," said Barney, his blue eyes twinkling.

They soon had quite a good piece of the middle of the square cleared. "It's big enough for a helicopter to land here now," said Roger, considering it carefully. "Though it would be a pretty near thing. Mrs. Tickle, what about you and Diana going to get those dark curtains now, and we can lay them round the clear patch as soon as we hear the noise of the helicopter. We don't know when it will come, but we'll go on digging hard till it does."

Mrs. Tickle and Diana disappeared indoors. They came out in half an hour with armfuls of the dark curtains, taken down from the upstairs rooms.

They laid them down in a heap and joined the boys
in their digging. No helicopter arrived, and soon the
diggers felt as if they simply MUST have another rest.
Barney was digging in his shirt-sleeves now, and seriously
considering working bare-backed, he was so hot.

Mrs. Tickle went indoors and brought out some buns
and ice-cold lemonade. Nobody wanted a hot drink
just then! They ate and drank eagerly, for the exercise
had made them very hungry and thirsty. Then they set
to work again.

"It's a quarter to twelve," said Mrs. Tickle, at last.
"I think I'd better go in and make some soup, and peel
potatoes, and so on. With three extra lunches, we'll need
plenty of food. Diana, you come too; you've done enough
digging."

"Yes, go and help Mrs. Tickle," said Barney, who saw
that Diana was getting tired. "We've not much more to
do. There's a fine big clear place for the helicopter to
land now."

Diana went in to help Mrs. Tickle, and the boys
resumed their shovelling. Certainly they had made a
big enough landing-place now. Barney felt quite proud
of it.

Then, through the clear, frosty air, there came a distant
throbbing. The boys looked up. It must be the helicopter.

"Quick! Spread out the dark curtains!" shouted Barney,
suddenly excited. "And don't you dare to run off with
any, Loony—or you either, Miranda!"

Mrs. Tickle and Diana came running out as soon as
they heard the helicopter, and helped to put the dark
curtains all round the big, cleared square of lawn. They
could now see the machine quite clearly—not a very big
one—its vanes spinning above it.

It came nearer and nearer, and the noise grew louder.

"It's coming down! It's seen our marked-out square!" shouted Snubby, in intense excitement. "Here, helicopter, here; this way, this way!"

Carefully and gracefully the helicopter descended to the clearing. It came to earth with hardly a jerk, and the sergeant, who was piloting it, jumped out first. He grinned round at the excited children.

"Fine!" he said. "We saw our landing ground miles away. Splendid!"

Then came Barney's father, Mr. Martin, and last of all the trim, burly inspector, with a grim mouth, but kind eyes twinkling under bushy brows.

"Well!" he said. "Good morning to you all. You've had a little excitement, I hear."

Mr. Martin smiled round, glad to see everyone looking well and cheerful. "I'd never have let you come if I'd known you were going to be snow-bound like this," he said. "Come along—let's go into the house and talk."

Off they went, and Mrs. Tickle became very busy indeed in the kitchen, while the others filed into the sitting-room to exchange their news.

The inspector and the sergeant listened to everything with great interest, the sergeant taking notes all the time. The children had to tell the story over again right from the very beginning. The inspector asked many questions, and was pleased with the clear, ready replies.

"Intelligent children, these," he said, turning to Mr. Martin, who had sat silent, astonished once again at the strange story. He turned back to the children.

"Mr. Martin says you tried to find the boxes, after the men had taken them away, but couldn't," he said. "Have you any idea at all where they *could* have been taken?"

"Yes, sir," said Snubby eagerly, and he told him of their latest idea—that the men had slid the toboggans across the lake, taking the boxes to the other side. "But the snow hid their tracks across," he said, "so we actually thought that they had taken the toboggans no farther than the boat-house; we never thought of them going across the frozen lake. And I found a half-full packet of cigarettes out on the lake, too; they must have dropped it there on their way across."

Now the inspector and the sergeant were sitting up straight. "Ah!" said the Inspector, "now this is something. It's obvious that the men couldn't *carry* the boxes far, so . . ."

"Sir, what's in the boxes, do you think?" asked Snubby, longing to know.

"We'll have to wait and see," said the inspector

tantalisingly. "If it's what we hope it is, we shall be very, very pleased."

Mrs. Tickle appeared in the doorway. "I hope I don't interrupt, gentlemen," she said politely. "But I've got a meal all ready to bring in, if you'd like it now. Or I'll keep it hot for you."

"No, no—we'll have it now, Mrs. Tickle," said Mr. Martin at once. "Very good of you to think of it. Have you much more questioning to do, Inspector?"

"None," said the inspector, and the sergeant snapped the elastic band round his black note-book, and put his pencil away. "But we'll do a little searching this afternoon, if you children will show me the lake and the boat-house and all the rest. We may be able to find those boxes."

"Oh, good!" said Snubby, rubbing his hands. "I say, things are getting pretty exciting, aren't they?"

"Very," said the inspector, smiling at the red-haired, freckled boy with the spaniel at his heels.

"I'll go and help Mrs. Tickle," said Diana, and Roger went too. Miranda leapt off Barney's shoulder and scampered out of the door as well, much to the astonishment of the two policemen.

"She's gone to help herself to something she fancies," said Barney, grinning. "She's probably lifting the lids off the dishes to see what's inside."

Mrs. Tickle had provided a very good lunch indeed— "quite smashing," as Snubby said—and stayed in the room to help to serve such a large company. The two policeman stopped being rather ponderous and sharp-eyed, and joked and laughed as cheerfully as Mr. Martin did. Altogether it was a most enjoyable meal, especially for Loony, who was provided with an astonishing amount of scraps under the table.

Miranda was thrilled, because besides a big steamed

jam sponge pudding, there was a dish of pineapple and tinned cream, and Barney had to keep his eyes on her. She loved pineapple and would help herself out of the dish whenever she thought there was nobody looking.

"And now," said the inspector, having thoroughly enjoyed the lunch and the company too, "now I think we'd better get down to business. We will all go out and you will show me the boat-house, and anything else I need to see. Then we will trek across the frozen lake to the other side, and see if we can find where those boxes are hidden."

All was excitement immediately. The four children rushed to get their coats and scarves, while the three men lighted cigarettes and waited for them.

Soon they were all ready, with Loony rushing about madder than usual, holding a small duster in his mouth, and defying everyone's efforts to get it from him. Miranda waited her chance and dropped down on his back as he rushed past. In anger and surprise Loony turned on her and barked, and the duster dropped from his mouth.

In a trice Miranda had it in her paw, and was up on Barney's shoulder again, stuffing it down his neck for safety.

"What a pair!" said the inspector, chuckling. "As bad as a couple of children." Everyone laughed—and then out of the house they went, stopping to show the inspector the enormous lion's head knocker on the front door.

"H'm. Those fellows badly wanted you out of the house, didn't they?" said the inspector, eyeing the knocker. "Well, come along; we've got a lot of work to do this afternoon."

CHAPTER TWENTY-THREE

Snubby Stubs his Toe

THE CHILDREN TOOK the three men down to the boat-house first of all, and showed them the broken window there, and the place where the toboggan tracks had ended.

"And that's where we found the toboggans, over there, almost hidden by the snow," said Snubby, pointing.

The policemen went into the boat-house and searched for a while, saying very little. They came back, and shook their heads.

"Impossible to hide anything much there," said the inspector. "But there's no doubt the *men* hid there, by the number of cigarette ends and spent matches. Now, let's go across the lake. Scrape the snow away a bit here and there, in case we can find any tracks on the ice underneath."

They scraped here and there, but could find no tracks of the toboggan runners. They reached the other side of the lake and began a systematic search. The inspector allotted searching spots to each of them. The drifts of snow were high in places, and it was just possible that the boxes might have been hidden there.

It was tiring work, stamping in the drifts and searching in the snow for anything hard, such as a box. They soon exhausted the spots the inspector had allotted and went farther afield, but here the snow lay perfectly smooth and unbroken, and it was fairly obvious that no big boxes were hidden there, or the snow would have lain unevenly.

"Well, we don't seem very successful, do we?" said Mr. Martin, disappointed. "We've pretty well examined the whole of this bank of the lake. The rest of it has bushes growing down to the edge, and it's unlikely the men would go there."

"I think we'd better give up for this afternoon," said the inspector. "I don't imagine that the men will try to retrieve their boxes while it's so difficult to get transport—such as a lorry—to take them away by road. Wherever they are, those boxes will have to remain hidden till the roads are clear of snow. THEN the men will lose no time in collecting them from their hiding-place and getting them away one night."

"Right," said Mr. Martin. "We'll go back to Rat-a-Tat House for tea then. It is getting dusk now. We can hardly see what we're doing."

They turned to go back across the lake. The weather had turned warmer, and in places the snow was now melting fast. They came to the lake and stepped on it to go back to the boat-house.

Mr. Martin and the two policemen went first, talking together. Snubby and Loony came last, shuffling through the snow that lay on the frozen surface.

Snubby suddenly stubbed his foot against something hard, and gave a yell of pain.

"What's up?" said Barney.

"I've stubbed my toe," said Snubby, standing on one foot and holding the other. "Oooh, I felt it right through my rubber boot!"

"Don't make such a fuss," said Barney. "Just a bit of frozen snow, that's all."

"It was *not*," said Snubby, indignantly, and immediately began to hunt for whatever it was he had stubbed his toe on. He soon found it, and uncovered it.

"Here, look, Barney!" he shouted. "It's a great piece of solid ice. LOOK! *Not* a bit of frozen snow. No wonder it hurt my toe."

Barney turned back impatiently, and looked at the piece of ice Snubby had uncovered. It was rather curious —large, circular, and thick, and lay flat on the frozen surface of the pond. Barney stared at it in surprise.

"Why is it round like that?" he said. "What a *peculiar* piece of ice." He looked at it more closely and then gave a yell that startled Snubby considerably.

"Hey, Dad! Inspector! Come back here a minute— quick!"

Snubby stared at Barney as if he had gone mad, and Loony rushed round in circles, barking loudly as he always did if there was any excitement about. Mr. Martin and the two policemen turned in surprise and made their way back as quickly as they could. "What is it?" said the inspector. "Have you found something?"

"Yes, this piece of ice," said Barney. "Look—perfectly round, and quite large. It's been sawn out of the icy surface of the pond."

"Ah! *Now* we're getting warm," said the inspector, and knelt to examine the circle of ice. "Perfectly round— done with a saw, of course, as you say. But why? Aha! This is very interesting. What a pity it's getting so dark! Let me see, now. Could you boys run back to the house and get torches and some spades to shovel away the snow just here on the ice? We must see where this circle was sawn from."

Tremendously excited, the four children raced back to the house, grabbed torches, found spades, and raced out again, hardly replying to Mrs. Tickle's astonished questions.

Torches shone on to the snow near where Snubby had

found the round piece of ice. Shovels were used vigorously to shovel away the snow round about.

"We'd better be careful not to fall into the hole made when this piece of ice was cut out," said Roger.

"No fear of that," said Mr. Martin. "The water below would have frozen again almost immediately."

In under five minutes there came a yell from Barney. "I've found the place. This must be it. Look!"

They went to him, and shone their torches at his feet. There, uncovered by the snow was a circle of ice clearly defined on the surface of the pond, showing where a round piece had been removed, and where the water had frozen again.

"It looks rather like one of those round drain-covers you see in the road," said Diana. "Goodness! Do you think—do you possibly think—that the men shoved the boxes down under the ice, knowing it would freeze again and hide them safely?"

"Looks like it," said the inspector grimly, peering down at the new circle of ice, so neatly filling in the place where the first one had been removed. "What an ingenious idea! Stan and Jim are evidently men with brains."

"What shall we do, sir?" asked the sergeant, with great interest. "It's getting very dark."

"I think we can safely leave things till to-morrow," said the inspector. "The men are not likely to try to remove the boxes from the lake until the weather is good enough to arrange for a lorry to collect them. We'll be along here to-morrow and have a little excitement sawing out another piece of ice ourselves, and probing down into the water below."

Everyone felt very excited, but rather disappointed that they would have to wait till the next day. "I shan't sleep to-night for thinking of it," said Snubby. "Sir, we could do it all right now, surely. I'll get a saw, and there are plenty of candles."

"Ass! They'd blow out," said Roger. The inspector didn't even bother to reply to Snubby. He led the way back to Rat-a-Tat House, feeling very pleased. Nobody took any notice of the way Snubby limped, and he felt cross. If he hadn't stubbed his toe so painfully against that big round piece of ice, nobody would EVER have found that most ingenious hiding-place. He thought they might at least sympathise with him over his toe.

Mrs. Tickle had to hear the news of course, and was surprised and excited.

"To think of that now," she said. "Making a hole in the ice and dropping the boxes down. What a thing to do! Well, I must say those men are full of ideas. What with hammering at the knocker in the middle of the night to scare us away, and pretending to be the snowman walking round and about! I'll be glad when you've got them safely under lock and key, Mr. Inspector, sir."

"So shall I," said the inspector grimly. "Very glad indeed. Of course, we don't know for certain that we *shall* find the boxes down there, nor what they contain. But I'm hoping—yes, I'm certainly hoping."

"Fancy having to wait a whole night before we find out," complained Snubby bitterly. "Loony, what about you and me slipping off at midnight and finding out for ourselves? Are you game?"

Loony was game for anything, of course, and said so, but the inspector did not approve of such fantastic suggestions.

"Nobody is to go near the pond again until the sergeant and I go to-morrow morning," he announced. "We will all have a nice quiet evening, and look forward to some good luck to-morrow."

Certainly the evening passed pleasantly enough, for the inspector proved to have a fund of astonishingly interesting stories. Snubby listened open-mouthed to the ways of the police in tackling crime.

"My word!" he said, in awe, as the inspector described the capture of a particularly clever spy. "I'm *never* going to do anything wrong, *never*. Nobody has any chance at all against people like you, Inspector. I think I'll join the police force when I grow up. Loony would be awfully good at tracking thieves, I bet he would."

"He's just tracked down another of Mrs. Tickle's brushes," said Diana. "Look—it's her hearth-brush again. Loony, have you no interests in life besides brushes and dusters?"

Loony deposited the brush at Snubby's feet as if he were bringing him a really fine bone. Snubby frowned at him.

"Idiot! Here am I praising you up to the inspector and you do a silly thing like this. Take it back at once, and apologise to Mrs. Tickle. Quick, before Miranda gets it!"

Mr. Martin laughed. Snubby always amused him. "Time you went to bed," he said. "Remember, we may have some difficult work to do to-morrow."

CHAPTER TWENTY-FOUR

The End of the Mystery

SNUBBY WAS UP first the next morning, with Loony racing round his feet. Mrs. Tickle came downstairs a few minutes after Snubby, and found him trying to rake out the kitchen fire and light it for her.

"I couldn't sleep a minute longer," he explained. "I can't think why the inspector isn't up. Surely it is his duty to get on with this job as soon as possible?"

"You're a caution, you are," said Mrs. Tickle. "Leave that fire alone, now. You've made ten times more mess than I do. Go and wake the others, because breakfast is to be earlier than usual."

"Thank goodness for that," said Snubby, and went back upstairs with Loony at his heels.

Breakfast that morning seemed a waste of time to the four children—even to Snubby, who liked a very big one, and could always be counted on to finish up the last piece of toast. But to-day he was as impatient as the others.

At last, armed with two saws and some thick rope, the little party set off to the lake. Miranda was on Barney's shoulder and Loony was finding that now the snow had melted on the lake, the surface was slippery again, and his legs most unaccountably slid away in all directions, making him feel most ridiculous.

They came to where they had discovered the newly-frozen circle of ice on the lake; close beside it was the loose piece on which Snubby had stubbed his toe. The inspector nodded to the sergeant, who knelt down and tried to insert the end of the bigger saw into the ice.

It wasn't easy, but at last the saw was really working, and the sergeant was puffing and panting as he sawed round the frozen circle. At last it was done—the circle was complete.

The sergeant inserted a wedge and heaved up the round piece of ice he had sawed round. Up it came, and he deposited it beside the first one. Everyone peered down into the icy water.

"I can see *some*thing," said the sergeant, his head almost in the hole. "I can just about reach it, sir, I think."

He put his arm down into the water and groped about. His hand felt a rope and he pulled at it. Up it came and he dragged it out of the hole.

"It's fastened to something down below, sir," he said, tugging at it. "We'll have to heave hard, I'm afraid."

"Tie that rope to ours," said the inspector. "Double ours to make it strong. Come away from the hole, boy—you'll fall in."

Snubby removed himself in disappointment. The sergeant knotted the two ropes together, and then he and the inspector did a little heaving.

"Something's coming up," panted the sergeant, pleased. "Whoa-steady, here she comes! Anyone else like to help pull? It's very heavy."

The edge of a box now showed through the big hole—then the top of it. And with another heave the big box came right over the edge of the hole and slid along the ice. The sergeant promptly fell over backwards, much to Loony's joy.

Everyone gazed at the box. "Yes," said Snubby joyfully. "That's one of the boxes the men took out of the cellar. Hurrah!"

"Shall I open it now, sir?" asked the sergeant, getting up carefully. The inspector nodded, whereupon the sergeant produced a most interesting collection of tools in a leather case. How Snubby wished he had a set like that!

With a great deal of care and manipulation the sergeant at last got the lid open, and the children stared down inside. The box had been quite water-tight, apparently, for there was no moisture inside. Something gleamed up brightly as the children bent over to look.

"Guns!" said Snubby, in awe. "I say, look at those guns!"

The inspector and the sergeant looked at one another and nodded. Yes, this was what they had been hoping for and expecting. Mr. Martin nodded too.

"Good work!" he said. "Let's hope we've got all the guns down there that those fellows stole from the army camp. I suppose they were going to be shipped out of the country secretly, and used against us somewhere."

"I *say*! Mrs. Tickle won't at all like the idea of having had dozens of guns stored in her cellar," said Snubby. "She's really scared of them. Are we going to get up the whole lot? Look—there's a rope hanging down from this one, into the water. Is it tied to the next box? Are they all tied to one another?"

"Shut up, chatterbox," said Barney, eager to catch every word said by the three men. This was a serious business—traitor's business!

A thought struck him. Traitor's business—that rang a bell in his mind. Yes—what was that old legend?—the knocker, the lion's head knocker was never sounded unless there was a traitor in Rat-a-Tat House! And there *was* a traitor when that knocker sounded—it was sounded by the traitor himself. Barney made up his mind to tell the others this idea as soon as he got them alone. Very, very curious!

"Fetch your toboggan, boy," said the inspector to Snubby. "We'll drag this box back to the house for further examination. As for the other boxes, we'll leave them till I can get men down here to look at them. Their contents are probably exactly the same as this."

Snubby sped off and brought back his toboggan. They lifted the heavy box on to it and Snubby and Roger dragged it over the slippery ice. What a find!

"What about the other boxes, sir? Suppose the thieves come and get them!" said Snubby.

"They won't come until the snow has gone and they can get a lorry down the roads," said the inspector. "And a few men to help them."

"But aren't you going to set a watch, sir?" said Snubby. "I mean, you don't know when they might come."

"The first *lorry* that gets though to this district will be watched," said the inspector good-humouredly. "And just in case you think we don't know our business, I can tell you that as soon as the lorry is loaded with the guns, and the men drive off, it will be stopped, searched and driven off to the nearest police station. Does this meet with your approval?"

"Oh, sir!" said Snubbby, actually blushing. "I know you know your business—I just thought—well, those men may come along and get those boxes out, and——"

"But don't you think it is a good idea to let *them* drag them out, and load them into the lorry, so that we haven't anything to do but drive it to the police station?" said the inspector. "Or would you like to take on the job of getting them out yourself?"

"Oh, *no*, sir," said Snubby. "I—well,—er—er . . ." And he dried up completely, annoyed at being laughed at by the burly inspector.

The inspector and the sergeant, with the box of guns, took off in their helicopter after lunch. The children were sorry to see them go—everything had been so very exciting! They waved till the helicopter was a speck in the sky and then went indoors.

"Dad, are you going to stay on with us?" said Barney, delighted to have his father with them.

"Yes, I thought I would," said Mr. Martin, smiling. "If I shan't spoil the party."

"Oh, *no*," said Diana, who liked Barney's father very much. "We'd love to have you. I'm sorry the snow is going, though—there won't be much more tobogganing or snowballing—but there'll still be skating."

"My father skates marvellously," said Barney, with the note of pride that was always in his voice when he spoke of his father. "Dad, isn't Cousin Dick coming after all? Didn't his cold get better?"

"Yes, but there wasn't room in the helicopter for him too," said Mr. Martin. "So it will be just me and the rest of you."

"Good!" said Barney, pleased. "Jolly good! I wonder if we'll still be here when those men come to get their guns from the lake. I do hope so."

"Yes, I expect we shall," said his father. "That will be another bit of excitement to round off a most exciting holiday. My word, fancy your coming down here for a bit of winter sport just when the men had hidden their stolen guns in our cellars. What a shock it must have been for them to see lights in the house all of a sudden."

"Snubby *really* solved most of the mystery," said Diana generously. "If it hadn't been for him things wouldn't have turned out so well."

"You're right!" said Snubby, beaming. "*I* heard the noise in the night and went down and found the boxes ..."

"I bet it was *Loony* who growled or something," said Roger. "And don't forget that you managed to get yourself well and truly locked up."

"And it was Snubby who knocked his toe against that round piece of ice and made us realise where it came from and set us on the track of the guns," went on Diana. "Yes, and it was Snubby who found that cigarette packet half-full of cigarettes."

"In fact, we might almost say that Snubby solved the mystery of Rat-a-Tat House!" said Mr. Martin, smiling at Snubby's delighted face. "He deserves a reward. Anything you'd particularly like, Snubby?"

"Yes," said Snubby at once. "There's something I badly want to do—can I do it?"

"What is it?" asked Mr. Martin cautiously.

"I want to go and bang that lion's head knocker on the door," said Snubby. "CRASH it down, like Mr. No-One did that night. You've no idea what it sounds like, Mr. Martin."

"Ass," said Barney. "Let him do it, Dad. He won't be happy till he does bang that knocker. Little things please little minds, you know."

"That knocker is an ENORMOUS thing," said Snubby indignantly. "Come on, Loony—let's go and have a bash."

"Tell Mrs. Tickle what you're going to do, for goodness' sake," called Diana, "or she'll go up in smoke. And Barney, hang on to Miranda. Look, she's up on the mantelpiece with her snap-cards again, bless her!"

Snubby went to the front door and opened it, Loony at his heels. "Loony," said Snubby solemnly, "I and I alone, solved the Rat-a-Tat Mystery—and we're telling the world we did it. Stand ready!"

He lifted the huge knocker with both hands and then hammered with all his might on the door.

RAT-A-TAT-TAT! RAT-A-TAT-TAT! RAT-A-TAT-TAT!

All right, Snubby, we heard you. Now do go and sit down and be quiet!

THE END

The Rubadub Mystery

The Rubadub Mystery was first published in a single volume in the U.K. in
hardback in 1951 by William Collins Sons & Co. Ltd., and in paperback by
Armada in 1969.

CHAPTER ONE

PLANS FOR A HOLIDAY

"SNUBBY!" called a cross voice. "SNUBBY! Didn't I tell you to tie Loony up?"

Snubby came flying downstairs to his aunt. "Oh, Aunt Susan, I did! Has he got loose again? Oh, I say—did he make all that mess in the hall?"

The black spaniel sat in the middle of a few sheets of torn-up newspaper, his tongue hanging out. He looked exactly as if he was grinning.

"That's your uncle's morning newspaper," said his aunt. "He hasn't even read it yet. Snubby, you know that we're very rushed trying to get everything done before we leave to-day. I really *can* not have Loony rushing about loose."

" I'll shut Loony into my room, Mother," said Diana, coming up. " And I'll lock the door and put the key in my pocket. Then Loony will be safe."

" Well, nothing else in your room will be safe!" said Mrs. Lynton. " Do what you like with him—but keep him out of my way this morning! We shall never get off this afternoon, your father and I."

The Lyntons were going to America for a few weeks. The three children and Loony the dog were going off to the sea with Miss Pepper, Mrs. Lynton's old governess. She often had charge of them when the Lyntons had to go away.

Snubby had only arrived the day before, having spent the first week of the holidays with some other cousins. He had no parents and spent his time staying with various relations—but of them all he much preferred the Lyntons. He was very fond of his Aunt Susan, and admired and respected his Uncle Richard. His uncle, however, neither admired nor respected Snubby.

" I consider that boy to be the world's worst nuisance," was his continual description of poor Snubby.

Loony was led upstairs by a firm Diana. Sardine the cat was waiting for him at a turn of the stairs and leapt at him. He sprang back, almost pulling Diana down the stairs, and she squealed.

" This house is a mad-house," said her father, at the top of the stairs. " Where's Miss Pepper? Can't she take you all into some quiet corner till we've gone? America will seem a place of utter peace and quiet after this. Really, when you children come back from school, it's . . ."

" Oh, Daddy—you always say that," said Diana, hauling Loony up by his lead. " You know you'll miss us when you go. Daddy, I wish you'd take us with you to America."

" Not on your life!" said her father, horrified. " You'd

probably all fall overboard, to start with—and Snubby would spend his time down in the engine-room with Roger . . ."

"Oh, I say, sir—should I be allowed to?" called Snubby. "That would be smashing."

"Where do you get those awful words from?" said his uncle. "Can't you talk Queen's English?"

"I bet the Queen says 'smashing' sometimes," argued Snubby. "I bet she . . ."

"Move aside and let me pass," said his uncle impatiently. "What with Diana and the dog on the stairs, and now you—and is that Sardine I see waiting for me to fall over her as usual —this is a real mad-house."

"Richard dear—do come down and help me with the labelling," called Mrs. Lynton. "We'll go into the study and shut the door and the windows, and see if we can't keep out all the riff-raff!"

"Gosh—fancy Aunt Susan calling us riff-raff," said Snubby indignantly. "Hey, Aunt Susan . . ."

A door slammed down below. Snubby gave it up. He helped to push the reluctant Loony along the landing to Diana's bedroom.

Miss Pepper was there, pulling clothes out of drawers and cupboards. The children were to go off to the seaside the next day, and Miss Pepper was trying to do a little sorting and packing in between helping Mrs. Lynton.

"Hallo, Miss Pepper," said Snubby, as if he hadn't seen her for a month. He gave her a sudden squeeze round the waist. She gasped.

"*Don't*, Snubby! Why so affectionate all of a sudden? What is it you want out of me now?"

"Nothing," said Snubby, looking hurt. "I just felt sort of thrilled—holidays, you know—no more work for ages—going off to the sea to-morrow. What's the place we're going to, Miss Pepper? Nobody's told me anything yet."

Roger came marching in, his arms full of swim-suits. "Here

you are, Miss Pepper," he said, putting them down on the bed.
" I've found three swim-suits each. Is that enough?"

" Good gracious yes," said Miss Pepper. " Oh, don't let
Loony get hold of them. Snubby, take him away."

" He's supposed to be locked up here in Diana's bedroom,"
said Snubby.

" Well, he can't be," said Miss Pepper decidedly. " I'm
doing a lot of sorting out in here and I don't intend to be
locked in with Loony or any other mad dog either."

" He's not mad," said Snubby. " Are you, Loony?"

Loony promptly lay down on his back and pedalled his feet
in the air, looking sideways for Snubby's admiring remarks.

" Bicycle away," said Miss Pepper to Loony. " Stay there on
your back and pedal for the rest of the morning. That will suit
me nicely."

" Nobody's told me *yet* where we're going to-morrow," said
Snubby plaintively.

" Well, you only came yesterday," said Roger. " And considering that you spent practically the whole evening describing
the cricket match you played in last Saturday, and told us about
every run you didn't get, and how many sweaters the umpire
wore, and what you'd do if *you* were chosen for the Test team,
and . . ."

" That's not funny," said Snubby. " Miss Pepper, do tell me
about to-morrow."

" Well, we start off early, and we catch the train to Woodlingham, and we change there, and we catch another train, a slow
one, to Rockypool, and then we get a taxi to Rubadub," said
Miss Pepper. " There—now you know, so stop asking me."

" Rubadub! I don't believe it! There's not a place called
Rubadub!" exclaimed Snubby disbelievingly.

" There is," said Diana. " It's marked on the map. I think
it's a super name. I love thinking I'm going to stay at Rubadub.
Miss Pepper used to stay there when she was small—didn't
you, Miss Pepper?"

" Yes," said Miss Pepper, emptying another drawer. " Diana,

sort these out and put them over there. Yes, I often stayed there. It was the funniest little seaside village you ever could imagine then. Only a few shops, no pier, no promenade, a few cottages—and the old inn. You'll never guess what it was called!"

"Rubadub Inn?" said Roger.

"No. It was called Three Men in a Tub!" said Miss Pepper "You know the old rhyme—'Rubadub-dub, Three men in a tub.' Goodness knows why the inn should have been named that, but it was—and still is. Actually Rubadub village was called that because of a strange whirlpool place set between some queer-shaped rocks. One is like a scrubbing-board, and down below it the water boils and swirls and bubbles. . . ."

"As if it were in a wash-tub, I suppose!" said Diana. "Rubadub, See how we scrub . . ."

"That's right," said Miss Pepper. "The whirlpool is called Rubadub Pool, and so the village got its name, I suppose."

"It sounds jolly good," said Snubby approvingly. "I like the sound of all this, I must say. An inn called Three Men in a Tub, and a whirlpool called Rubadub Pool—I say, do we stay at the inn, Miss Pepper?"

"We do," said Miss Pepper. "I stayed there as a child and it was very comfortable. My niece stayed there last year and she sent such good accounts of it that when your mother suggested somewhere for you all these holidays, I thought of Rubadub."

"It'll be nice to stay in a dear little old-fashioned seaside village," said Diana. "No pier, no promenade, no . . ."

"Oh yes, there's a pier now *and* a promenade, and plenty of things going on," said Miss Pepper briskly. "And there's an enormous Secret Harbour built there, too, round beyond Rubadub Pool—where new submarines are tried out. Oh, Rubadub is no longer a tiny, sleepy village!"

"I say! A Secret Harbour!" said Snubby, thrilled. "I should like to go over that."

"I said 'Secret'" said Miss Pepper. "'Top Secret'

too, Snubby. So well guarded that no one, not even an inquisitive lad like you, could possibly get near it. So get that out of your head."

There came a call from downstairs. "Miss Pepper! Can you come? There are a few things I want you to do."

"Coming, Mrs. Lynton!" called Miss Pepper, and hurried out of the room. Loony immediately jumped up to go with her and leapt after her, quite forgetting he was tied to the bed-rail by his lead. He almost choked himself.

"It all sounds super," said Snubby, comforting poor Loony. "I'm sorry Aunt Susan's not coming, though. But I don't mind if Uncle Richard doesn't. Sooner or later I always seem to get a whacking from him."

"You got two, last hols," said Diana. "One for letting Loony chew up his best slippers, and one for cheeking him."

"Don't remind me," said Snubby. "I have to think twice now before I say anything to Uncle Richard in case he might think I am cheeking him. It's an awful nuisance."

"It's a jolly good thing," said Roger. "You want keeping down, young Snubby. And while you're about it, you can think twice before you cheek me, too. Oh, blow you, Loony —how did you get those swim-suits off the bed?"

A loud sound rang through the house, and the three children and Loony gave cries of joy. "The gong! I thought it was never going!"

"Race you downstairs! Come on, Loony!"

And down went an avalanche at top speed. Mr. Lynton groaned. "How *pleased* I shall be to see the coast of quiet, peaceful America. This house is Bedlam—never a moment's peace anywhere!"

CHAPTER TWO

GETTING READY

MR. AND MRS. LYNTON were to set off in their car after the meal. Everything was ready. The cases were packed and labelled. Big *Queen Elizabeth* labels were tied on, or pasted on. The tickets were safely in Mr. Lynton's wallet.

He was smiling as he said good-bye. He shook hands with Miss Pepper. "Don't stand any nonsense," he said to her. "And keep Snubby in his place. We'll write from New York. You've got our hotel address, haven't you?"

"Yes, thank you," said Miss Pepper. "Have a good time, and don't worry about the children. They'll be quite safe with me down at Rubadub. I'll see they don't get into mischief."

"No mysteries, please, and no adventures," said Mrs. Lynton, kissing her old governess. "Keep an eye on that, won't you—you know what extraordinary things can happen when these three are together."

"Good-bye, Mother! Don't forget to write!"

"Good-bye, Aunt Susan! I hope you don't get a storm that wrecks you!"

"Good-bye—and we'll be very good, so you needn't worry."

"Where's Loony?" said Snubby suddenly. "He wants to say good-bye too. Where on earth is he? Loony, Loony, Loony!"

"He *doesn't* want to say good-bye," said Miss Pepper firmly. "I've shut him in my bedroom."

The Lyntons got into the car. Snubby gave a yell and pointed up to Miss Pepper's bedroom window. Loony was there, his head squeezed through the half-open window, trying his best to see what was happening. He gave a bark.

"He did want to say good-bye!" cried Snubby. "Bark, Loony, bark!"

By a great effort Loony managed to push up the window a little way, and out came his shoulders and one paw.

"That dog will jump out next!" cried Mr. Lynton and jammed down the accelerator. The car leapt forward and was off down the road. Mr. Lynton had no desire to see Loony leap out of a high window!

Snubby tore upstairs and was just in time to stop Loony from flinging himself out of the window. "That dog!" said Miss Pepper, as they all went back to the house. "I can't imagine what the people at the inn will say about him. They said they didn't mind dogs—but they don't know Loony! Does he still go for brushes and mats?"

"Oh yes—and since he went to stay with your sister's dog, Loopy, last May, when we all went away with you after 'flu, he's taken to bringing down all the towels too," said Diana. " He caught that from Loopy."

" Well, we'll simply *have* to stop him doing things like that at the inn," said Miss Pepper, having a sudden vision of Loony piling all the visitors' towels out in the inn's garden, and then going back to fetch hair-brushes to put with them.

" I don't see how we *can* stop him," said Roger. " You simply can't reason with Loony. He just sits and grins at you with his tongue out, and thumps his tail on the floor. But you do love him, don't you, Miss Pepper?"

" I feel doubtful about that sometimes," said Miss Pepper. " Very doubtful. Now we'll all have to get very busy indeed, Roger and Diana, if we're going to be ready to go to-morrow. You'll have to help me to pack."

Loony came trotting down the stairs looking very pleased with himself. For once he had no brush or towel with him. Snubby followed.

" We're going for a walk," he announced.

" Oh no you're not," said Roger at once. " Trust you to try and get out of fetching and carrying, Snubby—and lugging heavy cases about. You're jolly well going to stay here and help."

" I'd much rather Snubby took Loony for a walk," said Miss Pepper hastily, thinking it would be marvellous to get both boy and dog out of the way together. " I'm sure Loony needs a walk."

" Pah! " said Roger in disgust. " Snubby always gets out of everything."

" Go along, Snubby—but be back by teatime," said Miss Pepper firmly, and Snubby went, followed by his faithful and adoring Loony, his long black ears flopping as he went—pad-pad-pad-pad.

The others spent a busy afternoon. Everything was packed. Diana neatly wrote a dozen labels. Roger tied rope round the trunk.

" I'll help you down the stairs with that," said Miss Pepper.

" I've just got to find Diana's sandals to put into this last bag."

Roger didn't want any help. He prided himself on his strength, and while Miss Pepper was hunting for the missing sandals, he dragged the trunk to the top of the stairs.

He set it flat and gave it a push. It cascaded down the stairs with a thunderous noise, arriving in the hall at top speed. Sardine the cat got the fright of her life as the trunk rumbled past where she sat on the stairs, waiting to pounce on someone coming down. She leapt in the air, and then tore like a streak of lightning into Diana's bedroom, as Miss Pepper was coming out in a hurry. Sardine shot between her ankles and landed on the bed, all her fur standing on end and her tail twice its usual size.

Miss Pepper rushed out on the landing. " Oh, who's fallen downstairs! Are you hurt? Whatever's happened?"

The cook was standing in the hall, brought out of her kitchen by the noise. She looked in disgust at the trunk, which had slid along the polished floor to the front door.

" Starting to throw trunks at one another now, I suppose," she said, and stalked back to her kitchen.

" What's the matter?" asked Roger, surprised. " I just shot the trunk downstairs, that's all. Jolly good idea—no lifting or carrying. I thought it would save us trouble, Miss Pepper."

Miss Pepper gave him such a glare that he disappeared into his room. Without a word she walked back to Diana's room, and picked up some socks.

" For two pins I'd leave them to themselves! " she thought, her heart still beating in fright. " Really, if Roger starts doing things like this my life won't be worth living. Snubby's bad enough."

Roger came humbly into the room. " I'm sorry, Miss Pepper," he said. " I didn't know it would crash down like that. Let me take those cases. I can carry them down for you one by one. You have a rest now, do."

" It's all right," said Miss Pepper thinking that the three children had their nice ways after all. " But I do wish you'd remember that you're in your teens, Roger, and be a bit more responsible."

"You sound like my form-master," said Roger gloomily. "Don't preach, Miss Pepper. You're too nice to preach."

Miss Pepper laughed and pretended to box Roger's ears. He ducked, grinning. He was very fond of her, as they all were, and hated it when she was vexed.

At last everything was finished. It was teatime and Snubby arrived back punctually with a tired Loony and an enormous appetite. He went straight into the kitchen to find the plump, good-natured cook.

"Cookie! Have you made any of your gingerbread for me? Don't say you haven't! I've been thinking of it all the term."

"Go on with you," said the cook. She opened the larder door and took out a tin. She lifted the lid and showed Snubby a great flat slab of sticky-looking home-made gingerbread. He gave her a hug round her waist.

"You're my very best friend," he said. "You don't mind if we eat it all, do you? I mean—it's a real compliment, really, if we eat up every single crumb. Isn't it, Cookie dear?"

"Go on with you!" said the cook again. "You'd talk the hind leg off a donkey, you would!"

"Why, is one of your legs coming loose?" inquired Snubby at once, and dodged out of the way as the cook took up a frying-pan and threatened him with it. Snubby's silly jokes usually went down very well with the good-tempered cook, and Mrs. Lynton always said that they had more and better cakes when Snubby was with them than at any other time.

"It's a wonder I did any work at all this afternoon," said the cook, taking the gingerbread carefully out of the tin. "That cousin of yours threw trunks down the stairs, and my word, they made a noise. I nearly had a heart attack!"

"Oh I say—good old Roger!" said Snubby, breaking a bit off the end of the gingerbread. "Strong man he's getting, isn't he? Wish I'd been there to see him throwing trunks all over the place."

"Now take your fingers away from the gingerbread," said the cook. "And take that dog out of my kitchen. I never in my life knew any animal that could slink into the larder when the door's shut, like that dog of yours can. He's a living miracle!"

"He is. You're right," said Snubby, wholeheartedly. "I'm glad you appreciate him. Oh golly, here's Sardine. We'd better go."

They left hurriedly. Sardine considered that the kitchen belonged to her, and hissed and spat spitefully if Loony stayed too long!

Teatime passed very pleasantly, because there were hot scones and honey, and gingerbread and some coconut buns. After that they all tidied up their rooms and put away everything. Loony helped by gathering together all the loose mats and putting them in a pile on the landing for people to fall over.

"I really think it's about time for Loony to grow up a bit," said Diana, picking herself up after stumbling over the mats in the darkness of the landing. "He's nearly two years old, and reckoning that in human years, it means he's in his teens. He ought to be more responsible."

Roger grinned at Miss Pepper nearby. "Another preacher!" he said. "Loony, do you hear what Di says?"

"What's the time?" said Miss Pepper, looking at her watch. "It's gone eight. I think you'd all better go to bed now. We've got a long day before us to-morrow. I want a bit of peace and quiet, too, to write letters."

"All right—we'll go," said Diana. "I always think it's thrilling, the night before we go away. Thinking about the sea and bathing and prawning, and walks. . . ."

"Woof!" said Loony, at once. He always joined in the conversation when he heard that word.

"Clever dog!" said Diana. "Come on—let's all go to bed."

CHAPTER THREE

OFF TO RUBADUB-ON-SEA

THE NEXT day was truly exciting. Usually the three children went off for their holidays by car, but they much preferred the train.

They found an empty carriage, and each bagged a corner. Loony shared everyone's corner in turn, breathing down their necks in excitement.

It was a long way to Woodlingham, where they had to change trains. The journey was a cross-country one, involving many long stops at various stations at which bits and pieces of the train were added or subtracted.

Snubby, of course, was intensely interested in these stops, and talked to every engine-driver, guard and porter that he could see.

"Do you know," he announced once, as he returned from a chat to the driver, "do you know that of all the fifteen carriages we started with, only two of the original ones are left now—ours and the next one? Such a lot have been shunted off. But some have been added, of course."

"You make it sound like a maths problem," said Diana. "So long as they leave our carriage on the train that's all I care about."

"Just like a girl," said Roger scornfully. "No interest in railways at all. I call it all very thrilling. We start with fifteen —we shunted off six at Limming and added five. We left another three at Berklemere, and got two more added on at Fingerpit. Now let me see. . . ."

"This sounds like a riddle now," said Miss Pepper sleepily. "If we shunt off six and add two, and leave five somewhere, and forget to take on the rest, please tell me the name of the engine-driver!"

"Ha, ha, joke," said Snubby politely. "I say, isn't it time for lunch yet?"

They got to Woodlingham at last and woke up Miss Pepper, who had fallen sound asleep. "It's a good thing we're *responsible* people," said Roger. "*Some*body's got to look out for the station we change at."

"Don't be idiotic, Roger," said Miss Pepper. "I can't imagine how I could have gone to sleep in this rattling, rumbling old train."

The train to take them to Rockypool came in at last. Snubby went to talk to the engine-driver, having found out that there was a ten-minute wait before it drew out of the station again.

He didn't notice that another engine came backing up to the end of the train. He didn't notice it being hooked on. He suddenly heard the whistle of the guard and the voices of the others calling him frantically.

"Snubby, quick, we're going. SNUBBY!"

Snubby leapt into the very last carriage, dragging poor Loony in by his collar. "Gosh!" he said to a surprised old country-woman there. "I nearly missed it! How was I to know the thing was going to go off the other way? Peculiar way trains behave here!"

"Ar," said the old woman wisely.

"I mean—it came in with the engine at the front, just as usual—and it leaves the station with a perfectly fresh engine, at the *back*," said Snubby, working himself up into a grievance because he felt so foolish. "It's time somebody spoke about these things."

"Ar," said the old lady, nodding her head. Snubby looked at her. In his experience people who said nothing but "Ar" made extremely good listeners. So he aired his views at great length and enjoyed himself thoroughly. He didn't even get out at the next station or the next, to find his way to the carriage

316

where the others were. He was afraid they would tease him unmercifully about being so nearly left behind.

Two men got in at the third station. Snubby looked at them closely. They were naval men, he saw. Aha! Probably they belonged to the Secret Submarine Harbour. What a scoop for him if he could make friends with them and get news of the harbour to retell proudly to the others. The men opened newspapers and began to read.

" Excuse me, sir, but are we very far from Rockypool?" began Snubby. " I've got to get out there."

" You'll see the name of the station when we come to it," said one of the men gruffly.

" I say, sir, I suppose you don't belong to the Secret Submarine place, do you?" Snubby tried again. " I've always been interested in submarines. Used to sail them in my bath, and . . ."

" You probably do still, I imagine," said the other man. " Shut up!"

Snubby subsided, grieved. He examined the men carefully, pretending he was a detective. Both clean-shaven. One with a mole on his right cheek. One with crooked eyebrows. Actually he thought they looked nice men. It was a pity they wouldn't talk. He sat and stared at them thoughtfully.

" Anything wrong with my face?" inquired one man at last. " What about looking out of the window for a change?"

Snubby scowled. He woke up Loony, who was sound asleep under the seat, bored with this long journey. He lugged him up on the seat and began to talk to him. He couldn't very well talk to the old woman, because she was now snoring in her corner, her mouth wide open.

" Shut up!" said one of the men again. " What a babbler you are!"

The old woman woke up unexpectedly. She gave a little wheeze of laughter.

" That's right, he is," she said. " Babbles like a brook, he do. I couldn't get a word in till you come along, misters."

317

Snubby glared at her indignantly. He got out at the next station with much dignity, and made his way to the compartment where Roger and Diana were hanging out of the window.

"Why didn't you come before?" demanded Roger. "Was there somebody interesting in that carriage?"

"Rather!" said Snubby, climbing in. "There were two men from the Secret Submarine place—and my word, the secrets they know!"

"As if they'd tell *you* any!" said Roger at once.

"All right. If you're feeling like that I won't tell you a word," said Snubby exasperatingly. He sat down in the opposite corner. Roger stared at him. He couldn't believe that any one would tell Snubby anything interesting in the way of secrets—but on the other hand Snubby was so friendly that people *had* been known to relate most amazing bits of information to him.

"Go on—tell me what you heard," said Roger. "Who were the men? What were they like?"

"They wouldn't tell me their names," said Snubby. "So I didn't press them. But I can tell you exactly what they were like. You just never know when it'll pay you to be really observant."

He described the men exactly, down to a mole, crooked eyebrows, two overlapping teeth, bitten nails on one man's hands, and misshapen little finger on the other man's.

"Jolly good," said Roger, thinking for the hundredth time that his fat-headed little cousin could be quite sharp, for all his idiotic ways. "You ought to go into the police force!"

Snubby was about to air his views on how lucky the police force would be to get him, when the train slowed down at a station.

"Rockypool!" yelled a porter, and Miss Pepper stood up quickly.

"Ah—here we are. Roger, go and see if our trunks and cases are *still* in the luggage van. I can hardly believe we have the

318

same luggage van as when we started, but still, you never know!"

Roger disappeared to find out. Snubby and Diana handed down the smaller cases and parcels, and they all got out of the carriage. Loony got his lead entangled round Snubby's legs as usual, and made him cross.

Roger came back. "The luggage is all there," he announced. "Safe as can be. What about a taxi, Miss Pepper? Shall I go and see if there's one?"

"It's already ordered," said Miss Pepper. "I asked the innkeeper's wife at Rubadub to order one for us. It should be waiting."

It was. As they walked to it Snubby nudged Roger and nodded his head towards two men walking nearby. Roger looked at them and immediately recognised a good many of the big and small characteristics that Snubby had recited to him. He stared at the men with interest. Like Snubby he thought it must be thrilling to work on anything secret.

Their taxi was waiting. The driver got down to help the porter in with their things. He strapped on the trunk, and put the cases in front.

"Is it far to Rubadub?" asked Snubby. The man shook his head.

"Matter of three miles," he said. "The railway don't go any farther than this."

They all got into the old musty-smelling taxi. Snubby stuck his head out of the window to take a look round. The country they passed through was rather wild and desolate—heath and moorland with pools of water shining here and there.

They rumbled along. Snubby looked at Loony anxiously. "I think he's going to be sick," he said.

"Oh *no*!" said Miss Pepper, in despair.

"He'd better go in front with the driver," said Snubby, and he knocked on the glass. "Hey—stop a minute, will you? I'm coming in front with you."

The taxi stopped. Snubby got out, carrying Loony, who looked very surprised. The two of them were soon in front with the driver, sitting on a pile of cases.

"Now I can see fine," said Snubby to the driver, and grinned happily.

"Well I never!" said Diana, who heard this. "I bet Loony wasn't feeling sick after all. It was just that Snubby wanted to sit in front and see everything."

"Well, never mind," said Miss Pepper, who was feeling tired, and not very anxious to cope with the inexhaustible and irrepressible Snubby. "We'll soon be there."

It didn't seem long before the taxi drove into a little town by the sea. It was set in a semi-circle of cliff, looking out to a small bay. There was a good promenade, a fine little pier, a stone jetty with boats and a sandy beach.

"It looks grand!" said Diana, pleased. "And oh, look—is this lovely old place the inn?"

"Yes—this is the Three Men in a Tub Inn, in the old town of Rubadub!" said Miss Pepper. "Out you get—we're here at last!"

CHAPTER FOUR

THE QUEER OLD INN

THEY ALL tumbled out of the taxi. The driver gave a shout to someone called by the queer name of Dummy.

"Hey there, Dummy! Come and collect these things, will you? Your people have arrived."

The children stood and looked at the Three Men in a Tub Inn. It had an old, old sign, but whether it was of three men in a tub, or of anything else it was quite impossible to tell, it was so dark and dingy.

The inn looked like something out of a story. "If you told me we were back in the Middle Ages I'd believe you!" said Diana, staring up at the inn. "I feel as if I've gone back hundreds of years when I look at this quaint old place!"

It was a rambling old inn, set back against the cliff, almost nestling into it. Its leaded, diamond-paned windows gleamed brightly. It had tall chimneys, and a roof so covered with grey-green lichen that the red tiles only showed through here and there.

The front door might have belonged to a castle! It was enormous, very stout and strong, and had a great knocker in the form of a sailing ship. Snubby, of course, immediately wanted to go and bang on it, but before he could do so the old door creaked open and a face looked out with round eyes and a button of a mouth.

At first the children thought it was the face of a child, but when the whole person appeared they saw that it was a grown-up! A grown-up not as tall as Roger, the head rather big for the body, and the face an odd mixture of child and grown-up.

"Come on, Dummy. Stir yourself," said the driver, un-doing some of the cases. Dummy ran out clumsily. He wore the dress of a hall-porter or odd-man—thick, navy-blue trousers with a line down the side, a leather apron and waist-coat over a dark shirt. He grinned at the children, holding his face sideways as if half-shy.

He appeared to be enormously strong! He lifted the trunk with ease, jerked it on his shoulder, and went back into the inn with it.

"That's old Dummy," explained the taxi-driver. "He's a good chap, but never properly growed-up, I don't reckon. Strong as a horse, and gentle as a child—unless he gets into one of his rages, and then all I say is, I'd rather meet a lion than Dummy!"

"I liked him," said Diana. "He had a nice sort of smile."

"He gets on well with children," said the taxi-driver. "But

when grown-ups go for him for being a bit slow, like, he mutters and mumbles and growls and scowls, and looks as if he'd like to throw them over the cliff. And see you don't ever laugh at old Dummy. Anyone who laughs at Dummy comes to a sticky end, so I've been told."

Miss Pepper thought that the taxi-driver had talked quite enough. She saw Snubby drinking in every word, eager to ask about the people who " had come to a sticky end."

" I think that's all," she said, taking out her purse. " Thank you for meeting us."

The driver touched his cap, and pocketed the fare and the generous tip that Miss Pepper had given him. Then he drove away.

Dummy appeared again to take the rest of the cases, and brought with him the innkeeper's wife. She was a large, plump woman with rather a gloomy face. She had so many chins that Snubby was quite lost in admiration. She did her hair high up on her head, and really looked rather majestic.

" Good afternoon," she said, advancing on the little company. " Your train must have been very punctual for once in a way. It's usually so late that I didn't expect you for another half-hour. Come this way. Your rooms are all ready."

" Oh, thank you, Mrs. er—Mrs. . . ." said Miss Pepper, rather taken aback by the ponderous plumpness of the inn-keeper's wife.

" My name is Glump," said that lady. " Mrs. Glump."

" What a wonderful name! " murmured Diana, as they all went into the big, dark hall, following Mrs. Glump. " And doesn't it suit her?"

" Yes—mixture of ' glum ' and ' plump,' " said Snubby with a giggle. " I wonder if there are any little Glumps. Come on—up the stairs we go. My word, aren't they uneven and steep?"

" Mind the bends," said Mrs. Glump, in her stately voice. " Oh my—what's that?"

It was only Loony, escaped from Snubby's hand, tearing up

the stairs, pressing himself against her legs as he passed her at sixty miles an hour. He liked this place. He knew he would find plenty of strange, unusual smells here.

" I'm so sorry—did he scare you?" said Snubby in his politest voice. " That was only my spaniel. He's excited because he's come to a new place. You don't mind dogs, do you? Miss Pepper said you took dogs."

" I take *well-behaved* dogs," said Mrs. Glump, leading them down a twisting corridor, lined with stout old doors. " I have a dog of my own, very well trained and most obedient."

" What's his name?" asked Roger.

" We call him Mr. Tubby, short for Three Men in a Tub," said Mrs. Glump. " My husband's idea of a joke. It took me a very long time to see it. But now that he—the dog, I mean— is old and fat, I must say that his name suits him very well."

She went up a few more stairs and came to a small square landing, out of which opened four or five doors.

" This is where I have put you," she said, and opened one of the doors. " This is the best of the rooms. Perhaps Miss Pepper would like it."

" Oh, I *should*!" said Miss Pepper in delight. " I once had it when I stayed here as a child. Oh, the view—it's exactly the same as it always was!"

She went to the leaded casement window and flung it wide open. The children crowded beside her.

The room looked out down a steep cliffside to the golden sands below. The sea was cornflower blue that August day, and the sound of the waves below came softly up to the window.

" Like someone sighing," said Diana to herself. " But I expect on a stormy day the noise of the waves would be terrific. Oh, I hope my room has the same view as this!"

It had. It was a much smaller room with a queer slanting ceiling. Big beams ran crookedly across the walls, which were whitewashed. There was almost the same view as from Miss Pepper's room, but a little farther west.

The boys pronounced their room to be " smashingly super," and called Diana to see it. It was a big room with a built-in oak cupboard, an old double bed that looked as if it had once been a four-poster but had had its four upright posts taken off, and a very uneven floor that would trip the boys up hundreds of times before their visit was over!

" This place has got a lovely old *feel*," said Diana. " Don't you think so, boys?"

" Rather," said Roger. " Like Hampton Court or the Tower or somewhere frightfully old. You can feel that things have happened here for years—the walls still remember them! "

" Funny. I feel like that too," said Snubby, rather astonished. " And I feel this has been a happy place, too—enormous meals and things."

" You *would* think that," said Diana. " If the walls could talk to you, all you'd want them to tell you about would be the meals people had downstairs."

" I wouldn't mind having a meal now," said Snubby. " Do we unpack? Where's Miss Pepper?"

Miss Pepper came in to see what the boys' room was like. She immediately shooed Loony off the big bed. " Snubby, you heard what Mrs. Glump said about well-behaved dogs, didn't you?" she said. " For goodness' sake tell Loony he can't behave here as if he was at home. Mrs. Glump would have plenty to say."

" It's a marvellous name, Glump," said Snubby. " Sort of gloomy and gluggy and gurgley and . . ."

" Oh, don't be *silly*, Snubby," said Miss Pepper. " Hurry up and unpack and come down to tea. Mrs. Glump said it would be ready when you are."

" Well, I am now," said Snubby at once.

" No, you're not. You've got to wash yourself and brush your hair—it's like a red-haired mop—and for goodness' sake brush your shorts too. You look as if you've been scrambling about under all the carriage seats on the train."

" I shall go all gloomy and glumpish if you scold me as soon as we get here," complained Snubby. "I feel glumpish already."

Diana gave a little squeal of laughter. "Oh, Snubby—that's a lovely word. Much better than gloomy. Do you feel down in the glumps?"

"Not really," grinned Snubby. "Hey, Loony, get off that bed. Didn't you hear what pepper-pot said?"

"You'll get into trouble with Miss Pepper if you begin calling her that," said Roger. "She won't stand cheek from you. I say, it's a shame our room doesn't look out over the sea, isn't it?"

"Yes. But it's got quite an *interesting* view," said Snubby, looking out of the small casement window. "Chimneys and roofs and other people's windows."

It was rather a peculiar view, really. Their part of the inn was higher than the other part, and they could see across uneven roofs and into attic windows here and there. They could see tall chimneys rising up too, one of them with wisps of smoke coming out.

"I wouldn't mind exploring this roof some time," said Snubby, washing his face vigorously. "I'm good at exploring roofs. You never know when that kind of thing comes in useful."

"You're an awful fathead, Snubby," said Roger. "Look, that dog's on the bed again. I think really it would be best to drape it with an old rug or something. I don't see *how* we're to keep Loony off it. Come on, Loony—teatime."

They called Diana and Miss Pepper, and went down the twisting, uneven stairs, moving rather cautiously because of the sharp bends in the stairway where one side of the stairs narrowed to an inch or two. Loony, of course, missed his footing and fell headlong down, bouncing merrily from stair to stair.

"Can't you behave, Loony!" hissed Snubby. "*WHAT* will Mr. Tubby think of you?"

326

CHAPTER FIVE

AFTER TEA

THEY HAD tea in the dining-room of the inn. This was a large, rather dark room, with heavy oak beams across the ceilings and walls. It had a colossal fireplace, now filled with foxgloves, and an amazing number of doors, all polished oak.

Snubby saw that the tea was good and fell upon it ravenously. New brown bread and butter and home-made damson jam disappeared down his throat without stopping.

"You're a greedy pig, Snubby," said Diana. "You get worse instead of better. I say, isn't this a heavenly room? It's got stags' heads all round, and big glass cases of fish. And look at those funny old prints—and did you ever see such a selection of horse-brasses hanging down each side of the mantelpiece?"

"Horse-brasses?" said Snubby, pausing in his munching. "I say—I collect those. I must have a look at them and see if there are any I haven't got."

"Ass! You've got about nine, that's all, and there must be seventy or eighty there," said Diana. "Look at that old clock, too, Snubby. It's enormous."

It was an old grandfather clock, the biggest the children had ever seen in their lives. It almost reached the ceiling, and its tick was so loud that it could be heard all over the room— TICK-TOCK, TICK-TOCK. When five o'clock came it burst into the loudest dong-dong-dongs that the children had ever heard, except from Big Ben. It was quite deafening.

"Miss Pepper, is everything just like it was when you came here as a child?" asked Roger. "Was that clock there then? Do you remember it?"

"Oh yes—and I remember someone hiding inside the big pendulum case at the bottom once, and frightening the life out

327

of me by growling inside there like a dog," said Miss Pepper rashly. Snubby had already pricked up his ears at this idea, of course.

"That's a smashing idea," he said at once. "I'll remember that."

"No, don't," said Miss Pepper, with a groan. "Please, Snubby, behave yourself here. I'm almost sure I knew Mrs. Glump as a child, and I don't want her to put you down as a lot of hooligans and think that I can't manage you all."

"Gosh—did you really know Mrs. Glump when she was a girl?" asked Snubby in wonder. "Was she older than you?"

"About the same age," said Miss Pepper. "She was a funny shy little girl then. See—what was her name now—oh yes—Gloria."

"Gloria Glump!" exclaimed Diana, in delight. "It can't be true."

"Sh!" said Miss Pepper, afraid that Mrs. Glump might hear Diana. "She wasn't Glump then. Her name was Gloria Tregonnan, as far as I remember. Her family have had this inn for hundreds of years so it's said."

Mrs. Glump suddenly appeared at the door. "Have you enough tea?" she inquired in her ponderous voice. "Oh dear —why, there's hardly anything left. Er—shall I send in some more?"

"No, thank you," said Miss Pepper, feeling suddenly certain that a good part of the tea had gone under the table to a ravenous Loony. That must have been why he had been so very quiet! She frowned at Snubby, who was just opening his mouth to protest that *he* could do with some more to eat. He shut it again.

"Now, while I unpack, you can go and explore the beach," she said. "And if it's wet, please tie your sandshoes round your neck. You hear me, Snubby?"

They rushed off. Miss Pepper poured herself out another cup of tea and drank it quietly. Mrs. Glump reappeared.

"Handful, aren't they?" she said sympathetically. "My,

children aren't what they were in our day, are they? We had to be seen and not heard."

"They're not bad children at all," said Miss Pepper loyally. "A bit high-spirited at times. Are you very full now, Mrs. Glump—many visitors here?"

"Well, we're not over-full at the moment," said Mrs. Glump. "There's a big new hotel built down in the town now, you know—near to the pier—and that's taken a lot of my custom away. We're old-fashioned here at Three Men in a Tub, and a bit out of the way."

Miss Pepper looked at one or two tables with napkins folded by the plates, and dishes of fruit. "You seem to have a few visitors besides ourselves," she said.

"Oh yes—I've two or three of the pierrots staying here," said Mrs. Glump. "There's a very good pierrot show on the pier every night, you know. They call themselves 'The Rubadub Rollicks,' whatever that may mean. 'Come to the Rubadub Rollicks for a Rollicking Show,' is on posters all over the place."

"Oh, the children will like to go and see them," said Miss Pepper. "Is there a funny man?"

"Oh yes—very funny," said Mrs. Glump. "They'll love him. He's staying here, as a matter of fact. And there's a conjurer too—queer thing to have in a pierrot show, but he goes down quite well, I believe. He's here too—and Miss Iris Nightingale, the singer from the show. That's not her real name, of course, she chose it because it's a good name for a singer."

"You've got some quite interesting people," said Miss Pepper, enjoying the chat. "Anyone else?"

"Well, there's an old fellow called Professor James," said Mrs. Glump. "I would like you to warn the children not to upset him, please, Miss Pepper. He doesn't like dogs, not even my well-trained Mr. Tubby. He's rather deaf, and he's got a very hot temper."

Miss Pepper made a mental note to warn all the children,

especially Snubby, and to keep Loony strictly under control
when Professor James was about.

"And there's Miss Twitt," said Mrs. Glump. "That's the
lot. She's all right, but she's what I call a *gusher*. Gushes
over children and dogs and cats and the pretty butterflies and
the darling birds, and all that. I wouldn't want the children to
laugh at her."

"Oh dear!" thought Miss Pepper. "I hope they won't. I'll
have to give them quite a talking to to-night."

She told Mrs. Glump how, long ago, she had known her as a
shy little girl, and the innkeeper's wife nodded her head in
pleasure. Well, well—to think she and Miss Pepper had
known each other as girls!

"The inn is very little changed!" said Miss Pepper. "I
shall love being here again!"

She went up to unpack. She looked at the glorious view
from the little window and sat down to enjoy it. It all looked so
very peaceful and serene! What a lovely quiet part of the world
this was!

Just as she got up again, a muffled explosion shook the inn.
Miss Pepper sat down again suddenly, feeling scared. What in
the world was that?

She went out on the landing, feeling alarmed. Dummy was
there, carrying somebody's case. He grinned shyly at her.

"What was that awful noise?" asked Miss Pepper.

"Boom-boom-boom," said Dummy, delighted. He put
down the case with a crash that made Miss Pepper jump.
"BOOM!" he said, and did it again.

"Don't," said Miss Pepper. "I just wanted to know what
made that loud noise."

Dummy took Miss Pepper by the arm and led her to a little
door. Behind it was a stairway. It led steeply upwards. He
went up it and beckoned Miss Pepper. In surprise, she followed. The staircase led up to the roof, through a small trap-
door which had a piece of glass set in it, like a small skylight.

"Boom-boom," said Dummy softly, pulling Miss Pepper beside him, their heads sticking out of the skylight trap-door.

She was now so high that she was almost on a level with the top of the cliff behind the hotel, where it suddenly slanted downwards. There was a deep cleft in it at one place, and the skylight opening looked directly through the cleft to the sea on the other side of the cliff.

It was surprising to see right over the cliff to the sea away on the other side. Miss Pepper gazed curiously. She remembered that the Secret Submarine base was somewhere over there, closely guarded on all sides, land and sea. Experiments, top-secret experiments, went on there. Perhaps the muffled explosion she had heard came from one of these experiments.

"Booooom-ooom!" The far-away noise made her jump again. Before the noise came she had seen a little cloud of either smoke or spray rising from the sea on the other side of the cliff. The noise made her certain it was an explosion of some sort.

"Boom-boom," said Dummy, who seemed quite unable to say anything else, pointing and grinning.

"Yes. Very interesting. Thank you, Dummy," said Miss Pepper. Dummy gave her his engaging sideways smile, and his bright blue eyes looked shyly at her. She patted him on the arm. What a queer little man he was—more like a gnome or brownie than a human being!

She made up her mind to tell the children what she had seen when they came home. They would be thrilled! She went to unpack once more, humming. The weeks seemed to stretch away before her, full of sunshine and walks and reading, and looking after three interesting madcaps of children.

They were having a lovely time by themselves. They had explored the sandy beach, which was studded with hundreds of pinkish shells. They had climbed a few rocks, and Snubby had slipped into a pool and sat down heavily. Now he dripped water wherever he went.

They went down the promenade, and came to the pier, where they examined all the notices.

" ' Come to the Rubadub Rollicks for a Rollicking Show,' " said Roger, reading the biggest poster. " I say, we ought to go and see them. I love pierrots. Look, it says there's a conjurer too. Matthew Marvels. We'll have to go and see *him*! "

They examined the photographs of the twelve pierrots. The children thought they looked fine.

" So long as the girls don't *sing* too much," said Snubby. " An awful waste of time when you've got a conjurer and a funny man as well. I don't mind the dancing so much—but all that singing's boring."

" Loony's gone on the pier," said Roger suddenly. " Loony, come back! Loony, Loony! "

Loony was half-way down the pier. He took absolutely no notice of the shouts. He had smelt an enticing fishy smell somewhere at the end of the pier and he was going to examine it if it was very last thing he did.

" We'll have to spend tuppence and fetch him," said Snubby in disgust. " Anyone got tuppence? "

" Yes. *You* have! " said Roger. " You don't get tuppence out of me that way. Spend your own pence on your own dog."

So Snubby had to fork out tuppence and go and yank a disappointed Loony out of a pile of decaying fish at the very end of the pier.

" Can't you hear the seagulls yelling at you, idiot? " said Snubby severely. " That's put there for them. What a dog you are! Can't even understand the rude names the gulls are calling you! "

CHAPTER SIX

THE OTHER GUESTS

THEY GOT back to the inn about seven o'clock. Miss Pepper
had said they must be in by then because the inn served dinner,
and everyone was expected to come in on time for that.

"You *are* nice and early," she said, hearing them come up
on the landing, and going to her door to greet them. "Did you
have a good look round?"

"Rather! It's a super place," said Roger. "Did you hear
any bangs, Miss Pepper? We did, and a man told us they were
from the Secret Submarine base. He says it's very hush-hush.
I wish we could see over it."

"People don't see over hush-hush places," said Miss Pepper.

"You might know that. Look, as you're in so early, I'll show you something. Dummy showed it to *me*."

She led the way to the door behind which was the little staircase. They all went up it wonderingly. Wherever did it lead to? Roger gave an exclamation when he reached the top and pushed up the trap-door to peer out.

"My word—we can see the Secret Base through that cleft in the cliff! How exciting!"

"Let me see!" said Snubby impatiently. "Di, do pull Loony down. He's pawing so hard at my shorts he'll make a hole in them. Gosh, Roger—what a view! I say, is that where the explosion came from Miss Pepper?"

"Yes. I actually saw the smoke—or spray, I think it must have been—from the second one," said Miss Pepper.

"I shall sit up here and watch for the third one," announced Snubby.

"No, you won't. You'll just come straight away down now," said Miss Pepper.

They all climbed down the little wooden stairway and went out of the door at the bottom, on to the landing. A man was just coming up to it from the lower stairs. He was a tall, thin man, with a long, cadaverous face, and deep-set, rather staring eyes. He looked in surprise at the children coming down the little stairway.

They stared back at him. Diana didn't like his eyes. She thought they seemed to look right through her, and she shivered. Who was he?

"Good evening," said Miss Pepper politely. She thought he must be one of the other guests.

"Good evening," said the man shortly, opened a door and disappeared into his room. He shut the door with a soft click.

Miss Pepper thought over the guests that Mrs. Glump had told her about, and came to the conclusion that the man could only be one of the pierrots who was staying there. Surely he wasn't the funny man, the comedian of the party? He didn't look as if he had ever laughed in his life. Then it must be Mr.

Matthew Marvels, the conjurer. Well, he certainly looked more like a conjurer than a comedian!

"That must be Mr. Glooomp," whispered Snubby with a giggle. "Didn't he look the picture of gloom? Lost a shilling and found a farthing, I should think."

"Hurry up and change into something clean," said Miss Pepper. "And do remember that you have dinner here, not supper, and are supposed to look washed and brushed and tidy, and must put on your best manners."

"Oh dear," groaned Roger. "Is it that kind of place? Anyway, Snubby'll *have* to change. Look at the drips he's made on the landing already. He fell in a rock-pool."

"He would, of course," said Miss Pepper. "Snubby bring me your shorts to dry when you've changed into clean, dry ones."

When the gong boomed out over the house, the three children were all ready. Loony was too. "I've brushed him and washed the sand off him," said Snubby, proudly. "He looks fine, doesn't he? I want him to make a very good impression on Mr. Tubby Dog."

They were the first down in the dining-room. A most appetising smell of tomato soup came from the kitchen. Snubby sniffed loudly, and then caught Miss Pepper's eye.

A very portly dog waddled into the dining-room. He was enormous—a bull-mastiff with a most gloomy and lugubrious face, wrinkles and folds of flesh hanging down his cheeks.

"This must be Mr. Tubby," said Snubby, eyeing the big dog with awe. "I say—look at his wrinkles. Good evening, Mr. Tubby, let me introduce you to Loony. Mr. Tubby—Mr. Loony."

"Woof," said Loony, scared but polite.

"Grrrrr," said Mr. Tubby, and lifted the skin from his top teeth in a horrifying manner. Loony backed hurriedly into a waiter who was bringing in the soup.

Mr. Tubby walked to a rug by the fireplace and subsided there gradually, with a few rather human-sounding groans. He eyed everyone with a superior and contemptuous air, looking extremely miserable. Then he laid his great head on his paws and let out a sigh that blew along the floor like a draught.

Loony gazed at Mr. Tubby in awe. What a dog! What a grandfather of a dog! Loony felt extremely small and decided to behave himself. He lay down heavily on Snubby's feet.

The waiter laid plates of tomato soup in front of everyone. They had just begun when the other guests walked into the room. Miss Pepper glanced at them, recognising them from Mrs. Glump's description.

Mr. Marvels the conjurer came first. He was the man they had met on the landing. Then came a man with a comical face, ears that stuck out and a broad smile. He winked across at the children, and joked with the waiter. He must be the funny man, decided Miss Pepper.

Then came a pretty girl of about twenty, who sat at the table with the conjurer and the funny man. She must be Iris Nightingale, the singer.

Finally came an old man with a beard, and a middle-aged lady fluttering with scarfs and bits of chiffon, and with a coy bow in her over-curled hair.

" Professor James—and Miss Twitt," thought Miss Pepper, drinking her soup. The children stared round at all the new-comers.

" Now," said the Professor, stopping just inside the room. " Where's that dog? Nowhere near my table, I hope."

Mr. Tubby didn't even deign to raise his head. Professor James stared at him with dislike and Mr. Tubby stared back sorrowfully and contemptuously.

" Ha! There you are!" said Professor James, advancing to his table. " Well, keep on the rug. Waiter, what soup is it?"

" Tomato, sir," said the waiter, a bright-eyed youth who had already exchanged a few winks with the irrepressible Snubby.

" What's that? Speak up, my man," said the Professor. " Everyone mumbles nowadays."

" Tomato, sir," said the waiter, a little more loudly.

" Bless the man—can't hear a word! " said the old fellow.

" He said ' TOMATO,' " said Snubby helpfully at the top of his voice. Everyone jumped violently including the Professor.

" Who's shouting? " said the Professor angrily. " Enough to deafen anyone! " He glared round at the children's table. Snubby got ready to confess at the top of his voice that it was he who had shouted, but Miss Pepper frowned so hard at him that he desisted.

" I should like some more tomato soup," he said in his normal voice.

A little laugh came to their ears. It was from Miss Twitt, who was sitting at the next table. She leaned over to Miss Pepper, one or two necklaces and bracelets jingling merrily.

" Isn't he *sweet*? Trying to be so helpful! And how nice to see such a healthy appetite! "

Snubby looked so completely horrified at being called " sweet " that Roger and Diana had to laugh.

" Such nice-looking children," gushed Miss Twitt. " Are you their mother? "

" No. I am merely in charge of them," said Miss Pepper, politely but coldly. Miss Twitt was the kind of person to avoid, she could see! She would rapidly drive the children to rudeness. " My name is Pepper. Miss Pepper."

" And mine is Twitt. Miss Twitt," was the reply. " We'll have to get together, Miss Pepper, when these rascals are safely in bed. I do *so* love children, don't you? *And* dogs, of course. Dear creatures! "

Loony decided to see who this gushing, talkative person was, and he appeared from below the table. This was the signal for a fresh outburst from Miss Twitt.

" Oh, the darling ! Oh, I *do* love cockers! Come to me, my pet. I'll take you walky-walkies one day, shall I? "

Loony gave her one disgusted look and retired under the table. Mr. Tubby gave what sounded remarkably like a snigger, got up very slowly, and lay down on his rug with his back to Miss Twitt.

"And what are the children's names?" went on Miss Twitt, who could apparently talk and swallow hot soup at one and the same time. "What's the little girl's name?"

"I'm Diana. And I'm not a little girl," said Diana. "You sound as if you think I'm six!"

"I'm Roger," said Roger gruffly.

"And I'm Snubby, Miss Twitter," suddenly beamed Snubby. Diana gave a giggle.

"My name is Twitt, not Twitter," said Miss Twitt. "And how do you like Rubadub, children? Such a very quaint name, I always feel!"

"Yes, so *twee*, Miss Twitter," began Snubby. "Oh, what pretty dinky beads you wear, Miss Twitter."

"Snubby," said Miss Pepper, in such a fierce voice that he subsided at once. Miss Twitt looked at her in surprise.

"Get on with your meal, children, and don't let me hear another word," said Miss Pepper, afraid of the effect Miss Twitt would have on them if they entered into any lengthy conversation.

Snubby was really scared when Miss Pepper's voice took on a certain tone. He began on a plate of cold chicken and ham and salad, unusually silent.

"Please, mayn't we talk now?" asked Diana after a while. "If we just talk to one another, I mean?"

Miss Twitt was now having an animated conversation with the funny man, who played up to her valiantly. Miss Pepper judged it was safe to let the three children use their tongues.

"Very well. But I've warned you," she said. "Don't go into the lounge after supper, please. Leave it to the other guests."

"Right. We'll all go for a walk then," said Roger. "*I* don't want to go into the lounge."

None of them did. Oh dear, thought Miss Pepper, this was going to be rather a *difficult* holiday!

CHAPTER SEVEN

FINE NEWS

THE THREE children and Loony set off once more for a quick walk. Miss Pepper had said it must only be a short one, as it was getting late. It was still light, of course—but as they turned down to the promenade they saw one of the buildings along it blazing with lights.

"It's a kind of fair," said Roger. "Let's go and have a squint at it."

"Oooh—it's got those Dodgem Cars," said Diana, thrilled. "Do you remember, we once had rides in them when somebody took us to a Play Camp. You kept crashing into me, Roger."

"Let's have a go now," said Snubby at once. But no one had any money on them, so they could only stand and watch. It was a very small fair—it could really hardly even be called that. There were automatic machines standing round the wall, where you could lose any amount of pennies. There was a stall to buy ice-cream and candy-floss. There was a machine that played tunes if you put money into it—loud, blaring tunes that never seemed to stop!

"A juke-box," said Snubby, airing his knowledge. He looked at the list of tunes on it. "Oh look—it can play twenty different tunes. How super! I wish they had one of these at the inn."

"Goodness—Professor James would have a blue fit!" said Diana.

"Yes—he'd go up in smoke at once," agreed Roger. "So would Mrs. Glump, I should think. Pity we haven't any money to-night."

"I don't believe Miss Pepper will let us come here much,"

said Diana, looking at the people who were swarming in. "They look a pretty rough lot, some of them."

A good many sailors had come in, and were climbing into the Dodgem cars with yells and whistles. One of them lurched rather roughly against Diana.

Roger immediately took his sister out of the place. He had been taught always to look after her, and he suddenly thought that this place wasn't right for Diana to be in at night.

"Here—where are you going, Roger?" asked Snubby in surprise. "We've only just come."

"Well, we're going," said Roger. "Come on. Let's go and see if the pierrots have begun their show."

They must have begun because a sound of very sweet singing came down the pier as the three children stood at the turnstiles. "That's Iris Nightingale," said Snubby. "I bet it is. I thought she looked sweet."

"Snubby's lost his heart to her!" said Diana. "*I* thought the Funny Man was the nicest of the three. I loved the way his ears stuck out—they were rather pointed too—like a brownie's!"

A sound of a banjo being played now came from the pier— jig-jig-jig-jiggy-jig-jig-jig! Snubby at once pretended he, too, had a banjo and began to play it earnestly, making a peculiar noise through his teeth as he did so.

"Oh stop it, Snubby," said Roger. "I suppose you think you're very funny."

"Well, I do rather," said Snubby, still going on with his banjo playing. "Everyone roars when I play my banjo at school—a pretend one, of course. I can play the zither too— listen!"

He pretended to be holding a zither, and twanged the strings with much feeling, imitating the sound of a zither as he did so. He really did it very well.

A man strolling down the pier suddenly stopped and listened. He was dressed in pierrot clothes and had obviously left the show for a breath of air. He watched Snubby with amusement.

"Hey there!" he called. "Aren't you the kids at the inn? You're not bad at that fooling, youngster. Why don't you go in for our kids' competition each week—I bet you'd win it!"

Snubby stopped his imitation of a zither, and grinned at the man. "I didn't recognise you in your pierrot get-up," he said. "You're the Funny Man, aren't you?"

The man suddenly waggled his big ears, which startled the children considerably. He also made a most peculiar face which Snubby immediately longed to copy.

"Yes, I'm the Funny Man," he said. "But it isn't always funny to be funny. I get bored, you know."

He did a few ridiculous dancing steps on the pier, fell over his feet and sat down suddenly with a surprised grin. The children roared, and Loony nearly went mad trying to get off the lead and streak through the turnstiles.

"You know, we have fun in these kids' competitions," he said, getting up in one quick movement. "Anyone can go in for them. Five bob prize for the best girl, five bob for the best boy. You ought to come along and try. It doesn't matter what you do—dance, sing, conjure, play the fool. That young fellow there would win the prize for playing the fool in no time!"

He nodded at Snubby, who didn't quite know whether to take this as a compliment or not!

"Snubby's *always* playing the fool," said Roger. "It's the one thing he really works hard at. Isn't it, Snubby!"

Snubby gave Roger a punch. The man grinned and turned to go. The dance music had stopped and he was due back in his place. He threw his cigarette over the side of the pier.

"So long!" he said. "See you in the morning at the dear old inn with Ma Glump seeing that we all use our knives and forks properly, and don't speak with our mouths full."

"Makes you feel quite in the glumps, doesn't it?" said Snubby, remembering the joke he had made before. The Funny Man laughed.

"You ought to come and be my partner," he said. "The Funny Man and the Scream of a Boy. So long!"

He went quickly up the pier. Snubby stared after him. He wasn't quite sure whether the man thought he, Snubby, really was funny or whether he was just making fun of him.

"Showing off!" said Roger to Snubby, in a tone of disgust. "How you can show off like that I don't know, Snubby. Come on—it's getting late. Miss Pepper will be sending out a search party soon!"

They went back to the inn. Miss Pepper met them at the door. "Roger! Diana! Who do you think has just telephoned?"

"Who?" asked everyone at once.

"Barney!" said Miss Pepper.

"BARNEY!" said all three children in delight. "Is he anywhere near then?"

"Come in and I'll tell you what he said," said Miss Pepper. She took them into the lounge which was now empty.

"I was sitting here," she said, "when Mrs. Glump came and said there was a Mr. Barnabas on the telephone for you— but would I like to go instead. I couldn't *think* who Mr. Barnabas was at first!

"I went, and it was Barney, of course," said Miss Pepper. "He's been ill. He sounded very lonely indeed, and I think he was longing to get in touch with the only friends he's got— you three. He gave me a telephone number and said would you ring him when you came in. It's a call-box and he's waiting there now."

"Quick—we'll telephone this very minute," said Diana. "What's the number? Dear old Barney! I'd so love to see him again!"

Miss Pepper gave them the number and they rushed off to the hotel telephone. Barney! How lovely! If only he was somewhere near and could come to Rubadub!

Barney was their circus-boy friend. They had met him by

accident, with Miranda, his clever little monkey—and had been firm friends ever since. He was all alone in the world, and kept himself by taking jobs in circuses and fairs. Now he had been ill—he was lonely. The three children longed to ask him all his news.

Roger and the others crowded into the little telephone box. Roger rang the number. Barney's voice answered at once. "Hallo! Is that you, Roger!"

"Hallo, Barney! Where are you? I hear you've been ill. Are you all right again? How's Miranda?"

"She's fine," said Barney. "I got a chill or something—sleeping under a hedge in the rain. I had to lie up in a barn for a week or two—and Miranda looked after me!"

"Good old Miranda!" said Roger, having a mental vision of the little monkey sponging Barney's face, and bringing him cups of water to drink! "Where are you, Barney? How did you know we were here?"

"I telephoned your home," said Barney. "Your cook told me. Listen—I can get a lift almost to your place to-morrow. Just a stroke of luck. I've been a bit lonely lately—that chill, I suppose."

It was so unlike Barney to admit that he felt lonely that Roger knew at once he must be feeling very miserable. He remembered how he had felt when he had the 'flu in the spring —and he had been surrounded by people eager to help and comfort him. Barney had had nobody but Miranda!

"You come down here," urged Roger at once. "Come and stay at our inn. Oh, wait though—I'm sure Mrs. Glump wouldn't have Miranda. Blow!"

"I can't possibly come and stay where you are," said Barney at once. "For one thing, I've no money and for another, they wouldn't have me there. But I can find some kind of a job, I'm sure, and I can always sleep on the beach in this fine weather. I'd like that."

"All right. Anyway—COME," said Roger. "We'll be on

the look-out for you. Oh, Barney, how super to have you here! Give our love to darling Miranda! Loony will be thrilled to see her."

" I'll come," said Barney. " Good-bye, Roger." There was a click in Roger's ear as the telephone receiver was put down at Barney's end. Roger put his down too. The others immediately plied him with questions.

Roger squeezed out of the box with the other two pressing on him, so eager to hear what he had to say that they couldn't wait to get out of the box properly.

They all went into the lounge, where Miss Pepper was waiting for them. Roger told them word for word what Barney had said.

" So he'll be here in Rubadub to-morrow," he said exultantly. " Good old Barney! It will be grand to see him again, and Miranda too."

" Smashing," said Snubby, who was very fond of the sturdy, self-reliant Barney, and his amusing mischievous little monkey.

" Now go to bed, please," said Miss Pepper, who was longing to go herself. " And please *DO* be down in time for breakfast! "

CHAPTER EIGHT

DEAR OLD BARNEY

THE CHILDREN slept so soundly that they didn't even hear the loud breakfast gong. Miss Pepper came bustling into their rooms just after it went, only half-dressed, with her dressing-gown still on!

"Wake up, do!" she said. "I've overslept as well. Dear me, we shall make a very bad impression on Mrs. Glump if we are so late the first morning. Can you be very quick?"

"No," said Snubby sleepily, and turned over.

345

"Barney may be here at any time," said Miss Pepper artfully.

Snubby shot out of bed at once. "I'd forgotten old Barney," he said. Miss Pepper left the boys dressing quickly, made sure that Diana was also getting up, and went to finish her own dressing. They were so late that only Miss Twitt was in the lounge!

She greeted them beamingly. "You poor things! Did you oversleep? The dear children must have been so tired—and the dear dog too!"

The dear dog was not in the least tired. He trotted up to Miss Twitt, removed her napkin from her knee and made off with it. It was a silly trick he had picked up, most annoying to everyone. Miss Twitt gave a little squeal.

"Oh, naughty, naughty! Bring it back then."

"LOONY!" roared Snubby, in his most stentorian voice. "BRING IT HERE!"

Miss Twitt almost fell out of her chair at this roar, and the noise brought the contemptuous-looking Mr. Tubby to the door. He gazed in inquiringly, looking more miserable than ever, with his baggy wrinkles falling over his doggy face. Loony backed away from him and dropped the napkin. Mr. Tubby sniffed at it, picked it up and took it to his rug. He lay down heavily on it, creaking and groaning.

"There, Loony! He'll take *you* next and drop you on his rug and lie down on you," threatened Snubby, hoping that he wouldn't have to go and rescue Miss Twitt's napkin from the formidable Mr. Tubby.

"Dear Mr. Tubby," gushed Miss Twitt. "Isn't he a *remarkable* dog? I do love dogs, don't you, Miss Pepper. I love cats, too, the dear dainty things!"

"You'd like our cat Sardine then, Miss Twitter," began Snubby. "She likes to trip people up on the stairs in a very dainty way. Oh, and Miss Twitter, you'd love a monkey that belongs to a friend of ours."

" Yes, dear, I'm sure I should," said Miss Twitt. " But my name is Twitt, not Twitter."

" I just *can't* remember," said Snubby, deliberately not looking towards Miss Pepper, who was wearing a fierce and warning frown. " It reminds me of a song I know—twit-twit-twitter little bird—something like that anyway. I do so *love* birds, don't you, Miss Twitter. I think they're sweet."

" Snubby, will you go and get me a handkerchief, please," said Miss Pepper desperately. How could she stop this awful chatter of Snubby's? It was sending Diana into helpless giggles, and Roger was grinning from ear to ear. Even Miss Pepper, angry as she was, couldn't help thinking that Miss Twitt deserved to have fun poked at her—how very, very silly she was! Twittering away like that.

Snubby gave a surprised glance at Miss Pepper. " 'Tisn't often you forget *your* handkerchief," he remarked. He caught her eye and decided to say no more. He went meekly off and returned with a handkerchief. Miss Twitt beamed and looked as if she was about to make a remark about helpful little boys. Miss Pepper charged in desperately before she could say a word.

" I wonder when Barney will arrive, Roger. Did he say any time? We must look out for him."

This was such an interesting theme of conversation that all three immediately forgot about Miss Twitt, and she soon left her table and went out of the room with a swish of skirts, a rattle of bracelets and a sudden waft of rather strong perfume.

" Pooh! " said Snubby. " What's that awful smell?"

Miss Pepper took the opportunity of explaining very clearly and concisely to Snubby exactly what she thought of discourtesy and impoliteness, and threatened such dreadful things that Snubby sank back in his chair, amazed.

" I say! " he said feebly. " I'm sorry. She kind of sets me off, you know, with her twittering. She's too good to be true. Miss Pepper, you don't really mean to say you'd make me go without cake for a whole week, and only let me have one helping of anything? You couldn't be so cruel."

"I could and I shall," said Miss Pepper severely. "I will not have rudeness even if you mean it to be funny rudeness. Now, finish up that toast and marmalade for goodness' sake. I don't want to sit here till dinner-time."

They all bathed that morning. The water was warm, and although there was little wind, there were very satisfactory waves some way out to dive through.

"I like to cut through a wave just as it's breaking," said Diana. "It spills its green colour all over me. I say—it's going to be super here, isn't it?"

They kept a look-out for Barney and Miranda, but they didn't appear that morning. They all went on the beach in the afternoon to read and laze. The sun shone down on them and they began to turn a lobster red. They were all in swim-suits and Miss Pepper thought they would feel very uncomfortable if they got much more burnt!

"Loony wishes he could take off his coat and wear a swim-suit too," said Diana, patting the panting dog. "Hasn't he got a long tongue when he hangs it out? Do you want an ice-cream, Loony?"

"Woof," said Loony at once, scrambling up. "Ice-cream" was one of the words he understood very well! But as everyone was too lazy to go and buy any, Loony lay down again mournfully. Fancy raising his hopes for nothing! He began to pant heavily once more, making Diana feel hotter than ever.

One by one they fell asleep in the sand. Diana lay on her back, her sun-hat tilted over her face. Roger lay on his side, curled up comfortably. Snubby lay on his tummy, and his back got redder and redder. Miss Pepper slept in a dignified manner in a deck-chair, with a sunshade over her head.

Somebody came scampering over the sands. Somebody leapt right in the middle of Snubby's back and jumped up and down there, chattering. Loony gave an enormous bark and planted his front paws on Snubby's back too.

Miss Pepper woke up with a jump. Snubby woke too and yelled angrily, " Get off, idiot! Who's that banging my back? Get off, I tell you, it's sore! "

He rolled over and somebody suddenly cuddled into his neck, making a little chattering noise of welcome.

" MIRANDA! " yelled Snubby. " Oh, Miranda, it's you! Hey, look, Miranda's here. Where's Barney? "

The whole group then became extremely wide awake and lively. Loony went mad, of course, and raced round and round them, kicking up sand as he went. Miranda leapt from one to another, chattering and hugging and snuggling.

Snubby stood up and looked along the promenade. He saw a figure he recognised at once. " Barney! Barney, here we are! Come on, Barney! "

By this time every one on the beach was aware that a boy with a monkey had arrived, and was being loudly welcomed by his friends! Barney jumped down from the promenade and made his way over the sand, grinning. Diana flew to meet him.

" Barney! You've come! Oh, Barney, you've gone thin! "

Barney sat down with his friends, his face beaming. His strange, wide-set eyes were as brilliantly blue as ever and his corn-coloured hair was the same thick mop. His wide mouth smiled happily as he looked from one to another of his friends.

" It's grand to see you, " he said. " It seems ages since May when we were at Ring O' Bells together. And now we're at Rubadub-on-Sea! You're looking fine, all of you. "

" You've been ill, poor Barney, " said Diana. " You look thin and you're not as brown as usual. "

" Oh, I'm better now, " said Barney. " Miranda looked after me, as I told you. I got a chill, I think—sleeping in the rain. I lay in a barn and coughed for days. The farmer let me be there, and Miranda fetched and carried for me! She went to the farmhouse each day and brought back the bread and stuff the farmer gave her. You should have seen her carrying mugs of milk too—never spilt a drop, did you, Miranda? "

Diana's eyes suddenly filled with tears. She could see

Barney lying alone and ill with only a little monkey to see to him. How *awful* to be alone as that—no mother, no father, no friends to rally round! Dear little Miranda—how worried and puzzled she must have been!

" You must have been awfully lonely," said Snubby who, because he had no parents, understood a little more than the others what it meant to be on his own—though Snubby had plenty of kind relations!

" Yes. I'm not usually lonely," said Barney. " I wished my mother wasn't dead. And I wished I could find my father. Just imagine having a father alive somewhere, and you don't know who he is or where he is! He doesn't know anything about me, I know—but all the same we belong, don't we?"

Miss Pepper was listening. She knew all about Barney's history, of course—how his mother, a circus-girl, had married an actor, and had run away from him after three months to go back to the life she loved, in the circus. Barney had been born six months later, but she hadn't bothered to let his father know, afraid that he might want to have Barney for himself.

So Barney had grown up thinking that his father was dead— and it was only when his mother was ill that she had told him her secret—how she had run away from his father, and had never even told him about his son! But no doubt his father was alive, and Barney must look for him, she had said.

And Barney *had* looked for him, but had never found him. What was he like? Was he still an actor? He had acted in Shakespeare's plays, that was all Barney knew. If only he could find the one person who really belonged to him!

" We'll find your father for you," said Diana, unable to bear the loneliness in Barney's voice. " We will, we will! *SOMEHOW* there must be a way, Barney!"

CHAPTER NINE

LAZY AFTERNOON

BARNEY FELT better at once when he had told his troubles and
fears and longings to his three friends. He had brooded over
them after his illness and hadn't been able to get them out of
his mind.

"But now you've told us all about everything, and we'll all
do our best to get things right for you, you'll feel different,
won't you?" said Diana anxiously. She could never bear
people to be miserable.

"I feel different already," said Barney, half ashamed of
telling his troubles. "I shall feel a mutt to-night when I think
of all I've told you."

"Well, what's the good of having friends if you don't share
your troubles?" said Roger sensibly. "It simply means you
trust us."

"Yes. It means that all right," said Barney. "But *you*
don't share your troubles with me—you never seem to have
any. Perhaps people don't when they've got families to belong
to."

"Oh yes they do," said Snubby feelingly. "You wait till
you get into trouble with Uncle Richard like I do—and get one
of his whackings. That's trouble all right. Unfortunately I
can't ask anyone to share it."

"Don't forget that friends share their good things as well
as their troubles," said Miss Pepper. "Seeing we're all friends
together, what about sharing our tea, and a few ice-creams?"

"Golly—is it teatime already?" said Snubby, sitting up
hurriedly. "Fancy—I was so pleased at seeing old Barney, I
actually forgot all about tea!"

"What a wonderful compliment to Barney," said Diana,

stroking Miranda, who was surely the happiest little monkey in the world at that moment. "I shouldn't think anything or anybody made you forget about a meal before."

Barney laughed. This was the sort of silly family talk he loved and never had unless he was with his three friends. All that answering back and idiotic jokes and teasing—it was lovely to him, though Miss Pepper, of course, often got tired of it.

The children had brought tea down to the beach. Mrs. Glump had graciously said that she would have it packed up for them, and had supplied a quite enormous number of sandwiches, buns, slices of fruit cake and some home-made shortbread biscuits that really melted in their mouths.

"This is some tea!" said Snubby, with much appreciation. "I wouldn't have thought Mrs. Glump would have given us such a spread. But she's not as glumpish as she looks."

"She probably hoped that by giving you far too much to eat at teatime, you would eat less at dinner," remarked Miss Pepper, with amusement.

"What a hope!" said Snubby. "It doesn't make the slightest difference as far as I am concerned. You know I always feel frightfully sorry for you grown-ups, Miss Pepper. It must be awful never to have a really good tuck-in because you feel it might be rude or greedy."

"You'll hate being grown-up, won't you, Snubby?" said Diana. "No big meals. No half-dozen ice-creams one after the other. No munching of chocolate bars half the day. No . . ."

"Don't," said Snubby in alarm. "Come on, Barney, have another sandwich."

But Barney's appetite was not what it once had been. Miss Pepper thought he must indeed have been very ill. She wondered what he was going to do now. She wished she could have him at the inn and feed him and look after him a bit. But that was impossible. Nobody there would think of having

Miranda, for one thing, and Barney would certainly not be parted from her.

Also, he was rather down-at-heel and untidy. He had done his best to look clean and neat for his friends, but he had had no money for some time, and it was impossible even to buy new sandshoes. So he wore none, and his feet were brown and bare. His shirt was torn and had no buttons, and his grey flannel trousers were patched about the knees and frayed at the ends.

But what a fine boy he was—good-looking, trustworthy, intelligent and straightforward. A boy any father could be proud of. Miss Pepper looked at Barney and sighed. She felt sure that Barney would never find his father, but she hadn't the heart to say so.

"Barney, I *wish* you could come and stay at the inn with us," said Diana.

"I couldn't," said Barney. "You know that. Anyway, I've got myself a job."

They all stared at him in admiration. A job already! How *did* he do it!

"What job?" asked Roger.

"Well, there's a kind of a small fair in the town," began Barney. "With Dodgem cars and things."

"Oh yes! We went there last night!" cried Diana. "Have you got a job there, Barney?"

"Yes. I'm good at machinery, you know," said Barney. "I'm in charge of the cars—got to keep the machinery oiled and all the cars in running order and so on. It's an easy job for me. I like fairs, too—it's my life and always has been, going about with fairs and circuses!"

"Well, you'll be able to be with us quite a lot, won't you?" said Snubby eagerly. "This fair isn't open till after tea."

"Yes, I guess I can be with you quite a bit," said Barney, pleased. "I won't come to the inn, though. They'd look down their noses at me—I don't look very ship-shape at the moment.

But when I've got a bit of money I'll soon spruce myself up."

All the three wanted immediately to offer Barney every penny they had, either as a gift or as a loan—but they said nothing. Barney was surprisingly proud. It made him feel ashamed and embarrassed if they offered too much.

However, Miss Pepper had an offer to make and she made it briskly.

"There's one thing you can certainly do, Barney. Borrow a swim-suit from Roger—and while you're bathing I can sew buttons on your shirt and mend the frayed ends of your trousers. They look quite clean, so I shan't need to wash them."

"Well—thanks," said Barney, flushing. "I'm not too good at doing things like that."

Roger rushed off and fetched a swim-suit from the inn. Barney went behind a rock and came out again almost immediately in Roger's bathing trunks. He handed his shirt and trousers shyly to Miss Pepper.

"Thanks a lot," he said. "You're really kind. Gosh, it's wonderful to be back with you all again. Loony too—mad old Loony!"

Loony's cup of joy was full and running over now that he had Barney and Miranda as well as everyone else. He raced round the beach at top speed, barked as he passed the others, dodged round Miranda, barked in her ear, and then went off again at sixty miles an hour.

"Express train act," said Snubby. "He'll probably be tired out in a minute and come and flop down beside Miranda —and she'll play a few of her tricks on him."

It happened exactly as Snubby had said. Loony, quite exhausted, and panting like a train going uphill, flung himself down on the sand by the others. Miranda leapt on to his back and pulled up his big, floppy ears. Up he got and tried to shake her off, but she hung on, chattering excitedly.

Loony tore off with her, hoping to jerk her off, much to the amusement of everyone else on the beach. But Miranda stuck on, enjoying her ride immensely, bumping up and down on Loony's back as if he were a little black race-horse!

He suddenly remembered how to get rid of the annoying little monkey! He rolled over on his back and Miranda promptly sprang off, afraid of being rolled on. She scampered back to Barney and leapt into his arms before Loony could catch her.

A man came slowly up to them—a tall, thin man whom the children recognised at once. It was the conjurer belonging to the pierrot show. He had watched Miranda and Barney and an idea had suddenly struck him. He saw that Barney was dressed poorly and guessed that he had to work for his living.

"You boy," he said, when he came up, pointing to Barney.

"Do you want a job? I'm a magician—a conjurer with the pierrot show on the pier. If you like to come there with your monkey as my assistant, I'll give you good wages. What about it, son?"

"Sorry, sir. But I've just got a job," said Barney. "Down with the Dodgem cars. But if it doesn't turn out well, I'll come and tell you. I've got to stay there a week though."

The conjurer nodded and walked away. Barney turned to the others. "Did you see his eyes?" he said. "I bet he's a queer fellow. I guess I wouldn't like to work with those piercing eyes on me! They'd send shivers down my spine. He's the kind of fellow who can see out of the back of his head!"

"All the same, I think it's marvellous to be offered a job just like that!" said Snubby enviously. "I bet nobody would ever offer *me* a job out of the air. I bet it would take me months to find one."

It was a lovely lazy afternoon. Miss Pepper went for a walk about six o'clock and left the little company alone. They told Barney all about the guests at the hotel, especially Miss Twitter. They told him about the funny little hall-porter, Dummy. Barney looked up at once.

"Dummy? What's he like? Tell me."

They described him. "Little—with a big head and round blue eyes—a button of a mouth—and frightfully strong," said Roger. "He's not properly grown-up, I think—sort of half-child, half-adult. I like him. The taxi-driver told us he got into awful rages at times. Why—have you ever met him?"

"Well, it *must* be the Dummy I once knew," said Barney. "He was in a circus with me some years ago. He was always very fond of my mother, who was kind to him. I left that circus and never knew what became of him. Dear old Dummy! I liked him—he was really just like a kind-hearted child—but he certainly could get into savage tempers. He was dangerous then, with his extraordinary strength. I've seen him pick up a man and throw him into the air!"

"Goodness!" said Roger, startled at this new light on Dummy. "Well, you'll have to go and see if it's the Dummy you know. We'll tell him about you."

Miss Pepper came back and called them. "Dinner time," she said. It was the one call that always made them hurry! "Good-bye, Barney, see you to-morrow!" Snubby yelled. "Look after yourself!"

CHAPTER TEN

A WORD WITH DUMMY

MISS PEPPER wouldn't let the children go down to the little fair after dinner. " No," she said. " It will be Barney's first night. He ought to have nothing to attend to but his job."

" We shan't disturb him! " said Snubby indignantly. But Roger saw Miss Pepper's point. It wouldn't be fair on Barney when he was busy learning a new job to have three friends, to say nothing of Loony, trying to get his attention, or embarrassing him by watching him at work.

They decided to go and find Dummy and see if he knew Barney. Mrs. Glump was surprised when they asked if they might talk to Dummy.

" We think we've met a friend of his," explained Roger. " We just want to talk to him and find out."

" But you won't get anything out of poor old Dummy," said Mrs. Glump. " He hardly ever says a word. He can imitate noises. Boom-boom—bang-bang—ch-ch-ch, like a train—mew-mew like a cat. But he doesn't talk."

" Could we see him, all the same, though? " asked Roger.

" He'll be out in the back-yard," said Mrs. Glump, not very graciously. They went to the back of the dark hall, pushed open a baize-covered door, and went into a great kitchen. A door led out from there into the back-yard. It was a horrid little place, full of piled-up rubbish of all kinds, empty bottles, crates, boxes, old decaying vegetables, and a large tabby cat.

The cat immediately vaulted up to a high wall when Loony appeared. Loony, of course, felt sure he could jump the wall and began to fling himself at it madly.

Dummy was there, sweeping up the rubbish when Loony

rushed into the yard, Dummy turned round and saw the children, and his face became just like an amiable child's.

"Woof-woof" he said, pointing to Loony.

"Hallo, Dummy," said Snubby. "We want to ask you something."

Dummy's face clouded over. He obviously didn't like being asked questions. They confused his mind. He didn't mind being told to do things—but he couldn't bear to be asked anything. That meant he had to think of an answer.

"It's all right, Dummy," said Diana, noticing his frown. "We just want to tell you something. We met a friend of ours to-day who thinks he once knew you. A boy called Barney."

Dummy thought hard and then shook his head. The children were disappointed.

"It can't have been the Dummy that Barney knew," said Roger. "And yet—Barney said he was exactly like our description of *this* Dummy!"

Diana suddenly had an idea. She turned back to Dummy, who was regarding the three children anxiously.

"Dummy," said Diana, "Barney had a monkey—a dear little monkey called Miranda. Do you remember *her*?"

A brilliant smile transformed Dummy's anxious face. He threw down his broom and clasped his arms together, rocking them as if he were holding some small creature.

"Monkey!" he said at last. And then with a great effort he brought out the word "Barney." He nodded his head up and down violently, swept with sudden memories. "Barney, Barney, Barney," he said. He pulled at Diana's arm. He pointed round and about as if asking where Barney was.

"He's got a job down at the little fair—where the Dodgem cars are, you know," said Diana.

"Is good, good, good," said Dummy in a transport of delight. Then he caught sight of Mrs. Glump at one of the windows and snatched up his broom again. He began to sweep wildly, sending the rubbish here, there and everywhere.

"Come on—we'd better go. We've excited him so much that he won't be able to sweep anything up properly if we don't go away," said Roger. "I wonder what time he goes off duty. I bet he'll go straight down to the fair to find Barney."

"I do like Dummy," said Diana. "I'm sure he'd be able to talk all right if people were kind to him."

"I'm going to be very very nice to him to make up for all the people who probably haven't," announced Snubby, rather fiercely. "I like him too. He reminds me a bit of Loony—sort of faithful and loyal and all that."

"He's not a *bit* like Loony," said Diana. "Loony's crazy! Look at him now, still thinking he can jump over that wall. Loony, come here. That cat is laughing at you."

They disappeared through the kitchen door, and came out in the hall. It was dark there. They debated what to do.

"Let's see if there's anyone in the lounge," said Snubby "If it's empty we might go in and play cards. But if Miss Twitter's there I shall run for miles!"

Miss Twitter wasn't there. But Professor James was. Fortunately, however, he was fast asleep in the big arm-chair. "We could bring our cards here and just play a *quiet* game for half an hour," said Diana. "He's asleep—and besides he's deaf. He probably won't hear a single sound."

Roger fetched the cards. They sat down round a little table to play, and Roger dealt out the cards. He glanced round at the old Professor to see if he was soundly asleep. If he still was, they could talk in normal voices.

They played two games and then gathered up the cards, wondering if there was time for more. Snubby remembered the little stairway up to the roof, where a view could be got of the sea on the other side of the cliff.

"I wish we could get out of that skylight, walk across the roof to the cliff, and then sit down in that cleft to see the Secret Submarine Base," he said. "We might spot something quite interesting."

"We shouldn't," said Roger. "It's too far away. It's a

funny little staircase, isn't it? I wonder what it was first used for—I mean—it doesn't seem to serve any useful purpose."

"There used to be smugglers here in the old days," said Snubby. "Miss Pepper told me. I wouldn't be surprised if that old staircase up to that roof had some use then—you know —signalling that a smuggling ship had come in."

"Or it might have been used by wreckers," said Diana. "The men who used to send ships on to rocks by wrong signals, so that they could make money out of the wreck."

"Horrible creatures!" said Snubby. "I can't understand people like that."

"You might have done it yourself if you'd lived in those days," said Diana.

"I would not," said Snubby, raising his voice. "How can you say such a thing?"

Roger was listening idly, flipping the cards in his hands. He happened to glance into a mirror opposite him, which clearly reflected the old Professor, who was in a chair a little way behind him.

Had he got his eyes open? It looked exactly as if he had! It looked as if he were wide awake—and yet he hadn't said a word to stop them playing or talking! Roger turned quickly— but no, the old man's eyes were fast shut.

Roger was puzzled. Had he been mistaken? It really had looked as if the reflection showed the old man with his eyes open—why should he pretend to be asleep.

The other two were still arguing. Snubby was angry—how could Diana think he would ever be a wrecker?

"Don't shout," said Diana. "You'll waken the old man."

"I don't care," said Snubby rudely. "I just wish Loony would jump on him and give him a fright. It's awful for a dog to have to lie as still as a mouse under a table!"

Roger looked into the mirror again. There—he was *sure* the old man had his eyes open again! He was looking at Roger's back, listening to what was being said about him.

Roger turned round quickly—but again the old man's eyes

were closed. When Roger turned round to the mirror the eyes were closed there too. He was puzzled. Why was he pretending to be asleep? Just to listen while they went on talking? But then, he was deaf, wasn't he? What was the point then.

Roger gave it up. If an old gentleman liked to pretend he was deaf and asleep, and listen like a sneak to what others were saying, then he could get on with it.

He suddenly determined to find out for certain if the old man was deaf—and asleep. He leaned across the table, and winked at the others. They knew something was up, and looked at him expectantly.

" Listen," said Roger in a sinister sort of voice. " There's no one about except that old fellow there, who is deaf and fast asleep. We can have a few words about What We Know."

" Aha, yes," said Snubby, wondering what was up but quite prepared to fall in with any silly game of Roger's. " About the Man Who Whispers, you mean. And the one with the False Passport."

" That's it," hissed Roger. "Once we find out their Password, we can get going. We must look out for a man in disguise."

" Yes. But you can tell him by one of his little fingers—it's crooked," said Snubby, remembering one of the naval men he had seen on the train and putting him into his silly story.

Diana stared open-mouthed at the two boys. What in the world was all this? Had they gone mad?

Roger looked hurriedly into the mirror. The old man's eyes were wide open. He was certainly listening now. Well, much good would it do him! If he began believing all they said it would give him a lot to think about!

A voice came in at the door, making them all jump violently. It was Miss Pepper.

" Haven't you gone upstairs *yet*! Oh dear—is that the Professor there? I didn't see him at first or I wouldn't have spoken so loudly."

" It's all right,'" said Roger, getting up. " He's fast asleep! "

CHAPTER ELEVEN

MORE ABOUT BARNEY

NEXT DAY was rather exciting. For one thing, Barney had
discovered that Dummy *was* the old friend he had once known.
He was very pleased about it.

They all met down on the beach in the morning. Miranda
was excited and talkative. She began to dig herself a little hole
to sit in, imitating the children. Loony watched her, his
tongue hanging out. Miranda suddenly reached up a quick
paw and pulled it hard. Loony yelped.

"Well, keep your tongue in then, Loony," said Snubby.
"It's just an invitation to Miranda if you stand over her,

hanging it out half-way down your chest. You're a very silly dog to let a monkey get the better of you."

Loony wandered away, offended. Barney began to tell them about Dummy. " I was just finishing my work at the fair last night," he said, " when my boss said ' Chap to see you, Barney.' And in walked old Dummy! "

" Was he pleased to see you?" asked Diana.

" Pleased! I should think so. He took both my hands in his and worked them up and down as if they were a pump handle! " said Barney. " Then Miranda spotted him and she knew him at once. Miranda never forgets anyone, you know. She took a flying leap on to his shoulder, and he cradled her in his arms just like he did when she was a tiny little thing. He crooned to her like he always used to. I nearly howled! "

" Did he talk to you at all?" asked Roger. " He doesn't seem able to talk very much."

" Well, he's not British, to begin with," said Barney, " and he never was much good at picking up our language. But he can talk when he wants to, if he's happy and people are friendly. He couldn't say a word to me at first but he said plenty later on, when he came back to my lodgings with me."

" What did you talk about?" asked Diana curiously. " Your old friends?"

" Yes. And my mother," said Barney. He paused. " Dummy didn't know she had died. He cried when I told him, because he was very fond of her. She was so kind to him. But he said I'd grown quite unlike her."

" How?" asked Roger.

" Well—she was dark and I'm fair. She had brown eyes and I've got blue. She was little and I'm tall. I am sorry I wasn't like her."

" You must be like your father then," said Diana, looking at Barney's strange blue eyes. " That will make it easier when we try to find him. We'll look for someone just like you! "

" I wish I *could* find him," said Barney. " A father's no end of a help when you're growing up. Of course—I might not like him. He might not like me either. He might even be ashamed of me."

" Why did your mother run away from him?" asked Diana. " Was he unkind to her?"

" I don't know. I guess she couldn't live in a house after she'd lived in a caravan all her life," said Barney. " I guess she hankered after the life she knew. But I wish she'd sent word to my father when I was born. It's awful to think he doesn't know about me. He might not believe my story, if I ever do find him."

" What's your surname, Barney?" asked Roger, suddenly realising that they didn't know.

" Lorimer," said Barney. " My full name is Barnabas Hugo Lorimer—what a mouthful! But Lorimer isn't my father's name—it's my mother's. She used her own name again when she ran away, and I never even knew it wasn't my rightful surname till just before she died. She didn't tell me my real name —I don't think she thought to tell me, and I never thought of asking her, because I somehow thought Lorimer was her married name, you see. I never realised it would be important."

" What about your birth certificate?" asked Diana, remembering hers. " That would have everything on it, wouldn't it?"

" What's a birth certificate?" asked Barney, looking startled. " I never heard of one before. Anyway, I haven't got one, whatever it is."

There was a silence. The three children were all thinking the same thing. How hopeless to try and find a man when you didn't know in the least what he was like, or how old he was, or even what his name was! Why, he might be staying in the same town and none of them would know!

Roger made up his mind to ask Miss Pepper's help. She would know how to set about things. Anyway, they did know that Barney's father acted—or used to act, in Shakespeare's plays. That was something.

Loony appeared, carrying some article in his mouth. " Now

what's he got?" said Snubby. "Loony, if you bring that dead crab again I'll make you eat it. It was a bad enough crab yesterday and to-day it'll be worse."

It wasn't a crab. It was a man's hair-brush! Snubby took it out of Loony's mouth and glared at him. "Bad dog! Didn't I tell you that when you come to stay at an inn or hotel you don't pinch people's brushes? You're not at home. Whose brush is this, I'd like to know!"

"Woof," said Loony, pleased with himself.

"Do you mean to say you've been all the way back to the inn, popped upstairs, found an open door and grabbed a brush?" said Snubby. "You must be mad!"

"He's just showing off," said Diana. "He's trying to show Miranda something she can't do."

"Don't say that!" said Barney quickly. "You know how she imitates every one. I don't want *her* arriving with brushes. I should get into awful trouble."

"So will Loony," said Snubby severely. He smacked the surprised spaniel on his nose with the brush. "Why have you always had this passion for brushes? You are *not* to take brushes, towels *or* mats away, Loony!"

Loony backed hurriedly away from another smack and sat down on Miranda. He got up again just as hurriedly, feeling sharp teeth in his tail. He yelped and leapt on to Snubby.

"Don't play musical chairs with me and Miranda," said Snubby, pushing him off. "I'm still cross with you." He examined the brush. It had the initials M.M. on it in silver.

"Matthew Marvel," said Diana, tracing them with her finger. "He's the conjurer. His bedroom is on the same landing as ours. Loony must have found his door a bit ajar, pushed it, and gone in. I believe he thinks that all the rooms there are his to wander round. I found him in there yesterday."

"Well, I'll return it to dear Matthew some time to-day," said Snubby. "I don't feel I can go back this very minute. Let's bathe!"

So they bathed. Miranda wouldn't go into the water, but

‿ ‿ed up and down at the edge of the waves, holding up her little red skirt, much to the amusement of all the children nearby. Loony leapt into the water boldly, trying to keep up with Snubby. Barney swam the best. He was already feeling much better, partly because he was happy again. He thought warmly of his three friends—no, four, counting Loony. Whatever happened, he would never, never lose them.

" Can you come out with us this afternoon, Barney?" asked Roger, as they lay drying in the sun after their bathe.

" Oh yes. I'm not on duty till half-past five," said Barney. " What are you doing?"

" We haven't thought," said Snubby. " I'd like to take a boat out, I think."

" Yes. Good idea," said Roger. " I say—let's row out to Rubadub Whirlpool—I'd love to see that."

" What's that?" asked Barney, interested.

They all told him at once. " It's not very far out—it's towards the cliff that separates our little bay from the Submarine Bay," said Snubby, when Barney had disentangled all the descriptions of the whirlpool.

" Right. We'll get a boat and go there this afternoon," said Barney. " I'd like to see that. I've never seen a proper whirlpool before."

It was lunch-time, so they parted and Roger and the others hurried back to the inn—not because they were late, of course, but because they were overcome with hunger! They ran upstairs to wash and tidy themselves.

" I'd better return Mr. Marvel's brush," said Snubby. " I hope he's not in. If he isn't I could steal into his room and put it back. Then I shouldn't have to explain Loony's idiotic behaviour!"

Snubby knocked quietly. He listened. There was no sound from inside at all. He turned the handle of the door quietly and slid in without a sound, the brush in his hand.

He stopped suddenly. Mr. Marvel was there after all. He sat at a table strewn with cards on which were many numbers of all kinds. He was studying them, and then writing rapidly. Snubby didn't quite know what to do. He gave a polite little cough.

Mr. Marvel leapt to his feet immediately and turned a furious face on Snubby, covering up the cards with his hand. "What is it, what do you want, how dare you sneak in like this?" he demanded in a harsh voice. Then he realised that it was only Snubby, and forced a smile on his long, lean face.

"You silly boy—you startled me! I was just working out one of my conjuring tricks—lost in thought—deep in meditation—and you gave me such a start. What is it you want?"

"I'm sorry to say, sir, that my dog took your brush out of your room some time this morning," said Snubby, still feeling a little scared of the furious face he had just seen. "I've brought it back."

"Oh, thanks," said the conjurer, and took it. He put it down and pulled Snubby to him. "Why don't you wash your ears, boy?" he said.

"I do," said Snubby indignantly.

"Well, well—you've got potatoes growing behind each one," said the conjurer, and removed two small potatoes from behind Snubby's ears. Snubby stared, open-mouthed.

"And why keep watches in your mouth?" said Mr. Marvel, with a little laugh. "Anyone can see them then and take them—like this!" And he inserted finger and thumb into Snubby's mouth and brought out two small watches.

"I say—look, I say," began Snubby, amazed.

"And whatever is that bulging out your shorts' pockets?" asked the conjurer. Snubby looked down, astonished. His pockets were bulging out untidily! He put in his hands and pulled out two carrots from one and an apple from the other. He held them, staring in amazement.

"Food for a little donkey," said Mr. Marvel, and laughed softly. "You do like carrots, don't you? Have them with your dinner!"

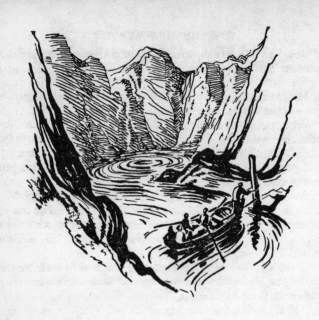

CHAPTER TWELVE

RUBADUB WHIRLPOOL

THE OTHERS had gone down to lunch. They couldn't wait for
Snubby. Nor could Loony, who was also feeling decidedly
ravenous. Miss Pepper looked coldly at Snubby.

"You've been a long time," she said. "What happened to
you?"

"Oh, nothing much," said Snubby airily. "Mr. Marvel
found some potatoes in my ears, and two watches in my mouth
and some fruit and vegetables in my pockets, that's all!"

"Do you mean he did some magic tricks on you?" asked

Diana. "You lucky thing! But I don't believe he took any watches out of your mouth."

"Well, I *wondered* what that ticking noise was that I heard this morning," said Roger. "Gosh, Snubby, you might have let *me* take them out of your mouth."

"He was pretty furious when he suddenly turned round and saw me standing there," said Snubby. "He shot out of his chair, and covered up some cards with his hand as if I'd come to sneak in on his magic. He said I'd disturbed him working out a magic trick. I can't make out if I like him or not."

Mr. Marvel came into the room at that moment, and Miss Pepper signed to Snubby to change the subject. The Funny Man also came in, with Iris Nightingale in a very pretty blue and white frock that took Snubby's eye at once. He grinned at her and she smiled back.

"She's *awf*ully nice!" he said. "I had a word with her this morning. She says we really must go to the show and she'll sing me my favourite songs."

"Well, I only hope she knows ' Ride a Cock-horse to Banbury Cross ' and ' Where did you come from, Baby dear?' " said Roger solemnly and rather loudly.

"Shut up. She'll hear," said Snubby fiercely. "You want a bang on the head, Roger."

"Snubby, behave yourself," said Miss Pepper, much to his indignation. He sat back, sulking, scowling at Miss Pepper. A bird flew in at the open window and fluttered round the room and then flew out. Snubby saw a way of annoying Miss Pepper, and paying her out for insulting him in public.

"Oh, did you see that dear little dicky-bird?" he said, turning round to Miss Twitt with a sweet smile. "I'm sure it twittered. I do so *love* birds, don't you, Miss Twitter."

For once in a way Miss Twitt looked at him coldly. "It's funny your little boy has such a bad memory for names, isn't it, Miss Pepper?" she said. "But there—not all of us can have brains, can we?"

"One in the eye for you, Snubby," said Roger in a low

voice. The Funny Man had heard all this and he gave a guffaw which exasperated Snubby. At all costs he must change the subject. "Miss Pepper, we're going to get a boat and row to Rubadub Whirlpool this afternoon," he said loudly.

"Then you must go with a boatman," said Miss Pepper at once. The three children stared in dismay.

"Oh, *why*?" asked Roger. "You *know* we can manage a boat by ourselves perfectly well."

"I don't know anything of the sort," said Miss Pepper. "And anyway you are *not* visiting whirlpools by yourselves."

"Quite right," said an unexpected voice. "A most dangerous place. Far better for children to keep away from it!"

It was Mr. Marvel speaking. Professor James put his hand behind his ear and spoke loudly.

"What's that? What's that you're talking about?"

"RUBADUB WHIRLPOOL!" shouted Snubby, and made everyone jump.

"Ah, very dangerous place," agreed the Professor. "Shouldn't let them go, Mam."

"Nor should I," said Miss Twitt, shuddering. "Whirlpools suck people down, don't they—and boats too. Down, down, down—it's terrible to think of."

"But, Miss Pepper—there are big advertisements all over the place saying it's just an afternoon trip in a boat," protested Snubby angrily. "We won't go alone if you don't want us to— but do be a sport and let us go with a boatman."

"Try Binns," put in the Funny Man. "He's the man I use. First-class fellow in a whirlpool. Always rows the boat the other way round in a pool so that you can keep quite still and watch it sucking things down. Binns for Brains, I say."

Nobody knew quite how to take this, but Miss Pepper came to the correct conclusion that he was merely being funny. She looked hesitatingly at the beseeching children.

"All right—I'll take you down to the jetty and see you safely into a boat myself with a boatman. In fact, I might even come myself."

"Good," said Roger. "That's settled then. We all go. Barney and Miranda are coming too."

They set off after lunch and met Barney and Miranda. The Funny Man stopped Miss Pepper as they went out.

"Why don't you bring the kids to our show to-night?" he said. "We've got our weekly competition on for children, and one of these might win a prize. Snubby's bright enough anyway! Tell him to bring his banjo and zither. He'll bring the house down with them!"

He walked on. Miss Pepper was surprised. "But you haven't *got* a banjo or a zither, have you, Snubby?" she asked. "What does he mean?"

"Oh, he's just being an ass," said Snubby. "Do let's go to-night, though, Miss Pepper. I'd like to go and see the conjurer anyway."

"And he *does* want to hear Iris Nightingale sing to him," put in Roger, and fled away at top speed as Snubby turned on him.

Miss Pepper found a boatman at the jetty who looked sensible, and strong enough to deal with whirlpools if necessary. She asked him if he could take them.

"Oh yes, Mam, that's right I can," he said cheerily. "And don't you be afraid of being sucked under, Mam—I can always pull you out again. I got a fine boathook, see?"

This didn't sound too good, but Miss Pepper felt that she couldn't possibly draw back now. So in they all got. Barney and Miranda had joined them by this time, so there was a real boatload.

"Do you mind the dog and the monkey?" said Miss Pepper.

"Not a bit. Only wish I'd brought my parrot. Be a bit of company for her, like," said the boatman with a huge guffaw of laughter. "Here you, lad—take an oar, will you?"

Barney rowed as well as the boatman. They shot out over the little bay and veered to the left.

"The whirlpool is round behind that clump of high rocks there," said the boatman at last. "We go between two sets of dark, high rocks, and then the way opens out—and there we are, on the whirlpool, if so be as I don't stop rowing!"

Loony was a bit of a nuisance. He kept racing from one end of the boat to the other, looking forward at the bows, and backward at the stern. Miranda sat on Barney's shoulder, enjoying the rhythmic to and fro movement as he rowed.

They rounded the clump of high rocks. As they came round them the children saw that there was a narrow, very crooked channel winding between them, down the very middle. It was as if the rocks had been cleft in half, letting the sea run right in.

The high rocks cut off the rays of the sun now and again, as the boat made its way carefully through the winding channel. After a little while the children heard a noise—a boiling, rushing, hissing noise that sounded excited and angry.

"Rubadub Whirlpool," said the boatman. "We goes careful here!"

And carefully they went, feeling a sudden pull on the boat as if the distant pool was putting out suckers to drag them to it!

They rounded a bend slowly—and the boatman slewed the boat quickly round to a ledge where a post stood. In a trice he had thrown a rope over it. The boat was held fast.

The whirlpool was not far from them. The channel had suddenly widened right out into a big rounded pool. It seemed alive and angry. It boiled and bubbled and threw up spray, it swelled up, and then, with a horrible sucking sound, it drained down low. Then up it boiled and bubbled again.

"That's one of the finest whirlpools I ever did see," said the boatman. "And I've seen a-many in my time. Anyone want to get out and walk along the ledge to see the pool properly? I'll show you the rock that gives the name of Rubadub—it's like a scrubbing board."

They all got out eagerly, even Miss Pepper, who was really fascinated by the restless, tortured waters of the strange whirlpool. They climbed up on to the ledge where the mooring-post was, and followed the boatman along another ledge that ran at the side of the high, enclosing rocks.

This ledge led them to a small platform of rock immediately over the pool. From there they had a truly wonderful sight of the boiling, sucking waters. The boatman took a piece of wood up and threw it down into the pool. The waters swelled up, bubbling, and then were sucked under again. When they swelled once more, the piece of wood was nowhere to be seen.

"Sucked down," explained the boatman. "It'll never be seen again. You be careful you don't slip any of you!"

Miss Pepper began to wish they were safely back in the boat, but the old man hadn't finished with them yet.

"Now you watch," he said. "Next time the pool swells up and then goes right down again, look across there to the rocky side opposite. You'll see Rubadub Rock."

They watched the waters swell and subside—down, down, down—exposing the rock on the other side. And sure enough, it was straight and oblong in shape—and ribbed just like a scrubbing board!

"Old Neptune's scrubbing board," said the boatman. "I guess he used to send the mermaids here to scrub out his best clothes—rubadub-dub!"

"They'd be sucked down!" said Diana with a shudder.

"Oh, they'd like that. That'd be a game to them," said the boatman, enjoying himself. "Do you know what folks say, Missy? They say that in the time of the smugglers and the wreckers, this was a mighty fine place to throw your enemies!"

"Don't!" said Diana. "I shall dream about it to-night! Is there anything else to see?"

"Oh yes—the Blow-Hole!" said the boatman. "I'll show you the Blow-Hole. Follow me—I'll show you something mighty queer."

CHAPTER THIRTEEN

THE BLOW-HOLE

HE TOOK them to the back of the little platform, and walked on another ledge alongside the high rocks. He came to some natural steps in the rocks and climbed up them to the very top of the outcrop of rocks.

It was windy up there. The breeze whipped Diana's hair across her face, and made Miss Pepper clutch at her scarf.

From this rocky height they could see over the Submarine Bay. "You know what goes on there, I don't doubt," said the boatman. "Secret Submarine work. No one's allowed there, not even us fishermen, though as a boy I knew every corner."

A stone enclosure guarded the whole of the bay. No ships could get in or out without the secret openings' being unlocked Men kept guard in little stone shelters along the top. There was a flash from one of them.

"See that?" said the boatman. "That's one of the guards turning his glasses on us. But he knows we can't get farther than this. If you go over the top of these rocks, any nearer the bay, you'll be blown up. They're mined."

"This all seems extremely dangerous," said Miss Pepper.

"Bless you, Mam, you couldn't get near the mined bit!" said the boatman reassuringly. "There's hundreds of yards of barbed wire."

"What about the blow-hole?" asked Roger.

"Ah yes. Now—you look over there, see?" said the boat-man, and he pointed towards the land, out of which ran the crop of enormous rocks they were standing on.

Suddenly they saw a great spout of water gushing up with a roar. It fell back immediately.

"What was it?" asked Diana, startled.

"I told you. A blow-hole," said the boatman. "Haven't you ever seen one before? There's a-plenty round our coasts, some big, some little. There's a long passage through the rocks from the whirlpool to the blow-hole—and when it's high tide—as it is now—the whirlpool waters get sucked down, and some of them are forced by the tide and the suction through the passage and out of the blow-hole. Watch—there'll be another spout in a minute."

There was. Snubby felt very thrilled. "Why is it only at high tide it comes?" he said. "Why doesn't it come always? Gosh—there goes another! It's like a whale spouting!"

"At low tide the level of the water sinks below the passage," said the boatman. "So no water gets along it. But when high tide swells up the waters again—whooooosh—they force themselves through the tunnel and out of the blow-hole!"

"Where's the entrance to the passage?" asked Roger. "I suppose it's not visible at high tide?"

"No. Not at all," said the boatman. "But I can show you just about where it is. There's a queer old tale about it."

"What?" asked Snubby at once. He never could resist queer old tales.

"Well, it's said that some smugglers once wanted to get rid of one of their enemies so that his body would never be found again," said the boatman. "And they carried him here at dead of night. They threw him into the whirlpool and fled away, back into the bay over there, where the submarines are now."

He paused, and Snubby urged him on. "Go on—what else?"

"Well, the fellow they threw in was a strong man, a giant of a chap. He wasn't going to be sucked down without a struggle. So, before the waters could suck him right down, he flung himself to the edge of the pool and got a grip on a rocky ledge. But he couldn't haul himself up."

"Did he escape all right?" asked Diana. "Do say he did!"

"The tide went down, and the fellow had to change his grip to lower and lower ledges," said the boatman solemnly.

"He couldn't seem to drag himself out, you see. The tide went down and down, and the waters of the whirlpool sank lower and lower. And then the man found himself standing on a ledge at the entrance to what looked like a dark little tunnel in the rocks. I guess it must have been moonlit that night!"

"It was the entrance of the passage that goes to the blow-hole!" said Roger.

"You're right. It was. And up that passage crawled the man right till he came to the blow-hole itself! He scrambled out, made his way back to land—and my word, didn't his enemies stare when they saw him walking down the street. They ran for their lives!"

"I bet they did," said Snubby, enjoying the tale. "Serve them right, the beasts. I hope they all got caught."

"I never heard tell," said the boatman. "There she blows!"

And once again they turned to see the blow-hole send out its sudden high gush of water. "That'll die gradually down as the tide falls," said the boatman. "Well, now, we'll go back. I'm not allowed to take you any farther, and even if I wanted to, there's too many mines about for my liking!"

They watched the blow-hole blow once more and then went back to where they had left the boat. The whirlpool was still performing its endless rhythm, and was boiling away merrily, making a strange, gurgling, groaning, rushing sound.

"Definitely glumpish," said Snubby. "Look at Loony—he's as quiet as a mouse. He's scared, aren't you, Loony-dog?"

Certainly Loony wasn't at all drawn to the whirlpool. He strained away from it as far as ever he could, held tightly on the lead by Snubby.

Miranda was curled up inside Barney's shirt, fast asleep. She didn't even wake when they reached the boat.

"You didn't show us where the entrance hole was," Snubby reminded the boatman.

"No. Nor I didn't," said the man. "Well, while I untie the boat you slip along and look down into the pool. When the water gets sucked down, watch out for a rock with a great knob-like piece on it. The entrance is below that."

Snubby and Roger and Barney went to look. They spotted the knobby rock at once, but could not see any sign of the entrance, of course, because the tide was still very high.

"A jolly interesting afternoon," said Roger. "Kind of trip I like. Something to write about when my form-master gives us his usual essay at beginning of term—'Describe an interesting day in your summer holiday.' I can let myself go about this. I'll put in the tale about the Fellow Who Came Back too. Horrible business it must have been, crawling through that tunnel in the dark—never knowing when the tide might turn and send a long arm of water after you."

"All this has made me hungry," said Snubby. "Anyone got any chocolate?"

Nobody had, so Snubby had to endure his hunger till they reached land. Miss Pepper paid the boatman and they went to have tea at a tea-shop Snubby had spotted that morning.

"It said 'Lobster Teas,'" he explained. "It's just about what I feel like. Why don't we ever have lobster teas at home?"

"Simply because it's easy to catch lobsters by the sea and it isn't inland, idiot," said Roger. "And let me warn you that if you eat more than one lobster you'll probably dream you're being sucked down in that whirlpool to-night."

"It'll be worth it," said Snubby, and was most bitterly disappointed when Miss Pepper refused to let him have more than half a lobster. Miranda liked lobster too. She daintly ate the little bits that Barney held out to her!

They all went for a good walk after tea. They examined the programme for that night's pierrot show as they passed the pier.

"Looks jolly good," said Snubby. "'Fred the Funny Man Keeps You Laughing. Matthew Marvel Mystifies you with Magic. Iris Nightingale sings like her name. Judy Jordan and John Jordan in their Wonderful Dancing Act. Bertram Deep the Baritone, and other talented Players. Philip Drew at the

Piano. GREAT WEEKLY CHILDREN'S COMPETITION
TO-NIGHT. LET US RECOGNISE YOUR TALENTED
CHILDREN EARLY. Two prizes of five shillings.' "

The others read the notice with Snubby. It certainly
sounded a good show. They all felt just in the mood for it.

" Super! " said Snubby, rubbing his hands together. " I
could do with five shillings. Can't think where my pocket
money disappears to."

" Well, I could tell you," began Roger, but Snubby didn't
want to hear. " Barney," he said, " if you went on the platform
with Miranda, you'd bring the house down."

" I'll be at work, you know that," said Barney.

" Yes, I know. Well, I suppose I'll have to uphold the
honour of the family," said Snubby, and began to pretend to
play his " banjo " again, making a horrible metallic, buzzing
noise between his teeth. " Zizz-ziz-ziz-ziz-ZIZZ, zizz-ziz-ziz-
ziz-ZIZZ! "

" *Not* here, please, Snubby," said Miss Pepper. " Is that how
you intend to uphold the honour of the family? I shan't know
where to look if *you* go up to perform! "

" I prefer your zither," said Diana.

" Or what about my mouth organ?" said Snubby, and
pretended to take a mouth organ from his pocket. He wiped it
and put it to his mouth. Terrific noise ensued, extremely like
a mouth organ. Anyone would really have thought that
Snubby was playing one!

" That's *enough*, Snubby," said Miss Pepper, as a little
crowd of interested children gathered.

" You know—I could really make a jolly good living at this
kind of thing, if I stood at a good corner," said Snubby. " I
could put a hat down. I bet it would soon be full of pennies! "

" You're too full of yourself! " said Diana. " Come on—
chase Loony and forget all the marvellous things you think
you can do—but can't! "

CHAPTER FOURTEEN

AT THE PIERROT SHOW

" I SAY! " said Snubby, at dinner-time that night, calling across to Iris Nightingale, " I say—we're coming to your show to-night. We'll clap like anything."

" Good," said Iris, smiling at him. She really was very pretty. " We'll put on our very best show for you."

" And be careful to wash your neck, young man, in case I find more potatoes growing there," said Mr. Marvel.

Snubby scowled as everyone laughed. He determined not to give the conjurer one single clap that evening. Mean fellow —talking about unwashed necks in public!

" I'm coming, too, to-night," put in Miss Twitt. " It's the children's competition, isn't it? I do so love seeing the little dears march up on the platform to give their funny little recitations and songs. The pets! "

Snubby's heart sank. He didn't at all like the idea of having Miss Twitt watch his performance. She would be so silly about it afterwards, he was sure.

Miss Twitt turned towards his table and spoke to Miss Pepper with her usual beaming smile. " And are any of your dear children going to perform? " she gushed. " The little girl, now—I'm *sure* she can dance beautifully."

If there was one thing Diana hated it was being called " a little girl." She glanced despairingly at Miss Pepper.

" Do you mean Diana? " said Miss Pepper. " I wonder why you call her a *little* girl, Miss Twitt? She is almost as tall as you are, and very grown-up indeed! "

Diana could have hugged Miss Pepper! She looked at her gratefully. Why didn't all grown-ups know that boys and girls hated to be referred to as " little "?

" Why don't *you* go up and sing on the platform, Miss Twitt?" asked Snubby innocently. " I'm sure you could twitter like a blackbird."

The Funny Man gave a guffaw and turned it into a coughing fit. Miss Pepper looked fiercely at Snubby, but Miss Twitt actually took it as a compliment.

" Well, I *did* sing beautifully as a child," she said coyly. " Fancy you guessing that! He's quite a cute little boy, isn't he?" she said, turning to Miss Pepper.

" You'll have to take Iris's place when she has a night off," said the Funny Man. " You would give everyone a surprise."

" Oh dear no, I couldn't sing like dear Iris," said Miss Twitt, fluttering nervously. " Ah, here comes the pudding— pineapple and ice-cream—how very nice!"

Miss Twitt was usually only silent when she was attacking her food, and the same thing applied to Snubby. Miss Pepper heaved a sigh of relief when she saw the young waiter put a really enormous helping of pineapple and ice-cream in front of Snubby. How did Snubby always get such big helpings? Miss Pepper supposed that, as usual, he had made himself well known to the staff, and as so often happened, made himself a firm favourite.

The show began at eight. The Conjurer, the Funny Man, and Iris had coffee quickly and then went to get ready.

" We'll have our coffee in the lounge together, shall we?" said Miss Twitt to Miss Pepper. But Miss Pepper had had quite enough of Miss Twitt.

" I'm not having coffee to-night, thank you," she said. " I'll go and sit outside in the evening sun with the children."

She found them wanting to start off for the show at once. " We do want good seats," said Snubby. " I can't see how a conjurer does his tricks unless I'm right at the front. Miss Pepper, let's go now. Have we got any chocolates to eat?"

" No, we haven't," said Miss Pepper. " There's no need to suck sweets or chocolate at the show—especially after such a good meal."

"Oh well, never mind. I think I've got a piece of chewing-gum," said Snubby, searching his pockets.

"Then please give it to me," said Miss Pepper. "If there's one thing I hate more than another it's to see people's mouths moving up and down, chewing gum—looking exactly like a lot of cows chewing the cud!"

"Gosh! Now I know why cows do that," said Snubby. "It's just as good as chewing-gum to them. I never thought cows could be so sensible. Anyway, Miss Pepper, you don't need to look at me while I'm chewing."

"Shut up, Snubby," said Roger. "You go on and on and on like a babbling brook. Let somebody else get a word in. And keep an eye on Loony. He's disappeared into the inn. He'll be bringing out something he shouldn't, I bet!"

Loony appeared, eagerly wagging his stump of a tail. He was dragging a small mat. He laid it down at Snubby's feet.

"Look at that!" said Snubby in disgust. "He's started his idiotic tricks all over again. Take it back, crazy dog!"

Loony tore off, but without the mat. "Now he's gone to get another!" said Diana. "Miss Pepper, can't we start now?"

"Yes," said Miss Pepper, getting up from the seat. "We'll leave Snubby to cope with the mats."

Snubby snatched up the mat and tore indoors. He collided with the Professor and Miss Twitt inside the hall.

"Oh—sorry," said Snubby. "Frightfully sorry. I didn't see you. Are you going to the show? See you there, then!"

"What that boy wants is a good caning," said the Professor, annoyed. "Always rushing about at top speed, shouting at the top of his voice—no manners at all!"

"Ah, yes—but children *will* be children," said Miss Twitt. "Dear little things. I do so love them, don't you?"

"No, I don't," said the Professor. "I should like to drown them all."

And having made this remark loudly and with much feeling, he said no more, but walked slowly off with Miss Twitt, who jingled and jangled as she went, and left behind her a very strong scent of Sweet Pea perfume.

Snubby soon caught up the others, with Loony tearing at his heels, his ears flapping wildly. He slowed down, panting. They came to the pier turnstiles and paid to go in. Then they made their way to the concert room, which was about half-way down the pier. There was a very good platform, and, in the open air, rows and rows of seats. The roof had been drawn back as it was so warm. In wet or cold weather it could be drawn right across, so that the concert room became an enclosed hall.

" This is fine," said Roger. " Are we going in the very front seats?"

They were all taken, however, so the children had to be content with middle seats in the second row. They sat down expectantly. Miss Pepper bought two programmes between the four of them. They studied them in silence.

Professor James and Miss Twitt joined the audience, but they sat half-way down the hall, as by that time all the front seats were taken. Evidently the Rubadub Rollicks were popular! Miss Twitt waved her programme to the children, and they waved back politely.

At exactly eight o'clock there was the sound of merry music from a piano on the curtained stage. Then the curtains swung back with a flourish, to reveal the twelve Rollicks on the stage, all looking very gay and bright, except for the conjurer, who looked his usual gloomy self. He did, however, manage a smile as they all rose to their feet for the opening song.

The pianist was excellent, a bright young fellow who immediately singled out Snubby, and gave him a broad wink which made Snubby feel very proud.

The programme followed a very usual course—songs, dancing, patter, a little sketch or two, much silly talk from the Funny Man, and, of course, the conjuring.

Iris proved to have a very sweet voice. Snubby clapped her so hard that his hands felt quite sore. He went on clapping long after everyone else had stopped. Roger poked him hard with his elbow.

"Shut up! Everyone's looking at you!"

"Encore!" shouted Snubby, undeterred. "Encore!" He was delighted when, at a word from the Funny Man, Iris got up to sing again. She gave him an amused smile.

The ordinary dancing was quite good, and the tap-dancing excellent. Snubby began to strum on his imaginary banjo when Judy Jordan began a tricky little tap dance with clicking toes and heels. Miss Pepper stopped him at once, hearing the familiar "Zizz-ziz-ziz" beginning.

But the best part of the whole show was the conjurer. He was quite brilliant. He didn't smile once as he went through his ritual, dressed for the act as an old-time Enchanter, with pointed hat and flowing cloak. He made Diana shudder, as with gloomy face and deep, gloomy voice he performed his act.

"He's really excellent," Miss Pepper whispered to Diana. "Absolutely in character with his magic! You could imagine him conjuring up genies and spirits and hob-nobbing with witches and goblins. He's really weird!"

The audience watched him in silence. He did unusual tricks. He picked most extraordinary things out of the air—a rose-spray—a pack of loose cards—quite a large book—a bonnet, which he presented to Iris with a deep bow!

He took his wand and announced that he was about to conjure up fire. He muttered a string of queer words that sent shivers down Snubby's spine—and then, hey presto! flames sprang up above his head, burning brilliantly. He really did the most extraordinary things!

"And now," he said, putting down his wand, "now I propose to show you my wonderful mind-reading act. Magic, my friends, pure magic!"

CHAPTER FIFTEEN

MR. MARVEL—AND SNUBBY

"YOU WATCH this," whispered somebody in the seats behind the three children. "It's marvellous!"

Iris stepped forward and bowed. Apparently she was to be Mr. Marvel's assistant. "Blindfold me," commanded the conjurer. Iris took a very large black scarf and blindfolded Mr. Marvel well and truly. Even Snubby was absolutely sure that nobody could see a thing under that scarf. It made the conjurer look very sinister indeed!

The mind-reading act followed the usual ritual. Iris collected articles from the audience, walking down the rows of chairs, smiling, putting her fingers to her lips.

"Mustn't give anything away!" she whispered. "No hints, nothing that might help Mr. Marvel. This is a true and honest test of his powers!"

She went back to the stage. Mr. Marvel, still blindfolded, was twisted round by Iris so that he stood with his back to the audience. She stepped to the front and held out a little gold brooch, given to her by a young girl.

"What do I hold in my hand, Mr. Marvel?" she cried. "Tell me! Let your mind read what I hold!"

Mr. Marvel began to swing his great cloak so that it flowed round him like black waves. He began to mutter in a deep, growly voice that made Loony, who was fast asleep under Snubby's chair, wake up at once.

"I see—what do I see—mirrity-marrity-mingle-o—I see, ah yes, I see—something small—something round—something that shines like gold—abblety-gabblety-mingle-o—it IS gold!"

"Ah, but what is it?" cried Iris, still holding up the little brooch. There wasn't a sound in the concert hall, as Mr.

Marvel began to mutter again. He suddenly swung right round, his cloak flying out round him.

" A brooch. A little gold brooch! "

There was a loud storm of clapping. Snubby forgot that he didn't mean to clap, and clapped hard; Roger and Diana clapped even harder than Snubby. Then Iris swung Mr. Marvel round with his back to the audience again, and this time she held up two things for them to see. One was a silver ring with a yellow stone in it and one was a watch.

" What do I hold now, Mr. Marvel? " cried Iris. " Two things I hold for your mind to read. Tell me what they are! "

There was muttering and mumbling again, and the cloak swung this way and that. To the three children it all seemed very weird and magical indeed. Mr. Marvel brought the house down by guessing both articles quite correctly. He waited till the applause had died down and then said:

" Wait—I see something else. The watch, I see the watch —on the back it has the letters A.G.S. Yes, I see A.G.S."

" You're quite right," said Iris in an astonished voice, looking at the back of the watch. Every one clapped again. A few more articles were held up and correctly described, and then came the last part of the magician's act.

" And now," said Mr. Marvel solemnly, his long thin face looking even longer beneath his pointed hat, " now we come to Numerology. My excellent assistant, Miss Iris, has a pack of cards with her. Each card bears a high number. She will shuffle the cards and pick one at random, showing it to you in silence. I will see it in my mind's eye within thirty seconds or less, and tell you the number she holds in her hand."

Iris took up a pack of cards. They all had plain-coloured backs of yellow. Snubby sat up suddenly. Why, these were the cards that he had seen in the conjurer's room when he had taken back his hair-brush. He must have been studying them then. But what good would any study do if he didn't know which one Iris was going to pick out?

Iris picked out a card and held it up silently. The number

on it was printed in black ink, in large figures across the card. Everyone could see perfectly. The number was 673589255.

The usual muttering noise came from Mr. Marvel. Then he groaned. "It is difficult. Where's my wand?"

Iris gave it to him. He made various passes with it in the air. "Come, genie of the numbers, come to my aid!" he cried, in such an anguished voice that the audience felt scared.

"Ah! AH! Now I see the number! Wait, wait—it comes! The number is 673589255!"

Iris was still holding up the number. Mr. Marvel had guessed it correctly. There was a shout of applause, and clapping and stamping of feet. Wonderful!

"Let's have another number!" shouted a voice.

"Only one more," said Iris. "This is a great strain on Mr. Marvel."

It certainly seemed to be by his writhings and mutterings and passes in the air with his wand. But he at last guessed the number correctly again.

"It is—it is—864592643!"

"Gosh—he scares me," said Snubby to Miss Pepper. "I'm going to be jolly polite to him in future. He's a wonder."

There was a merry song and dance next, to remove the tense atmosphere that Mr. Marvel had so cleverly created. Then Iris stepped forward again.

"Now comes the end of our programme and perhaps the best part," she said with her engaging smile. "The Children's Competition. As usual we have two prizes of five shillings, one for the cleverest boy, and one for the cleverest girl."

A jingling noise from the Funny Man proclaimed that the money was ready and waiting. "Can I go in for it, please, Miss?" said the Funny Man pathetically. "I can sing 'Three Blind Mice' well, I can, really."

Iris went on with her little speech. "We don't mind what you do—sing, dance, recite, play our piano, tell us a funny story—or even do a bit of conjuring that will put Mr. Marvel into the shade. Now come along—who will be first?"

Two small girls and a boy pushed their way eagerly to the stage. Another girl followed, and two more boys. Roger gave Snubby a nudge. "Go on! Do your stuff too, Snubby."

But Snubby was unaccountably overcome with nerves, and he glowered at Roger. "I'm not going to make a fool of myself, so shut up."

The children proved very ordinary indeed. Two of the girls played the piano, thumping hard and strong. One boy sang a comic song, of which nobody could hear a single word.

Another small girl did a competent little step dance, but was obviously so conceited that nobody clapped very much except her fond and admiring Mamma.

Then a boy about Snubby's age gave a recitation at top speed so that nobody could follow it at all. He then retired from the platform, also at top speed quite overcome by his effort.

The third boy refused to perform after all. He stood up on the platform the picture of misery.

"I've forgot me words," he kept saying. "I've forgot me words. Mum, what's me words?"

Mum had apparently forgotten them, too, so the small boy left the platform in tears.

"Now now, children!" said Iris reprovingly. "I'm *sure* there's somebody else who can try for the five shillings. We do badly want another boy."

"Let *me* try, Miss, do let *me* try," urged the Funny Man, putting on a little-boy voice. "I'm top of my form, I am, for singing and whistling." He pursed up his mouth to whistle, but hard as he blew, no sound came. So he produced a big whistle from his pocket and blew, making Iris jump violently. Everyone laughed, he was so idiotic.

"One more boy!" urged Iris. "Just one. Then we shall have had three girls performing and three boys."

The Funny Man came to stand beside Iris. He looked straight at Snubby. Then he pointed at him. "Look, Iris," he said, "there's the World's Wonder down there. See him? Chap with red hair, turned-up nose and freckles! Finest banjo player the world has ever seen. Pays a hundred pounds for each of his banjos. Whew!"

Every one craned their necks to look at Snubby. He went scarlet to the roots of his red hair. "Come on, son!" cried the Funny Man. "Come on up and play your banjo. Tell us your tune and the pianist will accompany you."

"Go on, Snubby," said Roger. "You've got to, now. Those other boys were frightful."

Snubby went up to the platform, half annoyed, half pleased at the Funny Man's patter. He stood facing the audience. The Funny Man solemnly placed a chair beside him. "To put your leg up on," he informed him. "That's a heavy banjo you have there. Rest it on your leg, mate. Now—what's your tune?"

Snubby suddenly entered into the fun of it. He laughed. "I'll play you ' What's the time when it's twelve o'clock,' " he announced, and put his leg up on the chair. The song was very popular just then, a silly jigging tune, admirable for the banjo. The pianist nodded. He knew the tune well.

"I must just tune up," said Snubby, and he solemnly tuned up the strings of his imaginary banjo, making twanging noises as if he really were screwing the wires to their correct pitch. People began to laugh.

"Right. Ready?" said Snubby to the pianist. "Not too loud, please. Tune all through, the chorus twice."

He brought his hand down on imaginary strings and made a startling twanging noise. Then off he went, twanging away with his right hand, and with his mouth making a most remarkable banjo-like noise he followed the tune absolutely correctly. Snubby could make his noises very loudly, and the pianist did not drown him at all, but followed him perfectly. They made an excellent pair.

"Twang-a-twang-twang-twang, twang-a-twang-twang," went Snubby, and ended off with what sounded like a marvellous chord. He put down his leg and bowed solemnly.

He got more applause than any other member of the show

had been given, even more than Mr. Marvel! Everyone yelled for more.

"One more—can you manage it?" asked the Funny Man, delighted. "Any other instrument?"

"I've happened to bring my zither," said Snubby solemnly, and put down his imaginary banjo and took up his imaginary zither. "I'll have to sit down for this, please."

He sat down, and once more he and the pianist gave an extraordinary performance together. Snubby reproduced the harp-like sounds of a zither perfectly, and instead of a jiggy song, he chose a romantic tune, "If I could only give you the moon." He didn't sing it, of course, but made the sound of a zither playing the tune. It was most remarkable. Everyone listened intently.

Fancy *Snubby*, the crazy, idiotic *Snubby* holding a big audience like this with just a little make-believe! Roger and Diana felt swollen up with pride in their cousin!

The tune ended. The Funny Man bowed to Snubby. "Quite a maestro!" he said, and Snubby wondered whether he was being rude or complimentary. He had never heard the word before. But the Funny Man was delighted with him. He turned to the audience. "And now to give out the prizes," he said. "We award the girl's prize to little Lorna Jones for her step dancing."

There was very slight applause. Certainly Lorna had been good, but nobody had liked the little show-off.

"The boy's prize goes—of course—to our young friend here, for . . ."

But the rest of his words were drowned in claps and stamps and cheers. Snubby, redder than ever, bowed, and took the five shillings. What an evening! Whoever would have thought that his crazy habit of strumming imaginary musical instruments would have brought Snubby such applause?

CHAPTER SIXTEEN

WHAT HAPPENED IN THE NIGHT

SNUBBY walked home in a whirl of excitement. "Now don't let all this go to your head," said Roger, afraid that Snubby might become quite unbearable. "After all, you can't *really* play the banjo or the zither—and you can only pick out 'chopsticks' on the piano. You're no musician, really."

"And for goodness' sake don't play banjos and things all over the hotel," begged Diana. "They won't like it a bit if you do."

Snubby took not the slightest notice. "I've been wondering if I could do an organ," he said. "Or a drum."

"*No*, Snubby," said Miss Pepper firmly. "Oh dear, here comes Miss Twitt. Hurry!"

But Miss Twitt was determined to pile praises on Snubby. "The little wonder!" she said, as she hurried up to them. "What a little marvel! The clever little boy. He's a born player, isn't he, Miss Pepper?"

"Well—I wouldn't say *that*," said Miss Pepper. "He can't play a note, actually."

"Fancy that! It just shows how wonderful he is to make people think he *can* play!" prattled Miss Twitt. "I *quite* thought it was a real banjo, you know. He really *ought* to join the pierrots, oughtn't he? Everyone would come to hear him!"

Miss Pepper glanced at Snubby and was horrified to see a pleased and fatuous smile on his face. He was drinking it all in!

"Snubby's little tricks are quite all right to amuse his friends at school," she said firmly. "But that's really all they are. It's silly to think them anything else, Miss Twitt."

Fortunately they had now reached the inn. "I want a drink," announced Snubby. "All that twang-a-twang has made me thirsty. Can I have a lemonade, Miss Pepper—two if you like. Oh, I say—wait a bit, though—I'd forgotten my five shillings. Drinks all round, please. What'll you have, Miss Pepper? Miss Twitt? Orangeade? Lemonade? Or go a splash and have a ginger beer?"

Diana began to giggle. Snubby really could be very funny. Miss Pepper ordered the drinks and then sent all three children, and a very sleepy Loony, up to bed.

"It's late," she said. "Very late. Take your orangeade with you. No, Snubby, I don't care if you have five shillings or ten shillings, you can't have more than one orangeade. No, Loony can't have one either. Water is good enough for him."

Snubby went off sorrowfully. He had hoped to stay downstairs until Iris, Mr. Marvel and the Funny Man came back, and also Professor James who had still not returned. Praise from them would be worth a hundred times more than fulsome words from Miss Twitt.

Snubby was too excited to go to sleep that night. Roger snored gently and peacefully while Snubby tossed and turned, his mind full of wonderful plans. He would practise more and more imaginary instruments to play. He would broadcast— perhaps he wouldn't though, because people might think he was *really* playing a banjo or zither or guitar—they wouldn't be able to *see* that he hadn't really got one.

Well, what about television, then? That would be the thing. And what about a drum? He was sure he could make that big BOOM-BOOM noise. He began to practise it very softly. Then he couldn't resist doing a very loud BOOM!

And then a most frightening thing happened. As soon as Snubby had delivered his BOOM, another BOOM came—a terrific one, muffled and very frightening. The inn shook. Snubby sat up in bed, scared.

"Bombs!" he thought. "No—can't be. Of course—it's an

explosion in the Submarine Bay. Some experiment like the one we heard the other day."

He thought for a moment. "But wait a minute—this is the middle of the night—about half-past two, I should think. They wouldn't experiment then, and wake everyone up."

The noise hadn't, however, awakened Roger, who was in his deepest sleep. It hadn't awakened Diana either. Miss Pepper had heard it, and had sat up, listening. But as there was no more sound she had lain down again.

Snubby felt restless. He couldn't possibly lie down and go to sleep to-night. A thought flashed into his head. He would go up that little stairway that led to the skylight, open it, and peer out. He *might* be able to see something through that cleft in the cliff—something down in the Submarine Bay!

He slipped out of bed and went to the door. He opened it and went out on to the dark landing. Nobody seemed to be stirring. Perhaps they hadn't heard the noise then.

Snubby stole to the little door that shut off the steep staircase. He opened it quietly. Yes—there was the staircase—he could feel it with his foot though he couldn't see it. He went up cautiously. It was a clear night and Snubby could see stars shining through the little square of glass set in the middle of the trap-door that opened on to the roof.

He opened it, pushing it back carefully, so as not to make a sound. He looked out.

Gosh! Something *had* happened down in the Submarine Bay. Snubby could see quite clearly through the cleft in the cliff. Far away, on the other side of it, was the bay, and something was burning there, on the water. Searchlights were playing here and there. Snubby held his breath. Something had happened. Some awful accident, perhaps. He wished he could see more.

"Perhaps if I climb right out of the trap-door I can find a higher place to see from," he thought. "It would be easy."

He climbed to the topmost stair and found it simple to get out on the roof, which, just there, was flat. Snubby looked round. There was a rise in the roof just to the right of him, where a set of chimneys rose up together. He could sit on the little rise, beside a chimney.

He made his way cautiously across the rise in the roof, and crawled up it on hands and knees. Now he was by a chimney. But the wind swept him that side, so he crawled round in between two chimneys where he was well protected. One chimney was warm—good!

But to his disappointment he couldn't see much more of the bay than he had seen before, although he was now a little higher. Searchlights were still criss-crossing, and the flames of whatever was burning were still as high. Perhaps a submarine had exploded and was on fire.

Snubby cuddled up to the warm chimney, feeling daring to be out on the roof in the middle of the night. He suddenly sniffed the air.

He could smell something. What was it? Cigarette smoke! Couldn't be! No one else was up on the roof in the middle of the night—smoking a cigarette too!

He craned his neck round the chimney, and saw, in the distance, a tiny glow, the red, burning end of somebody's cigarette. Somebody else had heard the explosion then and had come to see what could be seen.

He soon saw that the glowing end was just where the trapdoor opened on to the roof. Somebody must be standing on the stairs there, looking out and smoking. Snubby was just about to give a low call to tell them that he, too, was there, and had heard everything, when he stopped himself.

No. He'd get into a frightful row for being out on the roof at night. If Miss Pepper heard of it she would be furious. There wouldn't be any second helpings for the rest of the holidays! Silence was best. But *who* was it there? Snubby screwed up his eyes, but he could only make out a blob of a head with the glowing end of the cigarette in front.

After a while the smoker finished his cigarette and threw it down the roof. Snubby heard the soft creak of the stairs.

Somebody was going down them—but that somebody had shut down the trap-door first! Snubby's heart missed a beat or two. He could imagine himself sitting out on the roof all night —falling asleep—rolling down the roof—oh, how simply horrible!

He crept across to the trap-door. As he got there, a light sprang in the window of a room some distance away. Snubby stopped. Who was in there? Probably, whoever it was, was the smoker of a few minutes before—he must have returned to his room and switched on his light. Snubby decided to see who it was.

He crawled to another position, and found that he could look right across the roof into the lighted room. The curtains were drawn across, but there was a space about a foot left in the middle.

" Gosh! It's old Professor James!" said Snubby. "What a good thing I didn't let him know I was up here. He'd have told Mrs. Glump and Miss Pepper and got me into an awful row! "

He tried the trap-door with a trembling hand. Had the Professor slipped the catch into place, so that it could not be opened?

With an enormous sigh of relief Snubby found that he *could* open it. Thank goodness! He swung it back, and then clambered on to the narrow wooden stairway. He closed the trap-door quietly and then climbed down the stairs. He opened the door at the bottom, went on to the landing and back to his room. Roger was still fast asleep.

Just as he was about to shut his door he saw a line of light under a door nearby. It was Mr. Marvel's door. So he had heard the explosion too. Snubby debated whether to go in and have a chat about it—surely Mr. Marvel would welcome him now that he had given such a fine performance in the show!

He decided against it, however. Mr. Marvel wasn't quite the person to enjoy a midnight chat. He might start to do a bit more unpleasant magic on Snubby!

CHAPTER SEVENTEEN

THE NEXT DAY

IN THE morning the whole inn was agog with the news of the explosion in the night. So were the papers.

"GREAT EXPLOSION IN HUSH-HUSH BAY," said the headlines. "WAS IT SABOTAGE? ARE OUR SECRETS SAFE? INHABITANTS OF SURROUNDING TOWNS ALMOST HURLED FROM THEIR BEDS."

"What a lie!" said Snubby. "The bed just shook that's all. And you didn't even wake, Roger. I did."

"Did you?" said Roger. "Was it really a big explosion?"

"Terrific," said Snubby. "Tremendous. Louder than thunder. I got out of bed and went up that stairway to look out of the trap-door—and I saw something burning like anything. And searchlights going like mad over the bay."

"Sh! Miss Pepper will hear you," said Diana. "She'd be furious if she thought you went wandering about at night— especially up to the roof."

"She didn't hear," said Snubby. He glanced round. Old Professor James was nearby reading a newspaper. He was deaf so he wouldn't have heard either. Mr. Marvel and the Funny Man were also near—they would have heard, but probably they didn't know about the staircase anyway.

"I did something else too," said Snubby, lowering his voice. "I got out on the roof and sat beside a jolly warm chimney. Somebody else came up the staircase and looked out too. The old Professor, I think. Fancy him hearing the explosion and not you, Roger!"

"I expect the vibration woke him, not the noise," said Diana. "I say—it's pretty serious, isn't it? One of our newest submarines blown up to the surface—and then burnt to nothing! I do wish you'd woken me up, Snubby!"

"You'd have hated seeing it," said Snubby. "Is it sabotage, do you think? I mean—would it be possible for anyone to get into the bay and do a thing like that to damage us? I should have thought things were much too strict and closely guarded."

"It was probably an accident," said Roger. "You can't have successful experiments without accidents. Look at the things that happen in the lab. at school!"

"Oh well—we *plan* some of those," said Snubby. "A bit of well-planned trickery! All the same—I'd like to know if it *was* an accident. I don't want to think of people somewhere around planning to blow up more submarines—especially while we're staying here."

"Why? Are you afraid of being mixed up in another mystery?" asked Roger with a grin.

"*Afraid!*" said Snubby with scorn. "I *like* mysteries. I dote on them. But this isn't a mystery, it seems to me. I bet it's an accident."

Whether it was or not they didn't learn from any of the papers that morning or evening. The Press seemed to shut down on the incident, which annoyed the children very much.

That afternoon was wet. The rain poured down and the children looked gloomy.

"It's a glumpish afternoon," said Snubby. "What shall we do? Shall I practise my banjo?"

"Not unless you go up on the roof or somewhere far away," said Roger. Snubby had produced his imaginary banjo, zither, guitar and harp at different times that day, and Roger and Diana were getting a little tired of the remarkable twanging, zizzing, buzzing sounds produced by Snubby.

"Let's go up that little stairway and see if the poor old submarine is still burning," said Snubby. "I promise I won't take any musical instruments with me!"

They ran upstairs to their landing and went to the little door that enclosed the staircase. Snubby turned the handle. But the door wouldn't open!

"What's the matter with it? Is it stuck?" he said, and pulled violently. All that happened was that the handle came completely off in his hand and he sat down heavily on a startled Loony.

"Ass! You *would* do that!" said Roger.

"Things always come off in my hand," complained Snubby. "Now what shall we do?"

"You'll have to go and own up to Mrs. Glump," said Diana. "Go on, Snubby. If you were brave enough to get out and sit on the roof last night, surely you're brave enough to confess to Mrs. Glump."

So Snubby had to go and find Mrs. Glump. She was in a peculiar little den, adding up rows and rows of figures, and didn't look at all pleased to see Snubby. He explained what had happened.

" But why did you pull at the handle so violently?" asked Mrs. Glump, resting her face on her four or five chins, and looking most majestic. Snubby wished he had a few chins he could look majestic with too. He felt very small beside Mrs. Glump, and she made him feel like a naughty little boy.

" Well, I pulled hard because the door stuck," said Snubby. " It's locked, I think."

" Locked! But the key would be in the lock anyway," said Mrs. Glump.

" There wasn't a key. I looked," said Snubby. " I'm sure it's locked, Mrs. Glump. I thought *you* must have locked it. I'm sorry about the handle. I've still got one and sixpence left out of the five shillings I won at the pierrot show yesterday. Would one and six pay for a new handle?"

" I expect so," said Mrs. Glump. " But I'm sure Dummy has an old one he could fix on quickly. Go and ask him. And I hear I must congratulate you on winning the prize yesterday. Let me see—you played the banjo, didn't you?"

" Not a real one. My imaginary one. Paid a hundred pounds for it!" said Snubby with a grin, and immediately began to play a jigging, strident tune, twang-twanging in a most lifelike manner.

Mrs. Glump began to laugh. She had a very curious laugh. It seemed to begin somewhere deep down and then rumbled all the way past her magnificent chins, and came out as a very hearty affair indeed.

Snubby stopped, bowed and grinned. " You're a caution," said Mrs. Glump. " Get on with you! Go and find Dummy about the handle. And don't shut my door too violently in case the whole door comes off in your hand."

Snubby went out, pleasantly surprised. She wasn't really glumpish at all! He made his way to the kitchen to find Dummy. He was polishing some horse-brasses one by one and making a very good job of them.

" Hallo, Dummy. Can I help you? I collect horse-brasses

too," said the cheerful Snubby. " I say, did you hear about me winning the five bob at the show last night?"

Dummy listened and nodded. " You," he said. " You win. Good boy."

" My word, you *are* a chatterbox to-day," said Snubby, rubbing vigorously at a brass.

" What you do?" asked Dummy earnestly.

" This," said Snubby, and played his imaginary banjo again. To his enormous surprise, Dummy also picked up an imaginary banjo and began to twang it, making a most peculiar noise as he did so, almost as good as Snubby's!

" Here—what's all this?" said a voice, and the face of the young waiter poked round the door. " Some band performing here?"

Dummy fled at once, out into the back-yard. He sat down, blinking his eyes, confused. Years and years ago he had had a real banjo and he could play it. But when he had fallen from the rope, during a wire-walking act, he had hurt his head—and after that Dummy was different. Poor Dummy!

He sat till his mind cleared a little. He began to smile. Yes —he remembered his old banjo—and the tunes he played. He twanged imaginary strings again.

Snubby came into the yard to find him. " Oh, there you are, Dummy. I say, I forgot to tell you what I wanted you for. Have you got a spare door-handle? I've somehow pulled off the handle of the door that shuts in that little stairway leading to the roof."

" Roof," said Dummy. He stared at Snubby and then suddenly leaned forward. He whispered loudly in his ear. " Mind bad men up there! Bad men!"

Snubby drew back, startled. Dummy smiled and nodded at him. Then his face grew solemn again. " Bad, bad, bad," he whispered again. " Dummy see. Dummy watch. Dummy follow. Bad!"

Snubby looked at Dummy doubtfully. Poor old fellow—

what peculiar imaginings had he got now? He couldn't imagine Dummy watching people and stalking them! Snubby decided to humour him.

"Snubby see. Snubby watch. Snubby follow," he said, equally solemnly. "Gosh, we sound like Red Indians or something. Dummy, where's an old door-handle? Let's find one and go in. I'm not too keen on sitting out here in the rain— twang-a-twang-twang-twang, zizz-a-zizz-ziz-ziz. Ker-plonk! There—I knew a string would bust if I played out in the rain. See that?"

He held out his imaginary banjo, and Dummy laughed delightedly. It was the first time Snubby had heard him laugh. It was a ripple, just like a very young child's. Snubby patted Dummy on the back.

"That's right. Laugh your troubles away! Have you got a door-handle, for the third time of asking?"

Dummy had. He produced one from a shed and went upstairs. He was clever with his fingers and had soon fixed it on the door. He gave it a pull.

"Locked," said Snubby. "And the key's gone. Who did that? And why? I tell you, Dummy, there were mysterious goings on up here last night!"

"Indeed? And what were they?" said a voice.

Snubby jumped and turned round. Mr. Marvel the conjurer was standing outside his door. Snubby thought furiously. No—he wasn't going to give anything away and get himself into trouble.

"Oh, nothing," he said airily. "I was just putting the wind up old Dummy. I say, sir—that was a wizard act you put on last night. How did you guess those articles—and the initials on the back of the watch? Beats me!"

"That's *my* secret," said Mr. Marvel. "Did you hear the explosion last night?"

"Yes, I jolly well did," said Snubby. "Did you?"

"No, I didn't," said Mr. Marvel, which surprised Snubby very much. Hadn't he seen a line of light under Mr. Marvel's door when he, Snubby, had come down from the roof to go to bed again?

" I saw a light under your door though," blurted out Snubby, and could have kicked himself.

" Indeed? And what were *you* doing out on the landing at that time of night?" said Mr. Marvel at once.

" Just peeped out to see if any one was awake after the explosion," said Snubby. " I say, sir—how *did* you guess those numbers last night?"

But Mr. Marvel was gone. Snubby was left staring at a closing door. He made a face at it. All right—*be* snooty, Mr. Marvel! You *were* awake last night! Snubby shook a furious fist, marched into his own room, and slammed the door!

CHAPTER EIGHTEEN

THE TIME GOES BY

AFTER THE first few days the holidays began to slip away fast, as holidays always do.

A week had gone by before any of the children realised it. It had been a good week—bathing, boating, paddling, walking—messing about with Barney and Miranda. Loony had enjoyed himself too.

He dug violently every morning, covering everyone with sand. He then ran into the sea and got thoroughly wet. Then he came back and shook himself really vigorously, showering everyone with drops of sea water.

He had also developed a new and most irritating habit. Having been smacked hard for attempting to bring brushes, towels and mats on to the beach, he cast about for something that nobody could possibly object to.

He brought along a strange dog each day to play with him. The first time he brought a peculiar-looking mongrel with very short legs and a large head.

"Look at that," said Snubby. "Poor creature. If its legs were much shorter they wouldn't touch the ground!"

"Ha ha—very old joke," said Diana. "All the same, it *is* a peculiar dog."

"It's a bit of a smelly dog," said Roger, as the dog sat down heavily on his legs. "Get off, Smelly! Go away!"

But Smelly had no intention of leaving his good friend Loony. They went crazy together and nearly drove Miss Pepper mad as they tore round and round her deck-chair. They had to put up with Smelly all day, and were amazed to see Loony sharing all his tit-bits with him.

The next day Loony trotted off the beach and returned with

a second friend—a bulldog with a face a bit like Mr. Tubby's. He wasn't as bad as Smelly, and he liked to sit as near every one as possible.

"I wish you wouldn't *dribble* all over me," Snubby said to the bulldog. "You want a bib or something. Miss Pepper, do bulldogs always dribble or is this one just doing it on purpose?"

"He's dribbled over me too," said Diana. "I remember a teacher at school who had a bulldog and he dribbled as well. Loony, next time you bring a friend, bring one who doesn't smell *or* dribble!"

The bulldog was very sweet-tempered until he took a fancy to a bone that Loony was gnawing. Then he gave out such blood-curdling growls that even Snubby drew back. Miranda was with them at the time and she leapt on the top of Barney's head in fright.

"Go away," said Miss Pepper firmly to bulldog. "That's Loony's bone. Go away!"

The bulldog calmly picked up the bone and waddled off. Snubby gave Loony a poke with his foot.

"Coward dog! Couldn't keep his own bone! Cowardy custard!"

Loony hung his head. He crept off the beach when no one was looking. He returned looking quite a different dog, bright and cheerful, accompanied by three small dogs of the terrier type, all very alert and inquisitive.

"Oh, stop it, Loony! Have you gone potty?" said Snubby, surveying the four dogs in disgust. "What do you want to go and pick up half the town for? Shoo! Scat! Clear off, all of you. No, not you, Loony. You're going to be tied up to Miss Pepper's deck-chair for the rest of the day."

"Oh no, he's not," said Miss Pepper at once. "You did that two days ago and he made my chair collapse. Tie him to your foot!"

Barney was rather quiet after three or four days. He didn't encourage the others to go to the fair. "It's a rough place," he said. "Don't come. I don't like the men who run it either.

They're cheats. They're in some racket or other, too, but I don't know what it is."

"Why don't you leave them, Barney?" said Diana anxiously. "I *knew* you weren't pleased with the job. Don't stay with dishonest men."

"Oh, I'm used to that type," said Barney. "You can't knock about as I do without coming up against them all the time. Anyway—where would I get another job?"

"Don't you remember—the conjurer belonging to the pierrot show said he'd take you as an assistant," said Diana, remembering.

"But he's got Iris," said Snubby. "I don't know why he said he wanted another assistant!"

"No. Perhaps he doesn't," said Diana. "When's your week up, Barney? To-morrow, isn't it?"

"Yes. I get paid then," said Barney. "Two whole pounds! I can buy some new sandshoes and a shirt."

"Well, *do* leave then," said Diana. "I don't like that place either. I'm *sure* you could get a job somewhere else!"

But Barney wouldn't say he would leave. It wouldn't be easy to get another job in Rubadub, and he did so want to be near his friends.

That night Iris didn't go to the show. It was her night off. She sat in the lounge and played cards with the children, looking almost as young as Diana. Snubby sat next to her, wishing he could deal her the best cards in the pack. Loony sat on her feet. He agreed with his master that Iris was a very nice girl indeed.

"What will Mr. Marvel do without you to-night?" asked Diana, watching Roger deal the cards. "Does he do his mind-reading act when you're not there to help?"

"I don't know," said Iris. "I don't care either! Surly fellow. I don't like him."

"Why?" asked Snubby.

But Iris wouldn't tell why. "He used to have a helper," she said. "A youngish fellow. Then he suddenly went, I never knew why, and Mr. Marvel asked me to take over till he got someone else. I said I'd try for two weeks. But I don't like it, and I'm not doing it any more. The two weeks are up now."

Diana now knew why Mr. Marvel had asked Barney to be his helper. He had been afraid that Iris wouldn't go on with him after two weeks.

"Has he got anyone instead of you, do you know?" she asked suddenly.

"Someone came to see him to-day. I expect he was after the job," said Iris. "He'll probably get it, too, because Mr. Marvel must have someone. He can't do that mind-reading act without an assistant."

"Why not?" asked Snubby. "Anyone from the audience could be called up—or one of the other pierrots."

"No. He wants a proper assistant of his own," said Iris. "Look, are we playing a game of cards or is this just a chatter party? I've got such a wonderful hand that I'm longing to play it!"

Diana didn't play very well that night. She was thinking hard. Suppose they went to Mr. Marvel and begged him to take Barney instead of the other applicant? If they could tell Barney they had the job for him, surely he would give notice at the little fair to-morrow, and join the pierrots? He would make a wonderful assistant!

She could hardly wait to tell the others when they went to bed that night. They listened in silence.

"Yes," said Roger. "I think we ought to tell Mr. Marvel that Barney doesn't like his job, and will he take him instead of the other fellow, whoever he is. But *you'd* better ask him, Di. You're better at that kind of thing. You catch him all alone to-morrow morning and put your case!"

So, the next morning, when breakfast was over, Diana went to look for Mr. Marvel. He was sitting in a garden shelter, reading the paper. He looked up as she came shyly in.

"Please can I speak to you, Mr. Marvel?" she said. "It's about that friend of ours, Barney. He doesn't like his job. I'm sure he'd come as your assistant if you still want one. Please have him instead of any one else. He's a very hard worker and very clever. He'd do *anything* you want him to, anything."

Mr. Marvel put down his paper and looked at the earnest Diana. " I'm looking for a *servant*, really," he said. " Someone who will do errands for me, see after my clothes, take messages, as well as help in my act."

" He could do all that," said Diana eagerly. " Do try him, Mr. Marvel."

" What's his full name?" asked the conjurer, taking out a fountain pen and notebook.

" Barnabas Hugo Lorimer," said Diana. " Actually that's his mother's name. He doesn't know his father's."

" How strange," said Mr. Marvel.

Diana plunged into Barney's story, and Mr. Marvel listened with interest. " So you see," finished Diana, " Barney is all alone in the world, he can go where he likes and take what job he likes—but oh, I *do* so wish he could find his father!"

" I've no doubt I could do that for him!" said Mr. Marvel, putting away his fountain pen. Diana gasped and stared.

" What do you mean? How could you? How would you set about it? Surely you couldn't, if even Barney doesn't know anything about his father—not even his name!"

" My dear young lady, I have been in the theatrical world for more years than I like to remember," said Mr. Marvel. " I have only to ask a few of my friends if they knew of a Shakespearian actor some fifteen or so years ago, who is probably very like Barney in feature—he has a most remarkable face, that boy. I am quite certain I shall have news within a very short time!"

" Oh, Mr. Marvel!" cried Diana, her eyes shining. " Oh, it would be wonderful! Will you really do that?"

" If Barney comes to me, does what he is told and proves himself useful and trustworthy, then I shall certainly do my best," said Mr. Marvel. " It rests with the boy himself. I'm not likely to take any trouble though, unless he does well with me."

"Oh, Barney will do well, I know he will!" cried Diana joyfully. "Let me go and fetch him, Mr. Marvel. Then he can give in his notice to-day, and come to you to-morrow. Oh, thank you, thank you."

She flew off, her heart singing. Oh, Barney, Barney, suppose your father is found quite soon! Oh, wonderful Mr. Marvel, kind Mr. Marvel—why had she ever thought she disliked him?

She found Barney down on the beach, waiting for her and the others. She flopped down beside him and told him her news. "Please go to the inn now, this very minute, Barney!" she begged. "He's there, waiting for you. Barney, just suppose he really *can* find your father for you! He seemed quite certain he would!"

"You're a good friend, Diana," said Barney, his eyes shining. "Come on, Miranda—we'll go and try our luck!"

CHAPTER NINETEEN

BARNEY GETS THE JOB

BARNEY GOT the job. Mr. Marvel appeared to think he could try, at any rate. It seemed a wonderful job to Barney.

"I shall get you new clothes instead of those rags," said Mr. Marvel. "I will pay your lodgings for you. You will have three pounds a week—to start with. A good assistant is worth more than that to me, if he does what he is told!"

"Yes, sir," said Barney, hardly believing his ears. He'd be rich! He could save a bit of money! Miranda should have a new skirt!

"But you understand, of course, Barnabas, that I am a magician, a conjurer, don't you?" said Mr. Marvel. "You understand that my secrets are *my* secrets, and if I have to let you into any of them, you must never say a word to anyone about them. Not even to those three friends of yours."

"I wouldn't dream of it," Barney assured him.

"And about your father," went on the conjurer. "I think I can find him for you. In fact, I am certain I can. I shall cause inquiries to be made immediately and let you know where he is. He may no longer be an actor, of course."

"Yes, sir. I know that," said Barney. "Oh, sir—I'd do anything in the world for you if only you'd find out about my father—and make him believe I'm his son."

"I think I can do that all right," said Mr. Marvel. "I know many strings I can pull. Now, be a good boy to me in every way—and probably by the end of the season you won't want a job any more—because your father will want you instead!"

Barney walked unsteadily to the beach. He could hardly believe his good luck. What a job! And what a reward! He sat down and told everyone about the interview.

"Well, I must say that Mr. Marvel is going to do a lot for you," said Miss Pepper. "He must be a kindly fellow, although he looks so solemn and mournful. Well, it's time you had a bit of luck, Barney!"

That was a very happy morning. The sun shone, the water was calm and warm, and everyone was in high spirits. Loony disappeared, as usual, and all the children wondered what friend he would produce this time.

To their enormous surprise he brought back Mr. Tubby—the gloomy, lugubrious Mr. Tubby. How he had managed to persuade him to join the family circle nobody could think.

Mr. Tubby, however, drew the line at monkeys. Children he would put up with, and a courteous, polite dog like Loony, who deferred to him in every way—but not monkeys. Certainly not monkeys. He stared mournfully at Miranda, who stared back, surprised at such a big dog. She suddenly dipped her hand into a bag of peanuts Barney had bought for her, and threw a pawful at the surprised and annoyed Mr. Tubby.

He gave a deep, enormous "WOOOOF" that startled every one for some distance around. He cast a look of scorn at Loony, turned his back on them all, and lumbered back to the inn.

"There! Now he knows what awful friends you've got, he'll never speak to you again, Loony," said Diana with a squeal of laughter. "Oh dear—how marvellous of Miranda to throw those peanuts straight into his miserable face!"

Barney gave in his notice, and got his week's money. He didn't buy himself clothes as he had planned. If Mr. Marvel was going to buy those, he'd buy something else. So he bought a fine handkerchief trimmed with cobwebby lace for Miss Pepper, a book for Diana, a propelling pencil for each of the boys and a ball for Loony. That was so like Barney!

He went to his new job with delight. It would be easy after the one he had just had, which was a dirty one, as well as hard and heavy. And there would be the thrill of seeing how Mr. Marvel set about finding his father!

Mr. Marvel bought Barney some excellent clothes, and

Barney appeared at the inn looking very well dressed for the first time in his life. He grinned shyly.

"Do I look queer? I feel queer! Look at my tie. First time I've ever had one!"

He was full of Mr. Marvel. "He's a funny chap—his bark's worse than his bite. But my word, he's generous! He's already written to somebody who might know my father."

Every one's opinion of the conjurer had gone up sky-high. The children told Miss Twitt and the Professor all about how Barney had got his new job. Miss Twitt prattled away, as pleased as they were. But the Professor merely grunted.

"Well, if anyone wants to work with a conjurer I suppose he can! Dangerous job. Mark my words, young man, it's a *dangerous* job!"

He glanced sharply at Barney as he spoke. Barney smiled politely. "Oh, there's nothing out of the way about conjurers, sir. I've been at circuses with sword-swallowers, and fire-eaters and the like—they are all quite nice fellows, really."

The Professor gave one of his best snorts. He leaned back in his chair and shut his eyes. The chat was at an end!

Barney began work with the conjurer. He found it quite pleasant. He had to brush and sponge Mr. Marvel's very considerable wardrobe, and to do that, he had to go to his room in the inn. He had to do his shopping for him, and clean all his many pairs of shoes. Mr. Marvel was always complaining that Dummy didn't do them properly.

The conjurer frightened poor Dummy by shouting at him and calling him names that Dummy didn't understand. "Dunderhead! Nitwit! Fumblehands!" No wonder Dummy wouldn't clean his shoes properly for him!

Mr. Marvel initiated Barney into the mystery of his art. He told him what he wanted done on the platform, what cues Barney had to follow and so on. Barney was quick in the uptake and understood everything very easily. He was deft with his hands too, and soon felt that he could do some of the tricks himself that Mr. Marvel did.

"He's a better-class conjurer than you usually find in little shows like ours," he said to the children. "He could get a job in London easily. But he prefers the seaside in summer."

"Has he heard anything about your father yet?" Diana asked eagerly.

"There hasn't been time," said Barney. "But he wrote two more letters yesterday to old friends of his. It would be much easier if I knew my father's name, of course!"

A few days went by, happy and peaceful—and then a rumour flew through the little seaside town. "The police are here! Scotland Yard, they say. It's about that submarine that blew up. It *is* sabotage—someone got to know too much, passed it on—and the result was the blowing up of the submarine!"

The three policemen, all in plain, sober clothes, actually stayed at the inn! This was a terrific excitement. Everyone knew they were the police, of course, and Snubby spent ages staring at them. Had they found out anything? Did they suspect anyone in Rubadub? It was said they had visited the little fair. Had any of the men there something to do with the sabotage?

"Barney always said they were dishonest men," said Roger. "It might be one of them that the police are after."

Mrs. Glump placed a special room at the disposal of the solemn detectives. As Snubby passed the door once, he saw the Professor coming out. He didn't see Snubby, and went slowly up the stairs with bent head. Snubby watched him.

"I bet they've been questioning him! I bet they suspect him! And I bet they're right too! Wasn't he up on the roof that night, watching the blaze? Ought I to tell them?"

On second thoughts he decided not to. After all, he hadn't actually *seen* the Professor—he had only seen the glow of a cigarette, and noticed the Professor's light switched on in his room later on. Regretfully Snubby decided he had better not barge in. But he would keep his eyes open!

Dummy vanished completely when the police arrived. He

was absolutely frightened out of his wits. As soon as he knew the three men were detectives he went to earth like a rabbit.

Nobody could find him. Mrs. Glump was cross and worried. "He did that before when a policeman in uniform arrived one day to ask about a lost dog," she said. "Why he's so scared of them I don't know. Oh dear—just when we've got three extra guests in the house too."

Barney offered to help, if Mr. Marvel would let him. Mr. Marvel agreed at once, and went to the police to offer Barney's services if they wanted a good honest lad to clean their shoes and do any other jobs for them. Mrs. Glump, too, was only too glad to accept the offer.

"Thank you," said one of the detectives. "Right. If you can spare him we can make good use of him. We hear he was down at the fair. We'd like to ask him a few questions about the men who employed him."

But except that he knew they were dishonest, Barney could give the police very little information about the men.

"What about the men who go there?" asked one man. "Did you see any getting in touch with your employers?"

"Yes, sir. But I never heard what was said," said Barney. He gave quite a good description of one or two sailors who had visited the place two or three times and spoken to his employers.

"You're employed by a Mr. Marvel now, I believe," said the man. "Getting on all right with him?"

"Yes, sir. He's very good to me," said Barney. "It's a nice job."

"Right. You can go," said the man, and Barney went. He had a room high up in the attics now—he was actually living in the inn with the children, though he had his meals with the staff, of course. It all seemed very wonderful to Barney. Things were going well. And soon Mr. Marvel might hear news of his father. That would be the best thing of all!

CHAPTER TWENTY

NEXT MORNING

"Miss Twitt's all of a twitter this morning," announced Snubby, the next day. "The police have interviewed her. She's terribly excited about it. She says they asked her all kinds of questions."

"I bet they didn't get anything sensible out of her, then," said Roger. "I wish they'd interview *us*. Not that we've much to tell them. They've talked to Barney. I don't see why *we* should be left out."

"It was only because Barney worked down at the fair," said Snubby. "He thinks the police imagine he might have overheard some queer talk. I say—I do wonder where old Dummy's gone. I miss him."

"I expect he's streaked off at top speed, and is at the other end of the country by now!" said Roger. "Barney says most circus folk try to keep clear of the police. For all we know, Dummy may have thought they were after him for something."

"He's left all his things behind, the waiter told me," said Snubby. "Poor old Dummy. I did like him."

Miss Twitt sailed up, jingling as usual. A tremendous perfume of Gardenia came with her. She was, as Snubby had so aptly said, "all of a twitter!"

"Pooh!" said Snubby, under his breath, as he got the Gardenia full strength. He removed himself from the room at once, with Loony gasping at his heels. Snubby held his breath till he got outside the door, and then blew out vigorously. Miss Pepper, who was coming in, looked at him in amazement.

"What's the matter, Snubby? Don't you feel well?"

"A bit knocked out, that's all," said Snubby, leaning

413

against the wall, fanning himself with his hands. " Miss Twitt's in there—with a new smell! "

" Oh, don't be so idiotic, Snubby," said Miss Pepper. " I do wish she wouldn't use so many perfumes, I must say—but there's no need to make such a song and dance about it! "

" Good idea! " said Snubby, and produced his imaginary banjo. He began to strum, making his twanging noise, and did a ridiculous step dance in time all round the hall. Miss Pepper began to laugh.

" You're a born comic," she said. " Oh dear, I don't feel as if I want to hear about Miss Twitt's interview with the police all over again. I've just had a few words with them myself."

" Gosh! Have you really? " said Snubby, forgetting his banjo. " I say—why are they interviewing everyone here? Do they think anyone has got anything to do with the sabotage? "

" I don't really know," said Miss Pepper. " They've apparently got *some* clue they're working on. I think they're trying to find out how information and orders are passed out and into the Submarine Base. It's practically sealed off from the outside world, you know. Everyone is searched and checked before he goes out. But it can't be anyone *here*—nobody here has anything to do with the Submarine Base."

" I bet I know who it is," said Snubby mysteriously, his mind flashing back to the night of the explosion. " I bet I do! "

" No, you don't, Snubby," said Miss Pepper. " You're just being silly. Oh—good morning, Mr. Marvel. Have you been interviewed too? Snubby here thinks he knows more than the police! "

" And what do you know, young man? " asked Mr. Marvel, with his peculiar smile, that never reached his eyes. " Which of us is the saboteur? "

" What's *that*? " asked Snubby. " Oh—the fellow who did the damage? Aha! That's *my* secret! "

He sauntered off, strumming his banjo again. He wasn't going to tell either Miss Pepper or Mr. Marvel his suspicions of Professor James. They'd only laugh at him. But wasn't the Professor just the person to be mixed up in Big Secrets? He must know an awful lot about scientific things—and any information passed out he would understand—and he could learn it by heart, probably, and then tear up the message.

But how could any message get to him? Well, that was up to the police to find out. Or perhaps he, Snubby, could do a little snooping and find out something.

"I could creep over the roof and peep in at his window, to see if he's doing anything suspicious," thought Snubby, and a swirl of excitement came over him. "I *say*—that would be a smashing thing to do! I'll tell Roger. He could come with me."

Roger was rather doubtful. He agreed that the Professor was the most suspicious person in the inn. He had already told Snubby how he had seen him in the mirror a night or two ago, wide awake, listening to their conversation, although he was pretending to be asleep.

But all the same, creeping over the roof at night to snoop through his window didn't seem too good. "A bit sneakish," said Roger.

"Rot," said Snubby. "If he's a traitor of some sort he deserves to be spied on. If you're not game to do it, I'll do it with Barney. He sleeps up in the attics, and he could easily snoop about at night."

"You and Barney aren't going to have all the excitement," said Roger jealously. "I'm jolly well joining in."

They spoke to Barney about it. He agreed that it would be exciting to do some snooping round on their own. He thought the old Professor was up to something too.

"He's not such an old crock as he makes himself out to be," said Barney. "And he's not as deaf as everyone imagines either!"

"We know *that*," said Roger. "Right—we'll keep an eye on him—several eyes, in fact. When shall we do our bit of roof-crawling?"

"Wait till the bobbies are gone," said Barney. "I've no doubt they're doing a bit of snooping round too. I saw one of them coming out of the Professor's room yesterday—I bet he'd been doing a rummage round."

"All right. We'll wait a day or two," said Snubby. "They won't be here very long. I say, how does Miranda put up with staying in your room by herself?"

"She's as good as gold," said Barney. "She knows I'm on a job, and she just tucks herself up on a cushion by the window and waits till I'm free to go to her."

"We can always have her when you're busy, you know," said Roger. "Shall we have her now? We're going down to the beach."

"Right. You take her," said Barney gratefully. "I've got a lot to do. Dummy may have been a bit queer in the head, but he certainly managed to get through a lot of work! I must hurry or I shall never get done in time!"

Miranda was perfectly happy to go with Roger and the others. She knew Barney was busy and couldn't rush round with her on his shoulder all the time. So she played happily on the beach. Diana bought her a tiny spade and Miranda dug with it valiantly, scattering sand all over Loony as soon as he came near.

Loony was still bringing new friends. He brought a tiny Pekinese that day, with a funny little snub nose.

"Isn't that Peke like Snubby?" said Diana. "Miss Pepper, do look at him—he's got *such* a look of Snubby, same untidy mane, same turned-up nose, same . . ."

Snubby threw a bucket of water over her in rage and she screamed, "Don't, you beast! I've got hot in the sun and that water felt icy-cold!"

"Serves you right," said Snubby, pushing away the snub-nosed Peke. "Keep off. You're not my little brother, even though you think you are, after Di's silly remarks!"

Loony dug up a bone he had buried the day before, and

proceeded to lie down and gnaw it. The Peke immediately ran up. Loony growled.

"You be careful, Peke," said Roger. "The only time when Loony feels brave is when he's got a bone to protect!"

The Peke suddenly grabbed the bone from beneath Loony's nose and ran off with it. Loony barked in rage and ran after him. The Peke turned, dropped the bone, and faced Loony, yapping fiercely.

"Look at that!" said Diana admiringly. "What a tiny thing to be so lion-hearted!"

Loony ran at the Peke. But the little dog stood his ground and yapped and snapped. He suddenly ran at Loony, snapping his teeth and snarling.

And Loony put his tail between his legs and fled! The Peke picked up his bone and waddled off with it in triumph. He didn't appear again.

"*Well!* Loony ought to be ashamed of himself!" said Roger, disgusted.

"Oh, many a bigger dog than Loony has been put to flight by a Peke," said Miss Pepper, amused. "They aren't afraid of anyone or anything. Poor Loony!"

Loony arrived back after about twenty minutes, looking very much ashamed of himself. He sat down by Snubby and looked at him mournfully. Snubby put his arm round him.

"It's all right, Loony. I still love you though you really are a fathead," said Snubby, pulling Loony's long ears gently. "But don't bring any more strangers here—one dog's quite enough!"

Barney passed them, on his way to do some errands for Mr. Marvel. He had to go to the dressing-room at the concert hall on the pier to arrange Mr. Marvel's stage properties for the next show. He whistled gaily.

Miranda shot up the beach and was on his shoulder in a trice. "I'm going on the pier," shouted Barney. "I'll have a few minutes with you when I come back."

"We'll come with you," called Roger.

"No, don't. I can get on without paying now, but you can't," shouted back Barney. "It'd be a waste of money! See you later."

Barney sounded busy and happy. He had been a success with Mr. Marvel at the show. He had been provided with a small silken cloak with stars and moons on it and a round silken cap, rather like the pierrots wore, but with a brilliant star in front of it. He looked extremely handsome in cloak and cap, a simple black tunic and long hose!

"He's a better assistant than I was," Iris told the three children. "He gets on with Mr. Marvel better too. And I must say that Mr. Marvel is very good to him—much nicer to him than he ever was to me. Maybe Barney is cleverer at helping him with his tricks than I was. He's got some new ones since I helped him."

Barney felt that he had decidedly gone up in the world! A job at the inn near his friends—a job on the stage in fine clothes—other new clothes too—and a very fine wage! Barney was very pleased indeed with life.

CHAPTER TWENTY-ONE

A TRICK—AND A PLAN

Two or three days went by, days of brilliant August weather when the sea and sky were both deep blue and only a few cotton-wool clouds strayed overhead like lost sheep.

The children were burnt a deep red-brown, and even Miss Pepper began to turn colour too. They all had enormous appetites, and Mrs. Glump began seriously to wonder if she was making any money out of their stay at all! Snubby's appetite seemed quite insatiable.

"You're eating all day long," said Diana. "Honestly, I don't believe you ever stop. And when you can't find anything to bite and swallow, you take that horrible bit of chewing-gum and work on that!"

"Well, it's a comfort," said Snubby, chewing hard. "Though it hasn't any taste left now, unfortunately."

"You're disgusting," said Diana. She really did think Snubby was dreadful with his chewing-gum. She spoke to Roger about it. "Can't we get it out of his pockets and throw it away?" she asked him. "Couldn't you wait till Snubby's gone down to bathe and then take it?"

"No. He takes it with him in his mouth!" said Roger. "But Diana! I'll tell you what we'll do! Listen!"

He whispered to her. She chuckled. "Oh *yes*—that'll cure him! Go and buy some now."

So Roger sped off the beach while Snubby was bathing, and bought a little packet of plasticene. He opened it and took out a small stick. He broke off a bit and began to mould it and squeeze it to get it soft. When he squeezed it flat it really looked remarkably like Snubby's chewed bit of gum!

He and Diana waited their chance. Then Roger substituted

the new bit of plasticene for the old bit of chewing-gum, wrapping it up carefully in the bit of paper Snubby kept for his gum.

"Now we'll see what happens," he said to the delighted Diana.

But unfortunately Snubby did himself so well at meals that day, helped out by an ice-cream or two and some sweets, that he didn't remember his precious bit of chewing-gum. So the bit of plasticene stayed in his pocket, waiting.

After tea that day Barney came to them, his face shining with delight.

"Listen!" he said. "Mr. Marvel's had a letter back from one of his friends. He says he thinks he knows my father."

"*Barney!* Not really!"

"Oh, Barney—how wonderful!"

"Gosh—good old Marvel!"

Miss Pepper smiled at the excited boy. "How does the man who wrote to Mr. Marvel know that it's your father?" she asked.

"Well," said Barney, "he said that for one thing this man he thinks is my father used to be an actor and was very fond of Shakespeare's plays—and for another thing his Christian name is Hugo! And that's my second name, you know. My mother must have given me that name after my father!"

"That's very likely," said Miss Pepper. "What did he say your father's surname was?"

"He said it's Johnson, but he doesn't know if that's the name he chose for acting, or whether it's his real name," said Barney. "Isn't it grand, Miss Pepper!"

"Is he like you to look at?" asked Roger.

"He didn't say," said Barney. "He's trying to find out a bit more. He thinks my father was called up in the last war, so he's asking actor friends of his, who were also called up, if they heard of him anywhere."

"It's jolly exciting, all this," said Snubby. "I do wonder what your father's like. He might not be an actor at all now.

He might have stayed in the Army—or gone into the Navy or Air Force. He might be an admiral or a general or anything!"

"He might equally well have fallen on hard times and be playing a barrel-organ in the street," said Barney. "I wouldn't mind—so long as he was my father! To find someone who really belongs to me would be wonderful. I never even had an aunt or uncle on my mother's side, I never even remember a granny. You just can't imagine what it would be like to me to find people who were my own."

Barney thought the world of Mr. Marvel. To think he was taking all that trouble! He would be grateful to the conjurer as long as he lived. Barney shone all his shoes till they reflected everything around. He brushed all the conjurer's clothes till they hadn't a speck on them. He cleaned all his stage properties meticulously and never forgot a thing. Mr. Marvel had never in his life had such a willing and trustworthy assistant!

The police went at last. All three detectives slipped out one morning and were not seen again. They were there at breakfast, and then appeared no more. Mrs. Glump heaved a sigh of relief.

"There's nothing for them to snoop about here," she confided to Miss Pepper. "Down in the town perhaps yes—particularly at that Fair. Such a rough lot do go there—especially sailors. That's where any mischief is planned, I don't doubt."

Roger, Snubby, Diana and Barney met on the promenade that morning to discuss the departure of the detectives. They thought they might begin their snooping now. Snubby had dreamt about roof-crawling till he could hardly stop thinking about it.

"Let's have an ice-cream while we're waiting," he said. But no ice-cream man came in sight.

"Oh well—I'll have a spot of chewing-gum," said Snubby and put his hand into his pocket. Roger looked at Diana and winked. This was the first time Snubby had done any chewing since they had changed over the gum for plasticene! It had exasperated them considerably that Snubby should have shown no interest in his chewing-gum for the last day or two. Still, they could wait!

He took out the piece of paper and unwrapped it. He slipped the grey bit of plasticene into his mouth without even looking at it. He began to chew.

Diana felt she must begin to talk or she would dissolve into some of her helpless giggles. "Isn't the sea grand to-day," she began. "And look at the little frilly white waves at the edge— just like lace. And . . ."

Snubby looked at her in surprise. "What a lot of babble," he said. "You sound like Miss Twitt. She babbles like that!"

He was chewing hard. Then a peculiar expression came over his face. He chewed more slowly. Diana felt an enormous giggle forming in her middle. Roger began to talk fast now, much to Barney's astonishment.

"We'll have to make some plans. We might be able to do something to-night. I thought the Professor looked rather down in the mouth to-day. Maybe the police . . ."

Snubby wasn't listening. He wore a look of great disgust. His mouth fell half open, and he looked desperate.

"Ugh!" he said, and suddenly spat the plasticene right out of his mouth and on to the beach below.

"Snubby!" said Barney, amazed. "You nearly hit that woman on the beach. Whatever are you thinking of?"

"I'll have to get a drink of water," said Snubby, looking very green. "I'll be back."

Diana's giggle burst out of her and she sank back, holding herself tightly. Roger roared loudly. Barney, who hadn't been told the joke, stared in surprise.

Neither Diana nor Roger could explain what the matter was. "Snubby's face!" gasped Diana. "Oh dear!"

"Come on—tell me the joke," said Barney, beginning to laugh himself at the sight of Diana and Roger. At last they were able to tell him. "But don't say a word, will you, Barney?"

begged Diana. "If it cures him of chewing-gum it would be too marvellous for words. *Don't* tell him."

Snubby came back, looking better. He sat down on the seat again. "What was the matter?" asked Barney, trying to keep a straight face.

"It was my chewing-gum," explained poor Snubby, tickling Miranda under the chin. "I think I must have suddenly turned against it, or something. Instead of tasting all right, it was *horrible*. I just *had* to spit it out, I couldn't help it. I'm never going to chew gum again, never. Gosh, it made me feel as sick as a wet hen!"

Diana wanted to giggle again. But it would never do to give the game away after Snubby had made such a wonderful resolution. He was never going to chew gum again! It was too good to be true.

"I got a drink of water," said Snubby. "In fact, I drank the whole of the jugful that was on our table. I couldn't seem to get the taste out of my mouth. Who would have thought I'd turn against chewing gum like that? Well, I felt so sick at even the *thought* of chewing gum that I made up my mind I'd go up to my room, get the rest of the packet, and throw it away. So up I went."

"Good for you," said Roger, approving heartily.

"And listen to this," said Snubby, dropping his voice suddenly, and looking round furtively as if he thought the promenade might be full of listeners, "just listen to this. When I got up to my room, there was old Professor James on our landing! He must have been in somebody's room! He doesn't sleep on that landing. He's no business to be there."

The other three were extremely interested. Another black mark against the Professor! "Did he say anything?" asked Roger.

"I said to him, 'Hallo, Professor, lost your way?'" said Snubby. "He just scowled at me and didn't answer. He went downstairs then."

"He might have been trying to get up those stairs," said Roger.

"He couldn't. The door's locked and the key is lost—or stolen," said Snubby. "It all looked jolly suspicious, anyway. What about doing our snooping to-night? We might see something interesting if we crawled over the roof and peered into his window—always supposing he hasn't drawn the curtains right across."

"Yes, we will," said Roger. "Not Di, though. I'm not going to have her rolling off the roof!"

"I don't particularly want to come!" said Diana. "I'll keep a look-out for you, if you like. But how are you going to get on the roof if you can't get up that little stairway that leads there?"

"Easy," said Roger. "Our window gives on to part of the roof. We can easily get out there and crawl over to where we can peep into the Professor's window."

They all felt very excited. Snubby gave the surprised Loony a loving thump. "Roof-crawling, Loony!" he said. "But not for you, old chap! It's a shame—but I just feel you'll have to be left out of our trip to-night!"

CHAPTER TWENTY-TWO

ALONG COMES AN ADVENTURE!

MISS PEPPER couldn't think why the children seemed so mysterious that night. They gave each other winks and meaning looks, and Snubby kept talking about cats on roofs.

"Why do cats like roofs, Miss Pepper?" he said. "Do they go and warm themselves by the chimneys?"

"Why should they?" said Miss Pepper. "Very few chimneys are warm—only those that have a big fire down below. Don't be silly, Snubby."

425

Roger gave Snubby a kick to warn him to stop. But he went on. " I once knew a nice warm chimney," he said. " It was a lovely place to sit."

"That'll do, Snubby," said Miss Pepper. "If you've got one of your silly fits on, leave the table."

"But I haven't had any pudding," said Snubby. "All right, I'll stop twittering."

Miss Pepper made an exasperated click. But Miss Twitt was engrossed in cold meat and salad and didn't hear Snubby's silly remark.

Barney had a disappointment for them that evening. He met them after their dinner. " I've got to go to the show now," he said, " but I just came to tell you I won't be able to join you to-night. I've got to take a bag with something urgent in it over to the next town after the show."

" Well, you'll be back before midnight I should hope! " said Roger, surprised.

" No, I shan't," said Barney. " I've got to stay the night at Pearley, at the place I take the bag to. It's some clothes Mr. Marvel wants altering in a hurry—some of his stage clothes. He says the old woman I give the bag to will alter them that same night and give them to me to bring back to-morrow morning. Apparently she is always willing to do that for him. So I shan't be able to join you, unfortunately. I'm catching the last train to Pearley. I'm taking Miranda, though."

" What a nuisance! " said Roger. " Well, we'll roof-crawl without you. You can join us another time. I just don't feel we can put it off after getting so worked up about it."

" Of course not," said Barney. " I must fly. So long! "

The grandfather clock in the dining-room chimed a quarter to eight. " What shall we do this evening?" said Diana. " It's fine. Shall we go for a walk?"

" No. I'm tired," said Snubby. " All that swimming we did, I suppose. And I don't want to make myself any tireder because of to-night. I want to be jolly wide awake! "

"Well, let's read then," said Diana. "I've got a good circus story I want to finish. It's got a monkey in it, like Miranda."

It was decided that Diana need not keep awake or do any looking-out for the two boys. There wouldn't be much chance, they thought, of any one knowing they had crawled out of their bedroom window or of any one trying to stop them.

"Di, get Miss Pepper's alarm clock for us out of her room," said Roger. "We plan to roof-crawl after midnight, and we're sure to fall asleep before then. We'll have to have an alarm to wake us up."

"Well, set it and put the clock under your pillow then, or it will wake up every one on our landing!" said Diana. "I expect Miss Pepper will go to bed just after we do—she's such an early bird—and when I know she's asleep I'll creep in and borrow her clock."

Everything went as planned. They went up to bed at a quarter to nine, and Miss Pepper yawned and said she really thought she would come too. Diana winked at Roger. Good!

She slipped into their room with the alarm clock at just after half-past nine. "Will you believe it, Miss Pepper's asleep already," she whispered. "Here you are. I half wish I was coming now."

"Well, you aren't!" said Roger. "We'll tell you all about it in the morning, if we discover anything interesting."

Roger put the clock under his pillow. The alarm would go off and waken him but nobody else. It awakened him all right, and he sat up in bed, startled. Of course—it was only the alarm going off! He scrabbled under the pillow and switched it off. Then he woke the snoring Snubby.

It was difficult to wake Snubby, so Roger got Loony to do it instead. Loony leapt on to him and licked his face lavishly. Snubby sat up and pushed him off.

"What on earth . . ." he began, and then remembered. He scrambled out of bed.

"Don't make a row now, Snubby," warned Roger. "And

tie Loony to the bed leg or he'll try to jump out of the window after us. He won't howl, will he?"

"Not if I tell him not to," said Snubby, and tied Loony up firmly. Loony whined a little, but then lay down patiently.

The two boys climbed out of their window. There was a moon, but the sky was very cloudy, so the light was fitful. They sat on the roof outside their window and looked round.

Not far off was the Professor's window. It had a light shining in it, but to-night the curtains were drawn more closely together and only a small crack showed.

"Still—it's enough to peep through," whispered Roger. "Come on. Keep to the flat parts, or you'll roll away. It's easy going here."

They crawled slowly, dragging themselves along cautiously in a sitting position. There was no danger where they were, but still it all *felt* very dangerous and exciting. Snubby's heart began to beat quickly.

Just as they came really near to the Professor's lighted window, his light went out! The room was in darkness. How maddening!

"What shall we do?" whispered Roger. "Wait a few minutes, do you think?"

"Yes. Let's get by that tall chimney there. We'll be out of sight if he comes to the window," whispered back Snubby. So they crawled silently to the big chimney. Unfortunately it was not a warm one. Still the night was not cold, so it didn't matter!

They stood by the chimney, hoping against hope that the light would be switched on again. And then Snubby suddenly clutched Roger so violently that he made him jump almost out of his skin!

"Roger! Look! What's that!"

Roger looked in the direction that Snubby was facing. He stiffened in surprise. Some distance to the right, and higher up than they were, a light was flashing. Flash, flash, flash. Flash, flash.

"Signalling," whispered Snubby. "What window is it that the signals are coming from? I say, Roger—this is queer!"

"Let's get nearer that window," whispered Roger. "This is very important, Snubby. For goodness' sake don't make any noise. Let me go first."

Keeping in the shadow of chimneys when they could, they made their way very cautiously indeed towards the window from which the signals came. It certainly seemed very high up. What window could it be? It must be the highest one in the inn!

Roger clutched Snubby by the arm and put his mouth excitedly to his ear. "Snubby! That's not a window! That's the skylight trap-door opening off that little staircase! Why didn't we think of it before?"

So it was. The boys could now clearly see the trap-door thrown back, as the moon sailed out from behind a cloud.

"Who is it signalling?" said Snubby. "We *must* find out, Roger. Gosh, the police were right. There *is* someone here who's acting jolly suspiciously. Is it Professor James? It's funny his light went out just before we saw the signals. I suppose they *are* signals?"

"Of course," said Roger, watching for the next series of flashes. "Those flashes can be seen quite clearly by any watcher in the Submarine Bay if he is in exactly the right place to receive them. That cleft in the cliff might be *made* for signals to and fro! Maybe that is why it *was* made originally— for smugglers or wreckers to signal news or warnings. Whoever is out in a boat on the very spot that can be seen from that high trap-door window is no doubt receiving important messages!"

"It *must* be the Professor," said Snubby. "How can we find out for certain, Roger? We simply must!"

"Well, we daren't go any nearer than this," said Roger. "We don't want to be seen. It's important that the man shouldn't know we've been watching him. I know—you slip back into our room and hide somewhere on the landing. Then you'll see the man come down and spot who he is!"

" Jolly good! " said Snubby. " I'll do that. You stay here and watch."

He crawled away from Roger very carefully and quietly. He was strung up and excited. Why, this was another adventure! All of a sudden, in the very middle of the night, there was a smashing adventure! You just never knew when adventures might come along.

He came to his window and climbed in. He made his way to the door, fell over Loony, who was very pleased to see him again, and made much more noise than he meant to.

" Shut up, Loony! " he whispered, trying to push the excited dog away. " That's my face you're pawing. Be quiet. SHUSH! "

At last Loony quieted down. Snubby opened his door and looked out. The landing was in complete darkness. Not a sound was to be heard. Snubby debated where to hide. He wasn't afraid of being seen, the landing was so dark—but if the man had a torch, he might pick out Snubby in its light if he didn't hide himself well.

He shut his door softly. He tiptoed across the landing to a window hung with long curtains. He crept behind them and drew them carefully round him. He stood and waited, his heart working like a piston.

He waited there for a few minutes, his ears strained for any sound. Nothing happened. No noise came, not even the creak of a bit of furniture in the night.

Then Snubby thought he heard a sound. What was it? It was rather like somebody very cautiously clearing his throat. Surely that fellow hadn't come down the stairs so quietly that Snubby hadn't seen or heard him! He listened again.

There! The tiny noise came again—it was a little sniff this time. Snubby stiffened with fright. Good gracious! There was someone on the landing. He was certain of it. Where? Who could it be?

And then the door enclosing the little staircase opened slowly.

A little moonlight came through the skylight at the top of the stairway, enough to show Snubby that someone was creeping out of the door. Then it shut just as softly. Who was it? Snubby hadn't been able to make out—but he was absolutely certain it was old Professor James!

CHAPTER TWENTY-THREE

SNUBBY IS NOT LION-HEARTED

SNUBBY, HIDDEN behind the long curtains, heard the little creak-creak of the boards under the landing mats, as somebody went cautiously by. He longed to make absolutely certain that it was the Professor.

He would follow him and see if he went down to his bedroom on the next landing. So he slid out between the curtains and took a step or two towards the head of the stairs. He had completely forgotten there might be somebody else hidden on the landing!

He heard the creak of a stair some way down. He came to the head of the stairs and began to go down very cautiously himself.

But one of the stairs creaked so loudly that the man he was following heard it. He was now on the landing below. He took fright.

He ran down the remaining stairs at top speed and landed down in the hall. Snubby ran after him.

And somebody ran after Snubby! The somebody who had been hiding on the top landing, as well as Snubby, was coming down the stairs, close on his heels!

Snubby felt a hand clutch at him. He was suddenly terrified. He tore into the big dining-room, which was dimly lighted now and again by the moon. He must hide!

He heard a noise coming from the hall. Somebody was struggling there—struggling with somebody else, panting, trying to keep as silent as possible.

Snubby heard a gasp as one of the two fighters struck a blow. Then came a groan. He gazed desperately round the big dining-room. Where, oh where could he hide? Whatever was going on was something desperate, and he didn't want to be mixed up in it. Who was the Professor fighting?

He was standing by the grandfather clock. It suddenly made the loud whirring noise that meant it was going to strike.

Snubby almost jumped out of his skin. His hair stood on end —and then, with a wave of relief he realised that it was only the old clock. The old clock—why—the old clock would hide him!

Snubby felt for the clasp that fastened the door of the clock over the great pendulum inside. He opened it and got inside, almost falling in, he was so anxious to hide. The fighters were now in the dining-room, swaying this way and that, and they crashed against a table. Snubby pulled the clock door shut and stood trembling inside. The pendulum tried its hardest to swing to and fro with Snubby pressing against it, but it couldn't. It gave up, and the clock suddenly stopped its loud ticking.

But nobody noticed that, certainly not poor Snubby. He could only hear his heart beating, far more loudly than any grandfather clock!

There was a crash as a chair went over. Both the fighters fell on the floor, judging by the thudding and wriggling that went on. Snubby longed to peep out and see who the two were, but he didn't dare to push the clock door open even a crack. It was not Snubby's night for being lion-hearted!

A dog began to bark. It wasn't Loony. He was too far away to hear any noise. It was Mr. Tubby, shut up in Mrs. Glump's little den, with his enormous basket.

The fighters stopped for a moment. Then there was the sound of scampering feet, a click—and silence. One of the fighters had evidently gone. Which one?

Snubby listened with both his ears. The one who was left tiptoed to the hall. Snubby then heard him going up the stairs —creak; creak-creak.

He was gone. Snubby wondered whether it was all right for him to go and find Roger. He was simply longing for Roger! Snubby was always very brave in the daytime, but at night things were somehow different.

He pushed open the door of the clock. He climbed out. At once the pendulum began to swing again and the clock ticked once more. Tick-tock, tick-tock, slowly and deliberately.

Snubby tiptoed to the door in his turn. He didn't like it a bit. He wished he was safely back in the clock. He stopped, thinking he heard a sound. He had! Oh goodness gracious, who was that now? How many more people were there prowling about to-night?

It was somebody in the hall. The moon shone out at that moment and Snubby shrank back into a deep shadow, waiting there, shivering. If any one was in the hall he could jolly well show himself first!

A pair of curtains draped over a big hall window suddenly moved. Snubby nearly screamed. He stood there in his corner, hardly daring to breathe. Who was coming out of the curtains?

But nobody came out. Instead, something was poked through and a brilliant light suddenly shone on poor Snubby, making him gasp. He was caught in the beam of a powerful torch!

It was too much! He tore up the stairs two at a time, gasping and panting, fearing that the one behind the curtain would chase him. But nobody came after him. When he got safely to his room he sank down beside Loony, trembling and terrified. What an awful night! However many suspicious people were there creeping about the inn? It seemed suddenly to have become a perfect hot-bed of extraordinary happenings!

Loony licked him and licked him, whining because he didn't understand why Snubby was so scared. Snubby remembered Roger. He would still be out on the roof, wondering why in the world Snubby was such a long time. Snubby, feeling much better now, decided to go and get Roger and tell him of the astounding happenings down in the inn.

He climbed out of the window. The moon suddenly swept out again and he saw Roger standing by a chimney. Was he still watching for the flashing signals? Or was he looking into the Professor's window? He would be back in his room by now, no doubt.

He crawled to Roger. "What an age you've been!" said Roger crossly. "The flashes have stopped long ago and there's been no light on in the Professor's room, so there's been absolutely nothing to see. What have you been doing? Did you see who came down the stairs?"

"There's too much to tell you out here," whispered back Snubby. "Come back to our room. But, I say—let's peep into the Professor's room first. I've got a reason."

"Got a torch?" asked Roger. Yes, Snubby had. They could shine it quickly into the room.

"But suppose he's there?" said Roger. "He'll be angry."

"He won't do anything," said Snubby. "He'll be too scared! Come on—it's important."

They crawled to the Professor's room, and switched on the torch through the crack in the curtain. The light fell on the bed. No one was sleeping there. Snubby swept the light of his torch swiftly over the little room. It was quite empty, but the door was shut.

"Whew! He's not back yet! Where did he go to then?" wondered Snubby. "I certainly heard him creaking up the stairs after the fight."

"What fight?" asked Roger, astonished.

"Let's get back to our room and I'll tell you all about it," said Snubby. "Come on."

They were soon in their room, and once again Loony gave them an enormous, over-generous welcome.

"Before I tell you everything I must just see if the door of the staircase leading up to the roof is still open," whispered Snubby.

He and Roger crept out to see. They shone their torch on to the door. It was shut. It was also locked. And the key was gone!

"The one who has the key is the man we want to look for!" said Snubby. "He's the light-flasher—must be—because he's the only one with the key. And the lock must be well oiled too, because I never even heard him turn the key in the lock."

They went back to their room—but on the way Snubby paused. "What's that?" he whispered. They both listened. Roger gave a chuckle.

"Only the conjurer having a nice little snore!" he said. "I often hear him at night—don't you?"

"Little does he know all that took place here to-night," said Snubby. "I wish old Barney was here."

Once more they went back into their room and once more Loony flung himself on them rapturously. He simply couldn't understand what game the two boys were playing, but so long as they kept coming back to him he didn't mind a bit!

They sat on the bed, Loony between them. Snubby began to tell his story—how he had hidden on the landing—and had heard someone sniff, and had known there was someone else hiding there; how he had seen the staircase door open, but hadn't been able to see who came out; how he had tracked the fellow down the stairs, only to find somebody trailing him behind.

"And when a hand clutched me I got the wind up," said Snubby. "I flew into the dark dining-room and got inside the grandfather clock."

"*What!*" said Roger, hardly able to believe this extraordinary tale. "You got into the clock? You didn't, Snubby!"

"I did. And the pendulum stopped and the clock didn't tick," said Snubby. "And then the two fellows, whoever they were, began to fight. They rolled round the dining-room, they knocked over tables and chairs, they crashed into the clock, they . . ."

Snubby's imagination was beginning to run away with him. He went on, embroidering his tale as he talked. "They were getting quite desperate, and groaning and grunting, when Mr. Tubby barked. He simply barked the place down. I wonder you didn't hear him."

"Don't be silly. You know I was up on the roof. Go on," said Roger. "I can hardly believe all this. To think I was out of all the excitement! Weren't you scared, Snubby?"

"Pooh, *scared*! What do you take me for?" said Snubby grandly. "It takes a lot more than that to scare *me*. But that isn't all, Roger. When Tubby barked, one of the fellows shot away somewhere—towards the kitchen, I think, because I heard a door click. The other went upstairs. I heard him go. I'm sure it was Professor James, though where he is now beats me. Gone to do a spot more flashing perhaps!"

"Is that the whole story?" asked Roger.

"Not quite. When I got out into the hall, meaning to follow the Professor up the stairs, I heard a sound," said Snubby, thoroughly enjoying himself. "And gosh, there was a *third*

437

person hiding! He suddenly pointed a torch at me from behind those big hall curtains, and got me full in its beam. I just turned and hared up the stairs at top speed. I'd had just about enough."

" I should think so," said Roger.. " How very extraordinary! What *can* be going on? We'll have to do something about this, Snubby. My word, *what* goings-on!"

CHAPTER TWENTY-FOUR

A GREAT DEAL OF NEWS

THE TWO boys were so very tired after their late night that they both overslept considerably. Miss Pepper came to wake them just as the breakfast gong went.

"Well, really!" she said. "You'll have to go to bed much earlier if you oversleep like this. That's the breakfast gong, listen!"

They didn't remember the events of the night before as they stared sleepily at Miss Pepper. It wasn't until she had gone out of the room that Snubby sat up and suddenly remembered everything.

"Gosh! Do you remember last night? What are we going to do about it?"

"We'll tell Barney first, when he comes back from Pearley," said Roger. But they didn't see him until almost lunch-time. They debated whether to go to the police or not, as the morning went by and there was still no sign of Barney and Miranda.

Then at last they saw him. He was hurrying along the promenade, Miranda on his shoulder. He waved eagerly to them and then jumped down to the beach. Miss Pepper had gone for a walk, so the four children were alone.

"I say," said Barney, his eyes bright. "I've great news!"

"What?" asked all three.

"My father's been found!" said Barney. "Already! Isn't it marvellous. Look!"

He showed them a letter. Attached to it was a typewritten document, looking very official. Barney pointed to it. "Read it," he said.

"'Hugo Paul Johnson,'" read out Roger. "'Aged 40. Born in Westminster, London. Married Teresa Lorimer.

439

Worked as producer and actor, mainly Shakespearian plays. Called up to the Navy for World War. Remained in the Navy on Secret Service. Present whereabouts secret.' "

The typewritten document was signed by someone in the Services. The three children read it again and again. Well, how wonderful! Barney's father was found at last. Except, of course, that his whereabouts were secret.

"Oh, Barney—I'm *glad* for you!" said Diana, and gave him a sudden hug.

Roger and Snubby were very much moved too. They shook hands solemnly with Barney, feeling that the occasion called for some ceremony to mark it.

"What does the letter say?" asked Diana, "the one this document is pinned to?"

"Nothing much. It's just from one of Mr. Marvel's friends to say he's managed to get the information he asked for, and sends it herewith," said Barney.

"If only we knew where your father *was*!" said Diana. "That's the only thing missing now. Can Mr. Marvel find that out too?"

"He *has* found it out!" said Barney proudly. "And all because of something very extraordinary too—he doesn't mind my telling *you* this, but you must absolutely swear you won't tell any one else."

"We swear," said all three breathlessly.

"Well," said Barney, dropping his voice. "Mr. Marvel is more than he seems. *He's* in the Secret Service too."

There was a dead silence as they all took this in. Barney laughed at their astonished faces.

"I thought that would amaze you," he said. "He is a jolly good conjurer, and uses his gift for that as a cover for his Secret Service work. There's been spying and sabotage going on down here—and he was sent to see if he could trace anything. Extraordinary, isn't it?"

"Gosh, yes!" said everyone.

"*And*," said Barney, his face glowing even more, "*and* one of the men he's in constant touch with happens to be this very Hugo Paul Johnson—my father! Though he didn't know it! He says he's never seen him, only been in touch with him—and where do you think my father is now?"

"Where?" they all said, hardly able to take all this amazing news in.

"In the Submarine Bay!" said Barney. "Isn't that incredible! To think he's so near and I never knew it!"

"It sounds exactly like a story," said Diana. "Oh, I feel as if I want to hear it all again!"

She did hear it again. Barney repeated it from beginning to end—he couldn't talk about it enough. He was so happy about it, so glad that his father was alive and near him!

"Are you going to see him?" asked Diana.

"Yes," said Barney. "But I don't know how or when yet. Apparently there are some very hush-hush inquiries going on at the moment about this blowing up of the submarine. There are traitors among the men over there, and yet they have been checked and double-checked. My father is helping to track them down, and he hands the information on to Mr. Marvel, who sends it to the proper quarters."

"It's too exciting for words!" said Snubby. "I do hope you'll soon see your father. I bet he's exactly like you! You'll recognise him at once!"

"I hope so," said Barney. "I shan't know for a day or two how it can be arranged for me to meet my father—all the men in the bay are under close supervision since the explosion, and no one is allowed to leave the base on any consideration whatsoever. But Mr. Marvel says that if it's possible he'll arrange a secret meeting *some*how—he'll wangle it if he can. And he will too. He's a marvel, that man—and that's not a joke, it's the truth!"

"Barney, we've got some news too—and I bet it would interest Mr. Marvel," said Roger, remembering the night before and what happened. He began to tell him everything, helped and hindered by Snubby, who kept interrupting and adding various bits.

Barney listened in amazement. Diana had already heard it all, of course. "My word!" said Barney. "That really *is* news! What a pity I was away. I could have joined in it all! I had to take those clothes to the old dame who altered them. I didn't get back till after breakfast and then I had lots of jobs to do. My word—what a tale you have to tell!"

"We thought we ought to go to the police," said Roger. "What do *you* think, Barney?"

"I tell you that *I* think," said Barney. "Let me tell it all to Mr. Marvel and see what he suggests. Then, if he thinks you should go to the police, he could go with you. They'd be sure to believe every word you say if Mr. Marvel is with you!"

"Oh yes—that's a bright idea!" said Roger, pleased. "Will you tell him, then? Don't forget *any*thing, will you? Even the smallest detail might be important. It's a pity he slept through all the excitement—we heard him snoring away in his room when at last we went back to bed."

"Do you know it's a quarter past one?" said Diana suddenly. "No wonder the beach is so deserted. Oh dear—Mrs. Glump won't be at all pleased with us—late for breakfast and now late for lunch!"

"She'll give us her most glumpish look," said Snubby. "Come on, Loony—eats, boy, eats! Dinner, bone, biscuit!"

"Woof!" said Loony happily, and they ran back to the inn at top speed.

"Barney, come and tell us what Mr. Marvel advises as soon as you know," said Diana, as they parted. "We won't say a word to anyone till you've told Mr. Marvel."

Miss Pepper was thrilled to hear about Barney's father. She spoke to Mr. Marvel about it. The children hadn't told her anything except that Mr. Marvel had traced Barney's father and hoped to arrange a meeting. They hadn't, of course, said anything about Mr. Marvel's secret work.

"What wonderful news for Barney, Mr. Marvel," said Miss Pepper to him after lunch. "It's so good of you to take such an interest in him."

"He's worth it," said Mr. Marvel. "A good, trustworthy boy. There are difficulties in the way of arranging a meeting, but it can be done—it can be done! I shall do my best for Barney you may be sure!"

Barney himself appeared at that moment, eager to talk to Mr. Marvel and tell him what the children had related to him.

"Can I have a word with you, please, sir?" he asked. "It's rather important."

Mr. Marvel got up at once. "Excuse me," he said politely to Miss Pepper, and disappeared into the inn garden with Barney. They were there a very long time. Miss Pepper couldn't understand why the three children hung about so, instead of going down to the beach. At last she got cross and chivvied them all out.

"You won't even have time for a bathe before tea if you hang about much longer!" she scolded. "Whatever is the matter with you all? You *are* a lot of dawdlers!"

Barney joined them in an hour, looking really excited. "Sorry I couldn't come before," he said. He glanced at Miss Pepper, half asleep in her chair. "What about a walk? I could do with one!"

"Yes, do go," said Miss Pepper. "I'm getting tired of Loony digging holes all round me. Stay out to tea if you want to. I haven't brought it with me this afternoon as Mrs. Glump didn't seem very pleased about you all being so late for meals to-day."

"We'll have tea somewhere at a shop," said Snubby. "A lobster tea! And I shall have a *whole* lobster," he added as soon as Miss Pepper was out of hearing.

They went beyond the pier and found a very deserted spot. "Now," said Roger, sitting down comfortably, "what did Mr. Marvel say? Tell us every word!"

"Well, first of all, I must warn you that I can't tell you

*every*thing Mr. Marvel has planned, or is planning," said Barney. " It's so very secret. But I'll tell you everything I'm allowed to—and you must absolutely swear and promise not to say a word to anyone till Mr. Marvel says you may."

" We absolutely promise," they all said together. They sounded so solemn that Loony added a grave deep WOOF too.

" Well," began Barney, " he was *most i*nterested, of course, in the story you told me of last night. He could kick himself for being asleep! He was horrified when he heard about the signal flashes! He says something or other must be being planned again—another explosion, or a theft of valuable plans, or something."

" Did you tell him we suspected Professor James?" asked Diana.

" Yes. And he says we're right to. The detectives who came down suspected him too, but they can't prove anything against him. They told Mr. Marvel that. They know him well, of course. Mr. Marvel can't quite understand about the fighting. He says one must have been the Professor, of course. He doesn't know who the third person is, but he thinks it may be someone in the pay of the Professor. But do you know who he *does* suspect? You'll never, never guess! Have a try."

CHAPTER TWENTY-FIVE

MORE EXCITING STILL!

"Does he suspect Mrs. Glump?" asked Diana after a pause.

"No. Try again. It's someone we know quite well."

"The Funny Man?"

"Oh, no! Try again. And don't suggest Miss Twitt because it isn't her either!"

"Give it up," said Roger. "You tell us."

"*Dummy!*" said Barney. "He says Dummy isn't half as stupid as he seems to be. He's a very, very useful go-between, Mr. Marvel says. He's hand in glove with the Professor."

"I don't believe it," said Snubby, shocked to the bottom of his heart. "I liked Dummy."

"Well, do you remember how he disappeared immediately the police came? That was a guilty conscience, Mr. Marvel says," said Barney. "He was afraid of being caught."

"I just don't believe it," said Snubby. "I never never shall believe it. Dummy wasn't like that."

"It shows how much cleverer he was than we thought him to be," said Roger, amazed. "Yes—I believe it. I always thought it was funny that he ran away as soon as the police came."

"Well, I *don't* believe it!" said Snubby, getting into quite a rage about it.

"Don't work yourself up, Snubby," said Barney. "You don't know how dishonest and deceitful people can be, even when they seem to be quite the opposite. You haven't knocked about the world as I have."

"That isn't the point," said Snubby in one of his obstinate moods. "The point is not that I don't recognise *bad* people when I seen them—I grant you I may quite well be taken in by them—the point is that I know a *good* person when I see one. And I know Dummy was good, even though he was queer in the head."

"Well, have it your own way," said Barney. "As he's gone, there's not much point in arguing about him. It's quite certain we'll never see him again! He's probably a hundred miles away by now. I liked him too—but there you are! I was wrong."

"Are we to go to the police?" asked Diana.

"Not yet. Not till Mr. Marvel has collected one last bit of evidence he needs," said Barney. "I have a feeling it's the names of the men who are traitors and saboteurs that he's waiting for now. He says he hopes to get this last piece of evidence soon. Perhaps to-morrow. And *I'm* to be in that! I can't tell you how or why—that's really a terrific secret. I shall be able to tell you all about it afterwards. It's all tied up with how I'm to meet my father for the first time."

Barney was quite breathless after this long speech. Roger and Diana were too thrilled for words. Snubby still looked sulky. He simply couldn't believe that Dummy was bad.

"Let's go and have tea," said Diana, and Snubby at once looked more cheerful. Barney gave him a smack on the back. "Sorry about Dummy," he said. "But these things happen, you know."

Snubby didn't answer, but gave an awkward grin. After that he was more himself again, and he kept his word and ate a whole lobster for his tea.

"How you can do a thing like that I *don't* know," said Diana. "You'll dream to-night all right. We'll hear you yelling and calling for help! And it'll only be the lobster paying you out for your greediness."

They were all restless and excited for the rest of the day. Miss Pepper stood it until after dinner and then announced that they had better go to the pierrot show again. "I really must get rid of you," she said. "You're so fidgety and restless. Go along with you—I'm sure Barney will like you to see him helping Mr. Marvel, now that he's got used to it."

So off they went to the pierrots. The Professor was there again, too, but not Miss Twitt. They all looked with great scorn at the Professor. Ho! He didn't know that they knew all about his horrible doings! However, he took no notice of them at all, but merely sat slumped down in his chair, only waking up a bit when Mr. Marvel came on to do his conjuring, with a very handsome, finely-dressed Barney as assistant.

Barney certainly was excellent, deft, good at any patter necessary, and first class in the mind-reading. Once more the conjurer identified articles taken from the audience, and once more he guessed the long numbers correctly. There were more numbers to-night—six, instead of three. The audience clapped and clapped again, but Mr. Marvel would guess no more than six.

"It is tiring," he said apologetically to the delighted audience. "Mind-reading and number-guessing are the most difficult things to do!"

That night the boys quite meant to sit up and wait for anything else that might happen. But unfortunately they were so tired with the night before that they didn't wake, even when Loony had a bad dream and began barking in his sleep. "Yip-yip-yip!"

Snubby had terrible dreams. He was set upon by men behind curtains, he was involved in a terrific explosion, people sat hard on his tummy, somebody chased him up thousands of steep steps up which his legs could hardly crawl. Oh dear—that lobster tea!

Nobody heard anything during the night at all, not even Barney, who said he was so excited that he hadn't been able to sleep. Mr. Marvel had had another long talk with him, and had promised that when the morning letters came he might be able to tell him if and when he could arrange with him to meet his father.

Barney saw Mr. Marvel after breakfast. His eyes asked an

eager question. Had the letter come? Mr. Marvel nodded. "See me at eleven o'clock, when you can get ten minutes off," said Mr. Marvel. Barney went off whistling, Miranda on his shoulder. Not even a scolding by Mrs. Glump for taking things out of the larder made him down in the dumps.

"I took nothing," he said. "I never do. I'm not that sort. Sorry, Mrs. Glump, but if you think I'd take pie and cakes, when you give me them for nothing, don't keep me! I'll go!"

But Mrs. Glump didn't want to lose such a good worker. She still had no news of Dummy and felt sure he would never come back. So she said no more to the indignant Barney and began to wonder if the bright-eyed young waiter was quite as honest as he seemed.

Barney went off to meet Mr. Marvel at eleven o'clock, when he had a break of ten or fifteen minutes. The conjurer was impatiently waiting for him. He took the boy by the arm and walked with him to a deserted part of the promenade. They sat down in a shelter.

"I've arranged everything, Barney," said Mr. Marvel. "It's all planned out well. By this morning's post I had the letter from one of my men telling me that the names of the saboteurs, the men who blew up the submarine, have all been ascertained. But they're dead secret, of course."

"Yes, sir," said Barney.

"They are being sent from the Submarine Bay to me," said Mr. Marvel. "To-night. They will be delivered by hand. But not here, of course, with so many people like Professor James about. Too dangerous! I am to meet the man who brings the names, away out at sea."

"I see, sir," said Barney, excited.

"I can't row," said Mr. Marvel. "So I want you to row me out, Barney, and row me back. Can you do that?"

"Easily, sir," said Barney.

"And, as your reward, Barney, I will tell you this," said Mr. Marvel. "The man who brings the secret document is—your father!"

Barney couldn't say a word. He could only gaze excitedly at the conjurer. So Mr. Marvel had done what he promised! Arranged everything so that he, Barney, could meet his father face to face! His heart swelled with gratitude.

"Now, not a single word of this to anyone, my boy," said Mr. Marvel. "You understand that it has been difficult for me to arrange for it to be your father who brings the list—I have done it because of you. So on no account must you say a word, not even to your three friends, as I told you before—because I myself would get into serious trouble if my plans leaked out."

"You can trust me, sir," said Barney, looking straight at Mr. Marvel with his brilliant blue eyes, more brilliant than ever now, with excitement and happiness.

"Yes. I think I can," said Mr. Marvel. "Barney, be down on the beach at midnight. It will be moonlight then. I will tell you where to row. I shall be there with a boat which I will go and arrange for now. Good-bye, my boy—and remember—not a word to anyone!"

"Sir—before you go—just one more thing," said Barney. "Will my father know me? Does he know he'll meet me to-night?"

"As soon as he has given you the package safely, you can ask him," said Mr. Marvel. "I think you will find that he knows you, Barney! If he doesn't, then come back to me, and I will put things right. He may have found it all very difficult to believe. After all—he didn't even know that he *had* a son!"

He left Barney and went to speak to a boatman about a boat. Barney sped back to the hotel, afraid that he had taken too long for his break. The children were down on the beach. Nobody was about. Barney began to sing at the top of his voice as he polished up some silver.

Mrs. Glump suddenly appeared, looking extremely "glumpish" as Snubby would say, "Barney! What in the world are you thinking of, making a noise like that!"

Barney couldn't tell her what he was thinking, though he was bursting to tell somebody. He was thinking of that evening

—the mysterious trip in the boat—the meeting—the man who was his father! What would they both say? Would his father be pleased with him?

Barney looked at himself in the kitchen mirror. Would his father have his bright blue eyes and corn-coloured hair? He did hope there would be some likeness between them.

The day dragged along for Barney. It went quickly enough for the others. They bathed and swam as usual. They took a boat round the pier and back. They prawned after tea and caught a magnificent collection of enormous prawns which Snubby said he would ask Mrs. Glump to cook for them.

They didn't see Barney till just before dinner. He grinned happily at them.

" Any news?" asked Roger.

" Yes, plenty. Good news too," said Barney. " But I can't tell you any more. You understand why, I know. Things are going to happen to-night! I'll tell you all about it to-morrow!"

CHAPTER TWENTY-SIX

THE MEETING ON THE ROCKS

BARNEY went to bed at half-past ten that night. At least, he went up to his room—but he didn't even lie down or try to get a little sleep, because he was so excited. This was to be such an important night. He was helping someone in the Secret Service—he was also finding his own father!

Barney walked restlessly up and down the little attic room. Miranda was puzzled. What was the matter with him? She sat on his shoulder while he walked, occasionally nibbling his ear gently, just to let him know she was there.

"What shall I call him?" wondered Barney. "Dad? Father? Pa? And I wonder what he's like. Will he want me to go and live with him? Shall I find I've got aunts and uncles —and perhaps cousins. No—I mustn't hope too much. So long as I just find my father that's enough for me!"

Eleven o'clock. Half-past eleven. Twenty to twelve. Time to go!

The boy crept downstairs cautiously, Miranda still on his shoulder. He couldn't leave her behind, she would hate him going off at night without her.

He made his way quietly down the back stair and into the kitchen. He undid a little garden door and slipped out like a shadow.

Soon he was down on the little private beach belonging to the hotel. He knew the boat would be pulled up there somewhere, waiting. In the house the big grandfather clock chimed the quarter to twelve. Barney was early.

He waited on the beach. The moon came out from behind a cloud and flooded him with silvery light. It was a beautiful

451

night. The tide was rapidly going down. It would be easy to row out to sea.

Then he heard a slight noise behind him. It was Mr. Marvel. "You're there—good boy," said the conjurer's deep voice. "Let's go."

The boat was a roomy one. Mr. Marvel sat on one seat, and Barney sat on another, with an oar in each hand. A heap of tarpaulins lay in the stern of the boat, and coils of rope in the bow.

They were soon on the little waves that swelled up near the shore. Barney rowed strongly out to sea. This was one of the greatest nights of his life, he thought. What a piece of luck that he had met Mr. Marvel!

The moonlight dripped from the oars with the sea-water, as Barney rowed. "Over towards that great ridge of rocks," ordered Mr. Marvel. "Look—that ridge stretching out from the land."

"Why, that's where we rowed out to the other day," said Barney. "We went to see Rubadub Whirlpool. It was a fine sight."

"Ah, good," said Mr. Marvel. "It's just near the whirlpool where I am meeting this man—your father!"

"Oh, well—that's easy, then. I know the way perfectly," said Barney, and rowed vigorously. Farther and farther out they went, until they came to the end of the great ridge of high rocks. Now Barney knew he must find the entrance to the channel that led to the pool. He pulled over to the rocks and looked for the narrow, rocky entrance.

"There it is!" said Mr. Marvel. "Swing round a bit more, Barney. That's it. Now we're heading straight for the channel."

Soon they were right in the winding little waterway. It looked quite different now, from when Barney had last seen it, on a brilliant sunny day. It looked bigger, darker, more mysterious. The level of the water was much lower too, because it was now just about low tide. It would soon be on the turn.

Barney pulled right up the channel till he heard the sucking, gurgling sound of the strange whirlpool. Then he looked for the mooring post he knew was there.

"Ah—there it is," he said. "I'll just fling the rope over that post, sir, then we shan't get pulled along to the whirlpool. Once down there we'd never be seen again!"

The boat came to a standstill, held by its rope. Barney jumped out. "What do I do now, sir?" he asked. "How does my father get here—by boat down the channel too?"

"No. He swims here," said Mr. Marvel.

Barney was amazed. "Swims! But how can he? And why? The bay is completely built round by a stone enclosure, surely? And there are great gates built under water to prevent anything from coming in!"

"Your father is a remarkable man," said Mr. Marvel. "He will swim right under the gates and then strike out for these rocks. He has done it before now. It is the only way that he can bring secret information to us. He is a very brave man."

"But why must he do it all so secretly?" asked Barney. "He might be seen and shot by one of our guards on the stone enclosure."

"Quiet!" said Mr. Marvel. "I can hear someone coming. Now, you know what to do! Meet the man, say the password —'Moonlight Night'—and then take the parcel he gives you. It will be wrapped in waterproof cloth. Give it to me and then go back to talk to your father. I don't want to be present because it will no doubt be a thrilling meeting for you both."

Barney nodded. He was feeling tense and excited. He, too, could hear someone coming—climbing over the rocks, panting and exhausted after a long and tiring swim. He waited, his heart thumping painfully.

A man came over the top of the ridge of rocks. Except for bathing trunks, his body was bare and dripping with sea water. It glistened like silver in the moonlight. Barney gazed at him.

He was a big fellow with great square shoulders, and a head of dark, curling hair which was drying already.

"Password," he said sharply, when he saw Barney.

"Moonlight Night," stammered Barney. He couldn't see the man's face because the moon chose to go behind a big cloud at that moment.

The man took a package from the back of his bathing trunks. It was wrapped in waterproof cloth as Mr. Marvel had said. He threw it to Barney.

"Catch," he said. Barney caught it, and then hurried to give it to Mr. Marvel. The conjurer caught it deftly.

"Good boy. Now go and talk to your father!" he said. Barney turned, almost trembling with excitement. But the messenger was already climbing back over the rocks again! Barney called to him.

"Wait! Wait! Don't you know who I am?"

The man turned. "Why should I?" he asked.

"I'm your son," cried Barney. "Didn't Mr. Marvel tell you! He said you were my father!"

The man threw back his head and laughed. It was a harsh, mocking laugh. "What's he been stuffing you with?" he said. "You don't want to believe a word he says. I'm not even married."

The moon sailed out for a second and Barney caught a sudden glimpse of the man's face. He recoiled in horror. It was a mean, traitorous face—no, no, surely not his father! Barney stared in horror and dismay. The man laughed again, a contemptuous, amused laugh, and then turned to go.

"Just one of his jokes, I reckon!" he called as he went. He disappeared over the top of the rocky cliff, still laughing.

Barney felt suddenly sick. He sat down on a rock. He had left Miranda in the boat—but she suddenly came scampering up to him, chattering in her queer monkey way. She leapt into his arms, and snuggled to him.

"Oh, Miranda," said Barney. "It wasn't him. I can't make it out, I'm all muddled. I don't understand anything at all. Oh, Miranda!"

Then a sudden flame of anger shot him to his feet. Why had Mr. Marvel deceived him like that? What was the point of it? He would demand an explanation—and if Mr. Marvel couldn't give it, Barney would give away his secrets!

He went back to the mooring post, a furious rage making him tremble. But there was no boat there!

"Where's the boat? Miranda, what's happened? Where's the boat?" cried Barney, feeling as if he were in a nightmare.

He ran along the ledge that led to the exit of the channel between the rocks. If he could catch Mr. Marvel he would fight him, strike him till he cried for mercy, throw him out of the boat if he couldn't explain properly what all this meant!

The boat was rounding the end of the rocks as Barney got there. Barney leapt straight into the water, Miranda still with him, and began to swim towards the boat. He shouted.

"Mr. Marvel! Wait! I've something to ask you. WAIT, I SAY!"

Mr. Marvel went on rowing. Barney was a very strong swimmer, and so full of rage that he swam twice as fast as usual! He reached the boat, and tried to hang on to the edge.

Mr. Marvel hit out at him with an oar, and Barney got a crack on the head. "Keep off!" he shouted. "I've no more use for you, don't you understand that? You were a fool to believe all my pretty tales! You deserve all you got!"

"Mr. Marvel! Wait! I don't understand!" shouted poor Barney, still bewildered.

And then, quite suddenly, he *did* understand. He saw it all! Mr. Marvel had used him for his own purposes. He wasn't in the Secret Service. He was a spy, a traitor, in league with other traitors in the Submarine Bay. He had been afraid when he had found out that Barney and the others knew so much—so he had stuffed up the boy with the silly tale of his father. He had got the secret packet he wanted, and now he was off by himself with it, and would escape easily, because **Barney** would be left marooned on the Whirlpool Rocks.

"Traitor!" yelled Barney, beside himself with rage. "Spy! Wait till I get you!"

"You can't," called back Mr. Marvel mockingly, rowing away. "I've got what I want, thanks to your kind help—and now I'm off to give it to my headquarters—but *not* the names of those who blew up the submarine! Oh no! I've got the plans of the next secret submarine, not a list of names I already know! And long before anyone sees you on these rocks and rescues you, I shall be hundreds of miles away. You were a very stupid boy, Barney. Oh, VERY stupid!"

Barney could have cried with rage. He saw that he could not catch up the boat now. There was nothing for it but to swim back to the rocky reef with Miranda, and hope and pray that someone would rescue him in a day or two.

But wait—what was happening in the boat? There was a yell from Mr. Marvel, and the boat rocked violently. Whatever could be happening?

CHAPTER TWENTY-SEVEN

MAROONED BESIDE THE WHIRLPOOL

BARNEY CLAMBERED on to some rocks and stood up to see what was going on in the boat. The moon now shone as clear as day, and Barney could see everything.

There were *two* men in the boat, not one! Who was the other? Whoever it was, he had attacked Mr. Marvel and was struggling desperately with him. The two men rocked two and fro in the boat and the boat rocked too, almost overturning. Barney was amazed.

Where had the second man come from? Had he crept into

the boat out of the sea? Barney held his breath as the two men struggled together. He could hear their panting clearly. Miranda, wet through crept inside his dripping shirt, frightened.

There was a sudden splash. One of the men had fallen into the water. Was it Mr. Marvel? Oh, let it be Mr. Marvel; Barney strained his eyes to see.

But alas, Mr. Marvel was sitting down, rowing away for dear life. The man in the water was struggling and yelling for help.

" He can't swim! " Barney said suddenly, full of horror. In a trice the boy dived into the water again and was swimming strongly to the struggling man.

He slid his arm under the man's back, and began to life-save him, pulling him towards the rocks. Fortunately the man was now so exhausted that he didn't struggle with Barney or drag him under. The boy took him to a rocky ledge, climbed up and dragged the other man up too.

He looked down at him as he lay there, his eyes shut, his chest heaving up and down as he tried to get his breath. Barney saw who he was.

" Dummy! *DUMMY!* Why, it's you. Well, I'm blessed. This beats me. *DUMMY!* Where did you come from? Good gracious, is this all a mad dream? "

Dummy opened his eyes and saw Barney. He managed a very weak smile. Then he sat up suddenly and looked out over the moonlit sea. Away in the distance was the little black speck that showed where Mr. Marvel and his boat were, on their way to land.

Dummy sent out a string of foreign words after the conjurer, and shook his fist violently. Then he turned and patted Barney's knee.

" You save Dummy, " he said. " Good boy, Barney, he save Dummy. "

" Dummy—for goodness' sake tell me where you came from so suddenly, " said Barney. " I can't understand a thing! "

" Dummy in boat all the time, " said Dummy. " Dummy

know that man is bad, bad, bad. Dummy know he spy. He
flash lights, and then—boom-boom-boom. He makes bad
things come, that man."

"Go on," said Barney. "Why didn't you tell any one?"

"Dummy silly, Dummy not brave," said the little fellow.
"But Dummy watch and watch. And one day that man see
Dummy watching, and he say, 'Ah—I get police. They take
you away, Dummy.'"

"And then one day the police did come and you thought
they had come for you and you hid away. Poor Dummy!"
said Barney, suddenly seeing light. "Where did you hide?"

"Down in cellars," whispered Dummy, as if he thought
somebody might be eavesdropping on the rocks. "And at night
Dummy come up—eats pies and cakes in larder. Bad Dummy!
And Dummy watch all the time at night. Dummy fight with
that man too one night!"

"Gosh! So it was you who followed Mr. Marvel and
Snubby the other night—and fought the conjurer!" said Barney. "But who was the third fellow? Goodness, this is a
peculiar business—everyone watching everyone else! But I
still don't know how you got here like this to-night, Dummy."

"Dummy see that man with boat," said the shivering little
fellow. "Dummy hear him tell you things and Dummy afraid
for you. So . . ."

"So you slipped under the tarpaulins and waited to see what
was going to happen!" said Barney. "You must have given
Mr. Marvel a horrible shock when you pounced on him. It's
a pity he didn't fall into the sea, and not you. As it is,
he's won his little game nicely—got rid of me and all I
know—made me a fool—and now he's off with those secret
papers, and will escape to do a whole lot more damage. He's
too clever, that chap!"

Dummy put his hand into his shirt and drew out something
with a sly look. "Papers," he said proudly. "Dummy have
them!"

Barney gave a yell. "Dummy! That's the packet the

other fellow gave me! How did you get it away from Marvel?"

"He put in bag, and then put bag near Dummy," said Dummy. "So Dummy open bag and take package."

"Oh, Dummy—you're a wonder!" said Barney. "He hasn't got his secret papers after all! And unless he looks in his bag for them he won't even know they're not there! Dummy, I could hug you."

Miranda poked her head out of Barney's wet shirt and chattered a little. Dummy stroked her soft little head. "We stay here long, long time?" he asked Barney.

"Till someone picks us up," said Barney, gloomily. "Gosh, isn't it cold out here in the wind, for all it's a summer night! Let's get down into that sheltered channel. There's a little cave-like place near the whirlpool we could shelter in. I wish we had a boat! Then we could row to land, and catch that hateful fellow!"

They made their way down to the channel. It was certainly more sheltered there. They walked along the moonlit rocks almost to the whirlpool. "Come and have a look at it in the moonlight," said Barney. "I suppose it will be pretty low now it's low tide."

They went to the whirlpool. Certainly it was very low down in its ring of rocks now, and looked quite different from what it had looked the other afternoon. It sucked and gurgled away a good way below them, lighted brightly by the moonlight.

"Hole down there," said Dummy, pointing. "Big, big hole!"

Barney looked. "Yes—that's the entrance to the tunnel that runs all the way to that blow-hole, Dummy."

But Dummy had no idea of what a blow-hole was. He shook his head. Barney looked below the rock that had a great knob sticking out of it, watching the dark place that must be the entrance to the blow-hole tunnel. He suddenly remembered the old tale that the boatman had related to them.

He stood and stared intently at the hole. The whirlpool's waters were about six inches below the bottom of it. Was that old tale true? Was it really possible to squeeze through the blow-hole tunnel at low tide?

"Dummy, I'm going down to that hole. It leads into a rocky tunnel," said Barney suddenly. "The tunnel leads to land—we might be able to escape that way."

"No," said Dummy, shrinking back. "No."

"Well, listen—there's just a chance I could get back before Mr. Marvel escapes," said Barney. "He might think there's no hurry for him to escape immediately, as I'm marooned here. Dummy, I must take that chance. But you can stay here and I'll try to send out a boat for you to-morrow—if I get through safely."

"Dummy go too," said Dummy. "Barney brave. Dummy poor silly man, but Dummy go with Barney."

"Right," said Barney, only too glad to think he would have company in his dangerous struggle through the rocky tunnel. "We must go now if we're going. The tide is creeping in! Once it gets much above the level of that hole, the water will be pushed and sucked along it to the blow-hole—and that wouldn't be at all pleasant for us!"

Barney leapt down like a cat, and Dummy watched him stand in the entrance of the dark little tunnel. Then he bent his head and disappeared inside.

Dummy then dropped down, lightly but clumsily, almost missing his footing. He shuddered as he just prevented himself from dropping into the angry pool a few inches below. Dummy thought it looked alive and ready to clutch at him.

He went into the tunnel. "Barney!" he called suddenly overcome with fright. "Barney!"

"Here!" cried Barney. "Just in front of you. Follow me. Miranda has hopped down and she's leading the way, bless her! Her monkey eyes can see better than mine in the dark. Feel your way, Dummy—there are all sorts of unexpected knobs and ledges waiting to jab you or trip you up."

Barney sounded more cheerful than he felt. It was a horrid little tunnel, and he had to walk bent almost double. It was wet too, and smelt strongly of something sour and bad. Pooh!

Miranda kept running ahead, then coming back and touching Barney's knee to make sure he was following. She didn't seem a bit scared.

It was difficult work, going along the narrow, low-roofed tunnel. In one place it was so narrow that both Barney and Dummy had to go sideways to get through. Once or twice Barney became panic-stricken. Suppose they got held up somewhere? There wouldn't be time to get back before the tide came in—and they would meet the first big surge of water driven up the tunnel to the blow-hole! That would be horrible —they would surely drown! Or worse still, they might be dragged down by the water that ran back to the whirlpool, and end by being sucked into the pool itself!

Barney shivered with cold and fear as he made his way up the tunnel as fast as he could. It was pitch dark, of course, and he had to feel his way at every step. Miranda, however, had no difficulty at all. She went ahead and then came back, then went ahead again time after time.

"Wait, Dummy!" called Barney suddenly. "The roof's gone down low here. I can't even squeeze under it bent double. We'll have to crawl through it. I hope to goodness it doesn't go for far like this, I shall feel smothered to death!"

The roof went down to within two feet of the floor of the tunnel at this point. Barney wriggled painfully along on his tummy, hoping against hope that the tunnel would get no smaller. Why had he believed that tale of the boatman's? It was only a tale, probably. He began to doubt if he and Miranda and Dummy would ever get out of the dark, damp tunnel.

At last he was through the narrow bit. The roof rose up again. Thank goodness! Barney stood up once more and knocked his head against the roof. Then Dummy gave a shout. "There's water behind me, Barney! It's coming, it's coming!"

CHAPTER TWENTY-EIGHT

A NIGHT OF SURPRISES

WATER! That meant that the tide was coming in rapidly then. Water was being sent up the tunnel already! There was no return that way. They could only push on as quickly as possible, hoping that no great surge would race up the tunnel and overwhelm them.

Barney went on grimly, bruising himself badly as he struggled on as quickly as he could. Then he, too, gave a cry.

"The water again! That's the second time! It reached *my* feet then. Keep close to me, Dummy. We may have to help one another."

The water retreated again. The tide was not yet high enough or strong enough to send a wave all the way along the tunnel to spurt out of the blow-hole. But at any moment a bigger wave than usual might come, and they would be swept off their feet, smothered with the surging water.

"It's wider here," gasped Barney. "We can go more quickly. I'm getting so tired, my legs will hardly move along. Are you there, Dummy?"

"Yes, Dummy here!" came Dummy's scared voice. "Dummy hear water, Barney, water!"

The water ran beyond them that time and then retreated again. Barney stumbled on—and then, oh joy! What was that shining ahead of him? A moonlight opening! The blow-hole itself surely!

Dummy gave a shout of warning. "Big one coming, Barney!" Sure enough it certainly *was* a big wave that time. It almost felled them to the ground, and Dummy bumped right into Barney. Miranda leapt into Barney's arms in fright just in time to escape the swirl of water.

"Up to our knees that time," said Barney grimly. "Come on—just a minute more of this and we're out!" He struggled to the moonlit opening. It was quite round, and so big that he could easily get out. He climbed out thankfully, and pulled himself to a rock above the hole. He must have a rest for a moment, it was no good, he simply must!

There was a loud yell from the cave, and a roar of water. Dummy was caught! This was the first wave powerful enough to rush all the way down the tunnel to the blow-hole itself. It had terrific force.

In terror Barney waited. The water burst out of the blow-hole like a spout from a whale. With it came poor Dummy, yelling in fright. He was thrown up in the air like a ball, and then landed with a thud beside Barney, who was covered in spray.

"Oh, Dummy killed, Dummy drowned!" wept Dummy. "Oh, save poor Dummy."

"You're all right," said Barney. "We're both all right. Just did it nicely. Well, Dummy, I should think you are the first man ever to be thrown out of a blow-hole!"

Dummy went all to pieces. He wept and blubbered and sobbed like a child of three. Barney had to put his arm round him and comfort him. "It's all right now, I tell you. We're going to the inn now. We'll get something to eat and drink, and we'll feel fine!"

"Kind Barney," said poor Dummy, and nestled up to him like a child. Barney gave a weak grin. What a night! After all his great hopes, all he had was poor little Dummy sobbing on his shoulder!

He got up at last. His legs felt wobbly after his long struggle in the tunnel. "Come on, Dummy. Back we go. I'll look after you while you're with me."

Dummy followed him like a dog. Barney knew roughly where he was—at the beginning of the great ridge of rocks, where it jutted out from the land. He had only to make his way a little inland, and he would strike a path that led back to the inn.

The blow-hole was very active now. Giant spouts of water came up continually with a tremendous noise. Barney watched one or two. How weird it was—and how horrible it would have been to be caught in the middle of that tunnel when the blow-hole was in action!

He and Dummy and Miranda made their way landwards. It was not very far. There was a little path made by people who sometimes came to watch the blow-hole, and Barney followed it thankfully.

They came at last to the inn. "Let's go in the side gate," whispered Barney. "Do you know if any door is open, Dummy? Which one did you come from to-night?"

Dummy knew an old forgotten entrance, a low wooden garden door that led into a tiny passage. He opened the door and the two went silently in, with Miranda inside Barney's shirt, trying to sleep after her adventure in the tunnel.

"I wonder what's the best thing to do now," wondered Barney. "Telephone the police, I should think. Oh goodness, what's that!"

They had now made their way to the kitchen, meaning first of all to get themselves something to eat and drink. The moonlight shone in at the window—but standing by the larder was a stout, formidable figure, half in moonlight, half in shadow. There was a click—and the room was flooded with electric light.

"And what is the meaning of this?" said the furious voice of Mrs. Glump. "Raiding my larder again, I suppose? You too, Dummy! Where have you been all this time? I've a good mind to telephone the police! I was watching for my larder thief to-night—I knew I'd get him sooner or later. For shame, Barney! What will your friends say?"

Barney interrupted desperately. "We have got to telephone the police ourselves!" he said. "We want them to arrest Mr.

Marvel. He's a spy, a traitor! Mrs. Glump, let me fetch Miss Pepper—she'll tell you I'm not likely to tell you fairy tales!"

"I'd rather fetch someone else," said Mrs. Glump, astonished. "If there's anything in what you say, I'll certainly fetch him—or better still, we'll go to him! But mind—if you're lying to me, you'll have the police on your track immediately. Such goings on in my inn! I never did hear the likes!"

"Who is it you want to go to?" asked Barney, puzzled.

"Professor James," said Mrs. Glump, which astonished Barney considerably. Professor James! Why, they had suspected him too! He was probably hand-in-glove with Mr. Marvel, so what was the use of getting *him*?

But Mrs. Glump was not to be argued with. She hustled them both in front of her and pushed them up the stairs, dripping wet as they were. She knocked at Professor James's door.

"Come in," said a low voice, and a light was switched on immediately. To Barney's amazement the Professor was sitting in a chair, fully dressed, in the darkness. Whatever for?

"These two have turned up dripping wet with some tale about Mr. Marvel, sir," said Mrs. Glump. "They wanted to telephone the police. So I thought the best thing to do was to bring them to you, sir—knowing what you've warned me to do."

"But what's the use of telling *him* anything," said Barney. "He may be hand-in-glove with Mr. Marvel for all we know! We've spotted him doing some very funny things anyway. I don't want to tell him what's happened to-night. It's absolutely urgent to find out if Mr. Marvel has come back and to arrest him before he gets a chance to escape."

"What do you know about him?" rapped out the Professor, in such a sharp, imperious voice that Barney got a shock. He looked at him sulkily.

The Professor spoke again, more gently.

"Listen, boy. You can trust me. I'm working for the police.

466

Mrs. Glump can tell you that. I'm here investigating some very queer things, and some very queer people. It's your duty to tell me what you know."

Barney was bewildered. "Mr. Marvel said *he* was on Secret Service work, working with the police too, sir," he blurted out. "He said *you* were one of the people they were watching. But oh, sir—this is very urgent. We've got secret papers here, sir. I don't quite know what they are—plans, I think. They ought to be taken care of quickly."

"Where are they?" demanded the Professor, who suddenly seemed years and years younger, eyes, voice and everything! Barney was astounded at the sudden change in him.

"Here," said Barney and put them on the table beside the Professor. He pounced on them, ripped open the waterproof case and pulled out a folded document. He opened it hurriedly and pored over it. He let out an enormous sigh of relief and leaned back in his chair.

"Thank God!" he said, and it sounded as if he meant it from the bottom of his heart. "Our newest and finest plans! Blue-prints worth a fortune to any enemy. We knew they had been copied—and that the fellow was only waiting to pass them out of the Base. Boy, you don't know what it means to have this document in my possession! But this is all very extraordinary! How on earth did you get hold of them?"

"Sir—it's rather a long story," said Barney. "Couldn't you arrest Mr. Marvel first and get him safely under lock and key?"

"You needn't worry. He was seen when he came in late to-night," said the Professor. "There is a man outside his window, on the roof—and one on the landing outside his door. He's safe enough. We were closing in on him anyhow. But this is just what we wanted to bring matters to a head. Now— what about your story? Would you like to tell it here, to me —or shall I get the police in just to satisfy you that I'm to be trusted?"

"It's all right, sir. I believe you," said Barney. "But I've been so taken in by Mr. Marvel that—well—I began to feel I couldn't believe anybody! I say, sir—was it you who shone that torch on Snubby the other night after he had come out of the grandfather clock?"

"It was," said the Professor. "I, like Snubby and Roger—and Dummy here—have been doing my little bit of snooping too. So *that's* where Snubby was—in the clock! Bless us all, what a boy! It beat me to think where he had gone to!"

Mrs. Glump noticed that Barney and Dummy had begun to shiver. "Sir," she said, "what about going down to the kitchen and letting me poke up the fire for these two? They're shivering. We can lock the doors on ourselves. These two ought to get dry clothes and something hot inside them."

"Down to the kitchen then," said the Professor obligingly. "I could do with something hot myself, Mrs. Glump. All this prowling about at night is cold work."

They all went down to the kitchen, and Mrs. Glump locked the doors. She gave Dummy and Barney dry blankets to wrap themselves in, while she dried their other clothes beside the fire. She set some milk on the stove to heat, and got some meat-pie from the larder.

"Not so bad, Mrs. Glump," said the Professor, eyeing the pies. "Now—what about a heart-to-heart talk while we put away these? You begin Barney!"

CHAPTER TWENTY-NINE

IN THE MORNING

IT WAS a strange hour the four of them spent, down in the
warm kitchen. Barney told his whole tale, and Dummy
occasionally added a few words. He was scared of the Professor.

"It seems to me that you children have been doing quite a
bit of investigating yourselves," said Professor James. "All
that roof-crawling! Extremely dangerous, I should think.
And trying to peer into my window! Well, well—you fancied
yourselves as a lot of detectives, I suppose?"

"Not really," said Barney. "I'm sorry we suspected you,
sir—but what with one thing and another—you know, not

finding you in your room that night—and feeling sure you weren't as deaf as you pretended to be—well, we were right on the wrong track, of course, I see that now! I say, sir—who locked that staircase door and took the key?"

"Marvel, of course," said the Professor. "He used that skylight at the top to signal messages to his friends in the harbour, and when he knew you children were messing about up there, he locked the staircase door! He is a bold and wily fellow, is our Mr. Marvel. His real name by the way, is Paulus, and he really *is* a conjurer—a very good one too."

"Yes, but, sir—he doesn't *really* guess those articles I held up," said Barney. "He taught me various ways of putting the question to him. 'What have I here?' meant something in the jewellery line, for instance, and 'What do I hold in my hand?' meant a watch—and so on. And sometimes, sir, he used to have a pal in the audience who lent something— usually with initials on, so that it seemed marvellous when he guessed them."

"I know all that," said the Professor. "In fact, much of his work in that guessing was only a cover for the giving out of code messages. For instance—those long numbers! They were merely a message in code to a sailor in the audience, who would pass on the code messages to higher quarters on his ship —a traitor there, you see!"

"Yes, sir. I see," said Barney. "But he didn't *guess* those numbers, sir. He told me which cards to hold up each night—they were marked in some way so that I knew—and he knew them too, of course. I thought it was a mean trick to play—but there, he was a conjurer, and tricks are their trade!"

"He worked the message into the number code first," said the Professor. "It took up a lot of his time! May I have another pie, Mrs. Glump? Thank you. Most delicious. Well, my boy, your tale is very interesting, and you must be very tired after your struggle through that blow-hole. You're a brave lad, very brave. I'm sorry about that father business— that false letter describing your father—the false meeting—

most disappointing for you. You'll have to try again somehow won't you?"

"No, sir," said Barney. "I'm not trying any more. One disappointment's enough. I don't want to talk about it, please, sir. Anyway—I'm glad that fellow I saw *wasn't* my father!"

"You can't give me any really good description of him, can you?" said the Professor.

"Not really," said Barney. "Just a big strong-looking fellow with a mean face, and I think his hair was curly—oh, and he had a crooked little finger, I noticed. Not that that's much use!"

"It may be, it may be," said the Professor, jotting down a few notes.

"Sir—what will Mr. Marvel do when he opens his bag and finds he's not got the secret package after all?" asked Barney.

"I've no idea. Go off his head, I should think," said the Professor. "However—he's safe enough now, even if he takes it into his head to creep down to hunt in the boat for his lost package! But I've no doubt he's fast asleep, thinking he has everything safe—and that you are well and truly marooned on the cliffs. Nice fellow, Mr. Marvel!"

"Can I tell Diana, Roger and Snubby about all this?" asked Barney.

"Not till to-morrow," said the Professor. "Then we shall have everything nicely finished up, I hope. Go to bed now, boy—what's your name—Barney. You've done well. Pity your father doesn't know it all—he'd have been proud of you."

Barney said good night to the Professor, Mrs. Glump and to Dummy, who was sitting blissfully half asleep in front of the fire. Mrs. Glump had told him she would be very glad to have him back in his old job, and that not another word would be said about hiding away in the cellars—or taking food from the larder at night!

Barney was soon in his attic, fast asleep, tired out with excitement and with struggling through the rocky tunnel. He would dream about that many times in his life!

471

Next morning Snubby and Roger were awakened by a great commotion outside on the landing. There were shouts and yells, and the noise of a struggle. Then it sounded as if two or three people had rolled down the stairs together!

The two boys leapt out of bed, and, followed by a barking Loony, they ran out on to the landing. They saw a peculiar sight. Mr. Marvel was struggling half-way down the stairs with two burly policemen! One had spent the night in a convenient cupboard, the other had come to relieve him—and had arrived at the very moment that Mr. Marvel, shocked to discover the precious package was not in his bag, was about to hurry downstairs to examine last night's boat.

He was in a great hurry—but the policemen were not. They stopped him and suggested he should go back to his room and rest a little longer. Mr. Marvel had no intention of doing this, of course, and a very interesting struggle had developed on the landing, resulting in all three falling headlong down the stairs together.

Barney, attracted by the noise, came running up the stairs to see what was happening. He had been helping Dummy with the before-breakfast jobs. Mr. Marvel suddenly caught sight of him.

It gave him a dreadful shock. What! *Barney* here, large as life, when he ought to be shivering out on the rocks waiting until the next boat trip came to visit the famous whirlpool? He simply couldn't believe his eyes. He sat up on the stairs and gaped at Barney.

"Where did you come from?" he said weakly.

"From the kitchen," said Barney promptly. "Lost something, sir?"

Those words, of course, told Mr. Marvel that he had not only lost something but that Barney had got it. He gave up at once and went quietly with the two angry policemen, wearing a most bewildered look.

"What's it all about, Barney?" said Snubby, in open-mouthed amazement. "Why have they taken Mr. Marvel?

472

Have they got the Professor as well? Did you row out to the rocks? What about your father?"

"I can't answer all those questions at once," said Barney. "But I've got a whole lot to tell you. See you after breakfast!"

Nobody saw Mr. Marvel again. That plausible, wily, traitorous rogue was dealt with in a way that made it quite impossible for him ever to do any damage to anything or anyone again. Every one in the hotel was horrified when they knew that the conjurer was a traitor and a spy.

Iris Nightingale wept and shivered. "I never liked him. He was deceitful and cruel."

The Funny Man stopped being funny for a whole day, and didn't smile once. He was truly shocked.

Miss Twitt sank back into a chair and said she knew she was going to faint. She had felt in her bones that that man wasn't what he seemed. But as nobody paid the slightest attention to what she felt in her bones, she soon stopped thinking she was going to faint and listened with open mouth to all the news going round.

The three children could hardly believe their ears when Barney told them of his night's adventure. "Crawling through that blow-hole! Ugh, how simply terrifying!" said Diana.

"Smashing! I wish I'd been with you," said Snubby.

"Fibber!" said Diana. "You'd have hated every minute."

"I'm sorry about your father," said Roger. "That was a hateful trick to play on you. Don't give up hope, though, Barney. We'll still go on looking."

"I'm not going to bother any more," said Barney, his face clouding over. "After all that looking forward to seeing him—and to meeting him for the first time—and then for it to be nothing but a trick! No—I've finished with looking for my father. If he wants me, he can look for *me*!"

"But he doesn't know about you!" said Diana.

"Then we'll never know one another," said Barney, and he looked very obstinate. "And listen, you three—I don't want you to mention my father to me any more! Do you promise?"

"No," said Diana. "Don't be silly, Barney. Oh, Barney, don't look like that."

"Well, I mean it," said Barney. "I tell you, I've realised it's just a stupid dream of mine. I've done without a father all these years, and now I've made up my mind I don't want one. I don't want any of you to mention him again. See?"

"All right," said the three reluctantly, seeing that Barney was really serious. What a pity! But after all, it must have been a terrible shock to have that awful, heartless trick played on him by Mr. Marvel.

"What was the fellow like, who gave you the package?" asked Roger.

"I couldn't see very well," said Barney. "I wish I'd noticed more about him—but the moon went behind a cloud just then. I know the Professor thinks I've fallen down a bit there—if I could have described the man properly, he'd have been able to put his finger on one of the main traitors in the camp. All I saw was that he was a biggish man, with possibly curly hair—and a crooked little finger."

Snubby suddenly gave a yell. "A crooked little finger! *I* can give a full description of him then—listen!"

He shut his eyes, visualising the two naval men he had seen in the train coming to Rockypool, where they changed for Rubadub.

"Yes—here he is—a clean-shaven fellow—with a big mole on his right cheek—two teeth overlapping each other in front —hairs growing out of his ears—and a misshapen little finger! There—if the police can find that man in the Submarine Service, he's the traitor who gave you the secret papers last night, Barney!"

CHAPTER THIRTY

WHAT MORE COULD ANYONE WANT

AN ASTONISHED voice spoke behind them. "And how do you know all that, young man?"

They all turned. It was the Professor's voice—but could this be the Professor! This spruce, upright, keen-eyed fellow with brown hair instead of grey and no beard?

He laughed at their astonished faces. "I can be myself now," he said. "Good disguise, wasn't it? I was always afraid that Snubby, in one of his wilder moments, might pull off my beard or my wig—but mercifully he didn't! Well, Snubby, what about it? Is that true what you were saying just now—or a little invention on your part? Actually, there *is* a man of that description, but we'd no actual proof of his being mixed up with this business."

"He was in naval uniform when I saw him, sir, and I noticed everything about him, just as I said," said Snubby. "You find him and pin him down—and tell him Barney saw him last night—you'll have got him all right!"

"I rather think you've hit on the right man," said the Professor. "Excuse me—I'm going to telephone and use your bit of information immediately—mole on right cheek—overlapping teeth . . ."

Out he went, quite a different man from the old Professor they had known so well. What a very extraordinary thing! Why, Miss Twitt might turn out to be a policewoman or something! Surely nobody could *really* be quite as silly as Miss Twitt always seemed!

"I'm going to see Dummy," said Snubby, getting up. "I was the only one of us who didn't believe it when Mr. Marvel said Dummy was bad. I'm going to shake hands with Dummy and tell him he's a fine fellow."

And off went Snubby to find Dummy. He was out in the shed in the back-yard, peeling potatoes, and looking very happy indeed.

"Shake, Dummy," said Snubby, holding out his hand solemnly. "Shake! You're a fine fellow! Loony, put up your paw and salute Dummy! That's right. Now, three barks for Dummy—yap-yap-yap, WOOF!"

Loony obliged at once. Dummy was really very touched. He patted Snubby on the arm.

"You good boy," he said. "Funny boy. Good friend to Barney."

"It's a pity about his father, isn't it," said Snubby. "He says he's given up all idea of trying to find him now. You know he really thought he was going to meet him last night, Dummy, don't you?"

"Meet father?" said Dummy, looking bewildered. "Barney have mother, not father."

"Oh, I forgot. You knew Barney's mother, didn't you?" said Snubby. "What was she like? I say—did she ever tell you anything about Barney's father?"

Dummy frowned, trying to think back so many years. "Dummy think," he said slowly. "Snubby—you play your banjo again, and that make me think."

Snubby guessed what Dummy meant. He had known Barney's mother in the years when he, Dummy, had played the banjo. The twang-a-twang-twang noise and the sight of Snubby strumming away would bring back memories of those years.

"Twang-a-twang-twang-twang, twang-a-twang-twang-twang!" went Snubby softly, and Dummy sat, lost in thought.

"She so kind to Dummy," said the little fellow. "She tell Dummy her troubles and she make Dummy tell his. She tell Dummy about Barney's father—just a little bit."

476

"Did she tell you his name?" asked Snubby quickly, resuming his twang-twang noise at once.

"Oh, his name was Barnabas too," said Dummy, his eyes lighting up as he remembered. "Barnabas Frederick Martin—so many times she said it."

"What was he like?" asked Snubby, breathlessly. "Have you ever seen him? Twang-a-twang-twang-twang!"

Dummy shook his read. Snubby strummed on violently. "Did you ever hear where he lived? Where his home was? Twang-twang-a-twang-twang, zizz-zizz-zizz!"

"He had home, yes—nice home, she said. In Cherrydale," remembered Dummy. "His mother cross because he married circus girl. Unkind to poor Tessie. Made her run far away."

"Now we're getting somewhere!" thought Snubby, exultant. "Who would have thought old Dummy could say so much. I'll know how to make him talk another time—twang-twang-a-twang!"

"Dummy!" called a voice, and Dummy jumped. He was brought back to the present so violently that he looked quite ill for a moment. It was the bright young waiter. "Hi, Dummy —where have you put the dusters? Eaten them or something?"

There was nothing more to be got out of Dummy after that. He put on the worried look that meant he wouldn't be able to answer a single question. But Snubby had found out enough. His first thought was to rush to find Barney and tell him the news.

But no, on second thoughts, he wouldn't. Barney might be still obstinate. He might refuse to listen. Of course, Dummy's story *might* have nothing in it. Perhaps, on the whole, he had better tell Miss Pepper. Grown-ups came in jolly useful at times. They always seemed to know what to do in matters of this kind.

So Snubby was soon pouring it all out to an interested and surprised Miss Pepper. She sat and thought for a minute.

"Cherrydale," she said. "I have a friend living near there. I could telephone her and see if there ever was—or still is—a family of the name of Martin, with a son called Barnabas Frederick. I'll go and do it now. Oh, Snubby, it would be too wonderful if it were true!"

It took half an hour to get through to her friend and find out that yes, there *was* a family called Martin living at Cherrydale —an old lady and gentleman, and a son called Barnabas, and an unmarried sister of his called Katherine. There was also a married brother with four children.

"Miss Pepper! Barney's not only got a father then. He's got a grandmother and grandfather, aunts and an uncle, and cousins!" said Snubby. "*MISS PEPPER!* This is smashing! What do we do next?"

"Leave it to me," said Miss Pepper firmly. "And don't say a single word to Barney about it, for goodness' sake. He couldn't bear a second disappointment."

So Snubby left it to Miss Pepper, and quietly and efficiently she went about the very delicate business of contacting Barney's relations. Four days later she called Diana, Roger and Snubby to her in her room. She shut the door.

"I've news for you," she said. "Barney's father is coming down here to-day. He's longing to see Barney and to know if he really is his son that he never even heard about. Oh, children—I've seen a photograph of the father—and he does look so like Barney!"

"Good old Barney," said Diana, with sudden tears in her eyes. "When's the father coming?"

"This afternoon," said Miss Pepper. "I've arranged for Barney to be on the beach with you. I shall send his father there when he arrives—and you three will simply disappear when you see him—and Loony too, of course. You understand?"

"Of *course*," they all said fervently. Dear Barney. It *must* be his father, it *must!*

All four were on the beach that afternoon. Miranda was playing with her little spade. Loony was waiting for her to put it down so that he could run off with it.

Diana was keeping a watch on the promenade. She suddenly gave Roger a nudge. He looked up.

A man was standing up there, tall and well-built. He had thick, corn-coloured hair, brushed back. His eyes were very wide set, and brilliantly blue. His mouth was wide, and his face was brown. He was a grown-up Barney! He stood there, looking rather nervous. The three children rose up silently behind Barney and went to the promenade. Loony followed, astonished at the sudden move. Barney looked round, also astonished.

The man jumped down to the promenade, and walked down the beach. Barney stood up and faced him, wondering what he wanted. Then he stared incredulously. Why—this man was so like him! Who was he? What did he want?

" Your name is Barnabas, isn't it?" said the man.

" Yes," said Barney.

" So is mine," said the man. " I'm looking for a son I've lost for fifteen years—and I hear you've been looking for me."

" Yes," said Barney again, almost in a whisper. " Are you —are you really my father?"

" Just as much your father as you are my son," said the man, deeply moved as he looked at this fine-looking boy with the brilliant blue eyes so like his own. " And you've got a monkey, I see. How strange!"

" Why strange?" said Barney, fondling Miranda, who had leapt up to his shoulder.

" Because your grandmother has a monkey too!" said his father. " How pleased she will be to have a new grandson, Barney. And your aunts and uncles to have a new nephew. And your cousins to have my boy for a cousin!"

Miranda suddenly leapt on to the man's shoulder with a little chattering cry. She began to nibble his ear.

" Let's go for a walk and talk," said Barney's father, and he took the boy's arm. " You've much to tell me. We've got fifteen years to catch up on! It's a long time! "

They walked off together, Miranda still on the man's shoulder. The other three watched them go from a distance. Diana swallowed hard.

" It's come all right," she said. " Barney's got what he wanted. He won't need us any more."

" He will," said Snubby. " Barney's our friend for ever. Isn't he, Loony? "

" Woof! " said Loony solemnly, gazing after the two walking alone on the sands.

" A holiday—a mystery—an adventure—and a happy ending for dear old Barney! " said Roger. " What more could anyone want? "

" An ice-cream," said Snubby promptly. " Who's coming to buy one? "

THE END

480